1970

GERMAN MEN OF LETTERS
VOLUME II
Twelve Literary Essays

GERMAN
MEN OF LETTERS

VOLUME II

Twelve Literary Essays

edited by

ALEX NATAN

OSWALD WOLFF (PUBLISHERS) LIMITED
LONDON, W.1
1963

First published 1963

© 1963 OSWALD WOLFF (PUBLISHERS) LIMITED, LONDON

Second impression 1966

MADE AND PRINTED IN GREAT BRITAIN BY
THE GARDEN CITY PRESS LIMITED
LETCHWORTH, HERTFORDSHIRE

CONTENTS

INTRODUCTION

by ALEX NATAN

Friedrich Nietzsche died on 25 August 1900, on the threshold of the twentieth century. He it was who, in the isolation of his last productive years, declared war on civilization when he warned his fellow-men : "Gott ist tot. . . . Irren wir nicht durch ein unendliches Nichts? Haucht uns nicht der leere Raum an? Ist es nicht kälter geworden? Müssen nicht Laternen am Vormittag angezündet werden? Hören wir noch nichts von dem Lärm der Totengräber, welche Gott begraben?"[1] These questions, which have not lost their poignancy during the last sixty years, reflect the increasing anxiety which pursued all thinking men at the turn of the century. An intellectual uneasiness was noticeable among those who recklessly believed in the optimism of progress, and among those who, terrified by the enormous spreading of civilization, prophesied the "Untergang des Abendlandes". The latter were convinced that man had lost his orientation, had betrayed his cultural achievements, and was now doomed to damnation. Was there still a possibility of leaving the wildly rocking boat with its cargo of materialism and relativism, scepticism and resignation? Did a chance still exist of reaching a sheltered anchorage, and hence a point of new departure to shores of firm creeds and established beliefs? Some writers of outstanding importance in the German-speaking world attempted a charting of unknown seas, each in his own individual way before the holocaust of 1914 finally destroyed all illusions.

The Dutch philosopher, Johan Huizinga, called Nietzsche a "homo ludens", a man who played many parts in a protean life without ever being able to identify himself with any of them completely. Nietzsche's inability to settle down, his innate loneliness, his refusal ever to become "engagé" foreshadowed the problematical position of the intellectual in modern society. "Nur wer sich wandelt, bleibt mit mir verwandt"[2] sums up Nietzsche's personality. His fight against God, against Christianity and its "Sklavenmoral" reflected the corrosive spirit of an age which was finally to develop the atomic bomb. Nietzsche's embittered fight against traditional religion and morality was identical with the protest of an individual's conscience against the shallow tenets of a class-bound society. But it was equally directed against the strictures of the coming managerial age. Hence Nietzsche's romantic longing for the

I

Superman, hence the tragic attempt by his countrymen to identify themselves with this widely misinterpreted apostate of irrational dreams.

The misinterpretation of Nietzsche's philosophy caused great havoc throughout the realm of Western thought. But it would not suffice to evaluate Nietzsche only as philosopher. He was a poet sui generis, who did not only write excellent poetry but produced a collection of aphorisms in *Also Sprach Zarathustra*[3] which testify to the original poetic disposition of Nietzsche. The poet in him yields here to his artistic instinct. The discipline of his previous ascetism, for which an Apollinic attitude became symbolic, gave way to a Dionysiac boundlessness, an unrivalled expression of his romantic self-indulgence. In "Zarathustra", a great poet paid homage to the unchained forces of life, and was even prepared to welcome the deluge which such a confession to a destructive creation might produce under the sway of the god Dionysos. Once more the tragic preoccupation with Greek notions destroyed a noble spirit before its time.[4] Nietzsche's demand for a "re-valuation of all values" ("Umwertung aller Werte") exercised an enormous influence on German writers of the following generation. They all understood the brittleness of the glossy façade of contemporary society, and they all condemned its social structure and the hypocritical mentality of the ruling oligarchy. To most of them the coming slaughter seemed inevitable. There were Nietzsche's thoughts which were reflected in their works, no matter whether they were steeped in a pessimistic mood or were hoping for the emergence of a new Ararat after the floods had swept away the waste land.

"Seit die Deutschen Goethe und Schiller gehabt haben, tun sie es nicht mehr mit der einfachen Einzahl, es müssen immer ihrer zweie sein."[5] Thus *Hermann Sudermann* was paired with Gerhart Hauptmann, although he had really nothing in common with the Silesian dramatist, not even the outstanding intentions of naturalism. Sudermann was predominantly concerned with the uncovering of false values, immanent in Germany's aristocracy and plutocracy. His social criticism derived from French originals, such as Dumas, Sardou and Scribe. His technique consisted largely in theatrical canvasses, painted black on white without many transitionary nuances. Fathers turned against children, employers against their workers. Through the clash of crass contrasts, Sudermann revealed the shallowness of his society. The public liked this dramatic technique and sided with Sudermann while literary criticism patronized Hauptmann. The vitriolic attacks of Alfred Kerr, at the time Berlin's leading critic, assumed such tormenting proportions through charging Sudermann with the production of superficial trash, that the playwright ceased writing for the stage. His subsequent novels and stories revealed the concern of the writer with the hammering out of new values. He was called "The Balzac of East Germany, the reflector of a fantastic, intoxicated, unrealistic existence, significant for people living between the Vistula and the Memel".[6] And yet rereading some of his early plays makes it comprehensible why they were called "colportage in evening dress", anticipating the coming expressionism of Georg Kaiser. It was the dichotomy of his own personality which caused the poet to oscillate between the devaluation of existing values and the search for new values of a rather irrational disposition, so significant for people living in what was then the Masurian lake district.

The fin-de-siècle period of Vienna, anticipating the final dissolution of the anachronistic Habsburg monarchy, wrote literary history through its peculiar blend of Austrian impressionism whose characteristic mood was tired melancholy, brilliantly illuminated through mordant wit and scintillating dialogue. It was *Arthur Schnitzler*, an observant doctor, who wrote a penetrating comment on Vienna's fastidious society which widely neglected its political and social duties. It would, however, be wrong to assume that Schnitzler made Vienna, with its ambivalent position looking East, West and South, the central leitmotif of his oeuvre. The city offered no fresh experience but provided a realistic background instead, against which Schnitzler created his characters and their adventures. For the poet, sensuous pleasure became identical with life born out of Eros, who received a new interpretation from the newly discovered world of Sigmund Freud. Schnitzler, temperamentally unable to work out new values, resorted to a scepticism which let him view the world with undisguised irony. His own world was detached from the world he described, an attitude also taken up by his younger contemporary, Thomas Mann. Schnitzler wrote erotic stories and plays in an objective manner without committing himself. His interest was always focused on the clinical dissection of people typical for a fragmented society. Schnitzler was the master of perfect dialogue which showed him less interested in the psychological development of his characters and more in the climactic dénouement of a scenic moment or a linguistic subtlety. His profound knowledge and revelations of the human psyche created dramas and novels which stunned his contemporaries without provoking any violent protests. His audience was too tired to object to the implications and too frivolous not to enjoy the dissection of ego and libido. And yet, Schnitzler knew always the right moment when to drop the curtain over the most intimate experiences of life. He was a master of the "Before and After" in the manner of Hogarth's copper engravings, probably the last of his generation who respected traditional moral values.

The last decade prior to the outbreak of the world war witnessed the experimental phases of expressionism, futurism and cubism attempting the evaluation of new values. The mole who was prominently undermining bourgeois self-complacency in Germany was *Frank Wedekind*. He created a type of drama which transcends the analytical criticism of the naturalistic drama. He was what Jakob Burckhardt prophetically called a "simplificateur" who was destined to destroy idealistic conceptions of culture. Wedekind, well aware of Burckhardt's pessimism, took the opposite view. In his optimism he deceived himself when he regarded his times as a turning point in human history. The traditionally tolerated pure intellect would be swamped by the uncontrolled flood of sensuality. Wedekind, in his attacks on the taboos of society, pleaded the cause of unreserved acceptance of physical beauty, and of sex, its highest perfection. Any scientific investigation of the problems of his world was daringly brushed aside. Wedekind canvassed for an irrationalism which ultimately proved anew a romantic attitude of existence. Wedekind's quest was for a new man and a new morality— Nietzsche's Superman—immune from the insidious influences of modern civilization. It was Wedekind's tragedy to overlook that the pose of a Rousseau of the twentieth century must turn out to be a pipe-dream, at least a fundamental error if not an acknowledgment of intellectual chaos.

In Wedekind's immediate succession stood *Georg Kaiser*. In one of his plays the heroine bursts into a veritable "cri de coeur" : "Das Wort tötet das Leben!"[10] This was a literary protest against the powerful persuasiveness of the human language which had become severed from its original purpose of expressing reality. For Kaiser the abuse of the word served as a deceptive veil to lead man astray. He pointed to the dangers which must arise from the separation of language and existence. Any naturalistic writer, realizing this dichotomic conflict, had the means of escaping into a world of make-believe or of presenting his material as a strictly photographic observer. Any expressionistic writer had no other alternative but to follow up this conflict to its logical conclusion. Since it was Kaiser's intention to achieve pure expression, any self-deception proved impossible, even if this attitude involved a lack of interest in man's destiny. His superb stagecraft showed the logical development of any human situation through dialectic antinomies, arising conclusively from initial premises. His dramatic conclusions were born out of the intellect and not out of compassion, because the poet distrusted the power of the word in its traditional uses and forms. But since he could not suppress true or undisguised feelings, Kaiser strove for a new linguistic style which displayed its individuality in all his plays. Convinced of the moral bankruptcy of modern society, Kaiser was much concerned with the detrimental influence of technology, for him a prime factor in the destruction of the soul. Thus Kaiser tried to pave the way for a new man, who would resurrect a better world by dint of an irresistible, dynamic inner urge. A new code of morality would then come into existence as a natural corollary. Georg Kaiser was a genuine revolutionary playwright, for he deliberately threw overboard all traditional principles of stagecraft and thus made the expressionist drama possible.

Carl Sternheim was not interested in creating new forms of drama. As long as he could translate the contemporary scene into the grotesque, and thus could take revenge for the defeats and subsequent scandals which his first plays produced, he seemed to be content. His artistic atheism, his native wit and satirical vein, made it impossible to expect contributions from him which might solve the dilemma of his time. He too practised successfully the destruction of the shop-worn expressions of the German language. "Wir müssen lernen, uns stenographisch zu verständigen."[8] Sternheim confessed to the intellect and discarded the substance. By trying to become a German Molière, he displayed an acute awareness for the comical and grotesque aspects of life. But his brilliant inspirations never achieved lasting effect, because Sternheim himself killed them through the artificiality of his own language. If God was dead, Sternheim certainly played the successful grave-digger when making his shallow "juste milieu" of German society the butt of his malicious satires. The playwright was often charged with his inability to create real characters. Reading his plays today one cannot but admit that this charge is unwarranted. On the contrary, the character Sternheim persiflaged grew into a prototype of general validity which dominated Germany and which the brush of the painter, George Grosz, has preserved. Sternheim, more pitiless than Ibsen, was much concerned with the debunking of "Lebenslüge" and, in this process, laid bare unwittingly the isolation of the modern artist. Of Sternheim's characters the critic, Franz Blei, said : "Ins Einzelfällige ist dieser Typus nicht mehr und nie mehr aufzulösen, er ist nur zu steigern zur Masse."[9] Sternheim's dramatic exposure of the ruling but stupid aristocracy, and of the down-trodden but ambitious bourgeoisie proved in the long run more dangerous in all its consequences than any other medium of communication then at the disposal of any German writer.

Jethro Bithell drew attention to the influence of the cult of Nietzsche's Superman on *Heinrich Mann* when he pointed out that "the qualities of the Renaissance-Man may be transferred to modern characters, with the main aspects of licentious egotism and

ruthlessness, particularly in erotic experience".[11] The poet Gottfried Benn, in his oration on the occasion of Heinrich Mann's
sixtieth birthday, also stressed the considerable influence of
Nietzsche's dictum on the writer: "Nihilismus ist ein Glücksge-
fühl."[12] Heinrich Mann was not averse to being called the
"German Zola". He set himself the task to dissect the bourgeoisie
of the German Empire. (Curiously the world of the aristocracy and
of poverty escaped Mann's comprehension completely.) While Zola
could master a cool detachment and show convincing compassion,
Mann remained a "bourgeois manqué" who engaged himself in
brilliant propaganda. The more he considered himself a renegade
to his own class, the more it fettered him through its almost
hypnotical fascination. When the events of 1933 proved to the
writer that a grossly extended caricature of this incubus had
succeeded in poisoning a whole people, Mann discovered the
meaninglessness of the nihilistic hebephrenia in Nietzsche's dictum.
Mann, who had endeavoured all his life to emulate the quintessence
of French precepts and Gallic style, finally purged himself from all
Nietzschean inheritance by confessing unreservedly to the virtues
and vices of Henri IV, the first Bourbon king of France, whom he
called "the first ambassador of reason and human happiness". The
intelligent humanity of Montaigne held Mann captive for the rest
of his life, and his final philosophy culminated in the statement:
"Goodness means the highest degree of popularity."

Stefan Zweig's life presents a poignant and a most tragical commentary on the futility of a bourgeois's existence in times of
transition. He, too, emerged from the Vienna of the fin-de-siècle,
steeped in the twilight of Austrian corrosion. Stefan Zweig was the
paragon of a good European, a compassionate man and the heir
of a vanishing culture. When the dawn of a new barbarism forced
Zweig into a seemingly unending exile, he found himself unable to
grow new roots in alien soil. The awareness of his drifting existence
coupled with a hopeless yearning for "The World of Yesterday"
(the title of his autobiography) threw him into utter despair and
drove him finally to suicide. Like von Hofmannsthal and Schnitzler,
Vienna inspired him to a poetry of exquisite sensitivity. Being a
voracious reader of history, whose protean aspects fascinated him,
Zweig turned to biography and drama. As an essayist and highly
individual story-teller who had greatly profited from a study of
Sigmund Freud, he showed an original, psycho-analytical approach
to the objects of his studies. For years Richard Strauss urged Hugo
von Hofmannsthal for a really comic libretto. "After all," the
composer wrote in 1916, "I am the only composer nowadays with
some real sense of humour and sense of fun." Hofmannsthal
showed himself unable to gratify this ambition to become "the

Offenbach of the twentieth century". Since the death of his librettist Strauss had been looking for a new sympathetic collaborator and his choice fell upon Stefan Zweig. In 1931 Zweig began the libretto for *Die Schweigsame Frau* based on Ben Jonson's *Epicene*. The opera was produced in 1935. But as Zweig was a Jew it was withdrawn after only two performances. Strauss was even forbidden to communicate further with Stefan Zweig and was afterwards served by a friend of Zweig. It is well known that the bulk of Strauss's Opera *Der Friedenstag* is Zweig's work though it appeared under the name of a different librettist. Mental agony of this experience filled Zweig's most delicate sensorium which proved a productive receptacle for all utterances of the hopelessness of a life which had lost its meaning.

There were other poets who tried to escape from the inexorable logic of Nietzschean prophecies. *Christian Morgenstern*, as a poet, showed a split personality. Tormented by consumption, which caused an early death, he was groping for some spiritual meaning of his earthly pilgrimage, showing increasing signs of a preoccupation with mysticism. His lyrical poetry of melancholy introspection is nowadays largely forgotten. Morgenstern is mainly remembered as one of the few German nonsense-poets. Unwittingly he became one of the founder-fathers of the expressionist movement through his grotesque and parodistic humour. It should be worth while one day to draw attention to another renewer of forms and contents of German Lyric, Arno Holz, and to compare both poets and investigate their influence on modern German poetry. Christian Morgenstern was a daring experimenter with language and metaphor. A tendency to dissolve traditional meanings of grammar, syntax and word interpretation foreshadowed the ecstatic explosion of August Stramm and anticipated the monosyllabic outbursts of expressionist poetry. Morgenstern delighted in juggling with words, in creating new ones with or without a hidden meaning, and in discovering an exhilarating logic in illogical constructions. The word emancipates itself from its original context and creates its own fantastic world, devoid of reason but full of its own sense. "But this word-comedy expresses in reality a profound earnestness and moral significance which was all too often lost on a hyper-intellectual generation."[7] His fragmentation of established linguistic values points once more to the rejection of any deceptive security of life within a bourgeois society.

There is evidence that Franz Kafka often read the writings of *Robert Walser* whom he greatly admired. There is certainly a kinship between the Czech and the Swiss in the almost maniacal exactness of expression and in the submerged irony which accompanied a description of any man's destiny. Robert Walser, however, can be read without intellectual torment, for he means what he writes, and nothing else. His stories and poems do not suggest different planes of experience and do not allow speculative interpretations. Walser is firmly rooted in this world where he found so much sense in the midst of nonsense and so much diction in contradiction. The devotion which Stifter looked for in nature, Robert Walser pursued in man. But this "earthly paradise" of the human world was bound to confuse his innocent senses. His integrity refused to register the manifestations of evil. When he finally realized the delusions and deceptions of the world he inhabited, he ceased to write. The blessings of a prolonged mental derangement prevented him from being contaminated with the iniquities of his world which strove for self-perfection but only succeeded in stressing its imperfection. But side by side with Walser's obvious "joie de vivre", the awareness of fright, the consciousness of the moral and mental decay of modern man is always present with the writer. Since the death of Gottfried Keller and Conrad Ferdinand Meyer, Walser has been one of the most important figures in the world of Swiss literature. His poetic prose, partly descriptions of real occurrences, partly inventions of his imagination, deserves better attention in England.

It may seem inconsistent with the purpose of this book to show the disintegration among German men of letters at the beginning of this century by including an essay on *Gertrud le Fort*. The fact alone that she actually published books prior to the outbreak of the world war would not be sufficient reason. But Nietzsche's fight against Christian tradition prompted a reaction among those who were aware of the implications of such a cold revolution. A distinct Christian writing began to stir and to take the offensive at a later date. Léon Bloy, Georges Bernanos, François Mauriac and Graham Greene realized that the antinomy of Good and Evil, Heaven and Hell, Sin and Sanctity no longer sufficed for understanding a vastly more complicated reality. They comprehended very well the new situation for which neither religion nor any preferred creed could shoulder exclusive responsibility. Therefore they showed a sensitive awareness of a border-country, unknown in the past and impenetrable to any ready-made dogma. Since modern life had become identical with a highly personal risk, the answers to its problems could no longer be left to the go-between of priestly ordination. "Christian writing is militant writing." Gertrud le Fort, today nearly 90 years old, recognized that "every dramatic hero is always a guilty man". She also admitted that any innocent soul, any man without guilt held no longer much attraction for a creative writer. "The Pharisee is the most un-Christian figure in the Gospels." All her problems conflict with belief, church and dogma; her solutions aim at a sensible balance between religion and art. Preferring usually the disguise of an historical action, the problems remain those of our times : the conflict between belief and doubt. Herself a convert to Roman Catholicism, she knew how to avoid the pitfalls of a zealot. "The convert is not a man who stresses a painfully confessional separation, but, on the contrary, is a human being who has left it behind. His real experience is not provided by the creed to which he has converted, but by the unity of faith which submerges him." Gertrud le Fort at least discovered a way to renewed faith.

"He thought it strange," one reads in Ernst Wiechert's novel, *Der Totenwald*, about the man in the concentration camp, "that, with the exception of Hermann Hesse, he felt no need for any other living human being." When *Hermann Hesse* died in the summer of 1962, many an obituary reminded us of "the sage of Montagnola", having been "the last knight of Romanticism whose rearguard he valiantly defended".[13] One cannot entirely agree with this statement. Three times in his life Hesse clashed with the grimness of reality before the catharsis of these shocks opened the way to his own salvation which he discovered in the message of a new humanity. To remember became his mission, but not to conquer. He always remained conscious of the trends of his time and never fled from them. It is this consciousness which renders Hesse's humanity very credible. The essence of his writings was concerned with the problematical facets of an existence in ambiguous times. For him spiritual values and sensuous demands lived in close proximity. Both strove for higher forms of expression and for a more harmonious amalgamation. His quest for a synthesis, based on his variegated subjective experiences, left the impression in his earlier years of being unfilled and of remaining unfilling. Hesse thought to find his synthesis in the communion with nature. He possessed strong pictorial gifts and a very intense visual relationship with nature. Clouds and mountains, space and landscape, produced a colourful and pleasing clearness. But an almost nihilistic despair of man's inner dichotomy burst open in the novels of his middle period. The primaeval instincts of man seemed to put up a desperate fight against the encroachment of a doubtful culture and civilization. "In ihnen ist Göttliches und Teufliches, ist mütterliches und väterliches Blut, ist Glücksfähigkeit und Leidensfähigkeit."[14] In his novel *Narziss und Goldmund,* which deals with the polarity of ecstasy and asceticism, there is only muted resignation left, the wisdom of the hermit whose contacts with the world have become fragile and slender. His last great works which achieved the synthesis of a true humanity and for which Hesse received the Nobel prize were spiritual adventures into Utopian realms where all dichotomy dissolved and the wisdom of Eastern profundity reigned. "'Das Glasperlenspiel' ist die entgültige Transposition und Ueber-höhung all jener Lebensläufe, in denen sich Hesse darstellte."[15] The poet, in his late novels, became a great magician, in whose hands the word achieved immanent appraisal and only needed to testify its own value. The arts of the prose writer, of the poet, and of the painter have become inseparable : they show the perfection of inner and outer vision, fused into harmony. His life came round full circle. The poet of the early "Romantische Lieder" showed now a mysterious affinity with his last phase, and, like a dream, the interim of his life must have rushed by. It was a long way from Nietzsche's nihilism to Hesse's final conclusion : "The realm where I dwelt, the dream land of my poetic hours and days, was mys-teriously stretching somewhere between time and space." And yet, the inability to face the quicksands of German reality fairly and squarely provides a distinctive link between most writers on the eve of the First World War.

TRANSLATIONS

1. "God is dead .... Do we not all wander through an infinite Nothing? Does the empty void not breathe on us? Has it not become much colder? Must street-lamps not be lighted in the forenoon? Do we not yet hear the din of the grave-digger who inters God?"

2. "Only he who knows how to change, remains my kindred spirit."

3. "Thus Spake Zarathustra."

4. viz. E. M. Butler, *The Tyranny of Greece over Germany*, Cam-bridge University Press, 1935.

5. "Since the Germans had Goethe and Schiller, they are no longer satisfied with singular numbers. They must now appear in twos." Otto Julius Bierbaum.

6. Paul Fechter: *Geschichte der Deutschen Literatur*, Gütersloh, 1960

7. viz. August Closs, *The Genius of the German Lyric*, London, 1962.

8. "We must learn to achieve an understanding by shorthand methods." Carl Sternheim in *Das Fossil*.

9. "It is impossible to dissect this type as an individual case in future. It can only be increased as a mass product." Franz Blei in *Essay über Carl Sternheim*.

10. "The word kills life." Georg Kaiser in *Die Flucht nach Venedig*.

11. Jethro Bithell in *Modern German Literature*, London, 1939.

12. "Nihilism means blissfulness."

13. Hugo Ball in *Hermann Hesse*, Suhrkamp Verlag, Frankfurt, 1947.

14. "In them there is divinity and devilry, maternal and paternal blood, and the faculty of being happy and to suffer."

15. "'Magister Ludi' means the final transposition and super-elevation of all those courses of life in which Hesse presented himself." Ernst Robert Curtius in *Hermann Hesse*.

Friedrich Nietzsche

Friedrich Nietzsche

by W. D. WILLIAMS

Friedrich Nietzsche was born on 15 October 1844 at Röcken near Lützen. His father died when he was five, and he and his younger sister were brought up by their mother. He was educated at Schulpforta and was destined to follow his father in the Lutheran priesthood, but turned at Leipzig University to classical studies. While a student he discovered the works of Schopenhauer and met Wagner, both of whom exercised an enormous influence on him. He was a brilliant undergraduate and was appointed at the very early age of 24 to the chair of classical philology at Basel. Here he became a close friend of Wagner, but provoked hot controversy with his first book *Die Geburt der Tragödie* in 1872. He served for a time as a volunteer in the Franco-Prussian War, but was invalided out of the forces. He was Professor at Basel for ten years, a friend of Burckhardt the historian and Overbeck the theologian. His *Unzeitgemässe Betrachtungen* (1873–76) contained strong criticism of the cultural values and institutions of the time. His friendship with Wagner ended finally in 1876 at Bayreuth in disillusionment with what he saw as the musician's capitulation to Christianity and to the demands of the commercial public. During this time Nietzsche's health grew steadily worse and after his resignation from the university in 1879 he was frequently unable to work for long periods, owing to very severe head-aches and partial blindness. He lived for the next ten years predominantly in Switzerland and Northern Italy, his works following one another rapidly, advancing now from criticism of contemporary attitudes to a much more thoroughgoing criticism of morality and human life as a whole. His isolation was relieved only by a few staunch friends like Peter Gast. In 1882 he met Lou Salomé, proposed to her, but was refused, and this episode led to a break with his mother and sister. *Menschliches Allzumenschliches* (1878–79), *Der Wanderer und sein Schatten* (1880), *Morgenröthe* (1881), all pursue the task of criticism, but from *Die fröhliche Wissenschaft* (1882) onwards, Nietzsche's ideals take a more positive form, expressed symbolically in *Also sprach Zarathustra* (1883–85) and critically in succeeding works (*Jenseits von Gut und Böse* 1886, *Zur Genealogie der Moral* 1887, *Der Fall Wagner* and *Der Antichrist* 1888, *Götzendämmerung* and *Nietzsche contra Wagner* 1889). At the end his autobiographical sketch *Ecce Homo* clearly bears the signs of madness. In January 1889 he collapsed in the street in Turin, was taken first to a Basel clinic (diagnosis: "progressive paralysis"), and then to hospital in Jena. He returned home in the care of his mother in 1890, but was oblivious of the world around him until his death in 1900.

"ALLES, was tief ist, liebt die Maske."[1] Nietzsche's words are an ironical commentary on the fate of his own works since their appearance. Seldom can an important thinker have been subject to more misrepresentation and misinterpretation; his "doctrine", reduced to a very few leading ideas—the Superman, the Eternal Recurrence, the division of humanity into "lords" and "slaves", the violently anti-Christian "immoralism"—has given rise to a whole series of fashionable attitudes on the one hand, or has been dismissed as nothing more than the ravings of an embittered neurotic on the other. The history of the spread of knowledge about his work has been in truth the successive penetration of one mask after another, each dominant for a time and then being discarded or radically modified as a different emphasis led to a more complete understanding. It is only in recent years that a balanced and critical assessment of his work has become at all current.

We have only to think of Nietzsche's early works, the *Geburt der Tragödie* (1872) and the series of *Unzeitgemässe Betrachtungen* (1873–76) to see how far the process of "masking" had developed even at the beginning. These were all written while he was still very much under the influence of Wagner and it is plain that he had to do a certain amount of violence to his thought to bring it into line with the admiration he felt for the Master at Tribschen. This is even true also of his passion for Schopenhauer, whom he continually exalts and to whom he devoted one whole enthusiastic essay (*Schopenhauer als Erzieher* 1874), but of whom we know he was sharply critical in some of his unpublished sketches of the time. If we look closely at the argument of the *Geburt der Tragödie* we can see how uncomfortably the mask fits in this case. This book represented Nietzsche's dearest hopes of making at one blow a reputation for himself, a great stroke in the campaign on behalf of Wagner, and a powerful protest against the uncivilized barbarity of his time. If we compare the many essays and sketches of this time with the work itself we can see that much has been left out. Everything, in the final version, is pointed to the glorification of the Master which forms the conclusion. In fact Nietzsche had to do some violence to his thought to harmonize it with his adoration of Wagner, and the fundamental contradiction between this and his interpretation of the Greeks, is apparent in the book.

The thesis is brilliantly simple, and is announced in the first paragraph. He sets himself against the view of Greek art which in Germany had held sway since the days of Winckelmann, which sees in the effortless ease of their statues and the superb majesty of their choruses and their epics a demonstration of the simple and noble faith which conceived beauty as a fine aesthetic harmony built on a pagan confidence in the goodness and joy of living. For

Nietzsche this "schöne Schein" was real, but was based upon a desperate and agonizing struggle to dominate tragic awareness of the evil and pain of life. Two opposing principles are in tension, which he calls the Apolline and the Dionysian, and characterizes as dream and intoxication. At the centre of all dream, all "schöne Schein", harmony and grace, the Greeks, he urges, felt the terrifying but fundamental principle of Dionysos, the final unity of man with nature, amoral, chaotic, unrestrained, which is an essential component of the greatest art. The ease and simplicity which we admire were only won by a sustained and heroic effort to transform the consciousness of this Dionysian quality into an illusion of peace and resolution. For life at bottom is will—the blind irrational and aimless Schopenhauerian will, ugly, terrifying and dangerous. The Greeks could bear this exalting but terrible knowledge in their art, as they bore it too by the creation of the Olympian gods, who justified life by living it themselves. The vision of Apollo, the formal illusion, could not subsist except on the basis of the Dionysian knowledge. We are reminded of Schopenhauer on every page. Nietzsche gives, for instance, a long analysis of music and its metaphysical significance which is deeply coloured by the latter's famous and profound thought on the subject. He describes the genesis of Greek tragedy in the tragic chorus, defining the earliest tragedy as the union of the Dionysian chorus with the Apolline world of images, and following its history in the light of the recognition that it consists essentially in the restoration of the broken unity of all being, the overcoming of man's individuation.

But this high activity, he maintains, was killed, or rather killed itself, by the appearance of Euripides, who, with Socrates, his master, represented the triumph of the new "theoretical" man, whose effort was directed towards knowledge and whose weapons were intellectual and rationalistic, over the old "tragic" or "aesthetic" man, whose whole preoccupation was with beauty and whose methods were instinctive and intuitive. Here we come to the crux of the book—the point where Schopenhauerian theory gives place to a much more profound and much more absolute revelation of Nietzsche's attitude. In common with many thinkers before and since, he felt that all the ills of the modern world were due in the last instance to the separation which has gradually grown through the ages, and especially since the Renaissance, between nature and mind, between the animal, instinctive life of man and his conscious intellectual life. These, he feels, we have allowed to become divorced, with all the diverse evil consequences which can be seen as much in the agony of a Pascal as in the malaise of the Romantics, and again in the automatic unhumanized life of modern machine-man. The essential then, he feels, is to reunite spirit and nature, to bring into harmony again man's instinctual life with his conscious intellectual activity. This union was a living reality in Greek civilization, but only in pre-Socratic times. Here the voice of Nietzsche is curiously like that of Rousseau, and Rousseau is indeed his great spiritual forebear. From this follows a conclusion no less shattering than the discovery of the Dionysian spirit at work beneath the Apolline repose of Greek art and tragedy—the conclusion that the Greek achievement should be entirely revalued. The traditional view sees Greek culture starting in the dim past with Homer, evolving gradually through Aeschylus and attaining its full grandeur in the period beginning with Sophocles and culminating in the fifth and fourth centuries, with Plato and Aristotle, the triumph of the city-state, ruled by rational values enshrined in the Athenian democracy and in the Socratic analysis expressed in the Platonic dialogues. But on Nietzsche's premisses it is precisely this period which shows Greek culture in its decline, because it is now that owing to Socrates, with his insistence on logical thought, on knowing rather than living, the tradition of tragedy is killed by the intellectual, almost psychological, art of Euripides. His heroes are no longer symbols of the great mysteries of life, but ordinary men and women, and art has given place to naturalism. Socrates is the extreme opposite pole to the mystic : he is the "theoretical" man. His appearance *seemed* to herald an advance in human culture, but his essential insufficiency, Nietzsche urges, is now, in the nineteenth century, at last apparent and Wagner has opened our eyes to it. Thus neatly does he link his interpretation of Greek history and art to the needs of his own life, his desire to support his friend to the fullest extent, his disgust and disappointment at the dead-end of erudition and stylelessness into which our whole intellectual culture has led us.

This book is characteristic of his early work. The other essays, on D. F. Strauß, on the use and abuse of history in our civilization, on Schopenhauer, and on Wagner himself, all spring from the same disgust and disillusion with all that we are taught to admire and all that our educational system teaches us to esteem. It is apparent that what he is attacking is basically the whole civilization of his time, the stylelessness, the barbarous philistinism, the belief that culture is a matter of knowledge, the notion that "mass-education" is a worthy ideal, the general obliteration of standards of taste, refinement and power in an amorphous mediocrity, the levelling-down he sees all around him glorified by the name of freedom and democracy. He is irate at these things, and particularly, as a university professor of classical philosophy, at the way in which the universities are lending themselves to the betrayal of their high and noble task.

The essay on Strauß springs from the fundamental and growing conviction in Nietzsche of the utter hostility and incompatibility of the genius on the one hand and the scholar on the other. Nietzsche was setting them against each other continually—so that he is inwardly torn by the irreconcilability of the two sides of his own personality. This condition is typical throughout his life. The driving force, the dynamic of his thinking, is always such a conflict —not simply a tug-of-war between his emotions and his reason, as we have, for instance, in a man like Heine, but an emotional desire to have his cake and eat it, to unite in his own consciousness elements which his whole emotional impetus brands as opposites. It is this polarity in his own spirit which gives all his writing its dramatic and often tragic quality. And it is this, or mainly this, which drove him mad. The conflict took many forms throughout his life; this antithesis between genius and scholar is the first, the crisis over Wagner sprang from another, and the final tension between Christ and Dionysos ultimately destroyed him.

One may say that all his work follows from this initial disillusionment and disgust. A very large part of it is essentially a repeated attempt to do something to right these wrongs. His writings are frequently classified into three periods—this early enthusiastic advocacy of Schopenhauer and Wagner, and what they stand for, as guides who might lead men out of the troubles he diagnoses so ruthlessly, followed by a "critical" and "positivist" period in which he analyses the values on which we base our civilization, and finally a series of works from his last years of sanity in which he sketches his doctrine for the salvation of mankind. This classification is very much too schematic, and it fails to emphasize the extraordinarily tentative nature of all his thinking from beginning to end. The most significant feature of all his work is its entirely experimental nature. His thought is not a series of statements or conclusions, but a continual leaping into the dark, an incessant sketching of possibilities, a continual hazarding of hypotheses, a sustained experiment in pushing any postulate as far as it will go. But it is true to say that it all starts from these early invectives against the world he saw around him. As the early enthusiasms fade—and the break with Wagner is a cruel and shattering experience which scars Nietzsche for life—so he tries first a sort of Cartesian reduction of all the beliefs we entertain to an irreducible minimum from which perhaps a coherent structure can be rebuilt (*Menschliches Allzumenschliches* and the succeeding books) and this he finds leaves nothing fruitful behind, and then finally, from *Zarathustra* onwards, he seizes the bull by the horns and elaborates a series of sketches of what might be if men began to take their eternal destiny seriously. This effort to civilize, to educate, to preach at men, this is one side of his work, and a very important one, but it is not the whole of it, and it has led to a great deal of misunderstanding, when interpreters have seized on this or that dictum of his and taken it in isolation from the very complex balance of significances in which Nietzsche had originally set it. And this, it must be said, has been aided by the exaggerated importance which has been attached to the unfinished sketches edited under the influence of his sister after his death and published under the title, *Der Wille zur Macht*. We shall have more to say of this later.

The disillusionment with Wagner in 1876 represented in Nietzsche's life far more than simply the recognition that his adored master was a charlatan and his music a sham, designed not to stir the German people to heroism and culture, but to pander to their innate spiritual laziness and their comfortable self-esteem. Nietzsche's disgust at Wagner's embracing of Christianity was only the symptom of a swing of his mind right away from Wagner and Schopenhauer and away from all that these men had meant for him as cultural ideals. And the disillusionment leads him to abandon all the enthusiastic mysticism of his youth and champion now a destructive and cynical positivism which appears to take delight in uncovering all that is base in the most noble human ideals and aspirations. Socrates, the villain of earlier days, is now exalted as the true guide. The earlier ideal of the genius, whether saint, artist or philosopher, who justifies human life by his very emergence, is now replaced by the ideal of the "freier Geist", a Voltairian spirit unconstrained by habit, convention, even by belief. And the acid analysis of human beliefs, spiritual, moral, scientific, religious, aesthetic, is now regarded as the only proper task of the mind, and pre-eminently a task for the intelligence, not the will or the heart or the emotions. The books from *Menschliches Allzumenschliches* (1878) onwards follow out the destructive programme in the most uncompromising way. We have continual reiteration of the same points. There are no absolute truths or values, all belief is a reflection of pain or pleasure. Morality is a necessary lie which protects man from his own animality. Moral choice is the sacrifice of one desire for the sake of gratifying another, justice is the product of the clash of equally matched forces. There is thus no real basis for the distinction between good and evil, and the same applies to all religious and aesthetic values. Religion is the importation of fictitious laws for human purposes. The "scientific" man, who carries out this task of seeing through all illusions, is a higher stage of human development than the artistic. The theory that the "good" is essentially the strong and healthy is implicit throughout. As a symbol of the thoroughly emancipated spirit he chooses the figure of the wanderer, who has severed all ties which restrict him, even his own roots. All idealism is abandoned in favour of "psychology", which involves the determination to isolate the essential deceit which is at the centre of personality. "Die Bestie in uns will belogen werden : Moral ist Notlüge, damit wir von ihr nicht zerrissen werden : ohne die Irrtümer, welche in den Annahmen der Moral liegen, wäre der Mensch Tier geblieben."[2]

With *Die Fröhliche Wissenschaft* (1882) Nietzsche's thought begins to take a more positive turn. He is here beginning to investigate and define the ideal of "life" to which he has so long paid homage, and he reaches the following formulation : "Leben—das heisst fortwährend etwas von sich abstossen, das sterben will; Leben —das heisst : grausam und unerbittlich gegen Alles sein, was schwach und alt an uns, und nicht nur an uns, wird. Leben—das heisst also : ohne Pietät gegen sterbende, Elende und Greise sein. Immerfort Mörder sein. Und doch hat der alte Moses gesagt : Du sollst nicht töten."[3] If life involves a continual killing of that which within and without the organism is weak or decadent or dying, then this Darwinian insight should be applied to culture too. So again hard and telling blows are struck at Wagner on the score of his decadence. But in a famous passage entitled "Sternenfreundschaft" Nietzsche is conscious how much he owes to Wagner and how much his attack on his old master is a cutting-off of his own dying hand. And it is in this book too that he tells the significant little parable of the madman who accuses men of having killed God because they could not bear His witnessing them continually. The description of the meaning of the killing of God shows how deeply Nietzsche feels the essential being of the God he will not admit to his thought : "Ist nicht die Größe dieser Tat zu groß für uns? Müssen wir nicht selber zu Göttern werden, um nur ihrer würdig zu erscheinen?"[4]

It is plain that these books of the central "positivistic" period of Nietzsche's development show him carrying out a programme of total destruction accompanied by a great deal of heart-searching, and they all point forward to the triumphant proclamation in *Also sprach Zarathustra* (1883–85) of his "message". But this book is extraordinarily difficult to come to terms with, since in contrast to all his other works, it is couched in poetic and prophetic terms rather than those of logical argument. The message so presumptuously heralded, so exuberantly welcomed and so reverently transmitted here is not in essence new. We have seen in previous works most of the points he makes here, but the creation of the symbolic figure of the prophet Zarathustra allows Nietzsche an enormous latitude of experiment and play, enabling him to carry a wide range of significance in an emotional and intuitive coherence that logical presentation would have forbidden. The central burden of

Zarathustra's teaching is in no doubt from the first. God is dead,
man is alone. But man is not the end. "Der Übermensch ist der Sinn
der Erde. Euer Wille sage: de Übermensch sei der Sinn der Erde."[5]
The human will alone must create its values for itself and the
ultimate creative force is that highest desire within the individual
which longs to realize the Superman. The Superman, then, is not
some future development of man but a potentiality given in our
human make-up which it is our duty to fulfil. The theme is the
metaphysical situation of man without God—exactly the situation
which for Pascal was a terror and an abyss, but for Nietzsche is a
challenge—since God is dead anyway, that is the transcendental
principle of an all-powerful creator-deity has lost its validity in the
modern "theoretical" world. But if there is no longer God, the
universe no longer has meaning. All this Nietzsche accepts, and
replies that the human task is precisely to create meaning, to put a
sense into creation. And the Superman therefore is the "sense of
the earth".

From this follow the various developments of the book. Nietzsche
considers the traditional values and rejects all which conflict with
what he calls "loyalty to the earth". A certain admixture of bad is
in all good, as death is in all life, but the creative will can, and
must, transform the one into the other. "Und nur wo es Gräber
sind, gibt es Auferstehungen."[6] This life here is all we have and
our duty is to stamp it with a significance which transcends it.
"Kannst du dir selber Richter sein und Rächer deines Gesetzes?"[7]
This is the supreme question he addresses to us. And the consequences are an extreme personalism and an extreme emphasis on
"self-overcoming". "Alles Lebendige ist ein Gehorchendes. Gutes
und Böses, das unvergänglich wäre—das gibt es nicht! Aus sich
selber muß es sich immer wieder überwinden . . . Und wer ein
Schöpfer sein will im Guten und Bösen: Wahrlich, der muß ein
Vernichter erst sein und Werte zerbrechen!"[8] The doctrine of
Eternal Recurrence, which is not announced until the middle of the
book, is presented as an affirmation of belief in life which turns
Zarathustra's deepest despair into confident certainty. It has been
argued that the notion of the cyclic nature of the universe makes
nonsense of Nietzsche's whole idea of culture and the Superman as
an ideal, since there can be no progress if the clock is put back to
the beginning at the end of each cycle. But this is to misinterpret
his conception of recurrence, since he is at pains to point out that
we come back again and again, not to a life exactly like this one,
but to *this very life*. Recurrence does not mean repetition. Indeed
the question of time is here irrelevant—the doctrine is a powerful
symbol of the element of eternity which is in all life, and it is this
eternity of which Nietzsche is so tragically conscious. This is

Nietzsche's attempt at escaping a purely humanistic "life for life's sake" attitude, which the denial of God would otherwise involve. And it carries too, of course, the implication of total human responsibility, not to God, who is dead, but to ourselves. We must answer for every moment of our lives by re-enacting it in eternity. Nothing is ever lost, every act is truly eternal and therefore transcendental. And lastly, a point Nietzsche was at pains to emphasize in later works, the doctrine of Recurrence is a touchstone on which each of us is judged and redeemed or condemned by our reception of it. The "strong" man, who can "bear the thought" will glory in his eternity, while the "weak" will be broken. Later Nietzsche further extended this by saying that the "weak" will be broken and *will die out*, and then the "strong" will inherit the earth. This of course is untenable : there can be no "dying out" where all life is eternal.

In the light of this conception Nietzsche can formulate his moral ideal in startling terms : "Tut immerhin, was ihr wollt—aber seid erst solche die wollen können."[9] But in the last part of the book, with its much looser construction and its allegorical characters and events, the doubts and hesitations are apparent. This is anxious questioning whether in fact the sustained denial of God is really possible, whether man can carry the awful burden of redemption which Nietzsche would put upon him. His attitude is mystical, but essentially problematic. At the end of the book Zarathustra's work is plainly not yet done. Nietzsche planned other parts; several of the sketches show Zarathustra triumphant, his teaching accepted and applied by men, and himself dying, like Empedocles, at the bliss of such a moment. This was never carried out, and this fact lends strength to the supposition that the whole book is in a very deep sense a confession on Nietzsche's part, an account of his own deepest experience rather than simply a symbolic presentation of his ideas. And this is what gives it its poetry and its tragedy.

The works after *Zarathustra* are all amplifications and clarifications of ideas expressed in it and the first of them, *Jenseits von Gut and Böse* (1887), is sub-titled "Vorspiel einer Philosophie der Zukunft". Here the *Wille zur Macht* is posited from the first as the essence of life. In his search for a quality in life which gives meaning to it, Nietzsche has rejected everything offered before, starting with the nineteenth-century shibboleths of progress and ending with the Christian conception of Heaven and the Kingdom of God. Life does not strive just to survive, to remain as it is, but is always trying to improve itself and enrich itself. The survival-theory of Darwin is essentially static, an equilibrium is theoretically possible where no change is needed for survival. This, thought Nietzsche, would not be life but death. Life cannot stop still,

so it must do more than just survive. So it must be will to power.
Power within the organism, *bien entendu,* spiritual, mental, and
only secondarily physical. And with this admitted, he argues that
psychology is the way to the fundamental problems, and considers
here the psychology of morals, rehearsing extremely cogently the
various ways in which men are driven to deceive themselves about
the real bases of their actions. But he goes farther than before in
his radical criticism of the most basic suppositions by which we
live :

Es ist nichts mehr als ein moralischer Vorurteil, daß Wahrheit
mehr wert ist als Schein . . . es bestünde gar kein Leben, wenn
nicht auf dem Grunde perspektivischer Schätzungen und Schein-
barkeiten . . . Ja, was zwingt uns überhaupt zur Annahme, daß
es einen wesenhaften Gegensatz von "wahr" und "falsch" gibt?
Genügt es nicht, Stufen der Scheinbarkeit anzunehmen und
gleichsam hellere und dunklere Schatten und Gesamttöne des
Scheins—verschiedene valeurs, um die Sprache der Maler zu
reden. Warum dürfte die Welt, die uns etwas angeht—nicht
eine Fiktion sein? Und wer da fragt : "aber zur Fiktion gehört
doch ein Urheber".—dürfte dem nicht rund geantwortet werden,
warum? Gehört dieses "Gehört" nicht vielleicht mit zur
Fiktion?[10]

This "perspectivism" is from now on his fundamental attitude,
and he considers the "natural history of morals" with this in mind.
He finds the roots of all morality in fear of one sort or another, and
this leads to the proposition of a double system, one for "lords",
that is men who dare to be themselves and have the courage and
confidence to obey only their own spirits, and one for "slaves", that
is the generality, who have to rely on rules, on "categorical imperatives", on presumptions with a sanction either in public opinion or
the law or the wrath of God or the hatred of humanity. This is a
new version of the old antithesis in his mind between the genius
and the ordinary man, which we have noticed before.

In his next book, *Zur Genealogie der Moral* (1887), he becomes
more specific. The work consists of three essays—on the double
system of morality, on the religious ideas of guilt and conscience,
and finally on ascetic ideals. It is the clearest of the works of these
last years, and Nietzsche's most sustained piece of connected closely-
reasoned argument. In the first essay he investigates the origin of
the words "gut", "böse" and "schlecht". He goes into a good deal
of etymological detail, most of it unsound guesswork, and comes to
the conclusion that the original power-morality, in which the
natural lords ruled their weaker brethren, was based on the antithesis "gut/schlecht". "Gut" meant noble, belonging to the ruling

caste, privileged, strong, fearless, egoistic, and "schlecht" meant common, plebeian, low, base, unprivileged. This "natural" system was upset by what Nietzsche calls "der Sklavenaufstand der Moral" —the process, rooted in the resentment of the unprivileged, by which they combined against the lords, setting up their own qualities as "gut" and stigmatizing those of the lords as "böse". So what was previously "schlecht" is now regarded as "gut" and the new word "böse" was applied to the exemplars of the old goodness. This *Sklavenaufstand* found its most powerful expression in the Christian ethic of meekness, forgiveness, humility, gentleness—all those virtues of the unprivileged which, equipped with a transcendental sanction and a hierarchy of priests as propagandists, finally came to dominate the earlier "natural" conceptions; and this, urges Nietzsche, we inherit today, this makes us so weak-willed and shame-faced, so unoriginal and miserable. The Jews and the Romans provide him with his types of *Sklavenmoral* and *Herrenmoral*. The second essay goes into the mechanics of this—the Christian conceptions which have triumphed and brought about men's decadence. The conscience, and the guilt-feelings which Christian priests have turned to their own advantage, have proved the most powerful weapons in their struggle to make men accept an "unnatural" ethic. The psychological experience of a guilty conscience was, he says, unknown to primitive man—it was only when he had been "tamed" by the reversal of moral values described in the first essay that all his natural aggression-instincts, in a word his "will to power", deprived of any outlet, were turned inwards and let loose on himself, on his own consciousness. And then, to make sense of the guilt-feelings, the whole panoply of avenging, jealous or loving god, transcendental punishment, heaven and hell, were introduced. So, in the end, the very Christian ethic and Christian attitude which stands against the morality of the lords, is itself only a subtle and highly sublimated product of the same will-to-power which issues immediately in the lords' morality. As indeed it must be, since all life is will-to-power.

In the last of the three essays Nietzsche devotes his most brilliant insights to the analysis of the ascetic temperament. On the face of it, this contradicts his reduction of all moral experience to will-to-power. He brings in Wagner continually as a man who finally succumbed to the attractions of asceticism. For the first step in the argument is that the ascetic is so because he likes it. Schopenhauer, for instance. There must be a supreme satisfaction in self-denial. Nietzsche analyses the artist as ascetic (Wagner) and the philosopher as ascetic (Schopenhauer) and in doing so, analyses himself most beautifully, if unconsciously, for his insight into the satisfaction of asceticism springs from his own innate tendency to it. But on this level his analysis applies really only to those who play at asceticism, who use it as a tool for the attainment of something else—spiritual peace, harmony, or what you will. The real ascetic embraces a contradiction, a resentment which attacks life itself, a force which seeks to overcome itself and destroy itself. How is this possible? There must be some deeper reason—life could not thus cut away the ground beneath itself. First, perhaps, this is a phenomenon of degenerating life—the ascetic feels himself out of harmony with life, seeks to place the blame, and is persuaded to place it upon himself. This fits the sheep who is governed by his priest, but what about the priest himself, who is not taken in by his own sophistry? Here we come to Nietzsche's final analysis. Man is metaphysically situated in suffering and the gap he feels is not that of a counterbalance to his suffering, but of an explanation of it and a significance which will justify it, "Die Sinnlosigkeit des Leidens, nicht das Leiden, war der Fluch, der bisher über der Menschheit ausgebreitet lag—und das asketische Ideal bot ihm einen Sinn. . . . der Mensch war damit gerettet, er hatte einen Sinn, er war fürderhin nicht mehr wie ein Blatt im Winde, ein Spielball des Unsinns, des 'ohnesinns', er konnte nunmehr etwas wollen—gleichgültig zunächst wohin, wozu, womit er wollte; der Wille selbst war gerettet." He sums up : "Lieber will der Mensch *das Nichts* wollen, als *nicht* wollen."[11]

His later books become more and more shrill. The two devoted to his old antagonist Wagner, for instance, use extreme terms in characterizing the composer as a charlatan and an exemplar of the *Sklavenmoral* he hates. By making this attack he is tearing something out of his own heart. "If thy right hand offend thee, cut it off." One realizes, as one reads these later books of Nietzsche's, that all his attacks are basically a repeated cutting-off of his own offending right hand. And nowhere is this more true than in this resurrection of a quarrel twelve years old, this embittered attack on a man who had been his great leader and friend and whom he had not seen since 1876.

We have left out of our consideration so far the enormous mass of aphorisms and fragments which Nietzsche left after his death and which were published under the title *Der Wille zur Macht*. There is no doubt that the editing and arrangement of this book was largely influenced by Nietzsche's sister, who did not shrink even from amending the text on occasion in order to present a much more systematic and unified picture of her brother's thought than it warranted.* The ideas contained in it are not in essence new and

* For a full discussion of this matter see the introduction and notes to the third volume of the most recent and most scholarly edition of Nietzsche ed. Karl Schlechta (Mauser 1955-60).

it is a mistake to try to pretend that this work offers a fully articulated "system" in any sense. This indeed is true of Nietzsche's work as a whole. He stands at the end of a long development. Progressively the human approach to comprehension of the world has narrowed—in the beginning all human faculties were admitted, then mainly the religious consciousness linked to the reason, and finally the reason alone. If that fails there is nothing left, no human key to the mysteries which surround us. In the climate of our time, experience is fragmentary and disparate, and we have no principle around which to unify it. This Nietzsche clearly saw, and as clearly realized that any such unifying principle was a piece of wish-fulfilment or dishonesty. He therefore throws his net as wide as possible, bringing to expression all the different facets of our experience, leaving them problematic and ultimately inexplicable. This is what has led his readers frequently to regard him as a poet primarily and a philosopher only incidentally. But such an attitude to him, as we shall see, is only shirking any real confrontation with his thought.

We have to do with an attitude rather than a "philosophy", a consideration of values rather than truths. This is particularly clear in his attitude to morality. When he calls himself an "immoralist" he is urging that it is the individual only which creates moral value and all moral ideas not rooted in individual experience are invalid. What then becomes of organized society? What guarantee is there against chaos? Leaving aside Nietzsche's retort that he is here only stating a fact, since all moral systems are really only the reflection of the personality of their creators, we are brought up against his radical emphasis on life as the only absolute. Organization, systemization, the construction of a social fabric and the conditioning of a set of social responses—all these are a denial of life, an easy way of avoiding living. And since living is difficult and dangerous men prefer it that way. But for a living man there can be no external authority, so that chaos, in the sense of ultimate absence of rules, is inherent in life and the greatest possible stimulus to it. "One must have chaos in one to give birth to a dancing star." This saying of Zarathustra's is fundamental in Nietzsche, the dancing star being his symbol of the plenitude and joy of living. Always he is concerned not so much with the truth or falsehood of the ideas he treats but rather with their *effects,* the sort of life they lead to and encourage. His main criticism of Christianity is not so much that it is a false construction based on resentment and wish-fulfilment, as that its effect has been in practice to blunt the fine point of living, to encourage those qualities of weakness and dependence which he considers responsible for our automatic mechanical life today. Hence his violence in attacking it coupled with his unfeigned admiration for Christ himself. He is on much stronger ground here than say Voltaire with his ridicule of Christian conceptions because they are absurd and illogical. This, of course, involves a radical reversal of traditional conceptions of truth. Truth for Nietzsche is not a body of knowledge towards which men move, by trial and error, the gradual approximation of hypotheses and so on, but is, like life itself, problematic, contradictory, illogical and partial. There are many truths, but no truth. In one of the posthumous fragments he puts his point thus :

> Moralisch ausgedrückt, ist die Welt falsch, aber insofern die Moral selbst ein Stück dieser Welt ist, so ist die Moral falsch. . . . "Wahrheit" ist soweit nicht etwas, das da wäre und das auf-zufinden, zu entdecken wäre—sondern etwas, das zu schaffen ist und das den Namen für einen Prozeß abgibt, mehr noch für einen Willen der Überwältigung, der an sich kein Ende hat : Wahrheit hineinlegen, als ein processus in infinitum, ein *aktives Bestimmen*—*nicht* ein Bewußtwerden von etwas, das an sich fest und bestimmt wäre. Es ist ein Wort für den "Willen zur Macht".[12]

This is, of course, nihilism—the following to its farthest conse-quences of the presupposition that the universe is literally sense-less. But it should not be thought that Nietzsche enjoys this situation. We have seen enough of his thinking to realize that the various "perspective judgments" he advances—the Superman, the eternal recurrence, and so on—are in essence mystical at bottom. "Wenn Skepsis und Sehnsucht sich begatten, entsteht die Mystik."[13] His formulation here is directed at the mysteries of the church, but it fits himself extremely closely, and we can see very clearly the direction of his longing. His tone of voice again and again makes this clear. "Es ist ganz und gar nicht die erste Frage, ob wir mit uns zufrieden sind, sondern ob wir überhaupt irgend womit zufrieden sind. Gesetzt, wir sagen ja zu einem einzigen Augenblick, so haben wir damit nicht nur zu uns selbst, sondern zu allem Dasein ja gesagt. Denn es steht nichts für sich, weder in uns selbst noch in den Dingen; und wenn nur ein einziges Mal unsre Seele wie eine Saite von Glück gezittert und getönt hat, so waren alle Ewigkeiten nötig, um dies eine Geschehen zu bedingen—und alle Ewigkeit war in diesem einzigen Augenblick unseres Jasagens gutgeheissen, erlöst, gerechtfertigt und bejaht."[14]

It is plain here, and in many other places, that nothing is so strong as his yearning for eternal life; the song to eternity in *Zarathustra* is a direct expression of his deepest desires. He is searching for the kingdom of God while denying God's existence. He is filled with reverence, he must worship. In his youth he wrote a significant poem, "Dem unbekannten Gott", which shows the beginning of this path, and the *Dionysos-Dithyramben* show him at the desperate tragic end of it. For his critical intelligence allowed him nothing to worship, no idols, no heavenly powers, nothing finally except what is near at hand and in himself, the principle of life itself and its personification in the Greek god Dionysos.

Dionysos, the god of wine, of intoxication, of sensual and sexual enjoyment, of that instinctive pre-logical process of life which was so present to the Greeks and to Nietzsche, related to Pan, the great god of nature, and to Orpheus, the god of the lyre—this is the symbol to which Nietzsche again and again returns. He represents the "Amor Fati", the "Pessimismus der Stärke", the immersion in the unconscious flow of life for which he calls. And Dionysos stands against Christianity, the acceptance of life against its denial in favour of the world to come.

Der Gott am Kreuz ist ein Fluch auf das Leben, ein Fingerzeig, sich von ihm zu erlösen;—der in Stücke geschnittene Dionysos ist eine Verheißung des Lebens; es wird ewig wiedergeboren und aus der Zerstörung heimgekommen.[15]

Again and again Nietzsche insists on the irreconcilable conflict between Christ and Dionysos, and he resolutely sets himself on the side of the latter. But things are not so easy. The desperate reiteration that these two are opposites, that man must choose which he will embrace, that he himself has chosen long since and cast out Christ from his heart—this is evidence only of the radical desperation of his thought. He has sought to eschew any transcendental values, and has been brought finally to a position where the natively religious bent of his mind and feeling finds it impossible to remain within the bounds of a *Weltanschauung* which erects life as its own ultimate. The Faustian element in his thought is finally brought to recognize the transcendental. So now at the end of his life Dionysos is once more enthroned in his splendour, as he was at the beginning; but now Nietzsche has all the accumulated weight of his own scepticism and positivism to carry. The attempt has to be made to make the certainty and unifying force of the Dionysian view dependent only on an act of will, since nothing else will sustain it. This is having the cake and eating it too. Man alone must set his values, his "truths"—this is the position of *Zarathustra,* and from this there is no going back. Yet in performing this task man conjures up Dionysos, at once the glorification of life and the admission of its relation to a world of eternity. The Eternal Recurrence is another side of this desperate effort to preserve the sovereignty of the individual personality and yet take account of those realities which it cannot finally comprehend. There can be no safe resting here. For in Nietzsche is the Dionysian and the Christian too. All the transcendental qualities which he could not deny, which indeed it was his purpose to underline, are brought into life itself and into the personality which lives and creates them. There is much of Rousseau in this, but Nietzsche's proud emphasis on the majestic potentiality and divine destiny of the human spirit is coupled with a ferocious insistence that man is indeed "fallen", that he has destroyed his God and condemned himself to wander in the wilderness, that daily he is abrogating his divine heritage, that the "lord" in him is faced with the ever-present temptation to relapse into the easy automatism of the "slave", that he is continually dragged down from the heights by those "human, all-too-human" qualities which dominate him by fixing fear in his heart. Man, simply as man, is a poor, wretched, weak and disgusting being. But man who attempts always to realize the Superman within him, he is indeed the lord of creation.

It is time to attempt a general characterization of Nietzsche's thinking. Perhaps the most striking quality evident in it is its paradoxical nature, the way in which for him the opposites continually coincide. He argues for instance that democracy tends to breed a race of "slaves", and yet the real "lords" are able to stand out all the greater in such company. He speaks of "ascending life" but with a full consciousness that the "decadence" he sees all around him is not mere decline, but a movement of the modern world which gives cause of hope. Always the positive and the negative go together, "every god has a devil for father". And this is fundamentally true of the basic colour of his thinking, which is nihilism. His most recent editor, Karl Schlechta, has powerfully argued that it is as a nihilist that he should be read, that his positive "doctrine" was a personal and idiosyncratic addition to it which we can now disregard, while as a voice which radically and honestly made European nihilism explicit he will continue to hold his place among the supreme thinkers of our age. This is an unduly restricted reading of his work (and it involves in effect disregarding the early books and also everything from *Zarathustra* onwards). It is certainly as a philosopher of nihilism that Nietzsche takes his stand, but here once again the positive goes with the negative, the nihilism itself generates the essentially mystical movement of Nietzsche's mind in the directions we have considered.

He was fond of summing up the intellectual history of recent centuries in Europe as a struggle to the death between the spirit of Voltaire and that of Rousseau, and this is not without significance. His own Voltairean irony and scepticism are met and balanced by a fervent Rousseauistic urge to salvation, his own nihilism drives him to affirmation. In himself the Rousseau-Voltaire struggle provides the dominant pressure of his thinking. Just as for him "ascending life" *requires* decadence, so the Superman, the "transvaluation of values" and so on, *require* nihilism as their basis. So that in a sense Nietzsche *welcomes* the terrible and catastrophic consequences of the nihilism he both abhors and is fascinated by. This accounts for the extraordinary savageness of his joy in denunciation coupled always with euphoric hope and innocent wonder. It is not that he offers a "solution" to the nihilistic consequences of his thinking, but that they must be accepted and turned to a positive direction. The world is meaningless, so we *create* a meaning. Just, he urges, as Christianity did. Only Christianity was a fraud, it created the *wrong* meaning. And perhaps, at times we almost hear him saying, perhaps Nietzsche's "meaning" is a fraud too. "Die Dichter lügen zu viel."[16]

TRANSLATIONS

1. All that is profound loves to mask itself.

2. The beast in us needs to be deceived: morality is a necessary lie to save us from being torn to pieces by it: without the errors which constitute the basis of morality, man would have remained an animal.

3. Life—that means continually expelling from oneself something that wishes death; it means being cruel and merciless to all that is weak and old in us, and not only in us. It means, therefore, being without respect for the dying, the miserable and the old. Being continually a murderer. Yet old Moses said: Thou shalt not kill.

4. Is not the greatness of our deed too great for us? Must we not ourselves become gods, in order to seem worthy of it?

5. The superman is the sense of the earth. Let your will say: may the superman be the sense of the earth.

6. And only where there are graves, are there any resurrections.

7. Can you be your own judge and the avenger of your law?

8. All living is an obeying. Good and bad as eternal values—do not exist! Each must continually overcome itself from within itself . . . And if you would be a creator in good and evil, you must first be a destroyer and break up values.

9. Do what you will—but first be such men as *can* will!

10. It is nothing more than a moral prejudice that truth is more valuable than falsehood . . . no life could exist except on the basis of perspective judgments and approximations. . . . Anyway, what forces us to accept any fundamental contradiction between "true" and "false"? Is it not sufficient to accept various degrees of probability, so to speak, lighter and darker shadows and tones of appearance—varying "valeurs", as the painters say. Why should not the world, in so far as it concerns us, be a fiction? And if it is asked: "But a fiction requires an author"?—could one not simply retort: "Why?" perhaps this "requires" is also part of the fiction?

11. The meaninglessness of suffering, not suffering itself, was the curse that until now oppressed men—and the ascetic ideal gave it a meaning ...man was thus saved, his life had a meaning, he was no longer like a leaf in the wind, a plaything of meaninglessness, he could now exercise his will—no matter in the first instance how or in what direction: his will itself was saved.

Man will rather will nothingness than not will at all.

12. Expressed morally, the world is false, but in so far as morality is itself a part of this world, then morality is false ... "Truth", then, is not something that is there and is to be found or discovered—but something to be created, the name of a process, or better a will to conquer, which intrinsically has no end: we put truth into things, as a *processus in infinitum*, an active defining of them—not a learning to know something fixed and definite. It is a word for the will to power.

13. When scepticism and longing are joined, mysticism arises.

14. The main question is absolutely not whether we are satisfied with ourselves, but whether we are satisfied with anything at all. If we once respond positively to any single instant, then we have accepted not only ourselves but the whole of creation. For nothing stands alone, either in us or in the world outside; and if once our souls have vibrated with joy like a violin-string, then all eternity was necessary to bring about this instant, and in this one instant of our acceptance all eternity was blessed, redeemed, justified and approved.

15. The God on the Cross is a curse on life, a pointer to us to redeem ourselves from it—Dionysos hacked to pieces is a guarantee of life; it is eternally reborn and brought back from destruction.

16. The poets lie too much.

SELECT BIBLIOGRAPHY

BENTLEY, ERIC. *A Century of Hero-worship*. London, 1947.

BRINTON, CRANE. *Nietzsche*. Cambridge, Mass., 1941.

COPLESTON, F. *Friedrich Nietzsche, Philosopher of Culture*. London, 1942.

HELLER, ERICH. *The Disinherited Mind*. London, 1954.

KAUFMANN, WALTER. *Nietzsche, Philosopher, Psychologist, Antichrist*. Princeton, 1950.

KNIGHT, A. H. J. *Aspects of the Life and Work of Nietzsche*. Cambridge, 1933.

KNIGHT, G. WILSON. *Christ and Nietzsche*. London, 1948.

LAVRIN, JANKO. *Nietzsche, An Approach*. London, 1948.

LEA, F. A. *The Tragic Philosopher: A Study of Friedrich Nietzsche*. New York, 1957.

MORGAN, GEORGE. *What Nietzsche Means*. Cambridge, Mass., 1941.

REYBURN, HUGH. *Friedrich Nietzsche*. London, 1948.

ROUBICZEK, PAUL. *The Misinterpretation of Man*. Cambridge, 1947.

WILLIAMS, W. D. *Nietzsche and the French*. Oxford, 1952.

Hermann Sudermann

Hermann Sudermann

by WILLIAM F. MAINLAND

"... ein Neugieriger, der gerne in die Karten
schaut, wenn Andre miteinander—spielen."
(an inquisitive man who likes to peep at the
cards when others are—at play)
Sudermann, *Noli me tangere*

Born 30 September 1857, at Matziken in the district of Heydekrug (ca
50 km north-east of Tilsit (Tilže); died 21 November 1928, in Berlin. His
schooling in Heydekrug was interrupted by financial difficulties, but he
was later able to continue and for a short time to attend the University
of Königsberg. Obtaining engagements as private tutor, he went to Berlin
where he took up journalism. His novel *Frau Sorge* and the collection of
stories *Im Zwielicht* were little known until in 1890 the drama *Die Ehre*
brought him fame. After this Sudermann devoted himself entirely to the
writing of plays, interspersed with prose-fiction. For the most part settled
in Berlin, he travelled extensively, spending periods in Stuttgart, Würzburg,
Zürich, Paris and Rome.

EARLY in the present century it was fashionable in Germany
to consider literature as a product of races and regions. One
sign of this was an increased interest in what had been done
far east of the Elbe, viewed as German cultural achievement on the
confines of Western civilization. It seemed to be a fascinating mode
of enquiry. It was acceptable to a generation which could still read
Gustav Freytag's *Soll und Haben* as a congenially liberal novel and
was not disturbed when the Poles, encountered by the honest young
German hero Anton Wohlfahrt, were presented as a lesser breed
without the law. The mischief latent in racial and regional study
has long been apparent, but there is still academic value in remaining
aware of locale and descent when we turn to one of the most
spectacular of the German novelists and playwrights from the
eastern marches.

Hermann Sudermann was born and spent his childhood in what
was then East Prussia. The Sudermann family is noticeably
migratory; it is one of those belonging to a confessional group
which, accepting the teachings of the sixteenth-century Frisian
Menno Simonis, has moved to widely scattered regions, seeking
asylum for its strict sectarian observance and for its social and
moral code. Mennonites, who have some affinity to the Society of

33

Friends, have also settled in Canada and the United States, where members of the Sudermann family may still be found. Hermann Sudermann's knowledge of his family's history was limited to a very few generations and he took no trouble to extend it, to determine for example whether, as some asserted, he had any connection with the seventeenth-century religious poet Daniel Sudermann. Nor had he, apparently, a dominant feeling of belonging to the region of his birth. Yet, when he was away, he found he had a certain pride in it. He was by no means sorry that he never entirely lost his East Prussian accent. In his *Bilderbuch meiner Jugend* (1922) he recalled how, as a young member of the Berlin theatre-club "Die Schleife" with a part in Wilbrandt's *Jugendliebe*, he had been interrupted by a cat-call from the audience, imitating his accent with what sounds like a stock-phrase from the halls : "Der kommt wohl frisch von Albing mit der Schnallpost."[1] Travelling extensively in Germany, to Dresden and the spas of the west and settling in Berlin, he had to adopt the bearing which assured his acceptance into society : ". . . eine gewisse schmachtende Grazie legte ich mir zu, die zwar mit meinen Boxerkräften nicht ganz übereinstimmen wollte, die aber problematischen Naturen nun einmal eigen ist."[2] The words "problematische Naturen" used lightly here, reveal, beside the ironical humour, something of that self-consciousness which made him sensitive of his relations to different locality and social environment and so increased his awareness of life's difficulties.

Problematic natures are those which are consumed by inner conflicts; they cannot cope adequately with circumstance, and so they nowhere find complete enjoyment or satisfaction. Many people —and Sudermann was probably one of them—are gratified to apply such a fine-sounding phrase to themselves. It was popularized, with the meaning given above, by Goethe. But it was probably Friedrich Spielhagen's revival of it as the title for one of his best novels that echoed in Sudermann's ears. He had a great admiration for this political novelist of the preceding generation, and even if there had been no brief specific reference in his own novel *Es war* (published in 1894, more than thirty years after Spielhagen's *Problematische Naturen*) we might still detect a reminiscence of the two leading characters—Oswald Stern and his old teacher, Professor Berger. In varying ways *déracinés,* these two men both embody and respond to the challenge of a time of social and political change—the time of the 1848 revolution. In Sudermann's early years a social and psychological revolution was on its way, and in one of his latest novels he cast his mind back to the Bismarck era. *Der tolle Professor* (1926) is set in a scene familiar to him, the city and university of Königsberg. The leading character, a professor of very humble origin, brilliantly expounds his subversive views on society and its institutions, and as the life he leads is very closely in accord with his views, he provokes disapproval and scandal, which increase when he is induced to engage in politics. Professor Sieburth, driven to suicide, is clearly Sudermann's interpretation of the "problematic character". Through the social conflict which is, in a sense, fought out in his mind and life, and through the story of his profound influence on his students, we catch glimpses of the Spielhagen pattern. From his early and his late works we may hazard a diagnosis of Sudermann's state of mind : we may say that with some inflation of purpose and mission, he saw himself, socially and regionally displaced, perplexed by the sign of decay and renewal around him, and compelled to find expression for it.

By birth he did not belong to a dominant caste. His father was a brewer, and for a time, because of straightened family circumstance, the boy was obliged to go as apprentice to a chemist, thereby losing face among his former school-friends. He reflected in later life that the sense of not belonging to the "Honoratioren" caused him in his childhood more distress than anything else, and was perhaps the origin of his socialite ambition. But it also sharpened his perception of what was "wrong" with society.

Criticism was of course in the air. By the time Sudermann became articulate as a writer, noted socialists had been spreading their doctrines for more than forty years. His so-called "conversion" to socialism did not reach any considerable depth. His way of life came to depend more and more on the capitalist system (the evils of which he of course criticized) and his disposition was not that of the political analyst. Karl Marx, he confessed, was beyond his horizon. One of his text-books seems to have been Schaeffle's *Quintessenz des Sozialismus* (1875, English translation by Bosanquet, 7th ed. 1901); but it must be remembered that Schaeffle disappointed the socialists of his time, who had thought to find in him a strong academic exponent of their doctrines. More closely akin to Sudermann was the spectacular physician, novelist, and publicist Max Nordau (1849–1923). The aristocratic, the marital, the religious, and other aspects of the "Kulturlüge" were exposed by Nordau in a lavish volume *Die konventionellen Lügen der Menschheit* (1883), which was banned and soon translated into a number of languages (Engl. *Conventional Lies of our Civilization*, 1895). Several "Kulturlügen" are thrown into strong relief by the theatrical talent of Sudermann.

His talent was that of the alert observer, expert in retailing the nuances of thought and expression which he encountered. This is true, in the first place, in a clearly technical sense. He noted with ease, yet with a growing discipline of practice, the varying modes of speech around him. The most remote from his own language was that of the many people who were genuine natives of the country of his birth. There seems to be no conclusive evidence of the extent of Sudermann's knowledge of Lithuanian. It may have been comparable to the knowledge of Welsh among many English people brought up in Wales—fragmentary, shallow, and unsystematic. But in his stories he introduced occasional snatches of Lithuanian speech, and to a greater extent songs, sometimes a few lines in the language, more frequently verses of songs in what purports to be translation.[3] This seems to have been the sign of a genuine and lasting desire to share with his readers a fascinated interest in the way of life of a people despised by many of his own race, but in whom he saw a naïve ethos which sometimes undermined his sense of superiority.

The Mennonite tradition in Sudermann's family, already mentioned, provided some linguistic interest in the writer's early days. For a time he was a keen church-goer, sometimes, with eclectic zeal, attending Mass. But the speech of the Mennonite brethren seems to have impressed him. Long afterwards, in the *Bilderbuch meiner Jugend,* he recalled the archaic phrasing of their German. Such archaisms continued to have a bizarre effect on the speech and school-exercises of a much younger generation of Mennonites settled in Canada.

But it was in the castes and classes of Germany as a whole that Sudermann found most abundant copy. There was the wide range of the military caste, from the impertinent and indomitable subaltern to the general, either as tired roué or as citizen with a high sense of responsibility, there was the ex-criminal, there was the lion of metropolitan élite society, and the Berlin underdog, the cultured business-man and the pushing upstart, the brash "Korpsstudent",[4] the disinherited (pattern of Magnus in the *Hasenfellhändler*—"Wo es mir Spass macht, zu verrecken, das ist meine Sache").[5] All these had varieties of idiom and tone which had so clearly assorted and defined themselves in Sudermann's memory that passages of dialogue became the easiest thing for him to construct. "Dialogstellen sind die Oasen in der Arbeit an einem Roman . . . überhaupt keine Arbeit sondern Spielerei. Man braucht den Leuten, wenn man sie erst auf die Beine gestellt hat, ja nur zuzuhören und aufzuschreiben, was sie sagen"[6] (quoted by Irmgard Leux, *Hermann Sudermann,* 1931). It is hard for us to see how this apparently automatic kind of composition was achieved. Perhaps, if we have experienced the imagined clamour of shouting voices as we have been falling asleep, Sudermann may help us to understand, when he notes that he refrained from any new stretch of composition before going to bed, lest the characters should go on talking and keep him awake! One of the most economical devices of characterization by speech is the repetition of a typical phrase or word. Sometimes Sudermann tends to overdo this in a Dickensian way, as in the repeated conversation-gambit of Wally, the generous light-o'-love in *Die Raschhoffs*: "Gnädige Frau glauben doch auch an—eine Göttlichkeit der Seele?"[7] But in the smooth speech of the vicar whom Leo visits in *Es war,* the word "eben" is very effectively introduced with such typical insistence that it seems in the end to dominate (and undermine) all he has to say, and Leo is hard put to it not to slip into the habit himself.

This careful technique of notation helps us to see Sudermann (of the early years at least) as a literary craftsman in tune with his time. What there was and was not of so-called Naturalism in his works has often been discussed. It is not a matter of the highest importance now, and a brief statement about it would not only be vulnerable; like much literary classification it would carry the infection of a false sense of secure knowledge. Of those writers who were for a time regarded as leading Naturalists it can be said, to their credit and their discredit, that they laid great store by differentiated dialogue. It was part of the deterministic notion of the time to insist that people's behaviour, in speech as in other matters, is patterned by their environment; if this sort of logic dominates a writer's mind, he will find it wrong to represent the speech of characters from different milieus in a homogeneous, educated paraphrase or by inaccurate convention of drawing-room and back-stairs speech; he must, he feels, be consistent in recording the little nuances of utterance. This system was followed by Sudermann in the essentially social plays, even down to *Das deutsche Schicksal* (1921), when other dramatists were experimenting with terse, expressionistic techniques. His talent was not so effective when he tried to adopt a classical convention of exalted speech in plays such as *Johannes* and *Der Bettler von Syrakus,* drawn from distant periods.

It can be said that in common with many of his generation, in Germany and in France, and with large numbers of dramatists who have been at work since, Sudermann was powerfully attracted by unsavoury things close at hand. As M. G. Conrad expressed it, "Man ist hässlich und schreibt hässliche Kunst"[8] because that is the way to be "interesting". For many years it has been customary for journalists to consort with denizens of the underworld and make reports on their way of living. In the 1890's this would seem to have been a somewhat new and daring adventure for a dramatist of rising fame. In March 1892 Sudermann wrote to his wife Clara that he had been with a chief of police on a most interesting visit to taverns where the criminals of Berlin gathered together. More

spectacular, and also less palatable for us in the 1960's is his bland
admission that in the course of a few hours he had heard six
"confessions" from women. This eager emotional tunnelling raises
for students of the writer's art the vexed question of proportion
between sentiment and sensation. It is a historical question, for
upon that proportion the varying taste of successive generations
may perhaps be judged. The lavish exposition of tender feeling
accepted by one generation may be almost intolerable to the next,
and vigorous or impassioned action in narrative or drama which at
one time is exciting and shocking is later judged insipid. It seems
as if the adjustment and proportion of the sentimental to the sensational helps to distinguish one period from another. In this there
is something analogous to what happens in the progress of fashions
in dress, and the two are no doubt closely related. A popular mode
becomes ridiculous or abhorrent; then it recedes into historical
perspective, is viewed with affection and seen to be quaint.[9] There
is much of Ibsen which achieved a goal in its time by revealing a
turmoil of feelings and drawing tragic conclusions; then it came to
be seen as forced and inflated, and later still it has become a
period-piece. In 1958 Sudermann's *Glück im Winkel* was produced
by the B.B.C. in translation and repeated in 1962. It was handled
with great care and insight, avoiding parody or exaggeration.
Baron Röcknitz, seeking refuge from women in hard work, and
finding again and again that he could not do without them, was
not just the hot-tempered, self-pitying, predatory male of all time,
but a genuine Sudermann period character. The conclusion of the
play, when Elisabeth finds shelter from the alarms of a desperate
passion in the love of her ageing husband, who has known and
understood, was no more credible or morally acceptable in this
interpretation than it had been for Kawerau or Heller in their early
retrospect. But by sensitive historical reconstruction in production
and acting it afforded pleasure, for it gave a picture of a matter of
social controversy ably handled by a dramatist nearly seventy years
ago, when many people found an abundance of truth in the sentimental paintings of Millais and Watts. Similarly the hopes and
disillusions which had poignant meaning in the immediate retrospect of Sudermann's sequence of plays *Das deutsche Schicksal*
(1921) have now the soft patina of an epoch. Indeed the first play in
the series may at times seem to merge with a much earlier treatment of a similar theme—Nordau's novel *Die Krankheit des Jahrhunderts* (1888) which, in its first section, presents the beginning of
the Franco-Prussian war. (Felix Stern, the young Jew in Sudermann's *Heilige Zeit* has a good deal in common with Wilhelm
Eynhardt in Nordau's novel.)

Some of Sudermann's novels which offended good taste in their time, and were immediately popular, have a manipulation of description, tender emotions and passionate episode obviously contrived to prepare and ensure a thrill. We, accustomed to a very different structure and rhythm, may accept them as patterns of a period; we greet the high-lights, the purple patches, and the lingering dalliance with a smile perhaps a little too indulgent. Such are *Der Katzensteg* and *Das Hohe Lied*. In the former there is the episode of the shooting in the night, when the hero, to protect himself, and perhaps also Regina, from the consummation of passion, fires his revolver and wounds her. We are led to expect this by the author's lavish preparations, a prying into the hero's tangled emotions, a display of the dog-like fidelity of the woman, and the contrivance of a storm to make her own bedroom uninhabitable. In *Das Hohe Lied* there is such a sequence of love-affairs, of anguished lingering and capitulations that we begin to suspect a scheme somewhat heavily imposed on reportage. Yet it is a work of serious artistic intent, over which Sudermann had thought for many years before he started the writing. It is easy to understand why the dominant note in early adverse criticism of this, in its day, immensely popular novel, should be a moral protest : to the prurient minds of his readers Sudermann offered an occasional little reward in a brief, unequivocal statement: "Im nächsten Augenblick gehörte sie ihm",[10] the rest of the line being completed by the almost inevitable succession of dashes. The immediate causes of this kind of writing in Sudermann are complex and interesting. Among them are : the urge of the '80's to tear away at least some of the veils from human behaviour; Sudermann's early reading, including the very popular *Gartenlaube*;[11] and his own tangled temperament.

Enquiry into the life and personal experience of writers is usually somewhat distressing, but it can bring much needed illumination. Sudermann saw himself as something of a mountebank in closer personal relations—"Hochstapler der Liebe". The incident of the cat-call in the theatre, mentioned earlier in this chapter, has an echo in *Die Raschhoffs*, an unpleasant little comedy published in 1920. The perplexed and wayward young husband (from Sudermann's own region) has a mistress in Berlin, Wally, and she makes almost exactly the same comment on his East Prussian origin as the critic in the theatre-audience made about Sudermann. True, as Sudermann said, "Wir leben im Märchen",[12] but this merging of the substance of an author's experience with the texture of his work can become a little unsavoury. This is perhaps a particular risk in an age of full-time writers, for whom living tends to become conscious documentation for future reference. They may, as Sudermann did, lay claim to freedom, so that they can devote themselves

to their art. But this freedom will involve the purposeful gathering
of experiences, and these are not always vicarious. It becomes a
moral matter, and so is only partially relevant to the study of
literature. "Fragments of a great confession" is Goethe's often
quoted description of his imaginative works. But he pointed out
that what he set down as confession was not the original substance
of experience; this had undergone a change, and such change is
necessary if a work of art is to emerge. The writer must look to his
emotional metabolism. If, in reading a novel or in watching a play,
we find something that does not fit or harmonize, we suspect that
the author has either taken over something from another author,
or that he has introduced some raw material from his own experience. In either case he has not had due regard to the organization
of his work. There are elements of both these alien intrusions in the
play which first brought fame to Sudermann—*Die Ehre*. Here
Count Trast plays a heavy, dominant rôle, interpreting the theme
and leading the action, somewhat unexpectedly, to a happy ending.
He is thus "deus ex machina" and "raisonneur". The latter function, derived from French practice (e.g. Sardou), provides a somewhat ineffective mask for Sudermann himself to parade his
supposedly unbiased notions. It is cleverly done, but it is too
obviously the author's own cleverness in ironical little aphorisms.
And the freedom of the dramatist to dispose of his characters as he
will is a fiction made less credible by the circumstances of Trast's
own life. He arrives in the cramped and corrupt little world of
business magnates and their employees' families as Sudermann
imagines himself to arrive—a free commentator from outside. But
Trast, who has flouted the conventions of his own caste by refusing
to atone by suicide for an unpaid debt, is able to gain a hearing
and to shape other people's lives only by virtue of his own high
status. He has come back as a coffee-king, with enormous wealth.
He is *not* outside the structure of his society, any more than
Sudermann really was. He can be sure of a hearing, because money
talks, joining in the babble of "Kulturlügen".

Sudermann, propelled by fame and notoriety, developed something of the cult of the unique personality. Of impressive physical
stature, he grew an enormous beard, which proved a gift to the
caricaturists; in Wiesbaden a barber who, it is said, did not recognize his celebrated customer, remarked in admiration : "Why ! but
that is the genuine Sudermann beard !" In more complicated form
the carefully tended singularity of Sudermann emerges from certain
letters collected at his injunction and published in 1932. This is an
informative volume, especially interesting for its comments on the
contemporary theatre. But its underlying theme, modified, veiled,
and abridged by the editors, is still quite clearly the tragedy of a

woman—Sudermann's wife Clara. Her first husband had died, leaving her with three children. She and Sudermann were married on 14 October 1891, and only six weeks after the wedding he went away to Paris. This was the first of a series of journeys from which he sent her news about notable people he had met, about plays, impressions of places visited, about his state of health, his own feelings, sometimes buoyant, sometimes querulous. Early in December Clara wrote that she had not been able to see Franziska Elmenreich in the *Dame aux camélias* because she had not even had the money for a seat in the theatre; Sudermann arranged for the transfer of money, but seems not to have been deeply concerned : to him the matter was "ebenso fatal wie lächerlich".[13] Three days before the first Christmas, when Sudermann was still in Paris, Clara wrote enclosing a sprig from the Christmas-tree. "Es ist eigentlich dumm," she wrote, "aber ich tue es doch. Ich habe ihn vielmals für Dich geküsst."[14] In November Sudermann had written : "Ich habe das feste Vornehmen, als ein ruhigerer, festerer und widerstandsfähigerer Mensch in die Königsberger Verhältnisse zurückzukehren, und dann musst Du mir helfen."[15] And Clara, early in December : "Jedenfalls gebe ich Dir nochmals die Versicherung, dass Dir nie irgendwelche Verantwortung oder Verpflichtung aus allem erwachsen soll, und ich gebe sie Dir aus wirklich liebevollem Herzen und in der Idee, Dich in der Freiheit, die Du Dir wünschest, in keiner Weise zu beeinträchtigen."[16] Ten days later Sudermann to Clara : "Wir sind nicht Eheleute, wie andere, unser Bund setzt Notwendigkeiten und Bedürfnisse voraus, die in anderen Ehen nicht existieren."[17] A month before the birth of their only child on 14 June 1892, she repeated her assurance : "Ich will Dir schliesslich nur sagen, dass ich in jeder Beziehung aus Deinem Leben schon jetzt zurücktrete. Du bist absolut frei in jeder Beziehung, frei von jeder Verantwortung."[18] When Clara was disturbed by the opposition on moral grounds to Sudermann's tragedy on corrupt Berlin society and the degradation of the artist (*Sodoms Ende*) he attempted to reassure her : "Mein Leben ist naturgemäss eine Kette von Erregungen, ja, ohne diese Erregungen wäre ich gar nicht imstande zu leben. Das bürgerliche Gleichmass der Dinge ist für mich nicht geschaffen. Ich würde darin dumpf und stumpf werden"[19] (5 : 1 : 1892). Systematized hypochondria, the built-in spur and depressor of the artistic temperament, was recognized by Sudermann : "Für mich gibt es nur ein wahres Gesundsein, nämlich, wenn ich krank bin"[20] (23 : 2 : 1899).

From much of this correspondence we derive the picture of a man who was egocentric, opinionated, ebullient, and weak. This is not the full picture of Sudermann, yet it helps to explain many of the male characters of forceful temperament and physique whom he created, discovering in them a disturbing complexity of emotions not disciplined to withstand the attacks of prejudice and prevalent opinion, and of others, ennobled images of himself, who *were* able to overcome adverse circumstances, able, like Teja, the young king of the Ostrogoths in *Morituri* (1896), to bear privation and to face certain doom with high resolve: "Tomorrow I will take my spear and my shield and go forth to seize for myself my little share of death for which like a thief I have thirsted and lain in wait since ever you chose me as leader in your lost cause."

Such a mood was easier to imagine, might have been easier to achieve on the slopes of Vesuvius in A.D. 553 than in Berlin in the 1890's, where authority and a band of critics were massed against the playwright. He could to some extent cope with authority, even when faction in the Reichstag was persecuting him, for he was not the only writer of the time threatened by official censure. But the fierce onslaught of individual critics was a more serious matter. A certain young man, member of a highly talented Jewish family, found himself engaged in a literary skirmish with Sudermann, and drew blood. This was the brother of the famous professor of German literature, Georg Witkowski, and of the heads of the firm Witting in London. In tribute to Prince Hardenberg, who had vigorously defended the Jews in Berlin in 1812, he had adopted the name Harden. Felix Maximilian Harden tells how he received a copy of Sudermann's *Der Katzensteg,* inscribed in the author's own hand to "Kampfgenosse Maximilian Harden, in herzlicher Freundschaft".[21] Sudermann had seen the prospect of gaining an ally in the lively young critic. But however changeable Harden proved in his career as a publicist, there was a core of sincerity in him which made him refuse to be bought. As dramatic critic he had to deal with a performance of *Die Ehre,* and his account was for the most part unfavourable. Shortly afterwards he was walking along the street in Berlin and met Sudermann, carrying, he pointedly observed, a bouquet. To his friendly greeting Sudermann replied with a vehement outburst: "Ich kann mit Ihnen nicht mehr verkehren; Sie verderben mir meine Karriere."[22] This was their last encounter. The incidents are retailed in Harden's *Kampf-genosse Sudermann* (1903), a self-defence but at the same time an essay of considerable literary insight. Sudermann made the mistake of counter-attacking his critics. His essay *Die Verrohung der Theaterkritik* (1902) is a most useful document for the literary historian, but it did Sudermann much harm. Among his most ruthless opponents were Alfred Kerr, critic of the literary journal *Neue deutsche Rundschau,* and the essayist Hermann Bahr whose pungent comments were very nearly actionable; they were certainly scurrilous. Sudermann's resentment seems to have been chiefly

stirred by accusations of plagiarism. It was no doubt flattering for
him to merit praise abroad : an obituary in the Lisbon *Diario dos
Noticias* (1928) sums up widespread opinion in the phrase "the
most Latin of German authors"; early this century, in France, his
name was set beside those of Hoffmann and Heine. But for this
"Balzac des Ostens" to be told that he had been *copying* the French
was an intolerable affront. When he heard that he had "used"
Flaubert's story *Herodias* for his play *Johannes* he denied on his
word of honour ever having read the story. Harden's reply, flatly
questioning this "word of honour", might easily have led to a duel.
It is a pity perhaps that Sudermann and his opponents could not
perceive more clearly how the notion of plagiarism was giving way,
in the hands of progressive literary historians, to an academic
interest in influences. An offshoot of this in Sudermann studies
was Hubert Walter's dissertation *Sudermann und die Franzosen*
(Münster 1930) which is at points a little too speculative but provides much essential material. Balanced recognition of his debt to
the French helps us to see the nature of Sudermann's talent and the
formal trend of his style.

Revealing his weaknesses under provocation of the critics, Sudermann in another mood showed much estimable charity and understanding for his contemporaries. On Fontane, Max Halbe, Ricarda
Huch, Gerhart Hauptmann, Ernst Wiechert he bestowed praise all
the more substantial because it was acutely discriminating.

He was himself a deliberate craftsman, aware of the demands of
his art, and of his own shortcomings. A gourmand in his addiction
to words, he saw the need for rigorous restriction. In a letter to his
wife (29:5:1893) he mentions revision of *Es war*: "O weh. Da
gibts zu streichen.... Zuviel erfunden, zuviel hineingepackt..."[23]
Having read with pleasure Ricarda Huch's *Ludolf Ursleu* (1898) he
noted in it a congenial pattern, which, he said, would be his aim
if he turned again to writing novels. Zola, on the other hand,
though greatly admiring him, he criticized not only for his pessimism, but because the structure of his work was too diffuse. Such
comments could help to give us the measure of Sudermann's own
ideal of style. We cannot, it is true, expect to find in his narratives
the conciseness achieved by some of the generation which followed.
But his writing is not generally cumbersome, and there is little sign
in his latest novels—*Der tolle Professor* (1926) and *Die Frau des
Steffen Tromholt* (1927)—of that excessive elaboration which is one
of the common effects of senility on syntax. There *is* elaboration in
his writing, but it seems to be often the result of an almost obsessional preoccupation with certain themes, notably honour, fidelity,
the wanderer's return, and sex. He knew the fascination and the
fear, typical of the self-centred male, in contemplating the

corrupting effect of man on woman. "Wer birgt mir dafür, dass sie taktfest bleibt?"[24]—this, he confessed to Clara, was the niggling thought when he imagined her in the company of lewd men (he knew from his own disposition what lewdness was). Such anxious questioning, the substance of uncontrolled imaginative living, is a menace to artistic form. The balance of a picture, of a piece of writing, can be destroyed by that incomplete mutation of confession to which reference has already been made. In building up the character of Johanna in *Es war* Sudermann drew perhaps a little too lavishly on his own experience. She is seventeen, and at that age Sudermann as guest in a country-house, had had a swift and passionate affair with his hostess. He had read about adultery, and now he found *himself* involved, his imagination racing ahead to the novelistic consequences—the lovers' flight, divorce proceedings, and so on. But, by the lady's decision, the chapter was closed, only to be referred to later when Sudermann had to read the memory of his own consternation into Johanna's mind, and, with nice regard for her inexperience, to try to interpret her dismay as the suspicion dawned that her admired Leo had loved another man's wife.

Because the years since the 1920's have brought a mixture of the clinical and the barbaric into the literary treatment of sex, Sudermann's mode of presenting its problems nowadays appears sluggish, sultry, and unhealthy. In the *Katzensteg* he skirmished persistently on the fringe of incest. The use of a sister to promote illicit relations either schemingly or with baffled innocence (*Blumenboot*) is unsavoury. Sudermann makes an occasional expedition into the macabre, verging on flagellation, in *Das Hohe Lied* and *Der Katzensteg*. In the short story *Sterbelied* (published in the collection *Indische Lilie*), the young wife, compelled by the cruel religious obsession of her dying husband to read gloomy hymns to him, listens in the night to the whisperings and the singing of lovers in the adjoining room in the hotel.

But there are, as we have noted, other obsessional themes in Sudermann's works. In *Die Ehre* he had made incisive comments on the relativity of notions of honour, and he found himself again and again under a compulsion to return to the theme, and the specific nature of it merges in prolonged consideration of fidelity. There is fidelity to a person, fidelity to an idea; and they are both seen to have disturbing and disruptive effects, especially when the object of reverence is found to be illusory. This is worked out with varying intensity and on different planes. The hero of the *Katzensteg*, von Schranden, opposed by a whole community, tries to prove the honour of a father whose actions are shown, by documents and the testimony of his mistress, to have been dishonourable; and the pastor's daughter, for whom he has preserved unquestioning love, is revealed by the novelist (with vicious haste) to be using him to save his rival. Tragic disclosure of deluded idealism is the theme of the one venture Sudermann made into the mode of the "Märchen-drama"—*Die Drei Reiherfedern*. Here, with elements of fantasy which may perhaps derive from a non-Germanic (Balto-slavic?) source, King Witte pursues an ideal, only to discover in the moment of her death that the love he has sought is the Queen who broke her oath in order to marry him. In *Frau Sorge*, the first of Suder-mann's novels (1887), and the only one which has ever maintained a grip on the English and American school-curriculum, there is constant devotion in a cheerless life to an ideal of personal and family honour which leads the hero strangely through imprison-ment into marriage with the girl who has remained faithful to him. The satirical play *Sturmgeselle Sokrates* (1903), in which the "Stammgäste" assemble in the inn to honour the ideals for which they have fought, treats the matter of fidelity with light irony. With great pomp and circumstance, Beate, leading character of the tragedy of high life, *Es lebe das Leben* (1902), in whose household problems of personal and political integrity have reached menacing proportions, raises the poisoned cup as her final tribute to the one ideal of her doomed life—the fine art of living. The theme of the broken ideal is taken up by Sudermann in one of his rare excursions into the distant past, the beginning of the Christian era. In *Johannes* (1898) John the Baptist preaches against the sensuality of Herod, but, as he sees that the love in the teaching of the Saviour goes far beyond his own doctrine, and sees too the ill-will in all mankind, he cannot cast the stone against the tetrarch. The sanctity of a friendship, threatened by disclosure of an old misdeed, is the theme of *Es war*. Ulrich, Leo's friend, is selfless in his devotion and blind to the passion which his wife Felicitas had awakened in Leo when she was married to another man. By a somewhat forced dramatic irony the attempt to re-establish the bond between the two men after Leo's absence results in its undoing, for Leo is again ensnared by Felicitas. The characters are distorted to fit the exag-gerated nature of the plot—Ulrich is given a feminine frailty to contrast with the rugged determination of Leo never to give way to remorse, and the amoral character of Felicitas is stretched almost beyond the limits of credibility : in order to indulge in her planned love-affair she sends her little son to a boarding-school far from home, where, neglected at Christmas, he catches a fever and dies.

There are varieties of amoral women in Sudermann's works, from the bar-maids to Beate in *Es lebe das Leben* and Regina of the *Katzensteg*, and we catch glimpses of their prototypes in the *Bilderbuch meiner Jugend*. Sometimes they represent the illusory ideals in which men have put their trust. But the woman who has drifted away from moral convention or who has been forced by circumstances and the dictates of her own nature may also entertain illusory ideals. Thus Lili Czepanek (we note how Sudermann chooses a Polish name and so detaches her from any purely German tradition) keeps the picture of the young lieutenant who was the cause of her divorce, and imagines his continued love for her. Another admirer, a business-man with considerable patience, helps to maintain the deception and makes her believe also that the money she is receiving comes from the sale of little *objets d'art* she has been making. Even the song—the score of her father's composition, which gives the symbolic title to the story—the song which she has kept hidden away, she finds obliterated when, intending to put an end to her life, she takes one last look at it : mice have gnawed it, and it bears the brown stain of blood, her own blood, shed when her demented mother had snatched up a knife to kill her. The theme of this novel, called by Bartels (*Deutsche Dichtung der Gegenwart*, 8th edition, 1910) "ein widerlicher Dirnenroman", had, as we have noted, been in Sudermann's mind for many years and is not, for all its faults, to be lightly dismissed. It is the story of a woman who, as her favourite teacher had told her, had "too much love in her" : "Sie haben zu viel Liebe in sich. Von allen drei Sorten : Herzens-, Sinnen und Mitleidsliebe. Eine muss jeder Mensch haben, zwei sind gefährlich, alle drei führen in den Untergang."[25] She has histrionic and musical talent, but it is squandered on the frivolous "Bande"—the fast set with which she associates in Berlin. She is one of the countless women of Sudermann's time (for some of whom he found a place in his "comédie humaine") who, deprived of responsibility, became the toys of an affluent society. Frustrated longing for life with a meaning, which lead to the rebellion of Ibsen's Nora, is apparent in Sudermann's Lili. She leads an immoral life, and yet there is in her a naïve honesty, a kind of integrity. The symbol for this is the song—"das Hohe Lied". The score itself has been a talisman, and it is destroyed, but the song has become part of her.

One of the favourite female rôles in the high drama of social conflict at the turn of the century was Magda in Sudermann's *Heimat*, played magnificently, we are told, by Eleonore Duse and by Mrs. Patrick Campbell. Magda is the daughter of an army officer of stern moral outlook. She has left home and become a singer of international renown. She returns to her native place to give a recital, and it seems possible that a reconciliation may be achieved, if the condition she makes—that no mention be made of the past—is observed. The condition is broken, and it is revealed that her rebellion has involved her in a social predicament which

her father can never condone, and she is finally resolved to oppose
the convention which demands that the parents of an illegitimate
child should get married. If such a character provided material
for some of the greatest actresses of the time, she must have
embodied for that time the idea of the great artistic talent. Such
characters are expected to be flamboyant, but the airs of Magda,
and the paraphernalia which accompany her on her travels do
more than bring the breath of the exotic into the little provincial
nest; they feed our suspicion that this great emancipated woman is
a little too shallow to cope with the big social problem of relative
moral codes which Sudermann has thrust into her life. Sometimes
he shows up the illusory nature of his characters' ideals. Here,
where the courage of rebellion and hard-won success are intended
to break through the tinsel of convention, the illusion seems to
have possessed the author himself and so crept unawares into his
play.

The title *Heimat* has a significance for the precarious union of
art and life in Sudermann which is lost in the customary English
translation : "Magda". One of the most frequently recurring motifs
in Sudermann's works is the return home, with its conflict of meaning and effect. It is illuminating to see this ambivalence clearly
defined in Sudermann's record of his own experience : "Viel
Trübes, Schweres, Ängstliches in meinen Wesen stammt aus den
gedrückten, kümmerlichen Verhältnissen, die ich vorfand, wenn ich
in meinen zwanziger Jahren daheim eine Zufluchtsstätte fand. Und
Gott sei Dank, dass ich sie fand. Sonst wär' es mir noch schlimmer
ergangen"[26] (letter to Clara, 11 November 1900). We cannot piece
together all the circumstances which made these visits home both
pleasant and unpleasant. No doubt memories of his father's
dejection (uttered in the one syllable of tremulous misery—"äh!"
—"äh!" were reawakened. There were close kinsmen of widely
varying temperament, one uncle who was an Elder in the solemn
Mennonite congregation, and another, an amiable ne'er-do-well
who took to the bottle and had to be looked after by his nephew in
much the same way as the uncle in *Iolanthes Hochzeit*. It may be
that for young Sudermann, who had been finding his way in less
restricted society, the revival of contact with the Mennonites and
the memories of his early days of pious church-going were chasten-
ing and embarrassing. But on the other hand it is clear that apart
from the comforting familiarity of family life, the region itself had
a strong hold upon him. When he wrote of the pleasure he had had
in reading Wiechert's stories of Lithuania he criticized a lack of
attention to the setting. He himself had a lively and intense interest
in the detail of setting, interior and out-of-doors. Sometimes there
is a theatrical quality in his description, heightened when the

dramatic tempo of the story quickens, as frequently in the *Katzensteg*. But mostly he has a restrained and finely differentiated pattern, in which time and place, season and atmosphere are sensitively developed by the selective massing of detail. He rarely, perhaps never, reached the heights of "fine writing"—perhaps he lacked the talent. He had not the highest skill when he tried to give purposeful symbolic meaning to a setting as in the "Freundschaftsinsel"[(27)] in *Es war*; indeed his attempts at symbolism are apt to be a little maladroit, as for example in the plays *Stein unter Steinen* and *Schmetterlingsschlacht*, and in *Das Hohe Lied*. But because of this lack of the highest quality his descriptive passages are unobtrusive, and they are effectively adjusted to the march of episode. This is true of his descriptions of Berlin, but much more noticeable in the settings from his own region. In regional description, from *Frau Sorge*, through *Katzensteg*, *Es war*, to *Litauische Geschichten* there is a unison between the substance of experience and the gift and discipline of the writer's craft more nearly complete than when he looks outside East Prussia.

What is true of the landscape of these stories from the marchlands is true of the characters also. Not by a carefully studied heredity, such as that which stimulated Thomas Mann (of cosmopolitan descent) but by early environment and the inescapable memory of it, Sudermann was aware of what lay outside the vaunted heritage of the Germanic race. Sometimes he yielded to the theatrical urge, trying to pluck at the reader's heart-strings : in Regina, of the *Katzensteg* ("so jung und so verdorben"[(28)] and yet, in the hour of her death, how noble !) there is a managed concentration of qualities some of which were perhaps derived from Kleist's *Käthchen*; but at the centre of her character, perceived directly by Sudermann is—nature. This is the sign of an undeniably romantic response, but in Sudermann, who imagined her as a child of his own region, there is the strength of direct observation. All the fidelity of which he is capable—the fidelity of the artist to his craft —is seen in some of the characterization in the *Litauische Geschichten*. It has been suggested that for these stories Sudermann had learnt a lesson from Guy de Maupassant. If it is so, the lesson was absorbed and assimilated for the treatment of a theme in which he was at home. Sudermann had many startling and some effective things to say about society life in his time; and the years of travel and of domicile in Berlin, the eager exploration of contemporary French drama and fiction trained his sense of form. He managed with skill the bright repartee of the salon, the schemings and the languishings of a brittle civilization, living in its "Märchen". This furnishes the greater bulk of his fiction and his dramas. But the man who had drifted from sectarian traditions and freed himself from the cramping environment of a German province, may well have found his own melody, "die seine Seele immer mitsingt im Wachen oder Traum", in those lives more deeply rooted in his own region. Landscape and people of that country "wo der Strom stiller wird"[29] are the inspiration of his greatest work.

In the *Reise nach Tilsit*,[30] first of the *Litauische Geschichten*, the well-to-do Lithuanian Ansas Balczus, tiring of his wife Indre, has with the girl Busze devised a cruel plot. He invites Indre to come with him in their little boat for a treat in the town. Knowing the currents, and the precise spot where he can count on danger, he has made everything ready so that the boat will capsize in the night as they return, and he himself will be saved by floating on the rushes which he has stowed away in a sack by her feet. They have what seems a happy time together in Tilsit, and then there comes, very simply, a change of feeling in Ansas. In the inn, as they are eating and drinking together, in all the charm and gaiety of their peasant costume, the husband hears some words spoken by a German who has caught sight of his wife; the German is full of admiration and respect for the beauty of "these Lithuanian women". Late in the evening, the two get into their boat and set out for home on the quiet, moonlit water. There *is* a death on that voyage, and there is poignant sadness in it, but it is not tragic. With love and trust completely restored, the young wife has lost all the stifling apprehensions of the morning's journey. As they had set out for Tilsit Indre had seen the sack and had wondered what was in it. Her suspicions have been stirred; hanging on every syllable of her husband's words, every change of expression in his eyes, she lives from moment to moment of dread—dread giving way to hope, and hope stifled by mounting dread, a nightmare whirlpool of anguish from which there seems no escape. The passage, in itself and in the contrasting context, makes strangely impressive reading. It shows the artist's control of uncontrollable feeling in the heart of a woman far removed from the great and the petty order of civilization. It is exquisite tracing of the graph of elemental feeling, but in it there is a wealth of human sympathy. It is the anatomy of fear, which Sudermann, in spite of all his vigour and renown, his laughter and his wayward wanderings, must somehow have come to know.

NOTES AND TRANSLATIONS

1. He must have come express from Elbing. (Substitution of "a" for "e" is a sign of East Prussian dialect-speech.)

2. I put on a graceful, languishing air, which, it is true, did not quite assort with my pugilistic physique. But after all, it belongs to the problematic temperament.

3. Since the Lithuanian stories are of significance and great merit, it is regrettable to have found no systematic discussion of Sudermann's knowledge of the language and folk-lore of the country. I am therefore most grateful to Professor Velta Ruke-Dravina of Lund who, in answer to certain questions, has given me detailed and stimulating comments. These strengthen me in the belief that the matter calls for investigation by a scholar in that field. From Professor Ruke-Dravina's observations I draw tentative conclusions:

(i) that Sudermann was able to use genuine Lithuanian names and perhaps sometimes to invent names with true Lithuanian ring;

(ii) that on occasion a verse in German, purporting to be a translation, at least suggests by its motifs a Lithuanian original;

(iii) that, apart altogether from his now archaic spellings, occasional mistakes may have been printer's errors, or Sudermann's own mistakes in script; if the latter, then, taken in conjunction with the occurrence of dialect-forms,

(iv) that he drew directly upon his own recollection and did not depend upon some Lithuanian speaker to supply detail on request.

4. The "Korps" is one of a number of exclusive student fraternities, commonly associated by its name with a province, having strong traditions and observing elaborate ceremony.

5. After all it's my business where I choose to snuff out.

6. When you're working on a novel, passages in dialogue are the oasis in the desert. It's not work. It's just a game. Once you've got the people on their feet, all you have to do is to listen to them and put down what they're saying.

7. Doesn't madam also believe that the human soul is divine?

8. People are ugly and the poetry they write is ugly.

9. cf. James Laver, *Taste and Fashion from the French Revolution to the Present Day,* London, ed. 1945, p. 202.

10. A moment later she was his.

11. A very popular magazine in the second half of the nineteenth century, illustrated and containing stories, educative articles, and poems. The volumes Sudermann read as a boy had had some of the pages glued together.

12. We live our lives in the midst of a tale.

13. Awkward and ridiculous too . . .

14. It's silly, I know, but I'm doing it all the same. I've covered it with kisses for you.

15. I am firmly resolved to return to the Königsberg milieu more calm and stable, and less vulnerable, and you must help me.

16. But in any case I once more give you my assurance that you shall have no burden of responsibility or obligation whatsoever, and I give you this assurance from a truly loving heart and with the idea not to encroach in any way upon the freedom you want for yourself.

17. We are not like other married people. Our bond is conditioned by claims and needs which do not exist in other marriages.

18. Finally I only want to tell you that in every respect I withdraw

from your life now. You are absolutely free, in every respect, free from all responsibility.

19. My life is by its very nature a series of emotional disturbances. Without them I couldn't live. The even tenor of middle-class life was just not made for me. I should be stifled and stupefied.

20. There's only one good state of health for me, and that is when I am ill.

21. In sincere friendship to my comrade-in-arms M.H.

22. I cannot associate with you any longer. You are ruining my career.

23. Oh dear, oh dear! What a deal of crossing-out is needed. I've thought of too many things, and crammed in too much.

24. How can I be sure that she will be sensible all the time?

25. You have too much love in you. Of all three kinds—love of the heart, love of the senses, and compassion. Everybody must have one of them, two are dangerous, and all three together spell destruction.

26. Much of my gloom and melancholy and distress come from the wretched depressed conditions at home when I used to seek refuge there. But thank God I did, or things would have been still worse with me.

27. Island of friendship (an island where Leo and Ulrich had been together in the romantic days of their youth and had sworn eternal friendship).

28. So young and so depraved.

29. Where the river runs more gently (the title of Sudermann's posthumous novel).

30. Known in Lithuania as Tilžé, and on present-day Russian maps as Sovetsk.

THE WORKS OF SUDERMANN
and a
Selection of English Translations
(n. = narrative; dr. = drama)

1887 *Im Zwielicht/Zwanglose Geschichten, n.*
      Frau Sorge. n. (Dame Care, tr. Overbeck, London, 1891).
1888 *Geschwister. n.*
1889 *Der Katzensteg. n. (Regina* or *The Sins of the Fathers,* tr. Marshall, London and New York, 1898).
1890 *Die Ehre. dr.*
1891 *Sodoms Ende. dr.*
1892 *Iolanthes Hochzeit. n.*
1893 *Heimat. dr. (Magda,* tr. Winslow, Boston and New York, 1896).
1894 *Es war. n. (The Undying Past,* tr. Marshall, London and New York, 1906).
1895 *Die Schmetterlingsschlacht. dr.*
1896 *Morituri. dr.* (three one-act plays).
      Glück im Winkel. dr. (tr. Ashmore for B.B.C. production, 1958).
1898 *Johannes. dr.*
1899 *Die drei Reiherfedern. dr.*
1900 *Johannesfeier. dr.*
1902 *Es lebe das Leben. dr. (The Joy of Living,* tr. Wharton, London, 1903).

  Die Verrohung der Theaterkritik, essay.
1903 *Sturmgeselle Sokrates. dr.*
1905 *Stein unter Steinen. dr.*
  Blumenboot. dr.
1907 *Rosen. dr.* (four one-act plays). (*Roses,* B.B.C. production, 1959).
1908 *Das Hohe Lied. n.* (*The Song of Songs,* tr. Seltzer, London, 1910).
1909 *Strandkinder. dr.*
1911 *Die indische Lilie. n.*
  Spielhagen/Gedächtnisrede (memorial address).
  Der Bettler von Syrakus. dr.
1912 *Der gute Ruf. dr.*
1914 *Lobgesänge des Claudian. dr.* (sequence of scenes).
1917 *Litauische Geschichten. n.*
1919 *Romane und Novellen* (collected edition).
1920 *Die Raschhoffs. dr.*
1921 *Das deutsche Schicksal. dr.* (sequence).
1922 *Das Bilderbuch meiner Jugend* (memoirs). (*The Book of my Youth,* tr. Harding, London, 1923.)
1923 *Wie die Träumenden. dr.*
  Dramatische Werke (collected edition).
1925 *Der Hasenfellhändler. dr.*
1926 *Der tolle Professor. n.*
1927 *Die Frau des Steffen Tromholt. n.*
1928 *Purzelchen/Roman von Jugend, Tugend und neuen Tänzen. n.*
1930 (posth.) *Wo der Strom stiller wird. n.*

An amusing addendum is Edward Shelden's *The Song of Songs* (1914), an American dramatization of *Das Hohe Lied,* in which the already heady sentiment of the original gains added seasoning. The setting is New York, where Lily Kardos, daughter of the musician Dionysius Kardos, lives in a flat on East 59th Street. The closing scene is designed to be very touching: "Very softly, as if from a great distance, is heard the Song of Songs. . . . Dicky buries his face in her lap. Half unconsciously, she strokes his hair. But her eyes are still fixed on the face of the dream she lived for, and that she found, and lost"!

SELECT BIBLIOGRAPHY

Busse, K. *Hermann Sudermann/sein Werk und sein Wesen,* 1927. A useful analysis of works; discriminating comment on *Johannes.*

Duglor, Th. *Hermann Sudermann/Ein Schaffen zwischen Beifall und Schmähung* (*Schriften für die Ost- West- Begegnung*), 1958. Stresses significance of historical plays, e.g. *Johannes* and *Lobgesänge des Claudian.*

Gimmerthal, A. *Hinter der Maske,* 1901. Reference to Sudermann's use of allegories and symbols and to relation of poetry and religion in his work.

Goldstein, L. *Wer war Sudermann?,* 1929. Posthumous appraisal.

Hale, E. *Dramatists of Today,* 1906.

Heller, O. *Studies of Modern German Literature.* New York, 1905.

Jüngst, H. C. *Sudermann oder Liliencron?*, 1893. A brief attempt to strike a balance but: "Ein Drama Sudermann's wird nimmermehr veredelnd wirken".

Kappstein, T. *H. Sudermann und seine 17 besten Bühnenwerke*, 1922. Useful analysis.

Kawerau, W. *Hermann Sudermann/Ein kritische Studie*, 1897. Often listed. Subjective attempt to overcome bias.

Kerr, A. *Ein kritisches Vademecum*, 1903. Lively controversy.

Leux, I. *Hermann Sudermann*, 1931. Psychological study.

Rast, J. *Studien über den Aufbau des Dramas und Spielfilms*, 1942.

Scholz, K. *The Art of Translation*. Useful reference to English translations.

Selten, K. *Die Revolution in der Litteratur*, 1892. Sidelight on contemporary opinion.

Walter, H. *Sudermann und die Franzosen*, 1930. Detailed speculation on influences.

Briefe Hermann Sudermanns an seine Frau, ed. Leux, 1932.

Arthur Schnitzler

Arthur Schnitzler

by H. B. GARLAND

Turbulent though Schnitzler's inner life was, his biography is outwardly uneventful. He was born in Vienna on 15 May 1862. His father was a Jewish throat specialist who viewed his son's literary learnings with thinly veiled disapproval. Schnitzler's earliest works, derivative verse tragedies, the first of which was written when the boy was twelve, perhaps deserved and explain this parental attitude. An equivocal father-son complex persists through Schnitzler's life. Schnitzler studied medicine in Vienna, but continued to occupy himself with writing. With Hofmannsthal he frequented the literary circle in the Café Griensteidl.

After a short period of hospital service Schnitzler devoted himself to writing, though he never entirely abandoned medical practice. With *Liebelei* (1895) he broke through the Burgtheater barrier against naturalistic plays. After *Freiwild* (1896) he found himself the target of anti-Semitic attacks; and *Leutnant Gustl* (1901) led to the resignation of his commission in the medical reserve. Fiercely critical of himself as well as of others, Schnitzler nevertheless achieved general recognition in his native city in the 1920's. His last years were darkened by the suicide of his daughter. He died on 21 October 1931.

ONCE an image is implanted in the public mind it is not easily eradicated, continuing to live its own life, simplifying, falsifying or even obscuring reality. Arthur Schnitzler has been particularly unfortunate in the likeness which has long been accepted as a true-to-life portrait. It must be conceded that it is partly, though not all, of his own making. His cycle of one-act plays *Anatol* breathes charm, elegance, languor, and a fastidious yet irrepressible sexuality, seeming to reflect, discreetly yet unmistakably, an effete civilization—in a word, it may pass as the quintessence of Viennese decadence. Nor was Schnitzler helped by Hofmannsthal's charming and irrelevant prologue, with its

"Frühgereift und zart und traurig"[1]

and its peripheral allusions to the Vienna of Bernardo Bellotto. The image of the charming, frivolous Viennese, set against the background of the younger Canaletto's captivating architectural harmonies, accompanied by the titillating waltz music of Lanner and Johann Strauss, was thus established, and all the power and seriousness of Schnitzler's subsequent writing has never been able to do more than stir the veil which he had inadvertently drawn in front of his true self. The automatic responses which so irritate Georg von Wergenthin when he goes as conductor to Detmold, though there applied to Vienna itself, are a token of the public's preference for an easy and attractive semblance to the real Arthur Schnitzler.

"Denn wenn der Name dieser Stadt [Wien] vor den Leuten erklang, merkte es Georg ihren vergnügten Mienen an, dass, gesetzmässig beinahe wie die Obertöne auf den Grundton, sofort gewisse andre Worte mitzuschwingen begannen, auch ohne dass sie ausgesprochen wurden : Walzer . . . Kaffeehaus . . . süsses Mädel . . . Backhendel . . . Fiaker . . . Parlamentsskandal."[2]

Yet even the *Anatol* cycle contains more than the flavour of a captivating city and the echo of a dying age. Anatol's sentimental assessment of Bianca, his infatuation with the unseen "süsses Mädel" of *Abschiedssouper*, or the provocative charm and seductive erotic undertones of *Weihnachtseinkäufe* are only one side of the picture. Beneath the bloom of the surface, perhaps worn a little thin today, beneath the allurement, the lilt and the elegance, lurks a conflict, not of the sexes, but of sex. The seven women of these seven plays, together with many others whose brief dominance over Anatol is mentioned or implied, are all seen from without; all are symbols, differing in flavour and texture like chocolates in a box, but generically similar. The hand, tempted, reaches out for one, it is savoured, the taste delights, dissolves and the hand reaches out again. All are seen as existing solely in their relationship to the man, all are deceivers, potentially or actually, and the worthlessness of Emilie in *Denksteine* or of Else in *Agonie* is simply the crystallization, in circumstances of stress, of elements which are present in Cora or "das süsse Mädel" or the enchanting Frau Gabriele. This generic similarity is, however, not an objective constatation, but a subjective perception; it is an expression, not of them, but of Anatol himself, of his erotic life, describing a series of graph-like curves, each beginning in eager anticipation, rising to the glow and rapture of love, lapsing into dullness and stale repetition, ending in indifference or even hatred or disgust. The simple repetitive pattern of the cycle underlines the fundamental sameness of the experience beneath the surface of change.

The rhythm of Anatol's love affairs, from mistress to mistress, from rapture to boredom, represents the first chapter in Schnitzler's natural history of love. The scope of the pictures, however, is limited. The manner is often frivolous, the standpoint that of a rather spoilt, idle, well-to-do, Viennese bachelor, feckless but optimistic, cultivated but sterile. In his make-up appear from time to time elements which are not so much general aspects of male sexual behaviour as symptoms of a particular and specialized form of erotic response. In more than one of the plays there appears a dualistic attitude to women in which contempt and dislike are active even in the moments of attraction and exaltation. In *Die Frage an das Schicksal* Anatol strenuously ignores his suspicions, and in so doing emphasizes their strength. In *Episode* he is flattered by the thought that he has shattered Bianca's life—"Du, wenn ich mir's überlege, so scheint mir : Die habe ich wirklich zermalmt."[3] Over and over again, however, with Cora, with Else, with Emilie, there appears a jealousy which, if it cannot find an object in the present seeks it in the past, an attitude of mind which finds a more elaborate expression in Schnitzler's first, and rather dreary, full-length play, the naturalistic *Das Märchen*. For all Schnitzler's pretension to detachment and impartiality, his male characters constantly reflect a state of mind which is clearly his own—a completely egoistic attitude to the sexual process and its consummation, and a frustrated rage that the woman, as it seems to them, will not grant the selfless surrender which they themselves refuse. Though most of Schnitzler's characters focus their lives upon sex none of them can attain satisfaction in it. In this welter of conflicting tides come momentary interludes of clear vision, in which a moral judgment, surprisingly enough, is promulgated, only to be promptly submerged again in the whirlpool of passion. Such flickers of morality, which estrange because they are not integrated, hard lumps in the smooth texture of the *mousse*, occur when Anatol rebukes Frau Gabriele or Else ("verlogen und lüstern zugleich"),[4] and in Max's short-lived indignation with Anatol on his wedding morning.

The form of these plays is significant for the strength and weakness of Schnitzler's creative mind. The one-act play with its single climax of surprise, its brief *pointe* is akin to the Novelle. Its practitioners are not all short-winded, but it is a form in which shortness of wind, if it exists, is not revealed. Certainly Schnitzler's early plays are, for the most part, written with a brilliant first act, posing a situation, followed by two, three or four acts in which the matter is discussed at length; this is the structure of *Freiwild*, of *Das Vermächtnis*, and even, up to a point, of *Liebelei*. A clue to the weaknesses of the longer plays can be found in the dialogue, which serves perfectly to analyse motive and to evoke atmosphere, but can do little to further action. Such dramatic writing is effective in the limited scope of the one-acter; the longer plays reveal its deficiencies. It was therefore a true instinct or a correct calculation which led Schnitzler to achieve an evening's dramatic entertainment by a succession of connected short plays. Nor was *Anatol* an isolated experiment; *Lebendige Stunden* (1902), *Marionetten* (1906) and

Komödie der Worte (1915) are all groupings of short plays, with a common theme, though without the personal thread maintained by Anatol and Max.

Schnitzler's masterpiece in this form, however, is probably *Reigen*, the cycle of ten one-act plays which, in a film adaptation under the title *La Ronde*, has gone the round of the world. *Reigen*, written according to Schnitzler in the winter 1896–97, before *Lebendige Stunden*, and some seven years after *Anatol*, was published in 1900 but it did not appear on any stage until the First World War had relaxed some of the taboos which enveloped the presentation of sexual relationships on the stage, and even in 1922 it was reckoned pretty strong stuff.

Reigen bears the sub-heading "Ten Dialogues", and one of its principal original features is its circular form. Each character appears twice in succession, each time with a different partner, maintaining an overlapping link until the last character joins hands with the first in the manner of the round dance which gives the cycle its title. Schnitzler has in this way achieved a closed form, obviating the indeterminate and inconclusive end which is the usual defect of the one-act cycle. Its second and more notorious originality is the central climax of each episode, the consummation of the sexual act indicated by a series of dashes (and commonly pointed on the stage by the extinguishing of the lights). It is a pattern of recurring concupiscence, and assertion of the rise, fulfilment and decline of desire, not merely as an essential element of life, but as the determining factor of much human behaviour. It is a natural history of the *libido* and a delineation of the protective colouring which it assumes to achieve its end. The temptation to cynicism is obvious, but Schnitzler has resisted it; rather does he, with reticent irony, expose the pretensions and vanities, the hypocrisies and deceits of the egotistical and self-satisfied. The irony is at its most biting in the figure of "Der junge Herr", the portrayal is kindest in "Der Graf", with his innate decency of feeling. The whole is a commentary on human desire enveloped in human weakness, conceit and prevarication. What might at first sight appear to be a contribution to elegant pornography, proves to be a work of a moralist, a minor masterpiece of satire.

The moralist *malgré lui* is even more conspicuous in *Liebelei*, the work with which Schnitzler in 1895 gained for the play of contemporary life access to the Burgtheater, the jealously guarded home of classical drama. *Liebelei* is a large-scale tail-piece to the *Anatol* cycle. Divesting itself of the masculine egotism of Anatol's variations on a familiar theme, it recognizes the genuineness of a woman's emotions and contrasts them with the shallow good intentions of the philandering Viennese bachelor Fritz, a more earnest but still pluralistic version of the man of *affaires*.

The first act shows Schnitzler at his best. A sensitive master of mood, he brings his four characters to Fritz's flat for a little celebration, delineates them distinctly, establishes the two divergent love relationships and creates the atmosphere of gaiety, which expresses itself in each person differently and yet coalesces into a whole. Into this carefree circle intrudes the figure of fate. Termed simply "einen elegant gekleideten Herrn",[5] he tears, in his few minutes on the stage, the atmosphere to tatters. In the first production the famous naturalistic actor Mitterwurzer elected to play this minor part precisely because he saw its power and potency. "Der Herr" is the reality which by its mere presence shatters the meretricious jollity of the "celebration", and the whole tawdry structure of Fritz's aimless and foolish life. What follows is merely the unfolding of a predetermined pattern. The first act closes in an atmosphere of frustration and foreboding. The second provides a portrayal of mood in which, in contrast to the first, the emotions are real. Christine's love for Fritz is as genuine as the restrained fury of "der Herr", and it shows up by contrast the shallowness and inadequacy of Fritz's emotional world. So far Schnitzler was in command of his material. The first act had portrayed a "Stimmungsbild" destroyed by a lightning flash. The second act evokes a sweeter and truer mood, rendered more poignant by the knowledge of impending destruction which the spectator shares with Fritz. A situation is established, a lyrical scene, touched with irony, follows. But when he comes to the third act Schnitzler loses his grip. The delicacy and sensitiveness are discarded, and the avowed "Schauspiel" is lifted bodily on to the level of tragedy, at which elevation it can no longer maintain life. The language swells to the rhetorical and consciously poetic, and as it does so the genuineness of the play slides away into sentimentality and attitudinizing. *Liebelei,* perhaps, more than any other play, reveals Schnitzler's qualities and defects in crass contrast. It reflects the sensitiveness to atmosphere and the power to create it, the keen perception of human fragility and human self-deception; it betrays the inability to evolve any sort of large-scale structure and to communicate convincingly simple and powerful emotions.

The last act, which expresses indignation, is also symptomatic of something else. It shows the moral judgment in Schnitzler inhibiting artistic creation. Perhaps he felt himself so close to such a figure as Fritz that the open condemnation of him removed this most egocentric author too far from himself.

The faults in Schnitzler's dramatic construction (faults which are closely linked with peculiarities of his own mental structure) have

led him to write a number of mediocre plays which have never been
able to come to life on the stage or in the study. Apart from several
early plays, *Komtesse Mizzi, Zwischenspiel* and *Der Ruf des Lebens*
all belong to this category of still-born works. And his efforts at
verse drama, from *Der Schleier der Beatrice* (1900) to *Der Gang
zum Weiher* (1926), though often psychiatrically interesting, remain
entirely derivative in language and structure.

From time to time, however, Schnitzler has been able to overcome his limitations as a playwright and has created a work of
warmth or strength. *Der einsame Weg* (1903) rises above the usual
run of Schnitzler's plays just because he has accepted his own
limitations and, in so doing, turned them to positive account. The
work makes scarcely any attempt at dramatic coherence. It is
inhabited by a characteristic group of Schnitzler's Viennese—the
middle-aged man whose wisdom derives from the widest experience,
the perpetually unsatisfied, ageing philanderer-artist, the respectable
and faintly comic deceived husband, and the frank and clear-eyed
hussar subaltern who represents youth and the future; and for the
women, the actress who is a waning star and the determined,
independent, psychic young woman. There is no action. The whole
play consists in a complex and subtle pattern of human relations
set in an atmosphere of gentle resignation harmonizing with
the background of autumn woods, slow decline, softly approaching
end—

> "Wenn die Wälder rot und gelb
> schimmern, der goldene Dunst über
> den Hügeln liegt und der Himmel
> so fern und blass ist, als schauerte
> ihn vor seiner eigenen Unendlichkeit."[6]

Yet the supposed necessity of bringing the play to a conclusion
has brought to this play also a touch of unreality. The touching
reunion of Wegrat and the young man who has counted as his son
is moral and uplifting, but it belongs to a less austere and astringent
view of human relationships than that which makes up the rest of
this play. Schnitzler's restless and searching mind can find no end,
he achieves one here only by inhibiting his vision and invoking
convention.

It is very possible that the autumnal sunset glow of *Der einsame
Weg* is illusory; but it is an illusion the author has at least felt as
his own. *Das Weite Land* grasps the problem of age in a brusquer
and angrier fashion. Friedrich Hofreiter, arrogant, irritable, nervous, refuses to come to terms with age. Not that he blinds himself
or pretends that he is still young. He recognizes angrily the decline
and asserts himself by a wanton act of destruction, shooting dead

his young acquaintance in a frivolous duel. But he knows, as clearly as the resigned Sala of *Der einsame Weg,* that he is finished. *Das Weite Land* is the clearest and harshest exhibition of Schnitzler's corrosive intellect operating upon the Viennese civilization to which he belonged. Beneath a surface of culture and elegance play the real forces of egoism, brutal impulse and ruthless desire. In this world the man of decency (Dr. Mauer) appears as a rather contemptible bumbler. It is not on the face of it a moral work, and yet the pitiless realism is more truthful than the sentimentalities which often mar his consciously moral plays.

The problems of love and age are interlocked. Love, as the prelude and fulfilment of sex, is the focus of his thought, the pole to which the magnet swings back, however often it is turned in other directions. And age is felt less to be a termination of life than an end to love. But if these were for Schnitzler the fundamental problems of life, there were others which he, as a Jew, could not ignore. The years of Schnitzler's youth and early manhood were also the years in which anti-Semitism grew into a political faction, at first economic in outlook and then racial. The 1890's saw the rise to power in Vienna itself of Prince Aloys von Liechtenstein and Karl Lueger; in 1897 the anti-Semite Lueger became Oberbürgermeister of Vienna, an office which he retained until his death in 1910. The broadest picture of anti-Semitism occurs in Schnitzler's novel *Der Weg ins Freie,* where it is part of an even broader survey, and it flickers in the background in many works. In 1912, however, it formed the subject of a play which is among the most impressive of his works for the stage.

Professor Bernhardi shows a Jewish doctor who unintentionally finds himself the centre of a *cause célèbre.* Bernhardi, as the chief physician and director of a hospital, refuses a priest access to a dying girl on the grounds that the girl does not know that she is dying, and will have a more serene last hour if she is left in ignorance. His action, which is a mere snap response to an unforeseen situation, arouses lukewarm assent or misgiving among the colleagues present. In no time, however, it becomes clear that it is to become a focal point for political forces. The anti-Semites ask a question in parliament, the minister intends to defend Bernhardi, but changes sides when he finds the tide running against him, the hospital board resigns in protest against Bernhardi's act, some intriguing colleagues turn the medical committee against him. Court proceedings ensue and Bernhardi is convicted of an act hostile to religion and sentenced to two months' imprisonment, which he serves.

Told thus the play has the air of a story of the "martyrdom" of an individual, the crushing of an innocent victim by vicious reactionary forces. Many contemporaries interpreted it in this way, and were in consequence nonplussed by the levity and relaxation of the last act. But Schnitzler did not wish to write a serious *pièce à thèse*. There is clearly indignation in this play and *ressentiment*, too. But fundamental to the work is a balance, which arises from a profound truthfulness. Probably in no other work of Schnitzler is the urge for truth so plain. And the truthfulness is matched by intellectual power. The cross-examination of characters and motives is turned by the author not only upon the figures he has created but upon himself also. Beneath this intense scrutiny pose vanishes, conventional attitudes evaporate. Schnitzler sees not one side, not two, but many. And since he is not here concerned with the, for him, all-absorbing and all-consuming passion of sex, he can come to terms with himself and see the antics of pro-Christian snobbish Jews, timidly servile Jews, Zionist Jews, of Christians envious of Jewish wealth, Christians egged on by the Church, or Christians mildly influenced by social prejudice, as elements in the human comedy. The play is full of shafts of irony which play upon Jew and Gentile alike. Bernhardi's gesture is quite futile, the girl learns from the ward sister that she is dying. Professor Filitz's anger against Bernhardi is much more a consequence of a snub to his wife by Princess Stixenstein than the result of either religious or political opinions. Bernhardi is dethroned by the tortuous and overconscientious scruples of a Jewish colleague who feels he must vote with Bernhardi's tormentors. The conduct of Flint, the minister of education and religion ("Kultus und Konkord—",[7] as he almost calls himself by a slip of the tongue), is one long turn of ironical comedy, a study of the quite unconscious gulf between private professions and public pronouncements. And the fifth act, so much deplored by some, admirably ends this elaborate pattern of irony in the only appropriate way, by a light and deft touch which affirms the note of sanity and proportion. Like *An Enemy of the People,* to which it has often been compared, this play lives along with its problem, it does not exist in virtue of it.

Not only is *Professor Bernhardi* a masterpiece of irony, it is a superb study of human behaviour, and a brilliant rendering of the speech of a large and well-differentiated group of highly educated professional men. As with all Schnitzler's works none of the characters is entirely fictitious, but the fact that Bernhardi himself owes something to Schnitzler's father, that Oskar has traits of Schnitzler himself and that Hofrat Winkler is a lightly touched portrait of Max Burckhard is, at this distance at least, irrelevant. These figures live and, in so doing, they triumphantly justify Schnitzler's method.

Structurally, too, this play is superior to most of Schnitzler's dramatic works. As usual it sets a situation in the first act and proceeds to talk about it through the next four. A comedy can live on "talk" (as *The Importance of being Earnest* so convincingly demonstrates), and what talk it is through the five acts of *Professor Bernhardi*! However, Schnitzler does not here *merely* talk, he uses the flood of lifelike yet ironical eloquence to such good dramatic purpose that the third act provides a crisis much more tense than the episode of the first act. Perhaps it was that the problem of the Jew (unlike the problem of love) enabled Schnitzler to achieve the ideal compromise between commitment and detachment; at any rate *Professor Bernhardi* is unique in his work as a fusion of power and harmony.

Schnitzler's predilection for short forms is made apparent by the high proportion of one-act plays in his dramatic oeuvre : thirty-one against sixteen full-length plays, of which one (*Die Schwestern, oder Casanova in Spa*) is denoted as "Three acts in one". The same tendency is even more strikingly demonstrated in his narrative works, a mere two novels set against more than fifty Novellen and short stories.

Schnitzler's success in conveying atmosphere and mood in his plays foreshadows one of the most important features of his stories. He constantly shows a sensitive awareness of temperature, humidity, sunshine and cloud. The early story *Sterben* begins with atmospheric scene setting :

"Die Dämmerung nahte schon, und Marie erhob sich von der Bank... Es war etwas kühler geworden, dabei hatte die Luft noch die Milde des entschwindenden Maitages."[8]

A similar evocation occurs in the opening paragraph of *Frau Berta Garlan* :

"Auf den Hängen, an die die kleine Stadt sich lehnte, flimmerte es wie ein goldener Nebel, die Dächer unten glänzten, und der Fluss, der dort, ausserhalb der Stadt, zwischen den Auen hervorkam, zog leuchtend ins Land. Die Luft war ganz regungslos, und die Kühle des Abends schien noch fern."[9]

Such examples can be found in every Novelle, right up to the last, *Flucht in die Finsternis*, the last section of which begins :

"An diesem grauumzogenen Dezembertage dunkelte es früh. Kaum war der Zug über die Vorstädte und die kleinen Villenorte hinausgeflogen, so setzte ein leichter, allmählich dichter werdender Schneefall ein, so dass Wald, Hügel, Landstrasse und Dächer bald in einem linden, herzberuhigenden Weiss schimmerten."[10]

These are outwardly passages of description and may seem at first sight akin to hundreds of passages in novels of the nineteenth century. The appearance, however, is deceptive. The atmospheric writing is only incidentally a portrayal of the external world. Its real function is psychological, the rendering of a state of mind. Always Schnitzler is concerned, not with fine writing or the elaboration of background, but with the suggestion, subtle, sensitive and indirect, of a state of mind. The psychological significance of the "lind" and "herzberuhigend" of the mature passage last quoted is inescapable, but the full context of the earlier atmospheric writings establishes their mental co-ordinates, too.

Frequently the interplay of mind and atmosphere is emphasized by the perceptive character, as in the opening lines of *Die Frau des Weisen* :

"Hier werde ich lange bleiben. Über diesem Orte zwischen Meer und Wald liegt eine schwermütige Langeweile, die mir wohltut. Alles ist still und unbewegt. Nur die weissen Wolken treiben langsam; aber der Wind streicht so hoch über Wellen und Wipfeln hin, dass das Meer und die Bäume nicht rauschen. Hier ist tiefe Einsamkeit, denn man fühlt sie immer."[11]

In *Die Toten schweigen* Schnitzler goes a step farther :

"Er sah auf die Uhr ... Sieben—und schon völlige Nacht. Der Herbst ist diesmal früh da. Und der verdammte Sturm."[12]

Here there is complete fusion; wind and darkness are present as part of the perception of Franz, not as objective elements.

In this form of psychological narration lies a distinguishing characteristic of Schnitzler's stories. The narrator as a father-figure, remote and detached, austere and reproving, or genial and playful, has no part in Schnitzler's conception of technique. The story is always told from the standpoint of one of the participants. Yet it rarely takes the form of speech in the first person. If we disregard the early stories, collected posthumously under the title *Die kleine Komödie,* there are only five which use "ich" form as narration, and they all belong to the earlier phase of Schnitzler's career. Clearly Schnitzler aimed at a fine and delicate balance, in which the vision is that of a single person yet without the obvious endorsement which an overt indentification with the writer confers. The typical Schnitzler story makes use of narration, uses dialogue with restraint, and nevertheless contrives to imply a personal savour, not of the author but of the principal character, who is the percipient at each point. There is no mobile author, no roving camera-man. *Ein Abschied* affords an early example. Albert enters the room in which his mistress, the wife of another man, is lying dead :

"Er trat ein. Es war das Schlafgemach.—Die Fensterläden waren geschlossen; eine Ampel brannte. Auf dem Bette lag die

Tote ausgestreckt. Die Decke war bis zu ihren Lippen hinge-
breitet; zu ihren Häupten auf dem Nachtkästchen brannte eine
Kerze, deren Licht grell auf das aschgraue Antlitz fiel. Er hätte
sie nicht erkannt, wenn er nicht gewusst hätte, dass sie es war."[13]

The parenthetic enclosure of this description between actions and
mental processes of the character make it apparent that the description itself is a mental process, a record of his perception.

This psychological canalization of description and the prevalence
of atmospheric writing, which in itself denotes a psychological response, are indicative of a general tendency in Schnitzler's narrative
works, rather than the exemplification of a doctrine. The affinity
with naturalism is obvious, though the method differs from that of
acknowledged naturalistic writers. Schnitzler's manner is, no doubt,
the expression of his own mental characteristics and especially of a
scrupulous truthfulness, or at least striving after truthfulness, which
leads him to discard many literary conventions, including the convention of exact description.

On two occasions Schnitzler has diverged into a form which
augments this tendency to see through the character's eyes, and to
respond with his mind. These two Novellen, *Leutnant Gustl* and
Fräulein Else, exclude the narrator entirely, expressing their meaning exclusively in the form of monologue, mostly unuttered. The
words spoken aloud by Gustl or Else are isolated in inverted
commas; the things that are said to them are likewise in quotes or
set in italic, and are to be read, not as objective and external facts,
but as stimuli impinging upon the mind of the recipient. *Leutnant
Gustl* was a remarkable work in its day, employing the technique
of interior monologue at a time when James Joyce and Virginia
Woolf were still in their teens. Schnitzler's two stories, however,
remain isolated occurrences, separated by a quarter of a century;
it seems that the new form, for all the brilliance of these performances, was not really congenial to him. And the reason is probably
to be found partly in the difficulty of achieving atmosphere in
monologue form, and perhaps even more in a sense of inherent
untruthfulness, since the form makes articulate that which in the
real man is mostly *felt* and not resolved into words.

In the best stories the technique of monologue is held in reserve;
it is one of several devices which can be used with telling effect,
but it does not govern the story. In this form it appears in the later
stories, in *Casanovas Heimfahrt*, or *Spiel im Morgengrauen* or
Flucht in die Finsternis, where it is balanced with narrative, evoca-
tive and analytical elements.

The subject matter of Schnitzler's stories is, like that of his plays,
nearly always erotic. More clearly than in the dramatic works,

however, the theme of love appears as a part, and the most important part of human life. Schnitzler's natural history of mankind takes the shape it does, because of his own, almost oriental, preoccupation with sex. The persistence of the sexual impulse, the constancy of it, set against the waxing and waning of its attachment to any given object, give the basic pattern to his narrative work. The various *affaires* weave a melodic pattern above the ostinato bass of a powerful, vital and irrepressible sexuality.

In this portrayal of sexual life certain recurrent and individual notes suggest a personal preoccupation rather than a detached observation. The persistent refusal of Schnitzler's men to observe fidelity is matched by an absolute insistence on constancy and faithfulness in the women to whom they (temporarily) attach themselves. This contrast in standards in one whose intellect sought restlessly to shed prejudice in the pursuit of truth is an indication of how deep-seated in Schnitzler was the desire for possession, and how closely it was related to the desire for power. These tendencies occurring in his work are, moreover, credibly reported in his life. At the same time the analytical intellect denies the possibility of complete possession and so gives rise to the frenzied jealousies which prey upon Schnitzler's characters, as they preyed upon his own mind. It is a jealousy so insatiable that, if it is not offered an object, it must create it. And to this consuming and destructive passion every woman or girl offers a target. If she is faithful at the moment, the object of jealousy can be found in the past; if she is a girl who has no past then the object lies in the future. In this restless and corroding jealousy of present, past or future Schnitzler has an instrument always at hand with which to torment the beloved and himself. Such sadistic and masochistic motifs run through the plays, but they are much more perceptible in the stories, whose form permits minute and searching analysis. They reach their highest point in the dream symbolism of *Traumnovelle,* but they are clearly perceptible right through from the early *Sterben* to the final story *Flucht in die Finsternis.*

Schnitzler's deep personal commitment to sex is only one side of these Novellen, which, though monotonous in theme, are inexhaustible in variety. The author of the Austrian "doctor's dilemma", *Professor Bernhardi,* was himself a doctor and the son of an eminent physician. The medical aspect of the plays is, apart from this one obvious example, inconsiderable. But the stories are unmistakably clinical. *Sterben* is a case-history, an examination of the mental processes of a man in love, informed by his physician that he has not long to live. With remorseless detachment and accuracy Schnitzler traces the steps by which love, without diminishing, is distorted into something destructive and murderous. Alfred, no doubt, is very far from being every man, he is a facet of Schnitzler himself and subject to Schnitzler's devouring and many-sided jealousy. Yet within the self-imposed limits the medical history is convincing. Its special quality is the interweaving of physical disease and the emotional make-up of the patient, coupled with an austere rejection of every temptation to sentimentality. *Der Mörder* is a similar medical history, less probable, more violent, and, perhaps in consequence of its cruelty, tinged with a conflict of conscience in the apparently conscienceless young man; and ending on a note which satisfies preconceptions of aesthetic justice rather than an austere demand for truth.

"Study" is the term which could most properly be applied to Schnitzler's Novellen. From *Sterben* onwards a situation is given, the data are set out, the consequential developments are attentively observed and faithfully recorded, And these studies penetrate beneath accepted conventions, disregard customary labels and question traditional values. *Ein Abschied* reveals the essential cowardice of a "great lover". *Die Toten Schweigen* tears the veil of pretence from an illicit "grand passion". *Leutnant Gustl* displays the officer disregarding in secrecy the code to which he is publicly pledged. Though the revelations are scathing, their bitterness is relieved by slight touches of understanding and compassion.

The truly outstanding studies of Schnitzler are the larger-scale Novellen *Frau Berta Garlan, Doktor Gräsler, Badearzt* and *Flucht in die Finsternis*. All three are, in a sense, case-histories, the working out of subtle psychological changes. *Frau Berta Garlan* records the reawakening of sex in a young widow, the fulfilment of her desire and her subsequent revulsion. In this story Schnitzler evokes climatic atmosphere as an element of personal perception as in so many stories; but he also succeeds in doing something else : he communicates nameless, unanalysable half-tides of feeling which are as much physiological as psychological. The portrayal of Frau Berta herself represents outstanding achievement in a new mode of character rendering. Apart from this success *Frau Berta Garlan* is not on the highest level of Schnitzler's novellistic work. Written in one of his periodical brief revulsions against sex it weaves into Berta's story the contrapuntal account of a married woman, sexually deprived by the paralysis of her husband, and satisfying her desires by a discreet, illicit relationship. Frau Rupius, finding herself pregnant, seeks intervention for her husband's sake and dies of resulting sepsis. This sub-plot might be more readily acceptable as a story on its own; beside the history of Frau Berta its heightened tones appear forced, and the overt morality of the conclusion is heavy-handed and trite. The obtrusiveness of the moral elements which are occasionally embodied in Schnitzler's work suggest that they are transient acquisitions and not truly an integral part of his personality.

Frau Berta Garlan is a study of sexual maturity. *Doktor Gräsler, Badearzt,* written seventeen years later, when Schnitzler was fifty-four, is a story of oncoming age and incipient decline. Gräsler, a bachelor of forty-eight, has lived for many years with a sister who unexpectedly takes her own life. Oppressed by the tragedy, by a sense of the aridity of his life, and by an awareness of fleeting and almost lost opportunity, he turns to one woman after another seeking to replenish his sterile life, yet unable to shed the grey sameness of a life spent in drab and monotonous, though barely perceived unfulfilment. Inhibitions prevent him from asking the first, and finest of these women; the second, a sweet girl (though not, in the technical sense, "ein süsses Mädel") becomes his mistress but dies of scarlet fever; it is left to the third, an attractive, sympathetic and active young widow, to overcome his inhibited lethargy and make herself Frau Dr. Gräsler. There was material here for an ironical comedy. Schnitzler has not written it. He has preferred to give us a study, in subdued tones and lax tempo, of the human relationships of a sensitive man, muted by routine and age.

Schnitzler's last Novelle *Flucht in die Finsternis* also has as its principal figure a man in his forties; but the approach of age is not its theme. With a combination of professional psychiatric skill and poetic penetration and empathy Schnitzler traces the course of mental disease. Sektionsrat Robert suffers from persecution mania which leads him to fear and kill his anxious and well-intentioned brother. What distinguishes this story is its dynamic character. It traces with extraordinary subtlety and insight the imperceptible advances of the disease; it reveals Robert imprisoned within the limitations of his diseased personality, unable to follow well-meant advice, interpreting every action so as to foster the destructive delusion. The perversion of high intelligence, the plausible reversal of apparently plain evidence, the persistence of a subconscious will to attain that which is feared, are convincingly made clear and the reader himself suffers the combination of understanding and impotence which besets the witness of such conditions in real life. The medical knowledge alone could not have achieved this. It is Schnitzler's creative power, the ability to project himself, the power to evoke atmosphere and mood, which turn this case-book into a work of art. A sense of necessity, of powerlessness to avert a great impending and advancing calamity brings it very close to tragedy.

Of Schnitzler's two novels the later, *Therese,* is perhaps what might be expected of this gifted writer of Novellen : a long sequence of episodes which impart a sense of fragmentation and shortness of breath; the whole capped by one of those moral and righteous conclusions which seem the work of some other and less talented author. *Der Weg ins Freie,* written some twenty years earlier, is a very different matter. Unlike any other work of Schnitzler it unites breadth and grip; the wider horizon does not lead to loss of strength. It associates the two themes which lay nearest to Schnitzler: the relations of the sexes and the position of the Jew in Austria; and it makes plentiful use of his favourite modes of presentation—dialogue and atmosphere. The secret of its success probably lies in the author's interest in his wide range of characters. And that extended interest is possible because of the dual theme; those characters who are not involved in the complex history of love are implicated in the relationship of Jew and non-Jew.

In a sense *Der Weg ins Freie* is a social history. It is not comprehensive; it is limited to a section of Viennese society, marked by substantial means, private incomes, musical and literary culture, a liberal tone, and refined manners. The *Almanach de Gotha* is represented only in its lower reaches, the working classes hardly at all. The men are in business, or civil servants, or officers, or men of letters, or just "independent". The women are their wives and daughters. It is a picture which has no need to be all-embracing; it suffices that it is comprehensive within its self-imposed limitations.

The Viennese society which Schnitzler portrays is held together by its cultural interests and a sense of social style. It is not, however, homogeneous. Its constituent elements range from the noblemen Felician and Georg von Wergenthin and the hussar officer Stanzides to the rich and intentionally vulgar and over-Jewish Jew Salomon Ehrenberg. In between are a multitude of figures, who express various shades of attitude to the Jewish problem. For this society, even when it ignores it, is only too well aware that the drift of events and the shift of ideas has created a problem of race. Old Ehrenberg truculently asserts his national characteristics, his wife and daughter self-consciously disregard the question, his son Oskar deludes himself, but no one else, in snobbish aspirations, playing the Catholic aristocrat. Willy Eisler, whose military and gentlemanly appearance belies the Jew, neglects no opportunity to remind his hearers that he is one. Dr. Berthold Stauber is the Jew in parliament, uncertain of himself and sensitive and truculent by turns. Leo Golowsky opts for the Zionist solution. The figure on the largest scale is Heinrich Bermann, the restless analytical intellect, the Jew repelled by the hostile or distant Gentiles and disgusted with many of his own fellows. The manifold subtle aspects of the problem are indicated not merely by realistic figures with symbolical functions, but also in endless, fascinating debate presented with all Schnitzler's brilliant powers of dialogue. There is no conclusion, no tilting of balances or shifting of stresses to achieve an end; with a transparent, if complex, honesty Schnitzler leaves the matter with the inconclusiveness of real life. Indignation is held in check by self-criticism, sympathy is balanced by fastidious distaste.

The breadth and the multiplicity of treatment which Schnitzler gives to the Jewish problem in this novel is equalled in his handling of the theme of love. Once or twice, as in *Frau Berta Garlan* and *Liebelei,* he had used a secondary motif to throw into relief the love relationship of his principal character. In *Der Weg ins Freie,* however, the manifold presentation of the erotic theme is there in its own right. This implies in Schnitzler an unusual clarity and detachment. It is usually apparent that, for all the coolness of narrative, the problems of the principal character, particularly if he is a man, are closely implicated in Schnitzler's own reactions. He has achieved sufficient distance in *Der Weg ins Freie* to be able to project facets of his own erotic life into two sharply differentiated characters. Heinrich Bermann, the Jewish author, has long been known as a self-portrait, and the tormenting relationship with the actress, the sadistic refusal alike to forgive or to relinquish, and the conclusion in her suicide are closely paralleled by an episode in Schnitzler's life. The power of illogical, cruel and ruthless impulses, to survive and operate, despite keen intelligence and conscientious tolerance, is a fundamental aspect of Heinrich Bermann's love-life. As soon as sex is involved sadistic and masochistic trends emerge and dominate actions, mocking the comments of the intellect, indeed often enslaving it.

Georg von Wergenthin's relationship with Anna Rosner is of a gentler kind, and in him it is generally believed that portraiture of another personage was intended. The young nobleman has qualities which stirred admiration in Schnitzler (though the elder brother Felician is much more a wish-projection of the author), but his erotic life is unmistakably that of his creator. The latent, ever-watchful jealousy, ready to pounce leopard-like at the slightest stirring of opportunity, the element of boredom and revulsion which sets in immediately after the first consummation, the restless, unstable attachment to a freedom which is simply a refusal of responsibilities, all these are elements of Schnitzler's emotional life. Sex was something which Schnitzler could only see in relation to himself; consequently Georg, though in background, gifts, mood, and mode of life modelled on another, assumes Schnitzlerian characteristics as soon as his emotions are engaged. Georg von Wergenthin's relationship with Anna Rosner, though not the thread on which the work is strung, is the most substantial element in it. It describes an arc, beginning in exploratory sympathy, passing through tenderness and harmony, declining in subdued but increasing estrangement. As always with Schnitzler a sense of the end is already contained in the beginning. More than in any other of his works this one is scrupulously fair in its treatment of love. It is not weighted on the side of the man as *Anatol* is, nor is it written in reaction like *Liebelei* or *Frau Berta Garlan*. Still less does it superimpose a moral, which is not inherent in the work. It is scrupulously fair to both parties and in concluding with Anna's bitterness and Georg's relief, it ends in complete integrity.

Der Weg ins Freie comes as a fresh surprise each time to the reader familiar with Schnitzler. In its balance, harmony and breadth it is so unlike the rest of his work. And yet the formulae themselves are not different. The problem of love is there as always and the variations on it, though subtle, are not new. A fluent, elegant and lifelike dialogue and an acute rendering of inner reflection display character, mood and response. What gives this novel such substance is the localization of these factors, without diminishing them, not only in place but in time. These sentient men and women belong to the world around them. Though the moral ideas and attitudes of Schnitzler and Fontane are poles apart, *Der Weg ins Freie* is nevertheless first cousin to *Der Stechlin*. Schnitzler has here succeeded in combining in himself the poet of human life and the historian of the age.

Schnitzler's oeuvre certainly contains elements and works that are meretricious and ephemeral. For a successful playwright he possessed astonishingly little dramatic power. His leaning to the short work might suggest that he was really a miniaturist. And his self-imposed restriction to Vienna and its environs would seem to limit his public. Yet when all the faults are conceded we are obliged to admit that both in the cyclical play and in the story of interior monologue he created new forms; that this dramatist, whose plots have so little stamina that they flag after the first act, proved that the creation of atmosphere could sometimes carry a play in default of action; and we see that this miniaturist could write Novellen of power and weight—there is nothing small scale about *Doktor Gräsler, Badearzt* or *Casanovas Heimfahrt* or *Flucht in die Finsternis*. As to the local limitation, which is anyway not exclusive (remember *Die Frau des Weisen, Der Mörder* or *Dr. Gräsler* himself), the background of Vienna is international currency and an asset rather than a liability. It may still perhaps be validly objected that Schnitzler's field of view is restricted; but the depth, in which the trained eye of the physician assists the penetration of the poet, is unrivalled. His idiom is limited by his age, but his poetic natural history of the most powerful human passion is written at first hand and impressively documented. In

Der Weg ins Freie he has used his shortcomings to enhance his qualities and so has given us a novel which comes very near to the first rank. And in all his best work he restlessly and persistently seeks truth in the field of the mind, ruthlessly exposing all mental shams and subterfuges, including his own.

TRANSLATIONS

1. "Older than our years, gentle and sad."
2. "When the name of this city (Vienna) was mentioned George noticed from people's smirking faces how, like overtones on the basic note, certain other words began to vibrate in sympathy, even though they were not uttered."
3. "You know, when I think of it, I really do think that I crushed her."
4. "Both deceitful and lustful."
5. "A well-dressed gentleman."
6. "When the woods shimmer in red and yellow and the golden haze lies across the hills and the sky is so remote and pale as if it were afraid of its own infiniteness."
7. "Religion and Concord at" instead of the proper title "Religion and Education".
8. "Dusk was coming on and Marie got up from the bench ... It had become much cooler and yet the air still had something of the softness of the fading May day."
9. "On the slopes against which the little town nestled, there was a gleam as of a golden mist, the roofs caught the sun, and the river which came into view in the meadows beyond the town shone as it flowed on into the countryside. The air was motionless and the cool of evening still seemed far off."
10. "Darkness came early on this overcast December day. Hardly had the train passed the outskirts and the suburbs than a light fall of snow began which gradually became heavier so that frosty hills, roads and roofs soon glistened in a soft consoling whiteness."
11. "I will make a long stay here. An air of melancholy languor which does me good attaches to this place between sea and wood. Everything is silent and motionless. Only the white clouds drift slowly past. But the wind is so high in the air above waves and treetops that there is no murmur from trees or water. A deep solitude is here which one feels all the time."
12. "He looked at his watch ... Seven—and already quite dark. Autumn is here early this year. And the confounded wind."
13. "He went in. It was the bedroom. The shutters were closed; a small lamp was lit. The dead woman lay stretched out on the bed. The quilt was drawn up to her mouth; on the bedside-table a candle burned and its light shone harshly on to the grey face. If he had not known that it was she, he would not have recognized her."

SELECT BIBLIOGRAPHY

I. WORKS

A new complete edition is in preparation. Several of his works have been translated into English.

Die Erzählenden Schriften, 4 vols. 1922–26.
Die Theaterstücke, 5 vols. 1922–26.
Komödie der Verführung, 1924.
Fräulein Else, 1924.
Die Frau des Richters, 1925.
Traumnovelle, 1925.
Der Gang zum Weiher, 1926.
Der Geist im Wort und der Geist in der Tat, 1926.
Spiel im Morgengrauen, 1927.
Buch der Sprüche und Bedenken, 1928.
Therese, 1928.
Flucht in die Finsternis, 1931.
Die kleine Komödie (collection of early stories previously unpublished or published in periodicals), 1932.

II. WORKS ON SCHNITZLER

L. FEIGL. *Arthur Schnitzler und Wien.* Vienna, 1911.
J. KAPP. *Arthur Schnitzler.* Leipzig, 1913.
T. KAPPSTEIN. *Arthur Schnitzler und seine besten Bühnenwerke.* Berlin, 1922.
J. KÖRNER. *Arthur Schnitzlers Gestalten und Probleme.* Zürich, 1921.
J. KÖRNER. *Arthur Schnitzlers Spätwerk* (Preuss. Jahrb., April–May; 1927).
J. LANDSBERG. *Arthur Schnitzler.* Berlin, 1904.
J. K. RATISLAV. *Arthur Schnitzler: eine Studie.* Hamburg, 1911.
T. REIK. *Arthur Schnitzler als Psycholog.* Minden, 1913.
K. ROSEEN. *Arthur Schnitzler.* Berlin, 1913.
A. SALKIND. *Arthur Schnitzler, Studie.* Leipzig, 1907.
O. P. SCHINNERER. *Systematisches Verzeichnis der Werke Arthur Schnitzlers* (Jahrbuch dtscher Bibliophilen 18 & 19. Jahrg.), 1932–33.
O. SEIDLIN. *Der Briefswechsel zwischen A. Schnitzler u. Otto Brahm.* 1953.
R. SPECHT. *Arthur Schnitzler: Der Dichter u. sein Werk,* 1922.

Christian Morgenstern

Christian Morgenstern

by LEONARD FORSTER

Morgenstern was born as the son of a painter in 1871. He began his career with lyric, dithyrambic and parodistic verses which showed great technical skill. It soon became clear that he was an incurable consumptive. In 1905 he began the serious study of Western and oriental mysticism which is reflected in much of his verse and which finally led him to the anthroposophy of Rudolf Steiner. He died in 1914.

S O she went into the garden to cut a cabbage leaf to make an apple-pie; and at the same time a great she-bear, coming up the street, pops its head into the shop. 'What, no soap?' So he died, and she very imprudently married the barber; and there were present the Picninnies, and the Joblillies, and the Garyulies, and the grand Panjandrum himself, with the little round button at top; and they fell all to playing the game of catch as catch can, till the gunpowder ran out at the heels of their boots.

This celebrated piece is generally supposed to have been written in order to baffle an eighteenth-century actor who had maintained that she could memorize anything after having read it once.[1] It is obviously constructed on the principle that it is easy to memorize something that makes logical sense and that conversely it is difficult to remember something which does not. One does not need cabbage leaves to make apple-pies, and people do not have their shoe-heels filled with gunpowder. The whole thing is nonsensical, and therefore unworthy of serious consideration. This train of thought may be considered natural in the Age of Reason, but its falseness is shown by the circumstance that the piece has lived on—mainly orally—for nearly two hundred years, and that most of us probably have it by heart. Its attraction is quite plainly of a different order; we like it and we remember it precisely because it is nonsense.

By nonsense I do not mean the sheer absence of logical sense, but the creation of a structure which is satisfying in itself—for a variety of reasons—without reference to verisimilitude, logical sense or even intelligible words, though it may embody elements of all of them. In the piece about the cabbage leaf, there are recognizable elements of a rather inconsequential story, not unlike the end of some fairy-stories—the presence of the bear points that way too. It is also strongly rhythmical, with repeated and varied sound-patterns—"the Picninnies, the Joblillies and the Garyulies". It presents us with a fragment of a world into which we can enter and it does it in a linguistically satisfying way. The parallel with the fairy-tale is no mere chance, for nonsense of the kind I have in mind is familiar to us all from the nursery (the cow jumped over the moon), and there is folk nonsense in every country. A student from South Wales, who like many South Walians knew no Welsh, told me some years ago that when *Land of my Fathers* is sung in Welsh at patriotic gatherings and it is expedient for those present to go through the patriotic motions, those who have no Welsh sing an English version which keeps close to the Welsh sounds and begins: "My hen laid a haddock on top of a tree". An essential point here is that this version, on such an occasion, is not felt to be in any way irreverent or mocking. It is simply a perfectly functional form of words. But there can I think be little doubt that it is easily remembered because it is nonsensical.

The memorable property of nonsense is frequently put to use. Much medieval nonsense is mnemonic; the names of various figures of scholastic argument could be joined together in impressive-sounding formulae like "Barbara celarent" and thus committed to memory. There was a poem in hexameters of immense complexity designed to help people to memorize the feasts of the Christian calendar. The pairs of verses consist of the same number of syllables as the month has days; the syllables are the first syllables of the name of the feast day, with padding as requisite. The poem was known as *Cisiojanus* from its first words; here is the couplet dealing with the month of January; it has, of course, thirty-one syllables :

Cisio Janus Epi sibi vendicat Oc Feli Mar An
Prisca Fab Ag Vincen Ti Pau Po nobile lumen.

Cisio is the Feast of the Circumcision, which falls on January 1st; *Janus* recalls January; *Epi* (sixth syllable) Epiphany, January 6th; the thirteenth syllable is *Oc*, the octave of Epiphany, which falls on January 13th; *Feli* the feast of St. Felix on the 14th; *Mar* the sixteenth syllable indicates the feast of St. Marcellus on January 16th; *An* the seventeenth syllable, points to the Feast of St. Anthony on January 17th; and so on throughout the year. No one would have undertaken the immense labour of compiling this complicated work if it had not been plain that nonsense was memorable in itself. We are all familiar with the gender rhymes at the back of Kennedy's *Latin Primer,* which someone once called the purest poetry written in this country in the nineteenth century. The doubtless perverted pleasure that can be got out of repeating paradigms of irregular verbs is also familiar to many of us.

In all these cases, nonsense is put to use by ingenious persons, usually intellectuals, and indeed intellectuals have for centuries been the principal writers of nonsense. Rabelais, of course, the great early master in this field, was an intellectual. The peculiarly English brand of nonsense is that of Edward Lear and Lewis Carroll, both of them intellectuals; Carroll indeed was a professional mathematician, and thus presumably a super-intellectual. We are familiar with them from childhood, and they have received a good deal of attention from scholars of various kinds. Some years ago Miss Elizabeth Sewell wrote an interesting book called *The Field of Nonsense* (Chatto & Windus, 1952), from which it appears that this field contains two prize specimens of fat stock, Lear and Carroll, accompanied by a number of inoffensive field mice and rabbits in the form of nursery rhymes. There are other kinds of nonsense, and in particular a characteristically German brand of intellectual nonsense, associated with the name of Christian Morgenstern.

Morgenstern's work falls into two parts : the serious love poetry and mystical verse which he himself believed to be his chief contribution to literature, and the humorous, burlesque or purely nonsensical poetry for which he is remembered. He himself always insisted that there was no dichotomy, that the higher nonsense of the *Galgenlieder* (1905) was only another aspect of the higher insight of the mystic. This is undeniable, but the implied corollary, that both are of equal poetic value, is not; it is astonishing how unequal they are. Morgenstern's serious verse is usually characterized by the—fortunately—untranslatable word "innig". Its sincerity is not in doubt, but there is nothing fresh about its diction or its message; in this sphere he is an undistinguished exponent of a genre of sentimental mysticism all too common in Germany. (One remembers that Lewis Carroll's few attempts at serious verse were atrocious.) With the *Galgenlieder* he made a contribution to German literature that was unique in its day and has not been rivalled since—a brand of metaphysical nonsense as distinctively German as Lear and Carroll are English. His poetic craftsmanship in these books is remarkable for its range of styles, rhythms and metres and for its verbal felicity. It is all the more surprising that his skill should have failed him when he was hymning the great principle of love which he believed informed the universe, uniting the poet with all things in it.

Eins und Alles

Meine Liebe ist gross	Da ist kein Tier
wie die weite Welt,	vom Mücklein an
und nichts ist ausser ihr,	bis zu uns Menschen empor,
wie die Sonne alles	darin mein Herze
erwärmt, erhellt,	nicht wohnen kann,
so tut sie der Welt von mir !	darin ich es nicht verlor !

Da ist kein Gras,	Meine Liebe ist weit
da ist kein Stein,	wie die Seele mein,
darin meine Liebe nicht wär,	alle Dinge ruhen in ihr,
da ist kein Lüftlein	sie alle, alle,
noch Wässerlein,	bin ich allein,
darin sie nicht zög einher !	und nichts ist ausser mir ![2]

Repulsively sentimental as this expression of it undoubtedly is, it was precisely this belief which enabled him to create so convincingly his nonsensical world. The creatures who people it—Professor Palmström and Baron von Korf with their fantastic inventions, the Indo-Chinese Prickly Pig (*Hystrix grotei Gray*), the Moon-sheep, the lonesome knee, the lonely shirt—are as real as the Jumblies or the Pobble who has no toes, and are not unlike them. They are described with a peculiar plaintive charm; the jacket worn by day, taking its well-earned rest at night, harbouring a friendly mouse; and the unicorn which—outside this country—only survives as an inn-sign, are not far from the famous panther and the flamingoes of Rilke. And just as Rilke enters into the spirit of the creatures and the objects which he describes and shows us them as it were from the inside, so Morgenstern with a similar gift of loving empathy gives human qualities to everyday things and invents a whole fantastic bestiary. Here for instance is the "Rocking Chair on the Deserted Terrace" :

Ich bin ein einsamer Schaukelstuhl
und wackel im Winde, im Winde.
Auf der Terrasse, da ist es kuhl,
und ich wackel im Winde, im Winde.
Und ich wackel und nackel den ganzen Tag.
Und es nackelt und rackelt die Linde
Wer weiss, was sonst wohl noch wackeln mag
Im Winde, im Winde, im Winde.

I am a lonely rocking chair
And in the wind I am rocking.
Cool is the draught of the terrace air
And in the wind I am rocking.

I am rocking and knocking the whole day long,
And the lime branches also are knocking.
Who knows what else may be joining the song
Of rocking and ducking and knocking.[3]

Much of his effect is gained by playing with language, taking
metaphor literally and bringing it to life. He can start with the
simple sequence of sounds conventionally used in German for the
sound of church bells, like our "ding dong", and out of "Bim bam
bum" he conjures three characters, an eternal triangle, and the
lover desperately seeking his beloved—for ever in the wrong
direction :

Bim, Bam, Bum

Ein Glockenton fliegt durch die Nacht,
als hätt' er Vogelflügel;
er fliegt in römischer Kirchentracht
wohl über Tal und Hügel.

Er sucht die Glockentönin BIM,
die ihm vorausgeflogen;
d.h. die Sache ist sehr schlimm,
sie hat ihn nämlich betrogen.

"O komm" so ruft er, "komm, dein BAM
erwartet dich voll Schmerzen.
Komm wieder, BIM, geliebtes Lamm,
Dein BAM liebt dich von Herzen!"

Doch BIM, dass ihr's nur alle wisst,
hat sich dem BUM ergeben;
der ist zwar auch ein guter Christ,
allein das ist es eben.

Der BAM fliegt weiter durch die Nacht
wohl über Wald und Lichtung.
Doch, ach, er fliegt umsonst! Das macht,
er fliegt in falscher Richtung.

Bim, Bam and Boom

There flies a bell-note through the night
As if winged like a swallow,
Arrayed in Roman vestments bright,
High over hill and hollow.

He seeks the lady bell-note BIM,
Who flew the evening previous;

She has in fact deserted him,
Which BAM finds very grievious.

"Come back," he cries, "come back! Your BAM
Is suffering most severely!
Come back, O BIM, my love, my lamb!
Your BAM adores you dearly!"

But BIM, as everyone knows well,
Has given herself to BOOM,
Who is as good a Christian bell
As BAM, one may presume.

All through the night BAM flies on, sighing,
Without stay or deflection;
But oh how vainly! for he's flying
In quite the wrong direction![4]

In the same way he can start with the word "Werewolf"; look
at it from all sides, and dramatize it in a situation:

Der Werwolf

Ein Werwolf eines Nachts entwich
von Weib und Kind, und sich begab
an eines Dorfschullehrers Grab
und bat ihn: Bitte, beuge mich!

Der Dorfschullehrer stieg hinauf
auf seines Blechschilds Messingknauf
und sprach zum Wolf, der seine Pfoten
geduldig kreuzte vor dem Toten:

"Der Werwolf," sprach der gute Mann,
"des Weswolfs, Genetiv sodann,
"dem Wemwolf, Dativ, wie man's nennt,
"den Wenwolf—damit hat's ein End."

Dem Werwolf schmeichelten die Fälle,
er rollte seine Augenbälle.
Indessen, bat er, füge doch
zur Einzahl auch die Mehrzahl noch!

Der Dorfschulmeister aber musste
gestehn, dass er von ihr nichts wusste.
Zwar Wölfe gäb's in grosser Schar,
doch "Wer" gäb's nur im Singular.

Der Wolf erhob sich tränenblind—
er hatte ja doch Weib und Kind ! !
Doch da er kein Gelehrter eben,
so schied er dankend und ergeben.

The Werewolf

One night an errant Werewolf fled
His wife and child and visited
A village teacher's sepulchre
And begged him : "Conjugate me, Sir !"

The village teacher then awoke
And standing on his scutcheon spoke
Thus to the beast, who made his seat
With crossed paws at the dead man's feet :

"The Werewolf," said that honest wight,
"The Willwolf—future, am I right?
"The Wouldwolf—wolf conditional,
"The Beowolf—father of them all !"

These tenses had a pleasing sound,
The Werewolf rolled his eyeballs round,
And begged him, as he'd gone so far,
Add plural to the singular.

The village teacher scratched his head;
He'd never heard of that, he said.
Though there were "wolves" in packs and swarms,
Of "were" could be no plural forms !

The Werewolf rose up blind with tears
—He'd had a wife and child for years !
But being ignorant of letters
He went home, thankful to his betters.[5]

Or he can take the phrase "Fersengeld geben", to take to one's heels
(literally : to give heel-money) and in a poem called *Lebenslauf*
envisage a wild chase across Europe, in which the pursuer collects
the "heel-money" given off by the pursued. By the time they
reach North Africa the pursuer is a millionaire, and the two divide
the money.

Some of Morgenstern's poems are fantastic transpositions of
current philosophical views on ontology, etc. *Vice Versa*, for

instance, is close to Ronald Knox's limericks about the young man who said "God":

Vice versa

Ein Hase sitzt auf einer Wiese,
des Glaubens, niemand sähe diese.

Doch, im Besitze eines Zeisses,
Betrachtet voll gehaltnen Fleisses

vom vis-à-vis gelegenen Berg
ein Mensch den kleinen Löffelzwerg.

Ihn aber blickt hinwiederum
ein Gott von fern an, mild und stumm.

Vice Versa

In a green meadow sits a hare
Thinking that no one sees her there.

But with a gaze kind and intent
(Helped by a good Zeiss instrument)

From a far hillside opposite
A Man is keeping puss in sight;

And watching him in turn—how odd—
A distant, kind and silent God.[6]

There is more philosophy in Morgenstern than in either Lear or Carroll, but it is so transposed that it does not obtrude; here is a reflection on the nature of space:

Der Lattenzaun

Es war einmal ein Lattenzaun,
Mit Zwischenraum, hindurchzuschaun.

Ein Architekt, der dieses sah,
Stand eines Abends plötzlich da—

und nahm den Zwischenraum heraus
und baute draus ein grosses Haus.

Der Zaun indessen stand ganz dumm,
mit Latten ohne was herum.

Ein Anblick grässlich und gemein.
Drum zog ihn der Senat auch ein.

Der Architekt jedoch entfloh
Nach Afri- od- Ameriko.

The Slatted Fence
A fence of slats; between each two
There was a space you could see through.

An architect had noted this,
There, suddenly, one night he is,

Lifts out the spaces from the slats
And builds with them a block of flats.

The fence meanwhile stands quite confounded,
With slats by nothingness surrounded!

A horrid sight! In disapproval
The Council ordered its removal.

The architect made his escape
To California or the Cape.[7]

The naked slats, the lonely shirt and the rocking chair are symbols of human isolation, and there are many poems in which Morgenstern expresses a Thurber-like sympathy for creatures involved in an uncomprehended (though not *ultimately* incomprehensible) universe, like the hen which has somehow wandered into the hall of a railway-station, where it is "in the way" (*Das Huhn*). Mixed in with the gently ironical or charmingly whimsical nonsense verses there are sudden frightening visions like that of the fly planet (though the poem itself is a pastiche of Heine):

Auf dem Fliegenplaneten
Auf dem Fliegenplaneten,
da geht es dem Menschen nicht gut:
Dann was er hier der Fliege,
die Fliege dort ihm tut.

An Bändern voll Honig kleben
Die Menschen dort allesamt
und andre sind zum Verleben
in süssliches Bier verdammt.

In Einem nur scheinen die Fliegen
Dem Menschen vorauszustehn :
Man bäckt uns nicht in Semmeln
Noch trinkt man uns aus Versehn.[8]

and some in which anger and desperation crack like a whip-lash :

Schiff "Erde"

Ich will den Kapitän sehn, schrie
die Frau, den Kapitän, verstehn Sie?
Das ist unmöglich, hiess es. Gehn Sie!
So gehn Sie doch!! Sie sehn ihn nie!

Das Weib, mit rasender Geberde :
So bringen Sie ihm das—und das—
(Sie spie die ganze Reeling nass.)
Das Schiff, auf dem sie fuhr, hiess "Erde".[9]

The inaccessible captain and the nameless, impersonal officials
(fittingly referred to by an impersonal verb) who prevent access to
him, strike a Kafka-like note (Kafka was twelve years younger than
Morgenstern), but most of these poems do not get beyond abstraction and pastiche. The poem "Housemaids on Saturday" is another
Heine pastiche which looks at first sight like a straight piece of
social criticism :

Mägde am Sonnabend

Sie hängen sie an die Leiste,
die Teppiche klein und gross,
sie hauen, sie hauen im Geiste
auf ihre Herrschaft los.

Mit einem wilden Behagen,
mit wahrer Berserkerwut,
für eine Woche voll Plagen
kühlen sie sich den Mut.

Sie hauen mit splitternden
    Rohren
im infernalischen Takt.
Die vorderhäuslichen Ohren
nehmen davon nicht Akt.

Doch hinten jammern, zerrissen
im Tiefsten, von Hieb und Stoss,
die Läufer, die Perserkissen
und die dicken deutschen
    Plumeaus.[10]

But the injustice which is shown up here is not that of the housemaids, but that of the carpets, who are suffering undeservedly;
Heine or Klabund or Erich Kästner would have made them a
symbol of social injustice, they would have made us feel that the
blows ought to be reaching the master and mistress in the drawing-
room, who are referred to by an ironical *pars pro toto* as "the ears
in the front of the house". Morgenstern's last verse does not do this,

it does not encourage us even to think as far; yet he is not parody-
ing Heine but trying in his own way to do what Heine did. Here
his limitations are apparent; one is left with the impression that the
poet is more interested in carpets than in human beings, that the
"love, large as the wide world itself" somehow stops short of
servant-girls, and that the fantastically peopled world of his imagination is more important to Morgenstern than the social realities
among which he lives. He is happier in poems like this about the
gremlin who eats handkerchiefs :

Gespenst

Es gibt ein Gespenst,   vieles weg,—
das frisst Taschentücher;   nicht alles, nicht auf ein Mal.
es begleitet dich   Mit achtzehn Tüchern,
auf einer Reise,   stolzer Segler,
es frisst dir aus dem Koffer,   fuhrst du hinaus
aus dem Bett,   aufs Meer der Fremde,
aus dem Nachttisch,   mit acht bis sieben
wie ein Vogel   kehrst du zurück,
aus der Hand,   ein Gram der Hausfrau.[11]

This, despite its echo of Schiller, strikes an immediate chord in
readers of James Thurber or Ogden Nash. Though he always
strenuously denied it, many of Morgenstern's poems are pastiches
and parodies, usually of his contemporaries, and the trained ear
can pick them out, but they by now live a life of their own, just as
the verses from *Alice* do; most of us, I suppose, would be hard put
to it even to give the titles and authors of the poems which Lewis
Carroll parodied in them, but this does not spoil our pleasure. So
it is with Morgenstern; for instance the inconspicuous poem which
opens the *Galgenlieder* brilliantly reproduces the Olympian tone of
the maxims and reflections of the later Goethe :

Lass die Moleküle rasen,
was sie auch zusammenknobeln!
Lass das Tüfteln, lass das Hobeln,
heilig halte die Ekstasen.[12]

One of his most successful parodies is in prose; it is the introduction to the *Galgenlieder*, put into the mouth of a portentous
humourless academic called Dr. Jeremias Müller, who uses all the
clichés and the considerable resources of obscurity which the
German language possesses in order to throw a flood of light upon
I am not quite sure what. Here is an attempt at translation of the
first and last paragraphs :

We live in stirring times. One day follows another, and new

life burgeons among the ruins. Wherever we look, in the field of morals or medicine, poetry or patriotism, in trade and industry, in art and science, everywhere we see the same phenomenon, the same trend. Symptom follows upon symptom, symbol is ranged beside symbol. And just such a symptom, just such a symbol, was the idea which welded together, one fine day at the end of the last century, eight young men, the putative begetters of this modest volume, determined to face the cruel moment, wherever it might present itself, in season or out of season, in the spirit of the times, or precisely not in the spirit of the times—these times, like all others, considered not merely as times of absolute motion, but as a systole and diastole of rising tide and falling ebb, with an occasional predominance of the latter lamentable tendency with all the aversion from the ideal of undaunted progress which it brings in its train—and to set up against it as it were the Goon Show of their humour.

A wobbulable impulse.

And in sober fact, then, if at all, and only then, at that precise state of the great heart of the people, in which the spirit of the new age had most wonderfully roused the eternal unsophistication of the natural creature to proleptic pregnant meteor flashes and flutterings, could a particularly exocentric reaction against the "law in reason" be initiated by certain more excosely orientated spirits, thereby throwing one further shadow of evidence into the breach, whereby it appears that no age, however obscure in itself and to itself, can fail, if it but "lay bare its soul" with all the contradictions, tangles, wangles, broth and Bovril of its being, to summon the courage, nay more, the temerity, to rise at long last like a rosy-fingered prawn above the horizon of its own chaos—albeit as but a frigment of itself, with the most bravely smiling tear on its banner.

It is therefore with due confidence that we assert (what applies to all those who, being born under constellations which, as the poet sings, "singe, not shine", find their mental equipment sadly exsiccated) that we are confronted by—to use a phrase appropriate to the time, the latter considered as a hydra (under the negative aspect, of course)—a hydratherapeutic phenomenon of prime importance; always bearing in mind that, as we had occasion to observe, no one should summon the courage, nay more the temerity, to besmirch with rosy fingers the true inwardness of its essentially unprejudiced hope of a so to speak prawn-minded or existentious expansion of its natural sphere together with the freedom of the individual in the face of the great heart of the people and its unalterable principles—a phenomenon whose significance is linked with the same trends, the same propensities in trade and industry, art and science and whose value as a now more, now less wobbulable expression of a perfectly defined and in the broadest sense excose Weltauffasserraumwortkindundkunstanschauung can no longer be seriously called in question by any thinking person.

The whole is rather reminiscent of Mr. Peter Sellers' turn—"The Party Political Speech".

Justice cannot be done in English to the last paragraph, which in the original is one immense sentence of twenty-two lines of close print, with all the model auxiliaries in the language piled up in a crackling heap at the end; here are the last few phrases to give an idea of the whole :

als ein mehr oder minder modulationsfähiger Ausdruck einer ganz bestimmten und im weitesten Verfolge excösen Weltauffasserraumwortkindundkunstanschauung kaum mehr zu unterschlagen versucht werden zu wollen vermag—gegenübergestanden und beigewohnt werden zu dürfen gelten lassen zu müssen sein möchte.

Morgenstern's parody and satire is not restricted to literary style : many of his nonsense poems gently and indirectly satirize contemporary society and its figures. (We have seen that his attempts at direct social criticism are less successful.) Palmström and Korf invent astonishing and impossible machines—the Olfactory Organ, the day-night lamp, which turns the brightest day to night, the reading glasses which condense and abbreviate the text, and many other satires on the world of advancing machine technology. But Palmström himself is a parody—a parody of the learned, ingenious and totally unpractical academic, but one who is unfitted for the real world by a soft and sentimental heart. (Even his watch is a watch "mit Herz", that adjusts itself to the emotional state of its owner.) Here is Korf and Palmström's Mousetrap :

Die Mausefalle

I

Palmström hat nicht Speck im Haus,
dahingegen eine Maus.

Korf, bewegt von seinem Jammer,
baut ihm eine Gitterkammer.

Und mit einer Geige fein
setzt er seinen Freund hinein.

Nacht ist's und die Stern funkeln.
Palmström musiziert im Dunkeln.

Und derweil er konzertiert,
kommt die Maus hereinspaziert.

Hinter ihr, geheimer Weise,
fällt die Pforte, leicht und leise.

Vor ihr sinkt in Schlaf alsbald
Palmströms schweigende Gestalt.

2

Morgens kommt v. Korf und lädt
das so nützliche Gerät

in den nächsten, sozusagen
mittelgrossen Möbelwagen,

den ein starkes Ross beschwingt
nach der fernen Waldung bringt,

wo in tiefer Einsamkeit
er das seltne Paar befreit.

Erst spaziert die Maus heraus,
und dann Palmström, nach der Maus.

Froh geniesst das Tier der neuen
Heimat, ohne sich zu scheuen.

Während Palmström, glückverklärt,
mit v. Korf nach Hause fährt.

The Mousetrap

I

Palmström is very ill at ease :
He has a mouse, but has no cheese.

Korf, answering his heart's desire,
Builds him a cabinet of wire,

And with a fine-toned violin
He sets his boon companion in.

The night descends, the dog-stars bark.
Palmström makes music in the dark.

And while the sweet strains come and go
The mouse comes walking on tip-toe.

No sooner in than from aloft
The gateway drops down, secret-soft.

Half-hidden in the shadows deep
Sinks Palmström's figure wrapped in sleep.

2

Next morning Korf, with gloves and gaiters,
Loads this elaborate apparatus

(Complete, that is, with mouse and man)
On to a strong removals van

Which powerful horses bear apace
Towards a distant woodland place.

Here, in the leafy silence, he
Sets this unusual couple free.

The mouse trots out to take the air
With Palmström bringing up the rear.

She looks once at her chaperone,
Then wags her whiskers and is gone.

Their task achieved the happy twain
Immediately go home again.[13]

As for Korf, he has no real existence, which is a great advantage
in our complex society, especially when one is dealing with
officialdom :

Die Behörde

Korf erhält vom Polizeibüro
ein geharnischt Formular,
wer er sei und wie und wo.

Welchen Orts er bis anheute war,
welchen Stands und überhaupt,
wo geboren, Tag und Jahr.

Ob ihm überhaupt erlaubt,
hier zu leben und zu welchem Zweck,
wieviel Geld er hat und was er glaubt.

Umgekehrten Falls man ihn vom Fleck
in Arrest verführen würde, und
drunter steht : Borowsky, Heck.

Korf erwidert darauf kurz und rund :
"Einer hohen Direktion
stellt sich, laut persönlichem Befund,

untig angefertigte Person
als nicht-existent im Eigen-Sinn
bürgerlicher Konvention

vor und aus und zeichnet, wennschonhin
mitbedauernd nebigen Betreff,
Korf. (An die Bezirksbehörde in—)"

Staunend liest's der anbetroffne Chef.

The Official Form

Korf has been besieged by swarms
Of grim official-looking forms
Adjuring him to make reply
Who he is and what and why.

Where he resides, what his address is
And what profession he professes,
Where he was born (with day and date)
And whether he is celibate.

Why he had come into this town
And if he thought of settling down
And how much money he possessed
And what religion he thought best.

Contrariwise if he declined
To answer with an open mind
He'd be arrested without fail
And promptly taken off to jail !

Korf sent an answer mild and bland :
"Your letter of the 10th to hand.
The undersigned herewith presents
His most obsequious compliments,

But would apprise you of the fact
That, in the strict sense of the Act
As touching personal matters, he
Is a complete nonentity

And that, officially at least,
He much regrets not to exist."
The High Official gasped—and read
With eyes fair bursting from his head.[14]

So Korf in his own person may be said to be an extreme satire, the negation of ordinary civil existence, but none the less a person who leads in his absurd way a happier life, just *because* he does not "exist".

Korf and Palmström and similar figures, like the lonely knee, the rocking chair and the rest of them, become alive and credible because of Morgenstern's mystical doctrine of universal love out of which they spring. The adept of this doctrine, "Der Wissende", as Morgenstern says in his poem with this title (one of his serious ones), can *play* :

Ein Spiel bedünkt
ihn nun die Welt,
ein Spiel er selbst
und all sein Tun.[15]

So it is that what so often started as parody and satire acquired a life of its own, almost contrary to the intention of the author. "We mock at emotions," said Morgenstern, "in the cause of *higher* emotions." (Wir treiben mit Gefühlen Spott um höhere Gefühle.)[16]

Because I have so far illustrated my remarks mainly with translations or paraphrases, it may not have become apparent to how very great an extent Morgenstern actually plays with language. His play with language leads him in fact far beyond whimsicalities like the werewolf and the heel-money to verse composed entirely of incomprehensible sounds. This is a step beyond *Jabberwocky*, which does after all retain the framework of English grammar and syntax. In *Das grosse Lalula* we have not merely nonsense words but a whole nonsense language, which seems to have its own coherence within the framework of the poem. The first step towards it was Morgenstern's translation of one of the early *Galgenlieder*,

"Das Mondschaf" (The Moon-Sheep) into Latin—by the twentieth century almost a nonsense language in itself for most of Morgenstern's readers—under the title *Lunovis*.

> Kroklokwafzi? Semememi!
> Seiokrontro—prafriplo :
> Bifzi, bafzi; hulalemi :
> quasti basti bo . . .
> Lalu, lalu lalu lalu la!
>
> Hontraruru miromente
> zasku zes rü rü?
> Entepente, leiolente
> klekwapufzi lü?
> Lalu lalu lalu lalu la!
>
> Simarar kos malzipempu
> silzuzankunkrei (;)!
> Marjomar dos : Quempu Lempu
> Siri Suri Sei []!
> Lalu lalu lalu lalu la![17]

And one step farther comes the poem with no sounds at all— *Fisches Nachtgesang* :

Both these may have been invented as satirical jokes, but like many such, they foreshadowed serious *avant-garde* experiments made since, from which modern poetry has greatly profited.

There are two aspects of Morgenstern's thought which underlay his nonsense verse : the fundamental harmony of divinely ordered existence, which can even comprehend the absurd; and the complement to this—the absurdity of existence, pointing to God as the only solution.

Both these aspects were present in the work of younger men working in Morgenstern's last years, who carried the experiments which he had initiated to a much further point. The Dadaists and the Surrealists began where Morgenstern left off. But in other ways too his work was oddly in step with the vanguard of his contemporaries in other fields; I have mentioned Rilke, whose "Evangelium der Dinge" Morgenstern so strangely puts into practice, and Kafka; one could go on and say that *Fisches Nachtgesang* could almost have been written to be sung by one of those fish which the young Paul Klee was to paint, some fifteen years after the poem was written. But Morgenstern's continuing vogue does not depend on his having been abreast or slightly ahead of his own time; it is due to the perennial attraction of nonsense itself. Morgenstern has become a part of the inheritance of educated Germans because he offers an escape world—an uncommitted world in a committed age —much as Lear and Carroll do for us, but it is a different world; it is a world of half-tones, of gentleness in an age of conflicting ideologies and concentration camps; there is pathos in it but no tragedy, there is absurdity in it but no hopeless frustration; there is love and charity in it.

NOTES

[Part of this essay was incorporated in the author's inaugural lecture in Cambridge. I am greatly indebted to the Cambridge University Press for granting permission to reprint it. I would also like to thank Mr. W. R. Hughes for allowing me to use his unpublished translations of Morgenstern's poetry—ED.]

1. W. Gurney Benham, *Book of Quotations*, London, 1924, p. 440b.

2. "My love is as large as the wide world, and nothing is outside it; as the sun warms and illumines everything, so does my love my world.— There is not a blade of grass, not a stone, which my love is not in; there is no gentle breeze or little stream in which it does not move too.—There is no creature, from the tiny midge up to us human beings, in which my heart cannot live, in which I have not lost it!—My love is as wide as my own soul, all things rest in it, I alone am all, all of them, and there is nothing outside me!" Christian Morgenstern, *Auswahl*, ed. Michael Bauer and Margareta Morgenstern. Munich, 1929. For the connection between mysticism and nonsense in Morgenstern see F. Hiebel, *Christian Morgenstern: Wende and Aufbruch unseres Jahrhunderts*. Bern, 1957, pp. 129 and 160ff.

3. *Alle Galgenlieder*, Berlin, 1932, p. 37; translation by Ernst Rose, *History of German Literature*, New York, 1960, p. 328.

4. *Alle Galgenlieder*, p. 34; the translation is by William R. Hughes, to whom I am grateful for some other translations below; this one has not been published before.

5. *Alle Galgenlieder*, p. 86; translation by Richard Hull from J. M. Cohen, *Yet More Comic and Curious Verse*, Penguin Books, 1959, p. 220; I am grateful to Mr. Hull for permission to use this and several other translations.

6. *Alle Galgenlieder*, p. 192; translation by William R. Hughes from *Ye Cheerful Saints*, London (Robert Hale), 1959, p. 127, by kind permission of translator and publisher.

7. *Alle Galgenlieder*, p. 54; translation by William R. Hughes, not previously published.

8. *Alle Galgenlieder*, p. 194. "On the fly planet human beings are not well treated; for what man here does to flies, flies there do to him. Men all stick to papers covered with honey, and others are condemned to a slow death in sweetish beer. There is only one respect in which the flies are ahead of man: they don't bake us in cakes and they don't drink us by mistake."

9. *Alle Galgenlieder*, p. 270. "I want to see the captain," the woman screamed, "the captain, don't you get me?" "Impossible," they said. "Go away! Get out! You'll never see him." The woman, with a crazy gesture: "Then give him this—and this—" (She covered the whole guard-rail with her vomit.) The ship she was sailing on was called "Earth".

10. *Alle Galgenlieder*, p. 303. "They hang them up on the rail, the carpets large and small, they whack and whack, mentally whacking their masters and mistresses.—With fierce satisfaction, with true berserk rage they get their own back for a week full of worries.—They whack with splitting canes to an infernal beat. The ears in the drawing-room take no account of this.—But back in the yard, deeply wounded, the runners, the Persian cushions and the fat German feather-beds bitterly complain at each buffet and blow."

11. *Alle Galgenlieder*, p. 254. "There is a ghost that eats handkerchiefs; it goes with you on a journey, it eats away out of your suit-case, your bed, your bedside-table, like a bird eating out of your hand; it eats a lot, but not everything, not all at once. Proud traveller, you set forth upon the sea of foreign parts with eighteen handkerchiefs; you come back with eight or seven, the plague of the housewife."

12. *Alle Galgenlieder*, p. 13. "Let the molecules rage, whatever they may produce by random combination! Stop splitting hairs, stop planing boards! Revere ecstasies!"

13. *Alle Galgenlieder*, p. 128; translation by Richard Hull, *Yet More Comic and Curious Verse*, p. 125.

14. *Alle Galgenlieder*, p. 165; translation by Richard Hull from J. M. Cohen, *More Comic and Curious Verse*, Penguin Books, 1956, p. 45.

15. Christian Morgenstern, *Gedichte*, ed. M. Beheim-Schwarzbach, Fischer-Bücherei 152, Frankfurt 1957, p. 60. "Now the world seems to him but play, he himself play, and all he does."

16. Quoted by Michael Bauer, *Christian Morgensterns Leben und Werk,* vollendet von Margareta Morgenstern unter Mitarbeit von Rudolf Meyer, 5th ed. Munich, 1954, p. 69.

17. *Alle Galgenlieder,* p. 19. Morgenstern was not the first; his elder contemporary Paul Scheerbart (1863–1915) wrote a "Lautgedicht" *Kikakoku* in 1897.

SELECT BIBLIOGRAPHY

Morgenstern's humorous verse consists of the following collections: *Galgenlieder* (1905), *Palmström* (1910), *Palma Kunkel* (1916) and *Der Gingganz* (1919). These were all republished in one volume under the title *Alle Galgenlieder,* which has gone through many editions. In 1929 there appeared a further collection, *Die Schallmühle,* which was republished in 1938 under the title of *Böhmischer Jahrmarkt.* Among his volumes of serious verse are *Auf vielen Wegen* (1897), *Ich und die Welt* (1898), *Einkehr* (1910), love poetry in *Ich und Du* (1911); his last volume, *Wir fanden einen Pfad* (1914), was inspired by Rudolf Steiner. Anthologies are cited in notes 2 and 15 above. In 1953 the Insel-Verlag published a selection from the *Galgenlieder* with an "authorized English version" by A. E. W. Eitzen; some few of these renderings are happy, but in general the translator's command of English is insufficient for the extremely exacting task he has set himself.

The standard biography of Morgenstern is by Michael Bauer (see note 16 above) and there is a more recent study (in the spirit of Rudolf Steiner) by F. Hiebel (see note 2 above); the best studies of Morgenstern's *Galgenlieder* still remain Leo Spitzer, *Die groteske Gestaltungs– und Sprachkunst Morgensterns* (in L. Spitzer and Hans Sperber, *Motiv und Wort,* 1918), and Victor Klemperer, "Christian Morgenstern und der Symbolismus", *Zeitschrift für Deutschkunde* 42 (1928), pp. 39–55, 124–136 (reprinted in V. Klemperer, *Vor 33 nach 45, Gesammelte Aufsätze,* Berlin 1956), by two of the masters of stylistics. Of the few studies on Morgenstern in English the best is W. Witte, "Humour and Mysticism in Christian Morgenstern's Poetry" in *German Life and Letters I* (1936). See also Peter Härtling, *Palmström grüsst Anna Blume,* Stuttgart, 1961.

Frank Wedekind

Frank Wedekind

by ALEX NATAN

Frank Wedekind was born in Hanover in 1864, the son of a doctor. He grew up in Lenzburg (Switzerland) and completed his studies at the Gymnasium in Aarau. After working a short time as a free-lance journalist, Wedekind became advertising manager of Maggi Ltd. He settled in Munich in 1889 as private secretary to the art dealer Willy Grétor. In his company Wedekind travelled to France and England. Returned to Munich he became an actor and belonged to the "Simplicissimus" circle of Ludwig Thoma, Th. Th. Heine and Thöny. A poem lampooning Kaiser Wilhelm II got him three months' confinement in a fortress. He returned to Munich and joined the "Kabarett der Elf Scharfrichter". He married the actress Tilly Newes, by whom he had two daughters. He formed his own repertory company and toured Germany with his own plays. Throughout his life Wedekind had to fight for recognition which came late in life. He died in March 1918 from acute appendicitis.

FRANK WEDEKIND died on 9 March 1918. Friedrich Gundolf praised him as one of the few original dramatists in German Literature who belonged "zu den Geistern, die die Welt als eine in kämpfenden Gestalten gebärdete Bühne erfahren mussten".[1] As a kindred spirit of Lenz, Büchner and Grabbe Wedekind shared not only much of their lives' experience but also the agony of their final hour. An eye-witness has left a moving account of Wedekind's struggle against the inevitability of death which he fought with all the passionate force of his vitality : "Hoch reckte er sich auf, bäumte sich immer wieder dagegen, wehrte sich mit fanatisch gespannten Zügen gegen Etwas, das ihn feig von hinten packte, hinwarf, das man nicht in die Faust zwingen, nicht niederzwingen konnte."[2] In his last hour Wedekind, one of "God's devoted clowns", began to exorcize Death. Once more cracking the whip of his irreconcilable, rebellious spirit the puppeteer sang his own "Bänkellieder"[3] in his comatose delusion : "Lieschen sass auf dem Apfelbaum", "Der Tantenmörder", and the opening verse of "Erdgeist", which provided a leitmotif of Wedekind's earthly pilgrimage :

> "Greife wacker nach der Sünde;
> Aus der Sünde wächst Genuss.
> Ach, du gleichest einem Kinde,
> Dem man alles zeigen muss."[4]

Thus celebrating his own particular requiem Frank Wedekind sang himself to death, just as he had conquered life through play and song.

Since the death of Hebbel and Grillparzer German drama had only been a pale reflection of its great past. At about 1890, however, a spirit of fertile, if not revolutionary unrest began to make itself felt in Germany. A period of creative activity set in such as the German stage had rarely experienced before or ever since. A new "Sturm und Drang" burst forth using multiple forms of poetic expression and aiming often at diverse goals. Gerhart Hauptmann wrote his naturalistic plays and Hermann Sudermann dramatically chronicled the "juste milieu" of Wilhelminian Germany. At the same time the first poems of Stefan George displayed a tendency towards a Neo-Romanticism while the young prodigy, Hugo von Hofmannsthal, confessed to a new Symbolism in his remarkable verses. To this vanguard Frank Wedekind belonged but did not acknowledge any aesthetic doctrine, even though his first major play *Frühlings Erwachen* (Spring's Awakening) (1891) showed distinct naturalistic descriptions and confessed to a romantic mood. In the last act of his drama Wedekind undertook the breakthrough to a grotesque symbolism, which was destined to pave the way to German Expressionism and Surrealism, and which Friedrich Dürrenmatt's plays still re-echo seventy years later.

Frühlings Erwachen is the first German "Erziehungsdrama" and was followed by a number of similar plays. Wedekind has set his *Kindertragödie* among adolescents standing on the threshold of their so ambivalent puberty. Novalis had already observed that "We are too fond of calling children blessed, and are apt to forget that though they may in truth more lightly rejoice they suffer immeasurably more deeply than adults". The sufferings of awakening children is the theme of Wedekind's tragedy. Ten years prior to the beginning of the German "Jugendbewegung", which was to have such tremendous consequences in German history, Wedekind permits himself to be led astray, overwhelmed by his detestation of the moral hypocrisy of his times. He confronts his juvenile characters with somewhat unrealistic persons who, through their grotesque distortion, are unable to act as real antagonists. More than once in his plays Wedekind is carried away into dramatically dubious situations by his hatred for middle-class prudery and by his wrath against the mustiness of a mendacious bourgeois morality. But there can be little doubt that this tragedy belongs to the great plays of lasting importance because it admirably invokes the troubled spirit of young people worried by their

stirring sexuality which they cannot master physically or emotionally. This drama displays such a deep comprehension of the
adolescent psyche as Wedekind never again was able to show. Those
who see in *Frühlings Erwachen* no more than a call to sexual
licentiousness must surely consider the subject matter trivial and
dull, and its text insufferably old-fashioned. But this tragedy, echo-
ing the tormenting experience of the poet himself, embraces something imperishable, something which has remained dramatically
unparalleled because it stands in tragic contrast to a perishable convention. One must see through the text, the scenes and characters,
which were very likely conceived transparent on purpose, in order
to understand Wedekind's genius and his contorted intentions. To
grope for the hidden meaning, disguised under dramatic artifices,
is the only possible approach to an appreciation of Wedekind's
works in our times. "The primitive, eternal moral that the most
miserable life is preferable to death is proclaimed in an entirely
new way."

The lack of a unified style is already noticeable in this early
masterpiece. Moods prevail which create their own, permanently
changing style. In the sequence of scenes, which are really only
dialogues, a secret unity, a dramatic urgency are clearly dominant.
Actions and moods end together in this vernal storm of youthful
awakening. Wedekind's tragedy of childhood has remained his only
play which shows an intimate awareness of Nature. This mood for
landscape, his delicate reaction to the seasons present an essential
element in this drama of awakening eroticism, which shows the
poet a worthy descendant of Büchner's *Wozzeck* and brings to
mind his tremendous influence on the expressionistic plays of a
later period. *Wozzeck* displays a kindred mood for landscape,
Frühlings Erwachen is Wedekind's first, timid attempt to preach
the revolt of the male slaves against the "Feudalismus der Liebe".[5]
The poet does not yet crack his whip but lets the tormented
creature speak up for himself. But the last scene already contains
Wedekind's philosophy: only he who is willing to jump over
open graves will find life interesting and rewarding.

Melchior Gabor is already such an apprentice of the fine art of
living. It is not quite clear why Friedrich Gundolf calls him "einen
Nachfahr der reinen Toren, einen modernen Spross aus der Familie
der Parzival, Simplizissimus, . . . den deutschen Idealisten, der sich
fromm plagt um Erkenntnis".[6] The young man is simply interested in his physical changes, not because they indicate an inevitable search for some metaphysical absolute but because they
demand some personal responses which Melchior Gabor does not
eschew. After all, he finds his way into life all right, in spite of
the sultry and thundery atmosphere of the play. He instinctively

recognizes the magnetic life force in the character of the "Muffled Gentleman" and follows him, without questioning him closely, from the cemetery of youth out into the world of manhood. Eternal youth breathes in Melchior Gabor, in his love for Wendla Bergmann, in their mutual melancholic friend, Moritz Stiefel, and, above all, in Hänschen Rilow, the valiant knight of romantic illusions, who becomes the captive of his own sensuality so willingly. The boys linger and loiter in the school playground or stand at street corners then as now. The girls are still widely ignorant and cast uninhibited glances across to the boys. But their smile is already seductive, accompanied by an occasional innocent but telling gesture. Wendla Bergmann cannot understand why her beloved mother is so concerned to sew on "a handbreadth of flouncing" to her skirt which still shows her knees bare. The time comes when the boys stand apart wrapped up in secret speculations. The gust of spring has shaken them. They do not sense whence it blows into their blood. Moritz Stiefel gropes about like a blind man and suffers already "Lebensangst" which will become such a significant feature in German Literature. His friend Melchior is already worldly-wise by instinct, for he has observed a lot and drawn his own conclusions. He is quite prepared to take Moritz Stiefel in tow and provide the rudiments of sexual enlightenment. But his friend shows all the timidity of children in face of a sterling reality. He rather prefers to fathom the mystery of Nature from readings of forbidden books. Melchior provides him with the book of knowledge which turns out a fatal promissory note and will prove his doom. But nobody enlightens the girls. Wendla Bergmann does not know of whom to ask the meaning of the great physical changes which begin to stir in her. She complains to her stupid mother : "Wen in der Welt soll ich denn fragen als dich!"[7] The only answer in reply to the distress of the young girl sums up the dilemma of a mother of yesteryears : "Ich kann es ja nicht verantworten . . . ich verdiene ja, dass man mich ins Gefängnis setzt."[8] The impotence and hypocrisy of the respectable middle classes stand revealed as a telling accusation against a doomed society. The play is, however, also filled with pure, elemental poetry responsible for the delicate shades and rare moods of tenderness and budding love. When Melchior meets Wendla in the woods, the dark impulses of their blood interfere with their childlike stammerings. Melchior beats her with cruelty and passion, as he has not yet learnt the message of tender caress. In this and in other scenes the absurdity of expecting a logical behaviour of adolescents is underlined but also the disturbing oscillation between the Ego and the Thou proved. The unforgettable conversation between Hänschen Rilow and his friend Ernst Röbel in the vineyard, high above the river, when both boys drink the juice of ripe grapes and dream of the happiness of maturity, belongs to one of the outstanding confessions of modern German drama :

Ernst: Ich habe mich überarbeitet.
Hänschen: Lass uns nicht traurig sein! Schade um die Minuten.
Ernst: Man sieht sie hängen und kann nicht mehr . . . und morgen sind sie gekeltert.
Hänschen: Ermüdung ist mir so unerträglich wie mirs der Hunger ist.
Ernst: Ach, ich kann nicht mehr.
Hänschen: Diese leuchtenden Muskateller noch.
Ernst: Ich bringe die Elastizität nicht mehr auf.
Hänschen: Wenn ich die Ranke beuge, baumelt sie uns von Mund zu Mund. Keiner braucht sich zu rühren. Wir beissen die Beeren ab und lassen den Kamm zum Stock zurückschnellen.
Ernst: Kaum entschliesst man sich, und siehe, so dämmert auch schon die dahingeschwundene Kraft wieder auf.
Hänschen: Dazu das flammende Firmament . . . und die Abendglocken . . . Ich verspreche mir wenig mehr von der Zukunft.
Ernst: Ich sehe mich manchmal schon als ehrwürdiger Pfarrer . . . ein gemütvolles Hausmütterchen, eine reichhaltige Bibliothek und Aemter und Würden in allen Kreisen. Sechs Tage hat man, um nachzudenken, und am siebenten tut man den Mund auf. Beim Spazierengehen reichen einem Schüler und Schülerinnen die Hand, und wenn man nach Hause kommt, dampft der Kaffee, der Topfkuchen wird aufgetragen, und durch die Gartentür bringen die Mädchen Aepfel herein. . . . Kannst du dir etwas Schöneres denken?
Hänschen: Ich denke an halbgeschlossene Wimpern, halbgeöffnete Lippen und türkische Draperien. . . . Ich glaube nicht an das Pathos. Sieh, unsere Alten zeigen uns lange Gesichter, um ihre Dummheiten zu bemänteln. Untereinander nennen sie sich Schafsköpfe wie wir. Ich kenne das. . . . Wenn ich Millionär bin, werde ich dem lieben Gott ein Denkmal setzen. Denke dir die Zukunft als Milchsette mit Zucker und Zimt. Der eine wirft sie um und heult, der andere rührt alles durcheinander und schwitzt. Warum nicht abschöpfen? Oder glaubst du nicht, dass es sich lernen liesse?
Ernst: Schöpfen wir ab!
Hänschen: Was bleibt, fressen die Hühner . . . Ich habe meinen Kopf nun schon aus so mancher Schlinge gezogen. . . .
Ernst: Schöpfen wir ab, Hänschen!
Hänschen: Fängst du schon wieder an?
Ernst: Einer muss ja doch anfangen.

Hänschen: Wenn wir in dreissig Jahren an einen Abend wie heute
zurückdenken, erscheint er uns vielleicht unsagbar schön!
Ernst: Und wie macht sich jetzt alles so ganz von selbst!
Hänschen: Warum also nicht?
Ernst: Ist man zufällig allein . . . dann weint man vielleicht gar.
Hänschen: Lass uns nicht traurig sein! (Er küsst ihn auf den
Mund.)
Ernst: (küsst ihn) Ich ging von Hause fort mit dem Gedanken, dich
nur eben zu sprechen und wieder umzukehren.
Hänschen: Ich erwartete dich. . . . Die Tugend kleidet nicht
schlecht, aber es gehören imposante Figuren hinein.
Ernst: Uns schlottert sie noch um die Glieder.... Ich wäre nicht
ruhig geworden, wenn ich dich nicht getroffen hätte. . . . Ich
liebe dich Hänschen, wie ich nie eine Seele geliebt habe....
Hänschen: Lass uns nicht traurig sein! Wenn wir in dreissig Jahren
zurückdenken, spotten wir vielleicht! Und jetzt ist alles so schön!
Die Berge glühen: die Trauben hängen uns in den Mund und
der Abendwind streicht an den Felsen hin wie ein spielendes
Schmeichelkätzchen.[9]

This interlude, not at all necessary for the action of the play,
anticipates a major theme of the German "Jugendbewegung".
Never again has Wedekind written anything so tender as this
dialogue. Wherever the blind Eros will shoot his arrows like lightning out of the blue he will cause unfathomable havoc. This
central problem of the *Kindertragödie* explains sufficiently why
Frühlings Erwachen will stay alive when the rest of Wedekind's
work might only interest the literary historian. It is the gift of the
poet to convey the deeper meaning of groping conversations of
adolescents which is so revealing. There is the brief scene when
Wendla looks for Melchior in the hay-loft and surrenders to his
bewildered lust without resistance. Truthfulness cannot be uttered
more heart-wrenchingly. At the time Moritz Stiefel, the symbol of
a man who will always stay down, goes into the woods to finish his
young life. There he will find the way to freedom "ohne die
Pyramiden gesehen zu haben".[10] Life wants to rescue him when
the seductive Ilse, an embryonal Lulu, points out "den Weg
ungehemmten Genusses der Gelegenheiten".[11] In vain. This
juvenile suicide must atone for the parental shame of having a son
who was not moved up in school, another revelation of the shallowness of bourgeois respectability. Wendla too has no power of resistance left when "Mutter Schmidtin" knocks on the door to carry
out her dirty work. Like a terrified bird she hopelessly beats her
wings. "O Mutter, warum hast du mir nicht alles gesagt!" A
simpering sigh contains the telling answer: "Ich hab' an dir nichts

anderes getan, als meine liebe, gute Mutter an mir getan hat."[12]
One only perceives the shadow of the abortionist, a stroke of
dramatic genius. Everybody knows that the child will die from
her hands. Melchior Gabor will master his life. The school, having
destroyed many a child before and after him, can only expel him
for having distributed a guide to sexual enlightenment. The Borstal
institution into which his father has thrown him for shame and
from which Melchior escapes is also powerless to harm what is
good, decent and lasting in this boy. The play ends in the cemetery
when Melchior meets Moritz, carrying his own head under the
arm, at the foot of Wendla's tomb. This grandiose scene, worthy
of the imagination of a Shakespeare—shades of Hamlet addressing
Yorick's skull!—allows Wedekind to appear as "Muffled Gentleman" to explain the differential calculus of life to Melchior:
"Unter Moral verstehe ich das reelle Produkt zweier imaginärer
Grössen. Die imaginären Grössen sind Sollen und Wollen."[13]
Between these categorical imperatives opportunity is given "den
Horizont in der fabelhaftesten Weise zu erweitern".[14] Nobody
wonders when Melchior assesses this moral advice higher than the
dead wisdom of the phantom Moritz Stiefel: "sich an der Ver-
wesung zu erwärmen".[15]

Frühlings Erwachen is a tragedy of immature adolescents. It
purposely withholds justice from the narrow-minded parents and
the school authorities because the poet is convinced that they are
tainted by the curse of "summum jus summa injuria". Certainly
the staff meeting which expels Melchior is a conscious caricature.
Names of masters like "Flydeath", "Tonguestroke", "Hungerbelt"
speak their own language. This scene symbolizes the impotence of
an older generation in the face of the real problems of life, an attitude
which has only seen minor changes since the play was written. The
quarrel about the closed window at the same staff meeting is significant for the unbridgeable gulf between the generations. Its symbolism reminds us of the glued door in Strindberg's *A Dream
Play*. In more than one respect the Swedish poet was a tormented
brother-in-arms of Wedekind. They had met in Paris but did not
take to each other. Wedekind attempted in *Frühlings Erwachen*
to show the sexual instinct as an archetypal force of life, a theme
which he consequently treated and varied in all his other works. In
their centre stand men of impulse and instinct, unspoilt by the
shallow conventions of morality of doubtful value. Melchior Gabor
is wholly given over to his desires and enjoys instinctively the sport
of jumping over open graves. Moritz Stiefel represents the helpless
victim of life, whom his stunted instincts drive to his early death.
Wedekind, the missionary of a new morality, is therefore not afraid
to appear as Life and later, in the disguise of the sexual maniac

Jack the Ripper, as Death (*Pandora's Box*). The somewhat shadowy character of Ilse will soon ripen into Lulu, into Klara Hühner-wadel (*Musik*), into Effi (*Castle Wetterstein*) and finally into Franziska. The grotesque popinjays of the school staff will recur "im fünften Stand der Hochstapler, Dirnen, Ganoven und Ver-brecher, die nicht von moralischen und sozialen Bedenken beschwert sind".[16] They provide the sounding-board in almost every play of Wedekind, since he was not concerned with their moral or social significance but only with their appearance of serving as intellectual inventions. Wedekind always drew his effects from radical contrasts, even if the antagonists will not come con-vincingly to life. What mattered for him were the protagonists, "die Kinder, Künstler und Halbwüchsige, die noch nicht den Konven-tionen und Lügen der verspiesserten Moral und Religion erlegen sind".[17]

Wedekind's fame in Germany is based on his play *Lulu,* the original version of which was only to be published in 1962. In order to circumvent the rigid censorship against which the playwright fought a running battle throughout his life, he divided it into two separate parts : *Erdgeist* (Earth Spirit 1895) and *Die Büchse der Pandora* (Pandora's Box 1902). Of both parts various versions are in existence, as Wedekind was forced by the censor to make divers concessions before both plays could appear in book form. *Die Büchse der Pandora* could only be produced after the aboli-tion of the censorship in 1918 and scored together with the older *Erdgeist*—(what strange travesty of Goethe's all-embracing creative spirit in *Faust*!)—a remarkable success in all German-speaking countries, and served finally as libretto for Alban Berg's unfinished opera *Lulu.*

Wedekind, like D. H. Lawrence, was obsessed and possessed with the destructive power that sex so often exerts in a society which represses and abuses it. Wedekind wanted to be looked upon as the prophet of a new society. When the very society, however, whose shallow moral he pilloried, regarded him as a clown, he donned, like Grimmelshausen before him, the fool's cap to draw compelling attention to his message. This was not a voluntary disguise but forced upon him by his contemporaries, an act which made him suffer throughout his life. In *Lulu* he put the dregs of society on the stage, those confidence tricksters, sexual murderers, thieves, whores, white-slave traffickers and athletes, of whom Wedekind was convinced they alone still displayed natural, naked and genuine desires. They all move like puppets, manipulated by a fanatic seeker of truth, around Lulu, the woman identical with the elemen-tal principle of destruction. When tried before a court Wedekind referred to Christ as his "greater brother" who too had prophesied the return of Paradise. Walter Muschg has pointed out that "Wedekind wollte mit der *Büchse der Pandora* Goethe's Bajaderenballade fortsetzen und versah den *Erdgeist* mit einem Motto aus dem *Wallenstein*.[18] The meaning of the *Lulu* tragedy with its profound moral implications is already evident from the prologue, a biting satire on the prevailing naturalism of his times. It represents a deliberate attack on Gerhart Hauptmann who had abused Wedekind's personal confessions in his own play *Das Friedensfest* (Reconciliation 1890). A tamer of wild beasts appears before the curtain and orders the "Strong Man" of his circus to bring in the serpent : Lulu.

> "Was seht Ihr in den Lust—und Trauerspielen? !—
> Haustiere, die so wohlgesittet fühlen,
> An blasser Pflanzenkost ihr Mütchen kühlen
> Und schwelgen in behaglichem Geplärr,
> Wie jene andern—unten im Parterre :
> Der eine Held kann keinen Schnaps vertragen,
> Der andere zweifelt, ob er richtig liebt,
> Den dritten hört ihr an der Welt verzagen,
> Fünf Akte lang hört ihr ihn sich beklagen,
> Und niemand, der den Gnadenstoss ihm gibt.—
> Das wahre Tier, das wilde, schöne Tier,
> Das meine Damen !—sehn Sie nur bei mir. . . .
>
> Sie ward geschaffen, Unheil anzustiften,
> Zu locken, zu verführen, zu vergiften—
> Zu morden, ohne dass es einer spürt,
>   (Lulu am Kinn krauend)
> Mein süsses Tier, sei ja nur nicht geziert !
> Nicht albern, nicht gekünstelt, nicht verschroben,
> Auch wenn die Kritiker dich weniger loben.
>
> Mein Leben setz' ich gegen einen Witz;
> Die Peitsche werf' ich fort und diese Waffen
> Und geb' mich harmlos, wie mich Gott geschaffen.—
> Wisst ihr den Namen, den dies Raubtier führt?—
> Verehrtes Publikum—Hereinspaziert."[19]

Erdgeist is dedicated to Willy Grétor, a painter, writer, business-man and swindler whom Wedekind intimately knew when living in Paris.[20] Wedekind sets out to show the archetypal character of Woman whose name may be Eva, Lilith, Lulu : "The principle remains always the same." To outline the contents of the tragedy to an unprepared listener would invite today his protest, for they must appear to him as mere colportage from the back stairs. Wedekind introduces characters who just seem improbable : criminals who slit open their own and other people's throats while similar types brandish pistols and shoot sometimes in all directions. Husbands catch their wives "in flagranti" while their guests hide behind curtains or under the table-cloth. Shares fall and the daring hopes of the avaricious bourgeois are buried beneath. Even the cholera is invoked to enable Lulu to undertake an adventurous flight from prison, which comes dangerously near cheapest cinema. In short, Wedekind conjures up the grotesque world of a penny dreadful. It is the deliberate purpose of the playwright to blow up the action to gigantic proportions, in order to justify the reduction of the consequences to their utmost logical conclusions. Wedekind coarsens his characters to such an extent that they become puppets out of all dimensions, so that their shadows fall pointedly on the reality. Lulu breaks into the world of bourgeois respectability and this world turns into a macabre Punch and Judy show. Once more it will not do to judge this play from its external events. One must try to fathom the poet's intentions by analysing the meaning behind the action. The play is indeed called *Lulu,* but Lulu is no longer an acting part of importance, once the surfeit of eroticism has become simply pathetic, if not downright funny, as it must appear to an audience in our own times. Gundolf was right when he stated a long time ago : "Lulu selbst ist merkwürdig dürftig und ärmlich geraten."[21] The tragedy does not turn around Lulu but draws its profound meaning through her. All Lulu does, is the result of her dynamic originality, the emanation of a blind force of Nature. The biblical story of the alliance between Woman and Serpent assumes a new significance : both possess the irresistible charm of seduction and loquacity to deliver Man to his perdition, without desiring anything else but his virility. Both have possessed him completely when they succeed in destroying him. Their counterpart is therefore the man who is able, out of sheer impotence, to murder a woman, in order to possess her only in this dreadful moment. If man and wife act as destructive forces, both remain beautiful and terrible like real forces of Nature. Her childlike innocence drives Lulu to destroy Dr. Goll who had avidly followed her naked dances. Following entirely her unconscious impulses Lulu causes the death of her second husband, the painter Schwarz. Her third husband, for whose carnal love Lulu had struggled, is shot by her when he realizes the terrible force he has released. Again it is an instinctive impulse, this time of self-preservation, which makes Lulu a murderess. She senses darkly that she has to protect herself from the prowling male. When finally the male hunters bring the beautiful wild beast to bay, her defensive mechanism begins to slacken. The male sex does not fight the noble beast face to face but uses every trick to net this precious prey. Finally Lulu, tamed in spite of her inborn instincts, must render the meanest services as a street-walker, suffer the utmost degradation and sound the depth of human experiences. Because Lulu has challenged and flaunted all conventions of a bourgeois society she is doomed to finish her life in filth and in indescribable horror. It is the revenge of this society that Jack the Ripper, a sinister symbol of human depravity, becomes her butcher.

Lulu, a "somnambulist of love", means the naked manifestation of the everlasting sexual urge, always creating anew, always destroying afresh, always remaining the same. Therefore Man executes his obtrusive dance around this golden calf : the nakedness of Lulu. Who Lulu's mother was remains a speculation. Schigolch, a phantom born from Mephistophelian slime—his name rhymes with "molch"[22] in German—is presumed her father. (Wedekind, the moralist, believed in the existence of the Devil.) This old man without age and almost of eternity appears as her first and last master and was probably her early seducer. He stands on the touchline as the commentator who takes his own satanic pleasure in the destruction of human illusions. Dr. Schön, perhaps a mature reincarnation of Melchior Gabor, is a ruthless hedonist for whom any paralysis through the serpent's eyes means a sensuous pleasure. Because he recognizes nothing but undiluted power he must logically take cognizance of Lulu's elemental power which transcends even his own highly developed intelligence. He had picked up Lulu from the gutter where she sold flowers as a child. (One wonders how far Bernard Shaw drew on Lulu for his Pygmalion.) Instinctively Schön understands Lulu's sensuous attractions. The play begins anew, the old, old game. The more completely Schön perfects Lulu's arts and artifices, the more attractive the game becomes for him, the deeper his infatuation. He takes a delight in the tigress because he enjoys also the awareness of his taming power. He even thinks Lulu to be his toy whom he can hire out at will : to the lecherous Dr. Goll, to the sentimental artist Schwarz. But his own doom is inevitable, much as Schön may struggle against the final reckoning. Lulu's refined but still demonic forces prove stronger than those of the conquering male, too hopelessly enthralled by his own desires. For how can Man conquer Woman when tenderness, passions, sufferings and death are at stake? If a woman must fight with all means at her disposal, she will always appear invincible unless her male opponent succeeds in wounding her mortally. When Lulu kills Schön out of sheer necessity to survive, she who has never loved before, moans for the first time : "Ich habe keinen Menschen auf der Welt geliebt als ihn."[23] Lulu had to destroy her greatest lover because he was her only worthy rival who understood how to force out all the tricks of sexual seduction in her. This time it is the woman who leaps over corpses. What is changed in her after the death of her man is only the external garb, never her true self. Dr. Schön's son, Alwa Schön, is a weak image of his father, an early victim of hereditary degeneration. He too tries to defend himself against Lulu and only feels safe when she is imprisoned. Torn to pieces by his sexual longings for her he successfully plans her escape from prison, driven by his desire of identifying himself with Lulu's destiny. The remainder of this male dance of death consists of cowards and the lowest representatives of the fifth estate, all desiring Lulu, none worthy of her.

The Countess Geschwitz, a Lesbian whom Nature has not granted fulfilment, deserves particular attention, as she is Lulu's counterpart in the natural order of life. Gundolf is surely wrong in declaring her the real heroine of *Die Büchse der Pandora*.[24] If Wedekind had feigned this impression in the preface to this play, it was only to cheat the censor, not with much success, as the second part of the Lulu tragedy could only be performed after the fall of the German empire. The Countess Geschwitz, at the time a very daring creation in German Literature, is burdened with a curse, since her desires are limited within the problematical confines of unnatural love. This curse does not prevent her from assuming tragic greatness. Her readiness to make every sacrifice for Lulu does not know any bounds. The destructive force of the normal woman is here paired with the doom of the destroyed woman. The Countess Geschwitz, a true sister to Lulu in adverse circumstances, speaks the real epilogue in front of Schwarz's painting depicting Lulu's ravishing and ravished beauty: "Erbarm' dich mein, erbarm' dich mein!"[25] Alwa Schön once said about this painting, "dass es eine Seele vorstelle, die sich im Jenseits den Schlaf aus den Augen reibt."[26] Then follows Lulu's ghoulish murder by Jack the Ripper. "Du entkommst mir nicht mehr",[27] runs his cynical comment. Karl Kraus once spoke of "die gehetzte Frauenanmut der Lulu, der eine armselige Welt bloss in das Prokrustesbett ihrer Moralbegriffe zu steigen erlaubt".[28] Lulu, whenever asked whether she believed in love, truthfully retorted with a deadly monotony: "Ich weiss es nicht!"[29] Neither her life nor her death provided a definite answer. Perhaps her life is meant as a symbol of human questions to which no answers exist. At the end, as really at the end of every act, we do not comprehend any more what seems beyond human comprehension. Complete alienation dominates, and one begins to understand Bert Brecht's indebtedness to Wedekind. Lulu justifies Nietzsche's statement: "Die Liebe ist der Krieg, der Todhass der Geschlechter."[30] If Lulu's tragedy might easily appear as a show à la Grand Guignol, if its erotic contents are over-emphasized, it cannot silence Wedekind's basic contention that a woman who remains true to her instincts will only know physical love and only desire it if her male partner cannot resist her, even if such unconditional yielding entails his death. Seeing the tragedy against its contemporary background one must agree with the assessment that "Lulu ist die Trägerin einer neuen Moral, die nichts mit naturalistischer oder gar psychologischer Wahrheit zu tun hat."[31] Though the tragedy abounds with naturalistic details, Wedekind's interpretation of Lulu remains romantic, and the end achieves the effect of a truly expressionistic study, pointing to the future when Expressionism should celebrate its perhaps most telling triumph through the film *Das Kabinett des Dr. Caligari.* The psycho-analyst has learnt to interpret sexual murder as the revenge of the freely creative artist on those strata of society which wish to see him and his creative forces castrated.

As the Lulu tragedy means much more than erotic titillation I beg to differ from Friedrich Luft's recent verdict : "*Erdgeist* und die *Büchse der Pandora* sind eine Sache der Theatergeschichte, aber nicht mehr des Theaters geworden."[32] I also feel that the justification of the German film director Rolf Thiele, who has finished a new film version of *Lulu,* misses the point when he asserts : "Die Mädchen von heute sind allesamt Lulus. Sie kennen sich nicht, fragen sich nicht und sind daher entschuldbar wie Lulu."[33] The success which *Lulu* recently had on German-speaking stages proves that the theatre-going public understands that the erotic exploits of Lulu which excited our fathers have meanwhile given way to the deeper understanding that Lulu plays a principal part in the circus which life meant for Wedekind.

Between the two parts of the *Lulu* tragedy Wedekind wrote a comedy in praise of a confidence trickster. His character is a cynical mountebank who wages war against the stupidity of the "juste milieu". But the deceiver finds himself ultimately cheated. This conclusion only underlines the moral and social process of corrosion, clearly noticeable in Wilhelminian Germany. All traditional values become depreciated. The *Marquis von Keith,* completed in 1900, is "eine Kreuzung von Philosoph und Pfer-dedieb".[34] The hero amuses himself with stealing the horse of the bourgeois and, simultaneously, with parading his own hobby-horse : the philosophy immanent in the art of good and bad business. The Marquis is the prototype of the great, highly gifted adventurer. As a restless neurotic he is a telling product of times of profound transition. Thomas Mann described the final scene between the two protagonists in an essay : "Der Marquis stand nicht mehr auf dem Fussboden. Er war auf den Schreibtisch geklettert und hielt sich am Fensterkreuz fest! 'Geh! Geh!' stöhnte er. Und : 'Komm, Komm!' erwiderte der andere an der offenen Tür und winkte langsam-still mit dem ganzen Arm—und winkte gespenstisch und lockend in den Frieden, dorthin, wo man nur noch 'spazieren fährt und Billard spielt'.... Es ist grauenerregend. Der Schwindler und der Wahnsinnige bitten einander flehentlich : der Schwindler den Wahnsinnigen, dass er gehen—der Wahnsinnige den Schwindler, dass er zum Billardspiel kommen möge. Aber er hält sich nicht fest,—er, der zynische Idealist, der Abenteurer und inbrünstig Gläubige—er klammert sich fest dort oben an sein Fensterkreuz, er schreit endlich verzweifelt nach seinem Laufjungen und der Versucher verschwindet.... Es ist eine ungeheuerliche Szene. In einem nichts sagenden Zimmer wechseln zwei Männer in bürgerlicher Kleidung kurze und glasklare Repliken. Aber dahinter spukt und lockt ein Mysterium. Es ist das Mysterium der Abdankung . . . das Schrecklichste, Rührendste und Tiefste, was dieser tiefe, gequälte Mensch geschrieben hat."[35] This impression which Wedekind left as actor of his "Marquis" struck deep roots in Thomas Mann, which proved to be the seed of his own *Felix Krull*, a picaresque novel of a confidence trickster, whose fascination lived with Thomas Mann to the end of his days.

The daring spirit of the Marquis shows itself in his magnificent schemes and designs. This bold adventurer aims so high that he loses sight of the nearest hurdles. He leaps blindly across abysses where other people would fall in. But he comes to grief at the slightest obstacle which the average man knows very well how to circumvent. An opportunist like the Marquis who believes "gute Geschäfte lassen sich nun einmal nur innerhalb der bestehenden Gesellschaftsordnung machen",[36] will always lose to the stolid and consistent prudence of the "juste milieu". At the very moment when he transacts bad business, i.e. when he transacts his business badly, society will chalk it up as a sin : "Und Sünde ist dann nur eine mythologische Bezeichnung für schlechte Geschäfte."[37] The Marquis is confronted with a counterpart, another modern Don Quixote, a nobleman of fluid circumstances : Ernst Scholz, alias Graf Trautenau. He wants the Marquis to teach him complete enjoyment of life, and he does so : "als gälte es, eine Strafe abzubüssen".[38] The Marquis, accustomed to living on credit, welcomes the fortune of his friend which he intends to use for a new fraudulent coup in Munich, involving millions of marks. For he possesses the gift of creating scintillating illusions out of nothing. The world will always admire confidence tricksters as long as they do not commit any mistakes. It will never pardon stupidity, even if it understands it. For the cleverness of genius is the only justification for a criminal's existence. The title of Marquis is a pseudonym, necessary for the trade, just as the bourgeois surname is essential for the new mode of life of Count Trautenau. After the fraud stands revealed everybody goes over to the successful bourgeois speculator who, with a gesture of magnanimity and contempt, grants the Marquis the means of escaping abroad. To commit suicide seems to him just as inane as to be certified with Scholz in a mental home. The one who has just been on top, is now scraping the bottom of the barrel: "Das Leben ist eine Rutschbahn."[39] "Ein Unglück ist eine günstige Gelegenheit wie jede andere. Unglück kann jeder Esel haben. Die Kunst besteht darin, dass man es richtig auszubeuten versteht."[40] Scholz who did not learn the fine art of living dangerously sees the seclusion of a mental home as the identification with the flight from life itself, with the jettison of his own responsibility. His life's experience culminates in his sanest idea of having himself declared insane. It is therefore of compelling logic that Friedrich Dürrenmatt lets his play *The Physicists* (1962) begin where the Marquis refuses to find shelter: in a mental sanatorium. There a man's quest for intellectual peace will meet with adequate response. Wedekind could have written what Dürrenmatt has to say: "Entweder bleiben wir im Irrenhaus oder die Welt wird eines. Entweder löschen wir uns im Gedächtnis der Menschen aus oder die Menschheit erlöscht."[41] While Dürrenmatt's physicists have reached the logical conclusion of their experiences, the Marquis remains a beginner at the interruption of his career. He only reaches the conclusion that the love of God equals the love of one's own well-being: "Du kannst einzig mit dem Guten dauernd gute Geschäfte machen."[42] He who cannot successfully act Napoleon, has no right to bluff as a demi-God. This inner discrepancy prevents the Marquis von Keith from being the greatest character of adventure in German drama.

Wedekind's disciple, Bert Brecht, drew the logical conclusion and created the dominant adventurers of our times. One may, indeed, pose the question how profound the influence of Wedekind on Brecht has been. Brecht's formative years coincided with the high tide of Wedekind's successes: much of what has become significant in Brecht and in his dramatic technique had its roots in Frank Wedekind's approach to the theatre. Even today the *Marquis von Keith* will exercise a considerable effect when staged with a superb actor. Life has become a tremendous switchback since the death of the playwright, though our society still possesses sufficient moral discrimination to brand a confidence trickster as a permanent outsider of society. But as long as our form of society remains an unstable economic entity, a clever man will go on trying to outwit his fellow-man by means which the very society will supply him with. Far more than *Lulu* this play may prove in the hands of an imaginative producer to be one of the most essential and significant dramas of our times. Rightly Friedrich Dürrenmatt points out : "Wer so aus dem letzten Loch pfeift wie wir alle, kann nur noch Komödien verstehen."[43] Already Hofmannsthal cited Novalis who claimed that after a war there is only one possible form in which one can write—comedy. Wedekind's devotion to the *Marquis von Keith* stresses how much the playwright, a remarkable actor by instinct, was concerned to prove himself a genuine artist. This crusade for recognition in his own right was continued with *Hidalla* (1904) and with *König Nicolo* (1904)[44] : "Geschickt vermischte Wedekind Selbstreklame mit Selbstmitleid und verbarg den Zorn des Propheten hinter der Grimasse des Clowns."[45]

Among the later plays by Wedekind *Franziska* deserves mention. The poet called this attempt to create a female Faust a "Mysterium". Originally the title of the play was even to be *Faustine* which calls Swinburne's verses to mind :

> "You have the face that suits a woman
> For her soul's screen,
> The sort of beauty that's called human
> In Hell, Faustine."

A modern Mephistopheles stands by the side of an emancipated female Faust and wills a strange fusion of God and the Devil. His name is Veit Kunz and he seems to be the same gentleman from *Frühlings Erwachen,* who has at last discarded his disguise in order to reveal more biographical traits of Wedekind than, for instance, *Simson,* a still later work, which showed a return to the sado-masochistic tendency to which Wedekind remained prone throughout his life.

It was a challenge to write this play as a superficial imitation of Goethe's *Faust*. A comparison is superfluous, because Wedekind uses the adventurous action only as a parallel to modern life, in order to stress the fascination and message of the Faust-Saga. Franziska is a young woman whose Faustian longings reach beyond the possibilities of womanhood. The romantic yearning for the ambivalence of androgyny, i.e. for the amalgamation of all male and female instincts in a new human being, seems to equate the irrepressible urge for boundless freedom. Therefore Franziska seeks complete emancipation, unconcerned whether her journey will lead her into a new hell or bring her the bliss of a new heaven. Experience seems to be everything once more. Veit Kunz is determined to mould her fate. He acts as guide through the vicissitudes of modern life. He is ready to fulfil her every wish and every desire. He calls himself a "Sternenlenker",[46] a truly creative and destructive Mephistophelian spirit. Wedekind, delighting in a hundred disguises, plays a modern Phorkyas who transforms illusions into realities.

That she may taste the outer confines of freedom Veit Kunz lets Franziska's most daring wish come true : to live as a man for two years. The Devil's pact observed, Franziska shall be his, completely in body and soul. The descent to the worldly Hell begins. In a smart bar in Berlin Franziska is introduced to the tenor Eberhardt, the idol of the younger generation. It speaks for Wedekind's power of imagination that he turns the modern "Auerbach's Keller"[47] into a diabolic abode of uninhibited hedonism. To enhance the effect the playwright inserts his caustic song about the poet sitting at the loom of Time in frayed trousers, a bitter satire.

A second, highly problematical act follows. Franziska, assuming the disguise of her tenor-lover, has married a proud woman who demands her sexual satisfaction. She commits suicide when told of her disgrace of having been wedded to another woman. In search of new experience the hunt leaps across fresh tombs. A Duke's court—an allusion to Goethe's *Faust II*—provides the background, against which Franziska, tormented by the canker of eternal dissatisfaction, thirsts for an acceleration of the merry-go-round. It is the weakness of this play that even lust becomes so artificial that the tragedy which ought to result, never occurs. For a short moment, at the beginning of the fourth act, Wedekind returns to the pure poetry of his *Kindertragödie*, when Veit Kunz and Franziska linger for a while to sense the uplifting harmony of beauty in the midst of the wild disorder of their lives. Because of this fleeting moment of serene happiness Veit Kunz takes his precious possession for granted. He commits a fateful error, for the freedom of a human being is not for sale, since it would deny human destiny. Another deceiver is cheated. Franziska, compelled by her innermost resistance against domination through an alien will, destroys—another aspect of the Lulu obsession—Kunz's artistic work and throws herself into the arms of an actor. This act is Wedekind's "Walpurgisnacht", where the fools celebrate their Witches' Sabbath with a mad masquerade. Amid the whirligig Mephistopheles is cheated of his prize. Wedekind saw in Veit Kunz the prototype of modern man, endowed with superhuman possibilities thirsting for union with the perfect woman. Once more it is the man who must pay for his ambition because he attempted the impossible. Franziska, after two years under his guidance, has achieved normal maturity and thus recognizes the confines of human ambition. She marries a rather bourgeois painter, finds her happiness in motherhood and looks upon a contented married life as her seventh heaven. In this play, describing the boundless enjoyment of life, Wedekind parades once more the whole waxwork of his stock-in-trade. The clown becomes a philosophical commentator on the "Comédie Humaine" "Die Jugend wird verschönt durch den Urglauben an das Weib, das Alter verdüstert durch die Enttäuschung über den gleichen Gegenstand."[48] But does Life really end with a descent to Hell? Wisdom's last conclusion remains ambiguous. Is Franziska's bourgeois happiness with husband and child a deliberate satire, or did Wedekind finally become convinced of the senselessness of tilting against the windmills of discipline and order? The poet withheld a conclusive answer.

Wedekind's short stories have not found enough attention. Gundolf places them in the same high class as Kleist's.[49] They were written before 1900 and appeared in 1905 under the title *Feuerwerk* after publication in the German periodical *Simplizissimus*. In a preface "Ueber Erotik" the poet confesses his belief in a better education, if it were based on the moral precept that a free man should follow his instincts unimpededly. The flesh possesses his own spirit. The maxim that carnal instincts will always be of the flesh and, for this reason, contrary to the spirit, is anathema for Wedekind, who calls this assertion a bourgeois hypocrisy. At the time the Public Prosecutor denied Wedekind the right of calling himself a convinced moralist. The change in the evaluation of morals since Wedekind's death has proved him a true prophet. Among his short stories two, *Der Brand von Egliswyl* and *Rabbi Esra* stand out. Both stories deal with the confusion caused by sensuous passions. In *Der Brand von Egliswyl* Wedekind lets a former criminal confess his deed to the poet's father. The old convict had lived in the Swiss village of Egliswyl. At the age of nineteen "hatte er noch nicht von Männern und Weibern, nur vom Vieh, von Kühen, Kälbern und Stieren gewusst".[50] A precocious peasant girl had provided the inevitable initiation. Soon the peasant lad had become the lover of all the girls in the village, when he fell in love with a servant girl at the Castle who did not take him quite seriously. When she finally admitted him, and after he had left her, "war sie noch ebenso, wie sie gewesen war".[51] His excitement had rendered the lad impotent. Nothing offends a woman more than a man who is unable to give her what she desires. In this hour she cruelly let him feel her contempt for his predicament. Returning to the village in his incomprehensible perplexity, the boy roared like the cattle in the abattoir. Only one thought possessed him : to lay fire to every house where a girl slept who had set his blood aflame. The village perished in the arson of that night. The lad, however, returned to the Castle to vaunt his virility before the servant girl. She denounces him to the police with the hatred of a woman who feels cheated of her sexual satisfaction.

Rabbi Esra deals also with the sexual distress of youth. The Rabbi's adolescent son is about to become engaged. His father gives him an account of his own experience. He too had once been obsessed with the idea : "er wäre gewesen der König Salomo mit 5,000 Weibern". His desire had been consuming but the fear of God had proved stronger. He had known of the Talmudic wisdom : "zu den Weibern zu gehen, die dem Herzen gefallen, und nicht zu denen, die den Sinnen gefallen".[52] Therefore he had taken a wife without passions, in order to save himself from himself. After the death of his wife, the Rabbi had become anew a prey to his carnal desires and sought comfort from the daughters of the desert. There he had found his happiness. And the worldly-wise Rabbi took a second wife, following the desires of the flesh this time : "Man solle nicht kaufen die Katze im Sack and man habe doch mindestens so sorgfältig auszusuchen, wenn man sich eine Frau wählt, als wie Du aussuchest, wenn Du gehst in den Laden und kaufst Dir für eine Mark zwanzig eine Kravatte."[53] In this story young Moses is given the wisdom which did not exist in *Frühlings Erwachen* : to be conscious of his carnal lust and thereby to sense the harmony of flesh and spirit. Wedekind's protest against the overrating of the intellect and in favour of a healthy physical education can be read in the brochure *Mine-Haha* or *Ueber die körperliche Erziehung der jungen Mädchen.*[54]

Wedekind's poetry has been collected under the title *Die Vier Jahreszeiten*. He expressed his talent most naturally and most effectively as a singer of his own songs in the famous cabaret *Die Elf Scharfrichter*[55] in Munich, accompanying himself on the guitar. There he recited his ballads of horror and his love-songs with a compelling charm and force. Torment, lust and sensuality are usually their central theme. Some sound like French frivolities, others like laments for a world from which the gods have departed. In these poems one senses Heine's wit and derision.[56] It is again youth and its impudence which now leaps across the fallen and broken statues of the expelled gods. One is never quite sure whether it is mocking laughter or a veiled weeping which echoes from this poetry. Satyros is the final conquering hero and Wedekind his devotee. Even if the alluring tones of the lute in the evening or the note of pensive reflection are sometimes heard, Wedekind never displays the pure innocence of a real lyrist... in spite of his moving folk-song : *Ilse*

"Ich war ein Kind von fünfzehn Jahren,
    Ein reines unschuldsvolles Kind,
Als ich zum erstenmal erfahren,
    Wie süss der Liebe Freuden sind.

Er nahm mich um den Leib und lachte
Und flüsterte : O welch ein Glück !
Und dabei bog er sachte, sachte
Den Kopf mir auf das Pfühl zurück.

Seit jenem Tag lieb' ich sie Alle,
Des Lebens schönster Lenz ist mein ;
Und wenn ich Keinem mehr gefalle,
Dann will ich gern begraben sein."[57]

His "Bankelsänge" are usually ironical comments on Press reports or serve the glorification of notorious criminal cases. But they retain their own strange and moving effect over the years. They all are a classical "memento mori" and a reminder of Horace's exhortation to use the day since one can never be certain what the morrow will hold in store. Wedekind, more pathetic than the Roman poet, preaches here too his lifelong message : the flesh possesses its own spirit.

"Wedekind's Hass auf die bürgerliche Gesellschaft liess ihn als Propheten des gerade erlebten Untergangs erscheinen."[58] Hence his tremendous popularity in Germany after the revolution of 1918. As he had discarded the traditional psychological technique of a European playwright, he used unconsciously psycho-analytical approaches when he presented the sexual instinct as one of the archetypal forces of human existence. The theatre served Wedekind as his own peculiar "moral institution", which had little in common with Schiller's well-known definition of the functional stage. Wedekind was the prototype of the "Denkspieler",[59] who allowed his characters to speak monologues throughout, even in the interplay of a dialogue. He discarded every traditional style. "Er wollte nicht die Menschen 'wie sie sind' zeigen, sondern wie sie denken und fühlen."[60] This perpetual flight into the monologue quickly becomes monotonous. After the Weimar Republic had cemented its social foundations the vogue for Wedekind began to slacken. The bourgeoisie had undergone a new face-lift and felt safe from Wedekind's embarrassing disclosures. Although Wedekind was recommended to the National Socialist régime as a deeply moral prophet of a new Reich, he was banned from the stage. Though some of his plays have been given remarkable revivals since 1945, a Wedekind renaissance has so far failed to materialize. Ultimately immortality seems to have avoided the playwright because soul and mind will always triumph over the passions of carnal desires. Wedekind, blinded by social and time-bound prejudices, refused to recognize Schiller's dictum : "Es ist der Geist, der sich den Körper baut."[61]

Moreover, Wedekind did not possess the love of the creator but

only the dubious obsession of the destroyer. He showed little compassion for human nature. His almost pathological occupation of
"épater le bourgeois" has brought him only the thorny crown of a
clown. His "idée fixe" began early to bore people by its repetition.
Here lies the fundamental difference from D. H. Lawrence, with
whom Wedekind is often compared in Germany. Making up one's
mind about Lawrence is a task nobody has been able to avoid
since his death. As one reads Lawrence, one is made increasingly
aware of how he changed the lives of subsequent generations.
It is impossible to pass the same verdict on Wedekind. Lawrence
perceived life as a human struggle for a better, healthier future,
while Wedekind remained a grotesque reflection of his own generation. While Lawrence loved life in all its manifestations and
assigned to sex its rightful place, Wedekind distorted it by his
flirtation with death, which is the destruction of life. The discovery
of Lawrence is still a tremendous experience for young people
today, because they sense kindred moods and attitudes in his
novels. Wedekind's real and often tragic intentions remain incomprehensible to any young German reader if he finds his way to
Wedekind at all. Frank Wedekind, despite his importance as a
pioneer of modern German literature, shares only the fate of those
many German poets and playwrights, eager to set loose a new
"Sturm und Drang" : occasionally mentioned, insufficiently known
and hardly appreciated.

It was therefore only suitable that the clown, the tragedian of
the human circus, appeared at the burial of Frank Wedekind. The
mourners consisted not only of the family and the representatives
of art and literature but also of the fifth estate, the petty criminals,
the street-walkers, the rest of Schwabing's Bohème[62] and many
teen-agers, "die dem Dichter so etwas wie die letzte Ehre erweisen
oder doch wenigstens ihre Neugier befriedigen wollten".[63] The
poet Heinrich Lautensack, for whose recognition Wedekind had
done so much, became insane at the sight of the open grave. "Als
der Trauerzug sich in Bewegung setzte, geriet der Knäuel unwill-
kommener Zaungäste in wellenförmige Bewegung. Plötzlich haste-
ten sie dem Sarg voran, um nur ja die ersten am Grabe zu sein.
Wie die Wilden stürmten sie im Galopp querfeldein : glücklich
wer gesund und heiter über frische Gräber hopst !"[64]
This Dionysian interlude reached its climax, as only Wedekind
himself could have imagined it, when the representative of a
literary society approached the graveside, a sheet of white paper
in his black-gloved right hand, from which he read his eulogy :
"Frank Wedekind, Du warst uns teuer. Dein Geist ist über uns,"
cried the speaker with tear-drenched voice.[65] Then he looked down

to get his next cue from his script. "Hier stockend! Tränen!"[66] continued the unfortunate eulogist. In his panegyric for the deceased poet he had spoken by mistake those notes, which served for his private information, how his voice should sound at the appropriate climax. "Hier stockend! Tränen!"...

From a neighbouring tomb a film camera preserved for posterity this last scene from the tragic comedy of Wedekind's life. In the end it was the philistine who triumphed.

TRANSLATIONS

1. His was one of those minds that had to experience the world as though it were a stage abounding with fighting characters.

2. He reared himself up high, fought back again and again with all his power, with fanatically tense contortions of his face, struggled fiercely against something which seized him cravenly from behind and threw him down—something which could not be grappled with, could not be forced to the ground. (viz. J. Friedenthal in *Berliner Tageblatt,* March 1925.)

3. Cabaret songs.

4.   "Reach bravely out for every sin;
        For out of sin grows pleasure.
        Oh, you resemble a child,
        Who has to be shown everything."

5. Feudalism of love.

6. A descendant of the pure innocents, a modern scion of the ilk of Parzival, Simplizissimus . . . the German idealist who piously gropes for knowledge.

7. "Who in the world should I ask but you!"

8. "I could not answer for it!...I deserve to be put in prison."

9. Ernst: I have overworked myself.

Hänschen: Don't let us be sad! It would be a waste of time.

Ernst: There they hang and I have had enough...and tomorrow they will be pressed.

Hänschen: Tiredness is as unbearable to me as hunger.

Ernst: Alas, I have had enough.

Hänschen: Just those sparkling muscatels.

Ernst: I cannot produce the effort for it.

Hänschen: If I bend this tendril, it will dangle from mouth to mouth. Nobody needs to move a hand. We bite off the grapes and let the shoot rebound.

Ernst: Hardly has one made up one's mind, and behold, the dwindling strength grows anew.

Hänschen: The flaming sky also . . . and the evening bells . . . I have no great hopes of the future.

Ernst: I can see myself sometimes as a venerable vicar...a tender-hearted little wife, a copious library, duties and honours all round me. Six days will be given for meditation, and on the seventh day one opens one's mouth. When taking my stroll, boys and girls will hold out their hands, and when one returns home, the coffee-pot steams, a pound-cake will be served, and through the garden gate the girls will bring apples.... Can you think of anything more beautiful?

Hänschen: I am thinking of half-closed eyelashes, of half-open lips and Turkish drapings.... I do not believe in pathos. You know, our elders pull long faces, in order to hide their blunders. Among themselves they call each other blockheads like we do. I know all about it. If I were a millionaire, I would erect a monument to God. Think of the future as curdled milk with sugar and cinnamon. Somebody will upset it and cry; another will stir everything up together and sweat. Why not skim off? Or don't you believe that one can learn the art of skimming off?

Ernst: Let us skim off!

Hänschen: And the chickens can pick up what is left.... I have now got out of so many scrapes....

Ernst: Let us skim off, Johnny!

Hänschen: Must you start again?

Ernst: Somebody must begin.

Hänschen: When we remember like tonight in thirty years, it will appear perhaps as unutterably beautiful to us!

Ernst: And everything now falls into its right place without any special effort.

Hänschen: And so why not?

Ernst: If one happens to be alone ... one sheds perhaps even tears.

Hänschen: Don't let us be sad! (He kisses his mouth.)

Ernst (kisses him): I left home thinking of just talking to you and then returning home.

Hänschen: I expected you ... Virtue is not such a bad garb but mature characters must be clothed with it.

Ernst: And this garb of virtue is still flapping around our limbs.... I would not have been at rest, if I had not met you.... I am very fond of you, Johnny, as I have never been of any other soul....

Hänschen: Don't let us be sad! When we think back in thirty years, we may perhaps sneer at this evening! And now everything is so beautiful! The mountains are glowing: the grapes dangle in our mouth and the evening wind touches the rocks gently like a playful kitten.

10. Without having seen the Pyramids.

11. The path of unrestrained enjoyment of all opportunities.

12. Oh, Mother, why didn't you tell me everything?
I have treated you no differently than my dear mother treated me.

13. I understand by morality the actual product of two imaginary forces. The imaginary forces are "will" and "duty".

14. To enlarge your horizon in the most amazing way.

15. To warm oneself with putrefaction.

16. In the fifth state of impostors, whores, tricksters and criminals, not burdened by moral and social scruples.

17. The children, artists and teen-agers who have not yet succumbed to the conventional lies of a philistine ethic and religion.

18. Wedekind intended to continue Goethe's *Gott und die Bajadere*

with *Pandora's Box* and prefaced *Earth Spirit* with a quotation from *Wallenstein*.

19. What do these plays of joys and griefs reveal?
   Domestic beasts, well-bred in what they feel,
   Who vent their rage on vegetarian fare
   And then indulge in a complacent tear,
   Just like those others—down in the parterre:
   This hero cannot hold his liquor in,
   This one's uncertain if his love is genuine.
   You hear the third despair of this earth-ball
   (For five long acts he groans about it all),
   None gives the coup de grâce to do him in.
   The wild and lovely animal, the true,
   Ladies and gentlemen, only I can show you.

   Hey, August, bring our snake this way!
   She was created for every abuse,
   To allure and to poison and seduce,
   To murder without leaving any trace.
     (tickling Lulu under the chin)
   Sweet creature, now keep in your proper place,
   Not foolish nor affected nor eccentric,
   Even when you fail to please the critic.

   Against my life I set a joke's lightness.
   I throw away my whip and all these weapons
   And appear harmless as God made me once.
   Do you know the name of this wild beast?
   Honoured spectators, do step inside please!
      (Translated by Stephen Spender.)

20. Feuchtwanger writes of him that "Willy Grétor was the most brilliant forger of pictures of his time, no doubt many a picture by him hangs in many a gallery. He knew no scruples, acknowledged no restraint."

21. Lulu herself has turned out remarkably inadequate and meagre.

22. Newt, salamander.

23. I have loved no one in the world but him.

24. viz. Gundolf: *Frank Wedekind* p. 67.

25. Have mercy upon me.

26. This painting represents a soul which rubs sleep from her eyes in the beyond.

27. You are not going to get away from me again!

28. The hunted female gracefulness of Lulu whom a shabby world only permits to climb into the Procrustean bed of its moral conceptions.

29. I don't know!

30. Love means war, the moral hatred of the sexes. Nietzsche: *Der Fall Wagner* sht. 2.

31. Lulu is the bearer of a new morality, which has nothing to do with naturalistic or even psychological truth.

32. *Earth Spirit* and *Pandora's Box* belong to the history of the theatre but no longer to the theatre. (*Der Spiegel*, Hamburg 1962.)

33. The girls of today are all of them Lulus. They do not know themselves, do not question themselves and are therefore pardonable like Lulu. (*Der Spiegel*, Hamburg 1962.)

34. A cross-breed of philosopher and horse-thief.

35. The Marquis did not stand any more on the floor. He had climbed up on to the writing-table and held fast to the cross-bar of the window! "Go away! Go away!" he groaned. And: "Come, come!" the other replied from the open door and beckoned slowly-quietly with his arm— and beckoned phantomlike towards peace to that place where one only "goes for a drive or to play billiards".... It is ghastly. The swindler and the madman entreat each other urgently: the swindler the madman that he may leave—the madman the swindler that he may come to a game of billiards. But the swindler does not hold fast enough,—he, the cynical idealist, adventurer and fervent believer—he clings even tighter to his cross-bar up there, at last he cries in despair for his office-boy and the tempter disappears.... It is a tremendous scene. In a meaningless room two men in bourgeois dress exchange brief and clear replies. But behind it a mystery haunts and beckons. It is the mystery of abdication .... the most terrible, the most moving and the most profound that this profound, tormented man has ever written. (Thomas Mann: *Rede und Antwort*. S. Fischer Verlag. Berlin, 1922.)

36. One can only do good business within the existing social order.

37. And sin is then only a mythological term for bad business.

38. As if he had to serve a sentence.

39. Life is a chute.

40. Misfortune is a favourable opportunity like any other. Every ass can meet with misfortune. The whole ingenuity consists in knowing how to make the most of it.

41. Either we remain in the lunatic asylum or the world will become one. Either we erase ourselves from the memory of men or mankind becomes extinct.

42. In the long run you can do good business only with the good.

43. He who is as much on his last legs as all the rest of us can only comprehend comedies.

44. *Such is Life* is its alternative title.

45. Wedekind blended skilfully self-advertisement with self-pity and hid the wrath of the prophet behind the grimace of the clown.

46. A starry helmsman.

47. "Auerbach's Cellar" in Leipsic. viz. Goethe's *Faust I*.

48. Youth is brightened by the archetypal belief in woman, old age is darkened by being disappointed on the same subject.

49. viz. Gundolf: *Frank Wedekind* p. 5ff.

50. He had as yet no knowledge of men and women, only of cattle, of cows, calves and steers.

51. She was just the same as she had been.

52. To seek out those women who please the heart, and not those who please the senses.

53. Thou shouldst not buy a pig in a poke, and in choosing a woman, thou shouldst select at least as carefully as in visiting a shop when buying a tie for one mark twenty.

54. On the Physical Education of Young Girls.

55. The Eleven Hangmen.

56. viz. Gundolf: *Frank Wedekind* p. 33.

57.   I was a child of fifteen years,
        A pure and innocent girl,
        When I had first experience
        Of how sweet Love's pleasures are.

        He held my body tight and laughed
        And whispered: Oh, what delight!
        And at the same time he bowed back
        My head to the couch gently, gently...

        Since that day I am in love with everybody
        Life's splendid spring is mine;
        And when I don't please any more
        They may gladly bury me.

58. Wedekind's hatred of bourgeois society made him appear the prophet of the just experienced doom.

59. A conjurer of thoughts.

60. He did not want to represent men "as they are" but as they think and feel.

61. It is the spirit frames itself a body (*Wallenstein,* act III, scene XIII).

62. Schwabing was Munich's famous "Quartier Latin" before the First World War.

63. Who wanted to pay the poet something like the last honours or at least to satisfy their curiosity. (Kutscher: *Frank Wedekind* vol. III. 1931.)

64. When the funeral procession began to move, the throng of unwelcome intruders fell into an undulating movement. Suddenly they outpaced the coffin, in order to arrive first at the graveside. Like savages they rushed along at a gallop: Happy he who leaps across fresh graves hale and hearty! (Kutscher: *Frank Wedekind* vol. III. 1931.)

65. Frank Wedekind, you were beloved of us. Your spirit is with us. (viz. *Zwischenakt.* Heft 8. December 1927.)

66. Here falter! Tears! (viz. *Zwischenakt.* Heft 8. December 1927.)

SELECT BIBLIOGRAPHY

FRANK WEDEKIND. *Gesammelte Werke* (Georg Müller. Munchen, 1920).

FRANK WEDEKIND. *The Awakening of Spring* (tr. F. J. Ziegler. Philadelphia, 1909).

FRANK WEDEKIND. *Such Is Life* (tr. F. J. Ziegler. Boston, 1930).

FRANK WEDEKIND. *Earth Spirit* (tr. S. A. Eliot. New York, 1914).

FRANK WEDEKIND. *Pandora's Box* (tr. S. A. Eliot. New York, 1918).

FRANK WEDEKIND. *Tragedies of Sex* (tr. S. A. Eliot. New York, London, 1923).

Five Tragedies of Sex (Vision Press. London, 1952).

JETHRO BITHELL. *Modern German Literature* (Methuen and Co. London, 1946).

FRANZ BLEI. *Ueber Wedekind, Sternheim und das Theater* (Leipzig, 1915).

F. DEHNOW. *Frank Wedekind* (Leipzig, 1922).

BERNHARD DIEBOLD. *Anarchie im Drama* (Frankfurt, 1921).

H. M. ELSTER. *Frank Wedekind und seine besten Bühnenwerke* (Berlin, 1922).

PAUL FECHTER. *Frank Wedekind, der Mensch und das Werk* (Leipzig, 1920).

JOACHIM FRIEDENTHAL. *Das Wedekindbuch* (Georg Müller. Munchen, 1914).

H. FRIEDMANN AND O. MANN. *Expressionismus* (W. Rothe Verlag. Heidelberg, 1956).

H. F. GARTEN. *Modern German Drama* (Methuen. London, 1959).

FRIEDRICH GUNDOLF. *Frank Wedekind* (Langen-Müller. Munchen, 1954).

H. KERR. *Frank Wedekind, eine Studie* (Leipzig, 1908).

ARTHUR KUTSCHER. *Frank Wedekind, 3 vols.* (Georg Müller, München, 1922–31).

HEINRICH MANN. *Erinnerungen an Frank Wedekind* (1929).

THOMAS MANN. *Rede und Antwort* (S. Fischer. Berlin, 1922).

WALTER MUSCHG. *Tragische Literaturgeschichte* (Francke. Bern, 1957).

R. SAMUEL AND R. HINTON THOMAS. *Expressionism in German Life, Literature and the Theatre* (Heffer and Sons. Cambridge, 1939).

A. SOERGEL AND C. HOHOFF. *Dichtung und Dichter der Zeit.* vol. I. (Bagel. Düsseldorf, 1961).

Carl Sternheim

Carl Sternheim

by R. BECKLEY

Carl Sternheim was born in Leipzig on April Fool's Day, 1878, the son of Carl Julius Sternheim, a Jewish banker from Hanover, and his wife Marie, née Francke, of the Lutheran confession. He spent his early childhood in Hanover, where his father owned the newspaper *Hannoversche Tageblatt* and wrote the reviews for the most important theatrical productions. When he was old enough Carl was often allowed to accompany his father to the theatre and dates his first impressions of it from this time.

His school years were spent at the Friedrich Werder Grammar School in Berlin, to which city the family had moved in 1884 and where his interest in the theatre was further stimulated by the fact that his uncle ran the Belle-Alliance Theatre. By the age of fifteen he had written his first play, *Das eiserne Kreuz*, which, though never performed, was found to be of promise by Otto Brahm, the famous theatre director, noted for his sponsorship of the early naturalistic plays.

From 1897 to 1901 he studied philosophy, literature and history at the universities of Munich, Leipzig, Göttingen and Freiburg. After completing his studies he married and had a son, but was divorced five years later. His second marriage was to Thea Bauer, the stage designer.

Soon after his second marriage Sternheim built himself a large residence near Munich called *Schloss Bellemaison*, where he settled for the next five years. From this period dates his founding of the literary magazine *Hyperion* in collaboration with the critic Franz Blei, and also his first theatrical success, *Die Hose*.

From now until 1926 Sternheim wrote almost a score of plays, but because of continued difficulties with the censor he did not achieve his greatest popularity until the years immediately following the end of the First World War, by which time the rate of his creative output was beginning to slacken. The degree of his success at this time may perhaps be measured by the fact that Dohnanyi, following the example of Alban Berg with regard to Frank Wedekind's *Lulu* tragedy, composed an opera called *Der Tenor*, which was based on the text of one of Sternheim's most successful comedies, *Bürger Schippel*. Sternheim's third wife was the actress Pamela Wedekind, Frank Wedekind's daughter.

Sternheim had suffered all his life from a nervous complaint, the effects of which increased with age, making him restless and irritable and in frequent need of change of scene and society. After Hitler's coming to power in 1933 he emigrated and after much wandering finally settled in Brussels, where he lived in enforced retirement until his death on 3 November 1942.

CARL STERNHEIM is remembered in most histories of modern German literature chiefly as the author of a series of plays written between 1910 and 1922 and collectively entitled *Aus dem bürgerlichen Heldenleben*.[1] As the title suggests they comprise a satiric presentation of German bourgeois society in the late nineteenth and early twentieth centuries, although the period singled out for particularly searching scrutiny (Sternheim referred to himself as "Der Arzt am Leib meiner Zeit"[2]) is the Wilhelmine era of the years leading up to the First World War. The plays are not all equally closely linked in respect of character and incident. The main figure in one work quite frequently plays a subsidiary rôle in a later one, or a family relationship between characters in quite different plays may be indicated by the use of the same surname. Three of the plays, however, form a trilogy which follows the fortunes of a particular family through three generations. In *Die Hose*[3] the "hero" is Theobald Maske, in the sequel, *Der Snob*, his son Christian Maske, while the third play of the trilogy, *1913*, shows Christian in conflict with his grown-up children. Although the natural habitat of many of Sternheim's figures would seem to be the kind of provincial town large enough for its population to be divided by rigid social barriers but small enough to allow of the classes thus created coming into contact, the preference accorded the Maske family and the Wilhelmine era, is, in respect of place, given to Berlin—the little *Residenzstadt* that boomed in the years following the close of the Franco-Prussian War into Germany's first metropolis, and the only one comparable at the time with the other *villes tentaculaires* of Europe. The spate of speculative building in these years of urban expansion was executed in the style afterwards known as *Gründerbarock*—a coarse and vulgar imitation of rococo excesses, which had the same tendency towards elephantiasis and fussy detail as late Victorian architecture. And the *bürgerliches Wohnzimmer* or middle-class living-room, where the furniture matching this style of building would have the added ostentation needed to impress visitors, is almost invariably the setting for Sternheim's satires of bourgeois family life.*

There is no indication that Sternheim set out at the beginning of his career to write a planned series of plays which would bring a representative cross-section of contemporary German society on to the stage. The collective title is a comparatively late addition,

* Sternheim does not use the word "bürgerlich" in the rigid Marxist sense, or to define a social class distinct from the proletariat and the aristocracy. He seems rather to apply it to anyone whose attitude of mind is the product of the peculiar conditions of middle-class existence—the need to struggle for social recognition, conform to social standards, etc. It includes all but princes and beggars.

and the fortunes of the various characters who figure in more than one play were probably not systematically worked out in advance of their first appearance. The idea of uniting a series of works by establishing a loose connection between characters and events is of course as old as Balzac, who conceived the title of *La Comédie Humaine* to include all the stories he had already written, and then set about strengthening the narrative links between these by the addition of other stories. That Sternheim at no time aimed at a similar comprehension is probably indicated by the fact that the form he chooses for his title is *Aus dem bürgerlichen Heldenleben* rather than the more ambitious and all-embracing *Das bürgerliche Heldenleben*.

The vogue for epic surveys of social or political eras and family sagas running into several generations is typical of the period in which Sternheim was writing and natural to an age which was witnessing such spiritual change and upheaval. Thomas Mann's first novel, *Buddenbrooks*, which deals with the decline of a family over four generations, was written in 1901, almost ten years before the first part of Sternheim's trilogy of the Maske family appeared. On an even greater scale was Heinrich Mann's trilogy of novels, *Das Kaiserreich*, published between 1914 and 1925 and attempting to deal with all the main figures and events of the Wilhelmine era. Sternheim, however, seems to have been the first to present in dramatic form the history of a family of more than one generation. The great dramatic trilogies of the nineteenth century had tended on the whole to cover subject-matter too widely conceived to be confined within five acts, but with the interest concentrated on a single character, or pair of characters. Thus the figure of Wallenstein is central to the theme of all three parts of Schiller's epic drama; Grillparzer's *Das goldene Vliess* traces the fortunes of Medea in relation to that fatal prize; and in Hebbel's *Nibelungen* Kriemhild's love for Siegfried and Hagen's hate of him carry the action quite naturally past the point where Siegfried is murdered and Kriemhild plans her revenge on Hagen. In Sternheim's trilogy, however, Christian Maske, the hero of the second play, is unborn at the end of the first, while his father, Theobald, is long since dead and not even a subject for passing reference in the third play, in which his grandchildren appear on the scene for the first time.

Whether or not Sternheim was the innovator of this kind of dramatic trilogy, which seems to owe its peculiar form to the novel, his example was followed by two expressionist dramatists with varying success : by Georg Kaiser in the famous *Gas* trilogy, and by Fritz von Unruh in the unfinished *Dietrich* trilogy. Similarly, the technique of characterizing a whole era by emphasizing the same aspects of it in a series of different situations, which is

Sternheim's method throughout this group of plays, may have influenced Bertolt Brecht's conception of *Furcht und Elend des dritten Reiches*, where twenty-two independent scenes form a play only by virtue of the common underlying theme indicated in the title.

Like Kaiser, Sternheim made many attempts at dramatic composition before he found where his true bent lay. His early failures are interesting for his development, if only because they are so utterly different in tone and choice of theme from the satiric comedy in which he afterwards excelled. *Ulrich und Brigitte*, a play written in blank verse of the "Hiawatha" kind about 1907 and described as a "Dramatisches Gedicht", deals with the romantic agonies of two young lovers who discover they are brother and sister. The added attraction of incest grafted on to the Romeo-and-Juliet theme marks the work as a product of the Impressionist or Neo-Romantic movement which had already celebrated its greatest triumphs with the plays of Maurice Maeterlinck, but was now in its decline. The verse of this play is not merely bad. Its prosaic tone and wilfully awkward staccato rhythms are a ready-made parody of the romantic metre from which they struggle to escape, as the closing lines of the drama clearly reveal :

> *Brigitte:*   Ja, küsse mich. O du
> erstickst mich ja, und ich ersterbe
> im Glück. O du, du bist so kühl,
> Was ich für einen Himmel fühl,
> So kalt bist du. O lass, o geh,
> Du liegst in meines Lebens Näh,
> ich atme nicht, nun lass mich, Gott,
> ach Ulrich, ach, du drückst mich tot! . . .
> (Sie stirbt. Lange feierliche Stille)[4]

Don Juan, a more grandiose work of the same period, is ambitiously called a tragedy and divided into two parts, like Goethe's *Faust*. Once again Sternheim chooses a hero who, like Bluebeard and Casanova, was dear to the hearts of the Impressionists for his neurotic obsession with sex, but in the more serious moments of the play the sentiments tend to be expressed in prose, while the verse (especially in the form of songs or stanzas) is reserved for certain caricatured figures such as the king of Spain, from whom the audience's sympathy has to be alienated. Unlike *Ulrich und Brigitte, Don Juan* ends on an almost casual note. As the Don, at the head of a cavalry charge (he is engaged in one of Philip the Second's wars), falls in the thick of the fighting, an onlooker cheers him *sotto voce,* then goes over to the carriage where the Don's mistress is waiting and laconically conveys the news of his death with the words :

"Aussteigen. Es ist was los?"[5]

The radical change from Romantic tragedy to comic satire only hinted at in the cool tone and occasional grotesque characters of *Don Juan* is complete in Sternheim's next play. For a theatre-going public conditioned to the appearance in drama of monsters of human depravity, as long as they were dressed in historical costume, and prepared to accept the presentation of contemporary social evil only when seen with the passionate conviction and broad human sympathy of a Gerhart Hauptmann, the shock of encountering the cold passionless gaze with which Sternheim insolently views the older generation of his day in *Die Hose* must have been considerable. The potentiality of such satire to shock must depend on the seriousness with which it is taken. The effect of Gay's *Beggar's Opera* or Beaumarchais' *Mariage de Figaro* on the audiences they attacked was no doubt very different from the polite amusement these plays afford a modern audience, which does not feel itself personally attacked and whose sympathies in any case lie with the author. A recounting of the plot of *Die Hose* shows that, following the fortunes of all satire bound to a specific time and place, its power to make us laugh is greater than its power to arouse our indignation, righteous or otherwise.

Luise, the young wife of Theobald Maske, an ambitious petty official of the Prussian state, is of such a dreaming and impractical nature that one day while she is standing in the Zoological Gardens in Berlin amongst a crowd of people gathered together to watch the passing of the Kaiser, the fastening of her knickers, insecurely tied in a moment of romantic abstraction, snaps at the crucial moment and brings the royal progress to a scandalized halt. The play actually opens with Theobald beating his wife for her negligence, which is likely to cost him his position as state official. His rough behaviour characterizes him as "ein Mann aus dem Volk" just as Luise's sentimental quotation of the classical authors indicates that she has enjoyed a more refined upbringing, and is more conversant with the world of romantic fiction than the world of stern reality into which she has married. Sternheim's satiric intent is evident in the first unexpected twist he gives to events. Luise's mishap does not cost her husband his position. Instead, it brings two prospective admirers, titillated witnesses to the scene of her humiliation in the Zoological Gardens, in answer to an advertisement of two furnished rooms to let, which the struggling young newly-weds had inserted in the daily paper some days earlier. The one, Scarron, is a gushing poet whom Luise identifies with the ideal lover of her day-dreams. The other, a hairdresser, called Mandelstamm, claims to be filled with the same lofty sentiments as Scarron, but he fails so grossly in the expression of them, that his every utterance makes Scarron's behaviour appear ridiculous and insincere. Theobald seems to realize from the beginning that both men are infatuated with his pretty wife, but instead of being indignant, he confidently exploits the situation and overcharges his lodgers for their rooms. Luise has meanwhile persuaded herself that her husband's brutality gives her the right to seek love elsewhere. She feels she "owes it to herself" to experience the great romantic passion, which fate appears to have offered her in the figure of Scarron. Her resolve is fostered by an ageing spinster of a neighbour called Fräulein Deuter, who, too plain to have attracted the male, hopes to experience vicariously the ecstasy of mind and body preparing for Luise. The whispered scenes between the two excited women are among Sternheim's most striking conceptions for the debunking of the romantic dream, for Luise's tremulous expressions of joy and hope take on a perverse colouring from the participation of the old maid whose conversation frequently runs on the new frilled knickers that she is to make for Luise's first night with Scarron.

These scenes of expectation between Luise and Fräulein Deuter lead up to Sternheim's second surprise. As Luise stands waiting for Scarron to carry her off to his bed, the poet grabs paper and pencil, rushes into his room, and, locking the door behind him, tries to conceive in words the sexual act which even the inducements of a beautiful and willing woman fail to give him sufficient stimulus to perform. The only life which Scarron is capable of leading is, like Luise's, a life of the imagination, got second-hand from cheap romantic literature.

Theobald's confidence in the harmlessness of Scarron's advances to his wife, which made him appear naïve and foolish in the earlier half of the play, is now seen to be justified. Ironically, it is *he* who is able to establish real contact with Scarron—by engaging him in friendly conversation.

Luise, meanwhile, with the grosser part of herself roused beyond her own control, is now reduced to inflaming the desire of the hairdresser, Mandelstamm, whom she had at first treated haughtily as an obstacle to the privacy she desired with Scarron. Her humiliation is complete when he, too, absorbed to the point of hypochondria in his own health, fails her, preferring to spend a peaceful and refreshing night in his own bed. When her rage and disappointment have subsided Luise is only too ready to take the easy path of repentance and console herself with the very comforting thought that her husband, at least, is a man. At this point Sternheim presents his third and last surprise. While Luise is away at church performing her facile repentance with all the self-indulgence of her over emotional nature, Fräulein Deuter, innocent of the disappointing turn events have recently taken, comes to give Luise the finished underwear. Theobald is by chance there to receive her, and with the same eye to his own advantage as he had shown on an earlier occasion, whisks Fräulein Deuter into the bedroom.

It may be doubted whether Sternheim ever again arranged his subject so neatly or produced the maximum effect of irony with so light a touch. The offending garment which flutters so mockingly into the opening conversation of the play is never allowed to disappear from the imagination of the audience. Re-created with added magnificence under the assiduous fingers of the ageing spinster it takes on a malicious life of its own and directs the fates of the characters to the opposite conclusion of that which they had planned for themselves—fanning in Theobald the desire for the unprepossessing Deuter and gracing not the airy union of Luise and Scarron, but the very earthy relationship of a married petty official and his mistress (a relationship which Theobald loses no time in arranging on a regularly weekly basis).

The note on which Sternheim closes relies for its effect on a device much employed in the later propagandist phase of Expressionism. Like so much Expressionist technique it is an inconsistency or break in style which, while provoking a shock or protest as the audience's or reader's first reaction, enables a particular scene, situation or sentiment to be strikingly imprinted on the memory by means of its very incongruity. In satiric comedy or farce it often takes the form of a break in mood from the artificial or the grotesque to the real and serious. Shakespeare uses it in *Love's Labours Lost* when the news of the French king's death is brought unexpectedly and without a word of warning to break up the giddy flirtation between the princes and princesses, and to remind them that the world of wit and words in which they are living is being driven dangerously near the point at which it will lose all contact with reality. Similarly at the end of *Die Hose* Sternheim reminds us that farcical and manipulated though the characters and plot of his play may have been they nevertheless have their point of contact with reality and must be taken seriously. He does this by making Theobald say that the money he has obtained from Scarron and Mandelstamm, who have paid handsome sums in advance for their rooms, will enable him to afford to let Luise have the child which he so earnestly desires. Such a sincere expression of marital feeling and paternal hope sends in retrospect a warm glow through the harsh flattening light which up to the very last minute Sternheim has trained so mercilessly on his figures. It gives concreteness to the farcical situations which, smacking more of literature than life, have served up to this point to expose the theatrical unreality of the bourgeois world, and it also gives contour and colour to Theobald, who, in spite of his self-seeking and duplicity, seems like a solitary human being wandering amongst soulless puppets which occasionally catch a spark of life from his proximity.

According to Sternheim himself what most offended the audience of the day was to see their world and themselves presented as they actually were without having first been filtered through the transfiguring imagination of a lofty-minded poet. He says : "Als ich 1908 ein bürgerliches Lustspiel veröffentlichte, kannte nach Gerhart Hauptmanns Naturalismus die deutsche Bühne nur die Maskerade vom alten Fabelkönig, der jungen Königin und dem famosen Pagen, die unter mannigfaltigen Verkleidungen neuromantisch auftraten; reich kostümiert, abseits von Wirklichkeit Glanz sprachen, Erhabenheit handelten. In meinem Stücke verlor ein Bürgerweib die Hose, und von nichts als der banalen Sache sprach man in kahlem Deutsch auf der Szene. Ob solcher Einfalt fällte die Welt das Urteil : wie, war das Dichtung? Eine bürgerliche Hose und fünf Spiesser, die von ihr räsonierten? Wo blieb gewohnter Glanz (Ersatz), wo auch nur (Pseudo)—Naturalismus?"[6] The contemptuous tone detectable in Sternheim's play was, in fact, nothing new. Wedekind had been criticizing bourgeois behaviour and values on the stage for some years and Heinrich Mann had published in 1905 a novel called *Professor Unrat* which satirized contemporary society and presented scarcely a single character with any redeeming human feature. But both Wedekind and Mann showed their characters tormented with passions they could not control or vicious and revengeful to such a degree that they thereby acquired a certain stature.

In spite of some public displeasure, Sternheim undoubtedly found enough approval and encouragement to explore further the vein of comedy which he seems almost accidentally to have chanced upon. The second play of the Maske trilogy was not in fact the next work at which he tried his hand, but it is the next to reveal his development as an artist : the improved economy in his dramatic technique, the perfecting of his powers of characterization, and the increasing profundity of his critical insight. Moreover, it was quite a different kind of play, not a repetition of the earlier *succès de scandale*. *Der Snob* is a satirical study of the social entry of Theobald Maske's son, Christian, into the ranks of the aristocracy. Compared with *Die Hose*, the plot is simple, because Sternheim is here more concerned with the presentation and development of character. The opening of the new play is itself an ironic comment on Theobald's tender hope for a son, with which the earlier play had closed; for Christian has already, while still in his early manhood, worked his way up by sheer hard work, tenacity and ruthlessness, partly inherited from his father, to a position where, as a powerful business executive, he controls a considerable portion of the national wealth.

Sternheim's conception of the *parvenu's* rise, by way of commerce and industry to the point where he is able to buy his entry into the charmed circle of the aristocracy was appropriate for the age. His offer of marriage and wealth, to a daughter of one of the noblest and most impoverished houses, that of Graf Palen, reminds one of the marriage of the rich heiress of bourgeois origin to the prince of a bankrupt petty German state in Thomas Mann's *Königliche Hoheit* (1909). But whereas Mann uses the incident to show how a monarch helps his land and his people to economic prosperity, for Sternheim it becomes the means of exposing the deceit, callousness and eventual self-delusion which are practised in the struggle to ascend the social ladder.

Christian's first decisive step is to break off relations with the woman on whom he has lived hitherto and through whom he has made the contacts which have brought him to his present state of prosperity. Sternheim sketches her lightly, lest the tragedy of her situation (she still loves Christian) and the injustice done her should divert too much attention from the main subject of his study. Once again, Christian's insistence on repaying this woman every penny he ever had from her, including the interest which would have accrued over the years, and his attempts to assess in terms of money the value of her personal intervention for him in past years, illustrates Sternheim's thesis that for the bourgeois mentality the basic reality of everything in life can be translated into terms of hard cash.

Christian's next move in the breakaway from his past is to send his lower middle-class, and therefore socially unacceptable, parents to Switzerland, where they will be too far away to be able to embarrass him. There are two reasons for this. Graf Palen is extremely proud of his pedigree, and will only give his daughter to a man in all respects an aristocrat (Christian has so far managed to shroud his parentage in mystery); and Theobald, though now ageing, still has his occasional amorous adventure, which, with the appearance of an illegitimate baby, threaten to bring his name, and Christian's, into the newspapers. Sternheim cleverly reveals the measure of Christian's filial affection in the scene in which Theobald comes to protest at his being sent to Switzerland. Christian has just received a dinner invitation from Graf Palen, and when his father appears he is in a state of nervous excitement caused by trying to formulate an acceptance which will produce "the right impression". He feels the letter should commence with some many-syllabled high-sounding word. It then happens quite by chance that Theobald in his interview with his son uses the kind of word Christian thinks he is looking for, and when the interview is over he completely forgets his parents and their problems in the ecstasy of having found the word he needs. Sternheim, however, turns even his callousness to ridicule, for the word is really only suitable for a refusal, which Christian writes because the impression he makes on the Graf is more important to him than the dinner engagement.

Unlike his treatment of Luise and Scarron in *Die Hose,* both of whom he foils and unmasks before the end of the play, in *Der Snob* Sternheim seems to delight in leading his main character on to further folly until the measure he attains to is itself sufficient poetic justice. Accordingly, the first unexpected twist Sternheim gives to the plot turns in Christian's favour. His father quite unexpectedly returns from Switzerland when Graf Palen is in the house making the final arrangements for Christian's marriage to his daughter. Christian is immediately convinced that the discovery of his father's humbler background will put an end to his ambitious plans. It is only when he has, in the agony of the moment, lost his usual calm composure (which surprises the Graf more than the discovery of his humble parentage) that Christian discovers it has become fashionable to be of lowly origin. It seems that the Graf's definition of an aristocrat is not necessarily a man with a title, but one who completely identifies himself with the nobility and is thus best able to further its ends. Christian's reaction is, of course, to boast of the parentage he was at first so careful to hide, since it shows him to be a self-made man. However, Sternheim intimates that he is now less his own master than he was before. His attitude to his parentage is not of his own choosing : it is dictated by fashion, to which he must bow if he wishes to succeed socially.

Not that he does this unwillingly. When the marriage with Marianne Palen has taken place, Sternheim ends the play with a scene which catches up a theme broached at the beginning of the former play. Christian, flushed with his social success, seems unable to accept the fact that a man who is about to possess such a prize as Marianne should have no better pedigree than a humdrum middle-class couple with which to impress her. She, in her turn, and not unlike Christian's mother in the earlier play, has surrounded the man of her choice with an aura of mystery which ill accords with what she has since learned about his parents. It is at this point that Christian remembers his mother's mishap years ago in the Zoological Gardens, and, filtering this incident through the medium of his own transfiguring imagination, conceives the fairy-story of which both he and Marianne seem to stand in such need. He tells her of how, on a tour of France, his parents were once walking in the Bois de Boulogne when the great painter Auguste Renoir happened to be passing by. His mother stopped, and at this moment her knickers fell down. Renoir himself was so charmed by the scene that he called upon her the following day to paint her as he had first seen her. Quite by chance he brought a friend with him, a French viscount. When Marianne interrupts Christian to ask when all this happened, Christian replies meaningfully that the meeting with the viscount took place roughly a year before his own birth. To Christian's great good fortune his mother has recently died, so he is able to pass off a picture by Renoir as a portrait of her without fear of his deceit being discovered. The play ends with him speaking of the family country estate (the viscount's, one assumes) which he has been able to repurchase. This he does with a conviction which suggests he has completely persuaded himself of the truth of his story.

In its implications *Der Snob* is not just the presentation of a man determined to get to the top at all costs, but an exposure of the whole bourgeois attitude to life, as Sternheim saw it. It is the tragic theme of Ibsen's *Wild Duck*—man's need in this harsh world for a "Lebenslüge" to carry him through—treated comically, by showing that the need springs from man's own overweening pride and hypocritical desire to hide from himself the meanness of his own nature. It enables him to do shabby deeds from shabbier motives in the name of all the Christian virtues. But Sternheim also shows the penalty that must be paid. In being obliged to gain his ends by deceiving not only others, but also himself, Christian forfeits his own identity. He sells it for a pseudo-romantic fiction which has no existence in time or space. The practical disadvantage of this forfeiture is that if this fictitious world gains too great a hold on his imagination, it blinds him to his real situation and makes of him the kind of victim Luise and Scarron were shown to be in *Die Hose*.*

It may be questioned whether Sternheim's view of the society of his day was ever produced with greater clarity or wit than in these two plays. He himself said that every play after *Die Hose* offered nothing fundamentally new. It merely repeated what he thought could not be stated too often : that the age was spiritually dead.

There seems little doubt, however, that Sternheim attempted to broaden his vision to extend over the whole of bourgeois society and to present an epic survey of the problems and conflicts of his time.

* Like the names of so many of Sternheim's characters, the name *Maske* is particularly apt. It can be interpreted in two ways. (1) The hero is not what he seems: he hides his true nature behind a mask of pretence. (2) He is like a puppet without a soul: there is nothing real behind his mask-like features.

It was not only his plays that he collected under one title and linked in such a way that the whole attempted to be more than the sum of its parts. His short stories, too, when they had reached a certain number, were published together as *Chronik von des XX Jahrhunderts Beginn,* and a long essay entitled *Berlin oder Juste Milieu* tries to trace the essential history of that city in relation to its time and the rest of Europe, "ab urbe condita". But Sternheim's talent was probably too exclusively satirical to produce a more comprehensive survey at this stage in his career, and later on his sympathies, and the new problems and needs of a changing society, modified his artistic aims and intentions.

The third play of the Maske trilogy *1913,* bears witness to his attempt and partial failure to succeed in giving to his presentation the dimensions of a true saga. His difficulty lay possibly in the fact that he was unwilling to concede that there was anything more than banal in the bourgeois scale of experience and yet wished to convey that for such a society the end, if not terrifying, must be grisly. Significantly enough, Sternheim calls this play a *Schauspiel,* not a *Komödie*; the comedy it contains has something of a sour quality, and the laughs it affords are rather bitter. Christian Maske as an old man has an enormous fortune and a vision of his family's glorious future to bequeath to three highly unsatisfactory grown-up children. The father appears to have unwittingly and unwillingly visited his sins upon them. Christian's blind worship of the nobility has degenerated in his son Philipp into an exclusive preoccupation with fine clothes. The creations of an English tailor, Mister Easton, represent all that is most aristocratic in this line. Ottilia, his favourite child, is ironically enough, completely without ambition because of the wealth and social recognition she inherited at birth. Sofie, however, whom her father hates for reasons which are never very clear, is a monster of rapacity who possesses her father's vices several times magnified and who pits her strength against his in the world of big business.

The conflict of the play turns on the struggle of these two to transact a deal with the Dutch Government over ammunition for an impending war. The deal, the fight and the means employed are equally disgraceful, and the comedy is at its sourest when both parties change their religion in an attempt to wrest the prize from the other. It is an example of the struggle which some years later so intrigued and mystified Bertolt Brecht and which he at first took for a "Kampf um des Kampfes Willen."[7] Like the struggle in Brecht's *Dickicht der Städte* it ends with the death of the one who started it and first gave to the other the taste for blood. Christian momentarily clinches the deal with Holland, but the effort kills him, so that Sofie, against whose sheer genius for evil the other two children are defenceless, is left to reign darkly over the wealth which is all-powerful in the shaping of Germany's future. In the figure of Friedrich Stadler, a champion of the national cause in the more positive sense of that term and an opponent of the self-seeking capitalist Maske family, Sternheim pays a tribute to his friend, the young expressionist poet Ernst Stadler, who preached the spiritual rebirth of Europe through the conversion of each individual human being to the love and under-standing of his brother and a complete rejection of the materialism of the earlier generation which seemed to be responsible for the spiritual decay prevalent throughout society. In the play Stadler's great friend is Wilhelm Krey, whose socialist leanings have led him to take the post of secretary to Christian Maske, in order to observe and report on the various political and economic moves in the capitalist world. Sternheim uses Christian's relationship with Krey to reveal the enormous gulf between the world of Christian's idealistic imagination and the sordid practices of his actual life; for he exploits Krey's presence in his house to dramatize himself in his own mind into the heroic opponent of Krey and his socialism, while at the same time using the most unheroic and underhand means to thwart his own daughter. The lustre borrowed from this imagined conflict with Krey he then tries, in the con-fusion of his mind, to transfer to his jealous squabble with his daughter.

If this play fails to convince in the final instance, it is perhaps because Sternheim was too honest to pretend to a vision more compelling than that which he possessed, for there is no doubt that the work is grand in its conception. But the courage with which he begins to present the degeneration of the house of Maske seems to desert him as the plot develops to its climax. His attitude to his characters becomes ambivalent. There are moments when Christian, in conversation with his secretary seems to have changed from the early self-seeker to a man whose position has taught him a serious sense of responsibility towards his fellow-countrymen. This impres-sion is strengthened by Sternheim's intimation that Christian's secretary, Wilhelm Krey, has been seriously tempted and will be lured from his socialist cause by the wealth and success of his employer. This makes a mockery of young Germany's revolt against the materialism of its parents, which is symbolized by Friedrich Stadler's decisive exit from Maske's house at the end of the play, after his friend Krey has shown signs of going over to the enemy camp. Moreover, Christian's almost pathological hatred of his elder daughter, which has the important function of providing the motive for the external conflict of the play, is never very convincingly explained. Finally, *1913* does not sum up the underlying theme of the trilogy, as one expects it to do, because the trilogy was probably not conceived organically. It rather bears witness to Sternheim's realization that his vision needed constant modification.

All the plays of this period show signs of the mental struggle in which Sternheim's search for the truth underlying appearances involved him. In *Bürger Schippel,* the main character is again a man eager for acceptance in a higher social circle. Paul Schippel is an illegitimate brought up on the parish, who has a beautiful singing voice. The comic conflict arises when the local male-voice choir, which is patronized by the most respected inhabitants of the town, loses one of its tenors. How admit Schippel to the choir, in order to win the prince's laurel wreath at the annual singing contest, without actually having to accept the outcast socially? Sternheim seems to present Schippel with a mixture of pity, admiration and contempt. Schippel's savage anger at the insult and humiliation he has suffered all his life arouses a degree of compassion not often felt in reading Sternheim's work, and his refusal to accept in marriage the offer of a bourgeois young lady who has just been compromised by the local prince shows that he is not prepared to "buy" his entry into bourgeois society by sacrificing his sense of self-respect. However, the very fact that the bourgeois state is the ideal to which he attains seems to condemn him in Sternheim's eyes, for he gives many examples of his small-mindedness. Sternheim's attitude to the romantically minded bourgeois girl who falls in love with the prince is also ambivalent. Their love-scene is full of a tender, rather sad irony quite unlike that which may be found in the scenes between Luise and Scarron in *Die Hose* :

Der Fürst: Bist du Volk, Thekla?
Thekla: Bin's.
Der Fürst: Untertanin?
Thekla: Untertanin.
Der Fürst: Herunter mit dir! Wie bei Shakespeare trete ich hier auf. Habe eine Neigung auf dich geworfen und donnere dir den Befehl zu.
Thekla: Ach, Shakespeare ist hin. Wir sind drei Jahrhunderte weiter.[8]

The scene continues with Thekla telling the prince she only hesitates to give herself to him because her brother's pride will be deeply wounded by her shame :

Thekla: Ich liebe Tilmann. Sein Kummer ist mir das Härteste.
Der Fürst: So bin ich Eindringling in Frieden und Stille. Verleite Engel zur Lüge.

Thekla: Sündhaft von mir ist seit gestern jeder Atemzug. Aber ein Prinz! Ein junger, melancholischer Held. Zu lange habe ich mit dem Bruder Volkslieder gesungen, in denen er unablässig auftritt, dass ich ihm hingegeben war, bevor er noch wirklich kam.
Der Fürst: Entspricht er?
Thekla: Ganz.
Der Fürst: Das ist ein Geständnis, Thekla.
Thekla: Soll es sein. Spräche ich sonst nachts vom Fenster herab?[9]

The portraits of the philistine members of the male-voice choir, however, show Sternheim's attitude to his characters at its most unequivocal, and the cynicism with which the hypocrisy and cheap sentimentality of such small-town types are exposed becomes the dominant mood in *Die Kassette*. In this play two men successively neglect the women they love in order to dance attendance on a malevolent old lady who dangles before them the prospect of inheriting her vast wealth. As she has already secretly willed all her possessions to the Church both the servile flattery of the two men, and the grandiose plans for the future which they indulge in, appear doubly ludicrous and contemptible.

Signs of a definite change in Sternheim's attitude to the world around him may be found in the play *Tabula Rasa,* which was performed in 1914. It is the last of the "sardonic" comedies, and represents a clean sweep in more ways than one. As the representative of a workers' union, who has sold out to the employers in exchange for an easy job and a high salary, Wilhelm Ständer, the main character of the play, is a creation which reveals Sternheim at the very limits of his cynicism, for it is by means of this same character that the playwright gives some intimation of a dawning interest in the problem of the social responsibility of the individual. When the director of the factory where Ständer works offers him an active partnership in the business, he declines, knowing that the position would require much more hard work and self-sacrifice than he has been used to, without an equal increase in financial gain. His decision is interpreted by everyone as a sign that he will not desert the cause of the workers, and as Ständer had cunningly foreseen, they agree to his being accorded a handsome pension equal to the salary from the partnership but without the work and the responsibility.

In an attempt to understand the play some critics have interpreted Ständer's actions as an illustration of Sternheim's assertion that every man must have "den Mut zu sich selbst"—"the courage to be himself". It is claimed that to be oneself, and be selfish, is better than to be afraid of being oneself. "Den Mut zu sich selbst

haben" is certainly a theme which is central to all Sternheim's
work, but the aspect of it which interests Sternheim varies from
play to play. In *Die Hose* the main figure asserts himself in a world
of shams, but if in the process he exploits everyone and every
situation to his own advantage, he has the justification of being a
real human being with a real problem—the need to find the where-
withal to support a family. Ständer has no such problems. The
niece he spoils and pampers is, as he says himself, the luxury in
which he likes to indulge himself. That Sternheim condemns
Ständer for his selfishness seems clear from the opening and closing
scenes of the play, which are made to comment on each other.
At the opening of the play the woman who lives with Ständer as
his wife and looks after him as his servant demands an increase in
her weekly allowance. Ständer maintains she is not employed by
him and does not receive pay, but chooses to help him of her
own free will and is occasionally given unsolicited gifts. Ständer
is in fact exploiting his housekeeper-cum-bedfellow under the pretence of refusing to enter into anything so ignoble with her as a
master-servant relationship. However, when towards the close of
the play the director of the factory calls on Ständer, Sternheim
intimates by a repetition of certain expressions used earlier that
Ständer is being offered the partnership on conditions similar to
those he has forced on the woman he lives with. His refusal brands
him as the kind of man who is the continual butt of Sternheim's
satire—a hypocrite who propounds principals, but has none, and
whose actions are in direct contrast to his expressed ideals.

Exactly what factors contributed to the change noticeable in
Sternheim's work after *Tabula Rasa* has not been investigated,* but
his position in relation to the other writers of Expressionism may
not be without significance. Sternheim was older by at least a
decade than the generation of young dramatists who called themselves Expressionists, and his early satires of bourgeois life reflect
the mood of the preceding generation of the brothers Thomas and
Heinrich Mann. The period of Expressionist drama with which
the greater part of *Aus dem bürgerlichen Heldenleben* coincides,
was, in contrast to the latter, impulsive, emotional and idealistic.
It sought to establish the myth of "der neue Mensch"—the new
generation that would bring about the spiritual rebirth of decadent

---

* Sternheim began adapting the works of other writers about this time.
Der Geizige was a translation of Molière's *L'Avare,* and was followed by an
adaptation of Klinger's *Das leidende Weib* and a dramatization of the
Abbé Prévost's *Manon Lescaut.* This dependence on the work of other
writers may indicate not so much a lack of creative energy in Sternheim,
as his need to temper his rather rigid view of human nature.

Western civilization, and its normal vehicle of expression was certainly not the comic satire.

Yet Sternheim's work has much in common with that of the other dramatists of the time. For instance, the Expressionist preference for presenting general types of humanity rather than individualized characters, in an endeavour to get back to what were felt to be the more fundamental problems of existence, has its parallel in Sternheim's cultivation of the extreme caricature of bourgeois types for the opposite purpose of revealing that there is nothing fundamental about them whatsoever. Similarly, the stylistic innovations of Expressionism, which depend on the omission of all unessential words such as articles, pronouns and adjectives, and builds up its verbs and nouns into short explosive phrases, give to the conversation of Sternheim's characters a hollowness and rigidity which reflects their lack of humanity. What Sternheim does not share with his contemporaries, up to the writing of *Tabula Rasa,* is their preoccupation with the need to find a positive solution to the problems of the time.

The change comes, however, with *Die Marquise von Arcis,** written towards the end of the First World War and based on an idea from a story by Diderot. Conforming to the ideals of the Expressionist movement, it is yet an entirely original contribution, in that Sternheim develops further the themes which unite all his work.

Indicative of his desire to get away from contemporary social satire is his choice of a subject with an historical setting (Paris in the mid-eighteenth century), which enables him to give his theme greater universality. The play opens with a classic Sternheimian contrast. The Marquis d'Arcis and the Marquise de Pommeraye have been ardent lovers for many years, and their relationship is regarded by the whole of Paris as the ideal example of human constancy. The Marquise, however, has come to suspect that the Marquis' passion for her has cooled, and in order to trick him into confessing the truth she pretends to him that the intensity of her feelings has declined with the years. The Marquis swallows the bait, expresses his deep admiration for the Marquise's honesty, and suggests that from now on they should be as true in friendship as they were once constant in their love. The Marquise makes a show of accepting this new reality, but begins in secret to form a plan which will give her the revenge her wounded pride demands and also force the Marquis, disillusioned and contrite, to accept the

---

* *Die Marquise von Arcis* was translated into English by Ashley Dukes and performed in London in 1935 under the title *The Mask of Virtue.* Vivien Leigh made her West End début on this occasion in the rôle of Henriette Duquenoy.

continued validity of their old relationship. She is aided in her
scheme by the Marquis' determination to discover a new mistress
with whom he will be able to experience the spiritual rebirth that
will once again give purpose and meaning to his life. The Marquise
finds what she thinks will be the perfect tools for her stratagem in
the figures of Madame Duquenoy and her daughter Henriette.
Madame Duquenoy is a lady of gentle birth who has fallen upon
evil times, and in order to maintain appearances and continue
living in the standard of comfort to which she is accustomed, has
sold her daughter to a series of noblemen. Henriette, who is
notorious for her candour, has accepted the ugly truth of her
position, finding her best defence in an assumed cynicism.

After paying mother and daughter a handsome sum to move to
a part of Paris where they are not known, and to lead there for
a while a life of unimpeachable respectability, the Marquise de
Pommeraye introduces Henriette to the Marquis d'Arcis, who
immediately falls in love with her. Following the Marquise's com-
mands Henriette refuses to enter into any kind of relationship with
the Marquis until he has offered her his hand in marriage and
half his fortune. The Marquise's plan threatens to miscarry at the
last moment when Henriette discovers she is in love with the man
she has been forced to dupe. Only the bitterness of her experience
at the hands of society and the self-seeking she sees there drain her
of all courage and desire to attempt to live for her own happiness.
When finally the marriage has been celebrated and the newly-weds
have retired for the night Henriette discovers the enormity of the
deceit she has been forced to practise. The Marquis' trust in her
is so complete that he has surrendered himself to her entirely, by
placing both his possessions and his happiness in her hands. It is
at this moment that the Marquise de Pommeraye comes stalking
through the house to take her long-prepared revenge. While Henriette, terrified at the cruelty and indignity she has inflicted, packs
the few things necessary for the instant flight she has decided upon,
the Marquise reveals to her old lover that the girl whose form he
has invested with the radiance of an angel is in fact a common
prostitute.

The distress the Marquise occasions with this news is greater than
even she had anticipated. The Marquis is not merely wounded in
his pride : his belief in human nature is shaken to its foundations,
and the blow threatens to destroy him. What then follows is in
the nature of a miracle. When the agony of his despair and
humiliation is at its greatest and he is least able to see his own
situation objectively, the very intensity of his suffering shows him
the way of salvation : he suddenly realizes that his torment is
caused by something which has no foundation in reality. For if

Henriette is a prostitute, then he cannot accept society's low estimate of the prostitute; and if he cannot accept society's low estimate of the prostitute, then he has no reason to feel humiliation and despair on learning that Henriette is one. He now remembers that it was not Henriette's assumed air of respectability or virtuousness with which he fell in love, but the candour and innocence, which constantly broke through and gave the lie to these, and which she was able to preserve, in spite of the degrading uses to which her mother had put her. In rejecting the Marquise's and society's estimate of Henriette and refusing to react in the accepted way to the idea conveyed by the word "prostitute", the Marquis undergoes the first stage in his spiritual rebirth. In having the courage to meet a changing human situation with the new and unbiased attitude it requires he becomes the "neuer Mensch" of Expressionism. The Marquise's plan fails because it is based on an outmoded and ignoble conception of human nature. She had not reckoned with the Marquis' creative nobility of soul, which had enabled him to find the real human being behind the derogatory label. At the end of the play Sternheim stresses what might be considered his particular comment on the Expressionist ideal of the "neuer Mensch", for the Marquis' moral struggle and subsequent victory not only save him from spiritual suicide, but create out of Henriette Duquenoy, the social outcast, a "new woman"—the "Marquise von Arcis" of Sternheim's title.

There is no more impressive or exciting sequence in the whole of Sternheim's work than the Marquis d'Arcis' triumph over the prejudice of his age. The author himself seems to take the lesson of the play to heart, for in his last important work for the stage, written five years later on the subject of Oscar Wilde's fall from public favour, he brings to the task of presenting the English dramatist the same fervent sincerity which the Marquis d'Arcis brings to his "reconception" of Henriette. Wilde's homosexual activities, on account of which, according to Sternheim, his age condemned him both as man and artist, are not unduly stressed. Neither are they ignored. They are seen positively as one small part of the overwhelming evidence that Wilde was a giant among his contemporaries—the one man who had the courage to be himself at a time when public opinion, narrow, self-righteous and ignorant, made moral cowards of all other men. Like the Marquis d'Arcis Wilde turns his back on the conventional world, as represented by the frigid Lord Alfred Douglas and his implacable father, and finds among the social outcasts of London's all-night cafés the essential humanity which he had sought in vain elsewhere. The subsequent trial and imprisonment of Wilde are seen as the hysterically vicious acts of an age unhealthily obsessed with the word "immorality".

The problem of the individual and his relation to society is all-important for the German drama of the twentieth century, but it is possible that Sternheim's personal circumstances contributed greatly to his particular formulation of it. His conciousness of his Jewish background, and the mingled suspicion and fear with which society regards the minority groups in its midst, may well have increased the feeling of isolation common to so many modern artists. Most of his plays deal with the socially unaccepted or unacceptable—in the later phase with those who refuse to accept society. Probably only someone who has experienced acutely as a basic element of his existence the feeling of "not belonging" could present the unsympathetic picture of society we find in the early plays, or conceive the importance of the individual who has the courage to be himself, regardless of contemporary opinion, which gives such unexpected dignity to his later work.

TRANSLATIONS

1. From the heroic Annals of the Bourgeoisie.
2. The doctor examining the diseased body of the age.
3. A Pair of Knickers.
4. *Brigitte:* Yes, kiss me. Ah, but you are stifling me, and this death is bliss. Oh, your limbs are so cold—what heavenly rapture I feel! —so cold, so cold—. Oh leave me, go, your nearness threatens my life. I can breathe no longer, now leave me, God!—Ah Ulrich, Ulrich, you are squeezing me to death! (Dies. Long solemn pause.)
5. Better get out. Something's up.
6. When I published a comedy of middle-class life in 1908, all that could be seen on the German stage apart from Gerhart Hauptmann's Naturalism was the fairy-tale fiction of the old king, the young queen and the dashing page, which the Neo-Romantic writers adapted and presented in many guises. Dressed in gorgeous costumes, the characters of these plays expressed magnificent sentiments and performed sublime deeds far removed from the sphere of reality. In my play, however, a bourgeois young lady lost her knickers, and the characters talked in unadorned language of nothing but this banal matter. The world's verdict on such lack of sophistication was: Is this really art? A bourgeois pair of knickers, and five petty-minded characters who hold forth on the subject endlessly. Where was the (Ersatz) splendour they were accustomed to? Why wasn't there even any (Pseudo) Naturalism?
7. Fighting for the sake of fighting.
8. *Prince:* Are you "of the people", Thekla?
   Thekla: I am.
   Prince: My subject?

Thekla: Your subject.

Prince: Come down to me then! I've made my appearance here like a character from Shakespeare. I've taken a fancy to you, and I'm growling the order at you.

Thekla: (sighing) Shakespeare's age is past. We're living three centuries later.

9. *Thekla:* I'm very fond of my brother. His distress will be the hardest thing for me to bear.

Prince: Then I'm an intruder into peace and contentment. I tempt an angel to tell lies?

Thekla: Every breath that I've drawn since yesterday evening when I first saw you has been sinful. But a prince! A young melancholy hero! I've been singing folk-songs, in which he continually appears, for so long now, that I was head over heels in love with him before he actually came.

Prince: And does he live up to expectations?

Thekla: Completely.

Prince: That's a confession, Thekla.

Thekla: It's meant to be. Should I otherwise be talking to you at night from my bedroom window?

SELECT BIBLIOGRAPHY

(Note. There is no complete collected edition of Sternheim's works, but an almost exhaustive list of everything by him and on him, with the exception of his prose fiction, including English and American criticisms of his work, may be found in: *The Drama of German Expressionism. A German-English Bibliography,* by Claude Hill and Ralph Ley. The University of North Carolina Press, 1960. pp. 140–48.)

CARL STERNHEIM. *Aus dem bürgerlichen Heldenleben* (a selection including *Die Hose, Der Snob, 1913, Das Fossil, Bürger Schippel, Die Kassette, Tabula Rasa, Der Kandidat*). 2 vols. Berlin (Aufbau Verlag), 1947.

Lustspiele (contents: *Der Abenteurer, Perleberg, Der Nebbich, Der entfesselte Zeitgenosse, Die Schule von Uznach*). Berlin (Aufbau Verlag), 1948.

Historische Schauspiele (contents: *Das leidende Weib, Manon Lescaut, Die Marquise von Arcis, Oskar Wilde*). Berlin (Aufbau Verlag), 1948.

A Pair of Drawers (a translation of *Die Hose*) in *Transition,* 1927. Nos. 6–9.

A Place in the World (a translation of *Der Snob,* by B. Clark and W. Katzin) in *Eight European Plays.* New York, 1927.

The Mask of Virtue (a translation of *Die Marquise von Arcis,* by Ashley Dukes). London, 1935.

CAROL PETERSEN. *Carl Sternheim,* in *Expressionismus: Gestalten einer literarischen Bewegung,* edited by Hermann Friedmann and Otto Mann. Heidelberg, 1956.

ALBERT SOERGEL. *Carl Sternheim*, in *Dichtung und Dichter der Zeit. Neue Folge: Im Banne des Expressionismus.* Leipzig, 1927.

H. F. GARTEN. *Carl Sternheim*, in *Modern German Drama.* London, 1959.

OTTO MANN. *Bürger Schippel*, in *Das Deutsche Drama vom Barock zur Gegenwart*, edited by Benno von Wiese. Vol. 2. Düsseldorf, 1960.

FRANZ BLEI. *Über Wedekind, Sternheim und das Theater.* Leipzig, 1915.

ELISE DOSENHEIMER. *Das deutsche soziale Drama von Lessing bis Sternheim.* Konstanz, 1949.

FELIX BERTAUX. *Panorama de la Littérature Allemande Contemporaine.* Paris, 1928.

Georg Kaiser

Georg Kaiser

by H. F. GARTEN

Georg Kaiser was born in Magdeburg on 25 November 1878. After leaving school he entered upon a commercial career and spent three years, from 1898–1901, in Buenos Aires. Here he contracted a tropical fever which forced him to return, via Spain and Italy, to Germany. During his slow convalescence, he started writing plays. His first major success came with *Die Bürger von Calais,* in 1917. From then until 1933, he wrote untiringly, at times up to three plays a year, and became one of the most performed German playwrights. From 1921 onwards, he lived at Grünheide near Berlin. When the Nazis seized power in 1933, his plays were banned. He left Germany in 1938 and emigrated to Switzerland where he lived during the war years. He died in Ascona, on Lake Maggiore, on 4 June 1945.

THE total work of Georg Kaiser comprises more than sixty plays and two novels, besides a large number of sketches, fragments, and more than a hundred poems. He was carried to fame on the crest of the expressionist wave which swept German art and writing during and after the First World War, and he remained one of the leading dramatists until 1933, when his plays were banished from the stage. However, he continued writing untiringly, first in Germany, then as an exile in Switzerland, up to his death in 1945. His plays encompass every variety of subject and form : tragedy and comedy, social drama, history, legend, and even revue. This diversity has puzzled critics and public alike. and has laid him open to the charge of being no more than a brilliant technician of the stage, a *"Denkspieler",* who merely juggled with ideas to produce theatrically effective plays. Yet all his works bear the unmistakable stamp of his individuality; they turn, in fact, on one central idea which informs them all.

In one of his concise and self-revealing pronouncements on the art of drama Kaiser writes :

"Vielgestaltig sind die Figuren, die Träger der Vision sind... Sie würde zehn und hundert erdrücken—so müssen Scharen hinausgehen und Teile des Ganzen tragen, soviel ihre Schultern tragen. Aus allen Zonen holt sie der Anruf—kein Zeitalter, das nicht einen wichtigen und würdigen Boten lieferte... Von welcher Art ist die Vision? Es gibt nur eine : die von der Erneuerung des Menschen."[1]

This central idea, the "renewal of man" (incidentally, Kaiser never speaks of an "idea" but of a "vision"), links his work closely to the expressionist movement, from which it received its most vital impetus. It gives his writings the moral impulse which is the hall-mark of literary Expressionism. But while with most of the other Expressionists the force of this impulse shattered form and reduced language to an inarticulate stammer, Kaiser harnessed it to a rigid, almost classical form. These two principles—the driving force of expressionist zeal, on the one hand, and the rationally constructed, "cubist" form, on the other—actually merge in his plays. This antinomy is reflected in the very language of Kaiser—in the juxta-position of impassioned, rhetorical outpourings and terse, clipped dialogue. This unique language of Kaiser's, which he also uses in his narrative writings (including his private letters), is an essential ingredient of his work; it is as far removed from colloquial speech as is verse (to which it finally rose). With its repetitions, its sym-metries and climaxes, its precisely calculated dashes and exclama-tion marks, it has an intensely musical quality. However, it is not a music of half-tones and subtle shades but of glaring, white-hot passion and the violent clash of ideas. Kaiser admits of no distinc-tion between "feeling" and "thinking". For him both are one—merely different degrees of intensity. He speaks of the "sensuality of thought" and pronounces : "Denken heisst vital aufs äusserste sich gebärden."[2]

In this, and in this sense only, his plays are plays of ideas. These ideas are, however, not embodied in the realistic manner of Ibsen or Shaw. His characters are not psychologically differentiated individuals but abstractions or types—even when they bear indivi-dual names. This gives them an unreal, at the same time rigid and dynamic quality. They all act as though under a compulsion—obsessed by an idea which they carry to the point of absurdity. "Ein Drama schreiben ist einen Gedanken zu Ende denken",[3] runs one of Kaiser's axioms.

Like his language, his plays are shorn of all inessentials, all accidents of period and place. They are, in a way, bare outlines, geometrically balanced to the last detail. The dialogue moves in dialectic progression. Repeatedly, Kaiser cites Plato as a model for his dramatic technique : "Plato schreibt sein reines Ideenwerk als Dialoge nieder. Personen treten auf und sagen. Heftigere Dramen als *Symposion* und *Phaidon* sind schwer zu denken."[4] In one of his most accomplished, though lesser known plays, *Der gerettete Alkibiades,* he even enters creatively into the world of Plato and Socrates. But in his hands, it is transformed into something utterly different—an intensely personal, expressionistic drama turning on the antithesis of *"Leben"* and *"Geist"*, which bears the distinct mark of Nietzsche.

Whereas the reference to Plato applies mainly to a formal principle—the dialectic character of his dialogue—Kaiser's dependence on Nietzsche touches the very essence of his thought. This dependence is particularly manifest in his early works, several of which turn on the dualism of "Geist" and "Leben". Like Nietzsche, Kaiser stands on the side of "Leben", against the deadening "Geist". This dualism underlies such early plays as *Rektor Kleist* and *Der Geist der Antike* (both written in 1905). It recurs, on a higher plane, in his maturity, where it is fully embodied in the confrontation of Socrates and Alcibiades (in *Der gerettete Alkibiades,* 1920), and of George Sand and Musset (in *Die Flucht nach Venedig,* 1923). In the latter play, George Sand, who turns every life experience into literature, illuminates the tragic predicament of "Geist" in her last line : "Das Wort tötet das Leben."[5]

But Kaiser's indebtedness to Nietzsche reaches further. His basic concept of the "renewal of man", closely as it is connected with contemporary Expressionism, has its deeper roots in Nietzsche. It implies a total transformation of man from within, a "revaluation of all values". But while Nietzsche applies this ethical postulate only to the eminent individual, the "superman", to whom the masses are merely subservient, Kaiser fuses it with socialist ideas, extending it to each and all. He foresees a future when "fortschrittliche Einzelne werden von der Gesamtheit eingeholt. Der Berg wird zur Ebene, auf der *alle* siedeln . . . Der Mensch ist da."[6] For the Nietzschean "Übermensch" he sets the "Mensch"—a keyword throughout his work. Nevertheless, the idea of "Übermensch" haunts even those plays that turn on the renewal of society as a whole (e.g. *Die Bürger von Calais, Gas, Hölle Weg Erde,* down to *Der Soldat Tanaka* and *Das Floss der Medusa*). In every one of these, it is a single man who undergoes the transformation and sets out to impart his "vision" to his fellow-men. Indeed, the conflict between the single man and society, the inspired prophet and the dull, unhearing masses, is the central theme of all these plays. It is their basic tragic conflict.

These reflections touch on some of the main issues underlying the whole of Kaiser's work. It is now illuminating to trace these issues in a number of major plays. Such an approach is all the more appropriate in the case of Kaiser, as his work shows not so much a continuous development as a repeated restatement of two or three basic themes, running side by side and taken up alternately, sometimes almost simultaneously. Thus many plays are little more than variations on earlier works, and the detailed study of one sheds light on a whole series.

The observation that Kaiser's work has no "development" must be qualified at once. In fact, it took Kaiser an unusually long time to evolve his own unmistakable type of drama. He was nearly forty when the first performance of *Die Bürger von Calais,* in 1917, brought him his first, decisive success. But this was by no means his first play. From the beginning of the century, he had written, and partly published, a considerable number of plays, without attracting much attention. Most of these were comedies, or tragi-comedies, in the vein of Wedekind and Sternheim : caustic satires on the philistinism and moral hypocrisy of the petit-bourgeois. But their themes—the impact of sudden wealth, or the antinomy of "life" and "mind"—recur in his mature works. Two of these early plays, *Die jüdische Witwe* (1911) and *König Hahnrei* (1913), turn on legendary subjects—the stories of Judith and of Tristan and Isolde respectively, treating them from an ironic angle and in the light of modern psychology.

With *Die Bürger von Calais,* we stand on new ground. Published in 1914, the play was written on the eve of the First World War, anticipating some of its main issues and the spiritual revolution that followed it. When it was performed at the height of the war, it was at once acclaimed as a manifesto of peace and reconciliation against militarism, and as a supreme example of expressionist drama. Kaiser drew his inspiration from Froissart's chronicle and the famous sculpture of Rodin. But he turned to his own purpose the story of the six burghers who offered their lives for the preservation of the city.

Calais is besieged by the English, without hope of relief. The King of England sends a messenger announcing that "the city will be tumbled into the port" unless six chosen citizens appear in his camp next morning, with ropes around their necks, to hand him the keys of the town. A violent dispute arises. Duguesclin, the town commander, exhorts the crowd to fight to the last man, to save the honour of France. Against him, Eustache de Saint-Pierre, a citizen, proposes to accept the enemy's terms, in order to save the newly built harbour : "Euer grösstes Werk wird Eure tiefste Pflicht. Ihr müsst es schützen—mit allen Sinnen—mit allen Taten."[7] In this controversy, two ethical concepts are clearly opposed : the "old" concept of death for glory, and the "new" one of life for the sake of constructive work. Eustache prevails and offers himself as the first hostage. He is promptly followed by others—but instead of six, seven come forward (as two brothers apply simultaneously). Since there is one too many, one is requested to withdraw. At this point, Kaiser's particular dialectics set in. Eustache, who clearly emerges as the spiritual leader, at first proposes to draw lots. However, realizing that this only confuses the issue, he frustrates the plan by putting only blue balls into the bowl. He gives them one more night to reach a decision : at dawn, each shall set out to the market place. He who arrives last shall be free to live. In the morning, all arrive well before the time—only Eustache is missing. The crowd, enraged at his apparent cowardice, sets off to drag him from his house, when his aged father appears, preceded by a bier with the body of Eustache : he has killed himself during the night, welding the others, by this self-immolation, into a true community. Over his body, his blind father, ecstatically, pronounces the full significance of this deed : "Schreitet hinaus—in das Licht—aus dieser Nacht. Die hohe Helle ist angebrochen—das Dunkel ist verstreut... Ich habe den neuen Menschen gesehen—in dieser Nacht ist er geboren!"[8] Here, for the first time in Kaiser's work, the message of the "new man" rings out with full force. In the end, a messenger arrives, announcing that the lives of the six shall be spared as a son has been born to the English king. Eustache remains the only victim. His bier is raised high on the church steps while above it, over the cathedral porch, a relief of the Resurrection is lit by the first rays of the sun. The parallel to the expiatory death of Christ is clearly established—a parallel that was to recur at the culminating point of many a play of Kaiser's.

With regard to form, Kaiser reached full mastership in *Die Bürger von Calais*. The drama has nothing in common with the traditional kind of historical play. No attempt is made at reproducing a given period and setting. The subject serves merely as a parable to convey a timeless message. The language is fully expressionist, burning with exalted eloquence. The very grouping and gestures of the characters, as prescribed in the stage-directions, have the statuesque nobility of Gothic sculpture. The rich use of light and sound effects, and the calculated symmetry of speech and movement, give the drama the quality of a solemn ritual. Perhaps in no other work did Kaiser attain this perfection of form, and this artistic integrity. *Die Bürger von Calais* stands as a monumental arch at the beginning of his mature work.

The call for the "renewal of man" gains full significance where, stripped of any historical guise, it is embodied in present-day characters and applied to present-day social issues. This is the case in a long line of plays, written mainly between 1917 and 1923, at the height of the expressionist movement, vividly reflecting the social and spiritual upheaval wrought by the German revolution. Their scene of action is the world of today, factory, office, bank, prison; their characters : workers, clerks, policemen, judges, commissars—the functionaries and victims of a mechanized world, who have themselves become automatons. "Ich bin Automat, der die vorhandenen Gesetze anwendet",[9] says the lawyer in *Hölle Weg*

Erde. More deadening than the soulless apparatus of State, machine, and money is the routine of everyday life. "Man liegt tief gebettet. So ein Leben schaufelt mächtig. Berge sind auf einen getürmt!"[10] the bank clerk cries in *Von morgens bis mitternachts.*

This is the world from which "renewed man" sets out on his quest. The most trifling incident may cause his transformation : the smaller the cause, the more colourless the man, the greater the impact. Frequently his "setting-out" (*Aufbruch*) is marked by some legal offence, a fraud or even a murder. For the others, he becomes an outlaw, a man possessed—but he moves on a plane where the laws of society do not apply. The clash between his newly gained vision and society forms the nucleus of most of Kaiser's plays. This clash can take on two distinct forms : either, the "new man" seeks fulfilment for himself, outside and against society, or he tries to impose his vision on society. Both types are clearly outlined in Kaiser's work.

The foremost example of the first type is *Von morgens bis mitternachts,* probably Kaiser's most famous play (first performed in 1917, a few months after *Die Bürger von Calais*). Here an ordinary bank clerk, called simply the Cashier, acting on a sudden impulse, absconds with a large sum of money, abandoning his family and his daily routine. In the space of a single day, he strives to make up for a lifetime of frustration. After visiting a dance hall and a bicycle race, he ends up at a Salvation Army meeting. He realizes that his quest has been in vain : "Mit keinem Geld aus allen Bankkassen der Welt kann man sich irgendwas von Wert kaufen ... Das Geld verschlechtert den Wert. Das Geld verhüllt das Echte—das Geld ist der armseligste Schwindel unter allem Betrug!"[11] He scatters his bank-notes to the crowd and shoots himself.

Structurally, the play is a *"Stationen-drama"* : the action unfolds in a loose sequence of scenes, representing stages on the protagonist's way, while the other characters merely fill in the background. This pattern, typical of many expressionist plays, has its origin in the medieval Passion Play; its immediate model, within modern drama, is Strindberg's *To Damascus*. But while with Strindberg the religious connotations—the stations of the Cross—are still clearly felt, Kaiser's play moves exclusively on a worldly plane. The Cashier's quest is not for spiritual redemption but for the full exploration of "life". Yet even here the analogy to the Passion is implied : at the end, the Cashier "sinks with outspread arms against the cross sewn on the curtain", uttering with his last breath the words "Ecce—homo". Thus the play is precariously balanced between travesty and tragedy.

Von morgens bis mitternachts sets the pattern for several of

Kaiser's plays. The nearest variant is *Kanzlist Krehler* (1922). But here the central character—a minor clerk—experiences his metamorphosis within the four walls of his home Here, too, the sudden release from a humdrum existence leads to mental derangement and, finally, suicide.

The theme assumes a new dimension in *Nebeneinander* (1923). For here the "renewal", instead of being self-centred, implies the awakening of a sense of responsibility towards others. A nondescript pawnbroker comes across an undelivered letter, from which he gathers that the young girl it is addressed to is about to kill herself. So he "sets out" to save the life of this complete stranger. His search meets with indifference and derision. His appeal to the police falls on deaf ears: "Es wird alles ohne Sinn, wenn nicht alles jederzeit bereit ist, um einem einzigen Menschen das Leben zu retten!!!"[12] In the end, he returns to his pawnshop, a ruined man, and turns on the gas-tap. But his ordeal has not been in vain; he dies with "den Gewinn des wunderbarsten Gefühls: für einen fremden Menschen sich auf den Weg gemacht zu haben!"[13]

This play, ironically subtitled *Volksstück 1923,* is set against the background of the German post-war inflation, with its harsh contrasts of rich and poor. The irony is heightened through the parallel plot: the girl, unaware of the tragedy she has set in motion, overcomes her despair and finds happiness in a petit-bourgeois idyl. The harsh juxtaposition (*"nebeneinander"*) of these actions stresses the isolation of modern man in an unfeeling world.

The theme of "new man" finds its most forceful expression in a sequence of three plays which stand at the centre of Kaiser's work: *Die Koralle* (1917), *Gas I* (1918), and *Gas II* (1920). Though probably not conceived as a trilogy from the outset, these three plays form a coherent sequence ranging over three (or, to be precise, four) generations and encompassing, in bare outline, the evolution of industrial society. At the same time, they show a development from purely individual issues to those embracing the whole of mankind. *Die Koralle* has as its central character the *Milliardär*—a captain of industry who has ruthlessly worked his way to the top of the social ladder, acquiring immeasurable wealth. To assuage his conscience, he offers material aid to anybody seeking help in his office. In his frantic quest for peace of mind, he seeks to change places with his secretary (who is also his double): "In wen gehe ich unter—und verliere diese Angst und tobenden Aufruhr?!—Wer hat ein Leben—glatt und gut—für meines?!!"[14] With this single aim in mind, he shoots his secretary, to acquire, by a mental *tour de force*, the memories of a happy childhood. For this crime, he pays with his life. But he has gained a deeper happiness than he has ever known : "Ich habe das Paradies, das hinter uns liegt, wieder erreicht. Ich bin durch seine Pforte mit einem Gewalt-streich . . . geschritten."[15]

In *Die Koralle,* spiritual renewal is still attained by a single individual who breaks away from his former self and finds peace in escape. *Gas* shifts the issue on to the social plane. Its protagonist is the "millionaire's son", who, in the preceding play, had renounced his father's wealth and now runs the factory on the basis of equal shares for all. The factory produces "gas"—the symbol of the machine age. Against all rational calculations, an explosion shatters the works. Profoundly shaken by this event, the millionaire's son refuses to rebuild the plant and deliver man once more to the tyranny of the machine. Instead, he proposes to settle the workers on the land in order to restore man to his pristine wholeness. At a workers' meeting, his call rings out emphatically : "Menschen in Einheit und Fülle seid ihr morgen! . . . Ihr seid entlassen aus Fron und Gewinn!—Siedler mit kleinstem Anspruch —und letzter Entlohnung :—Menschen! !"[16] However, he is opposed by the Engineer, who urges the workers to rebuild the factory and resume work, even at the price of new explosions.

This fourth act, with its dialectic clash of ideas, its alternation of impassioned oratory and choral interjections, represents a climax of Kaiser's dramatic art and of expressionist drama in general. The Engineer prevails, and the workers unite in the single cry : "Gas ! ! !" The prophet has failed. Fatally wounded in a workers' riot, he sets his hope on a distant future when his vision of man will come true : "War er nicht nahe zu mir—kann er verlöschen— muss er jetzt nicht wieder und wieder kommen, wenn einer ihn einmal erblickte? ! . . . Soll ich noch zweifeln? ! !"[17] His doubts are answered by his daughter in the last line of the play : "Ich will ihn gebären!"[18]

Gas II, written two years later, carries the argument to its con-clusion. The automation of life is complete, men are reduced to "blue and yellow figures", tending the machines. The State has taken over the plant, and "gas" is produced for war. Owing to a decline in output, the war is lost, and the workers take over. Among them is the "millionaire-worker"—in fact, the grandson promised at the end of Part I. He exhorts his fellow-workers to renounce the production of gas and unite with the enemy in an all-embracing brotherhood of man. However, the enemy disregards the call and seizes the plant, forcing the workers to produce gas for his benefit. The Great-Engineer proposes to destroy the enemy with a poison-gas bomb he has invented. But the millionaire-worker objects : not through violence but by passive submission can true freedom be gained. His call re-echoes the Christian message : "The

Kingdom is not of this world!" Once again, mankind stands at the cross-roads. The workers decide for poison-gas, that is, for force. Whereupon the millionaire-worker offers to throw the bomb himself, destroying both friend and enemy. The curtain falls on a scene of total annihilation.

In this play, Kaiser's technique of condensation and abstraction reaches a *non plus ultra*. Although dealing with human issues at large, it is drained of all life-blood : the characters are reduced to mere ciphers, representing abstract ideas.

As in nearly all of Kaiser's social dramas, the end is steeped in deepest gloom. Mankind refuses to heed the call of its prophet, and the herald of "new man" dies a martyr to his creed. Only once does he succeed in realizing his vision : in *Hölle Weg Erde* (1919), written between the two parts of *Gas*. Here a man has attempted murder to save a friend in need. He is thrown into prison, but his persistent appeal gradually changes the hearts of men. From a single case, the action broadens into a general issue. The collective guilt of society is established, and each and all confess to their share in it. The prison-gates are thrown open, and convicts and guards alike pour out in an ever growing procession. Finally, the call of the prophet rings out across the sun-lit plain : "Die Erde klingt!!—Euer Blut braust—denn ihr seid die Erde!!"[19] The three words of the title correspond to the three parts of the play, each representing a stage in the social and moral evolution. "*Hölle*" stands for the present stage of society, with its rigid laws based on exploitation and egotism; "*Weg*" depicts the awakening of a sense of social responsibility; while "*Erde*" denotes the ultimate goal— the full realization of the ideal. Once again, the parallel with the Christian concept is evident—except that Kaiser substitutes for the transcendental Heaven of orthodox faith an earthly paradise. The alternation, within a single year, of fervent optimism with bleak pessimism reflects the emotional extremes which characterized the immediate post-war years in Germany.

In his later work, Kaiser repeatedly took up the theme of social renewal. However, there was a marked change in his style. Following the general trend of German drama, Kaiser abandoned the abstract constructions of his expressionist period. His language, too, drew closer to normal usage though it still retained its unmistakable idiosyncrasies. Yet it would be wrong to claim that he fell in with the *Neue Sachlichkeit* of the later '20's. In fact, Kaiser was the only one to maintain, to his very end, the moral fervour of Expressionism. But he now clothed it in more realistic fables, with well-defined, individualized characters. Instances of this type of drama are *Lederköpfe* (1928), an anti-militaristic play based on a story by Herodotus, and *Mississippi* (1930), where a community of

American farmers, inspired by early Christian ideals, rise against New Orleans, in their eyes the city of Mammon. During his exile, roused by the Second World War and the crimes of Nazi Germany, Kaiser wrote two poignant plays denouncing war—*Der Soldat Tanaka* (1940), in which a humble Japanese soldier has his eyes opened to the evils of militarism, and *Das Floss der Medusa* (1943), the tragedy of a group of children adrift in a lifeboat in mid-ocean. The eldest of them, a boy of twelve, grasps for the first time the full import of the commandment: "Thou shalt not kill!" He is the last, and the youngest, of the long line of prophets who are roused to a new concept of human values, and die for it.

At the close of *Mississippi,* the leader of the farmers, who have fought, and lost, their battle against the power of money, clasps his wife in the swirling floods of the river : "Du bist aufgebrochen aus allen Scharen, die sich nicht überreden lassen—allein. Ist es nicht viel? Kann mehr gewonnen werden?"[20] This end—the union of two lovers in the face of a hostile world—points to a type of play which occupies a prominent place in Kaiser's work. Alternating with his social dramas, there runs a line of plays of a very different kind. Confined to a small set of characters, they centre on the passionate union of two lovers. Essentially, it is always the same pair. Their love is not psychologically motivated; it is absolute, unconditional, and prepared to defy any intrusion from the outside world, even at the price of a crime. Curiously, these plays, whether derived from history or anecdote, or freely invented, are almost without exception set in France. In their outward form, they follow the pattern of the conventional "well-made" play, with its strict observance of the classical unities. But their thought-content is unmistakably Kaiser's own.

Among the earliest instances of this type of play are *Frauenopfer* and *Der Brand im Opernhaus,* both first performed in 1918, at the peak of Kaiser's expressionist phase. The title of the first could apply to any of them : usually it is a woman's self-sacrifice that raises a man to a higher plane of existence. The most perfect example is *Oktobertag,* of 1928. Here a young girl in a French provincial town, who is found to be pregnant but obstinately refuses to name the father of her child, utters during childbirth the name of an officer. The officer, a lieutenant in a crack Paris regiment, is summoned by her guardian, and recalls having spent a few hours, between two trains, in the town, but firmly denies ever having seen the girl. Yet, she calmly insists that he was her lover for one night. The two contradictory statements seem irreconcilable. Step by step, however, it emerges that she crossed his path three times that day and fell deeply in love with him without his knowledge. The strength of her conviction gradually draws him under her spell, and he accepts the child as his own. When the real father is discovered to be a butcher's boy who, unrecognized by the girl, had forced his way into her room that night, the officer kills him without a moment's hesitation. Completely disregarding the consequences of his deed, he embraces the girl with the words: "We can live!"

This action, balanced as it were on a razor's edge, leads into the very centre of Kaiser's thought. It turns on a clash of dream and reality, or, in other words, of subjective and objective truth. In this clash, the dream proves stronger than reality. The girl, through the intensity of her feelings, ignores all material evidence and succeeds in drawing the man into her dream world. Whoever dares to intrude upon their "mystic union", is ruthlessly destroyed.

This sets the pattern for a whole series of plays, leading up to the most extreme case, *Rosamunde Floris* (1940). Here the heroine commits no less than four murders, including that of her own child, to guard the secret of her love. Yet she acts with the conviction of complete innocence and purity. The night before her execution, she addresses her distant lover in a long monologue: "Ich werde rein sein, denn mich wäscht mein Blut rein. Es säubert, da es ausfliesst, das Gefäss, das ich bin—gefüllt mit Liebe—wie die Liebe alles ist—und das Vollkommene so selten, dass man es heilig hüten muss..."[21]

In this insistence on the prevalence of feeling over reality, Kaiser shows a close affinity to Kleist—the only German dramatist, besides Büchner, whom he acknowledged as his equal. What has been said of the characters of Kleist is equally true of Kaiser's: "They experience illuminations of consciousness which blind them to the realities of worldly circumstance. The entire drama consists in their stubborn adherence to the truth of vision. At the last their intense reveries prove stronger than material fact. It is not they who surrender but the world. Reality comes full turn and enters into the fabric of their dreams."*

At this deepest level, there is a close connection between those plays centring on the union of two lovers and those of individual or social renewal. In either case, there is a complete rupture with the accepted values of society for the sake of spiritual regeneration; except that in the first case, this regeneration is brought about by an intense experience of love uniting two beings and isolating them from the rest of mankind. In this form, and in this form only, Kaiser's vision of "Erneuerung" is fully realized. In his later work, this type of play predominates. It is as though the moral fervour, which had spent itself in vain against the hard facts of reality, shifted from the social plane to the innermost regions of the human

* George Steiner, *The Death of Tragedy*, pp. 222–23.

heart. The Absolute, unattainable in the outside world, can be realized only in the intimate sphere of a perfect love.

Between 1933 and 1938, when Kaiser was living in enforced isolation in Germany, his work outlawed, he wrote a whole series of "love dramas", such as *Adrienne Ambrossat, Der Gärtner von Toulouse, Alain und Elise, Rosamunde Floris.* All of these centre on the intense communion between two lovers who, through suffering and sacrifice, attain to a higher level of existence. It is no mere accident that several of these plays open in a hot-house—the scenic symbol of the magic isolation of the lovers in a chill and alien world.

To these plays must be added the two novels Kaiser wrote in the 1930's, *Es ist genug* and *Villa Aurea.* They are virtually dramatic-lyrical monologues—the second a single fictitious letter addressed to the beloved. Both deal with the passionate obsession of a man who, for the sake of his love, renounces his past, his name, indeed, his very identity, to enter into a new life. *Es ist genug* turns on the incestuous love of a man for his daughter, in whom he sees his dead wife reborn. He approaches her under an assumed name but, realizing that he is about to be entangled in unforgivable guilt and to destroy her life, removes himself for ever from her sight. In *Villa Aurea,* a Russian officer of the First World War, who survives defeat, assumes the identity of a common soldier, unable to face disgrace in the eyes of his betrothed. In the course of his wanderings through Europe, he crosses her way several times, without daring to reveal himself. In both cases, the hero finally shields the purity of his love from contamination. "Der Traum ist wichtiger als die Wirklichkeit" :[22] this sentence from *Es ist genug* could stand as a motto for many of Kaiser's works.

Kaiser's withdrawal from reality reaches its ultimate stage in the three "Greek plays" he wrote, in a single creative outburst, during the winter of 1943-44 in Switzerland, *Zweimal Amphitryon, Pygmalion,* and *Bellerophon.* In these plays, his language rises for the first time to verse. Kaiser's approach to ancient Greece has nothing in common with classical tradition. The themes of these plays re-echo, in mythological and poetic terms, the main themes of his entire work. In each of them, a deity—Zeus, Athene, and Apollo respectively—singles out a mortal being, to raise him, or her, above the rest. For the first time, superhuman powers intervene in the conflicts of men; but the conflicts are essentially the same as before. In the first play, Amphitryon, the general, loses his wife Alkmene to Zeus because he places military glory above love; in the end, he is condemned by Zeus to walk the earth, atoning for his vain ambition. *Pygmalion* is the tragedy of the artist who finds himself alone with his creative vision, his work debased by contact with a hostile world. *Bellerophon* centres on a pure youth, struggling in the snares of the world, until he is finally redeemed by Apollo, his guardian-god, and transformed into a star. After its completion, Kaiser wrote in a letter: "Yesterday I finished the third Hellenic play. *Bellerophon*. My swan-song. I have transferred myself among the stars."

Here, the author's identification of himself with his creation is manifest. His last three plays are no longer dramas in the strict sense but lyrical outbursts, personal confessions of a tortured mind. They thus form the link between his dramatic work and the sequence of more than a hundred poems he wrote in the last few months of his life. In these poems, cast in a strict metrical form reminiscent of Stefan George, Kaiser, who had hidden himself throughout his life behind the countless masks of his characters, stands at last fully revealed. Outcries of a tormented soul which has seen its vision scorned by a callous world, they burn with an unparalleled bitterness. Several of these poems invoke the Passion of Christ and His death on the Cross. One of them is entitled, *Die grosse Kreuzigung* (The Great Crucifixion):

> Genug—genug. Nicht mehr ist zu ertragen.
> Mehr nicht—mehr nicht. Der Beize ist genug,
> die mir die tiefen Wunden brennend schlagen.
> Es ist kein Segen mehr—es ist ein Fluch.
>
> Lass' doch in Dunkelkälte mich eingehen,
> wohin vom Schein der Widerschein nicht dringt.
> Lass' mich nicht aufrecht solchem Angriff stehen,
> der Riesen-Riesen in die Kniee zwingt.
>
> Dem Schrei ist Antwort heisseres Entzünden
> und das Erbarmen weicht noch weiter weit.
> Mehr denn. Triff mich in meinen tiefsten Gründen.
> Verbrenn' mich—glüh' mich aus. Ich bin bereit.[23]

The final evaluation of Georg Kaiser is still in the balance. Those who expected his work to be revived on a large scale after the end of the Third Reich found themselves disappointed. Some of his plays, it is true, have appeared here and there on the post-war stage in Germany, but they are usually his less significant, satirical comedies. His insistence on a "message", his demand for a spiritual renewal of man, as well as the white-hot glare of his diction run counter to the main trends of the theatre today. His work as a whole still awaits rehabilitation.

TRANSLATIONS

1. Manifold are the characters who carry the vision. It would crush ten or a hundred—so multitudes must go forth and carry parts of the whole, as much as their shoulders can carry. From every zone the summons brings them—no age fails to supply a significant and worthy messenger . . . What kind of vision is it? There is but one: the renewal of man.

2. Thinking means living with the utmost vitality.

3. To write a drama is to follow a thought to its conclusion.

4. Plato writes his work of pure ideas in the form of dialogues. Characters enter and speak. More violent dramas than *Symposion* and *Phaidon* can hardly be imagined.

5. Words kill life.

6. The masses draw level with the individuals who have gone ahead. The mountain turns into a plateau where all settle . . . Man has arrived.

7. Your greatest work becomes your first responsibility. You must protect it—with all your thoughts—with all your deeds.

8. Go out—into the light—from this night. The great day has dawned—darkness is dispelled! . . . I have seen the New Man—in this night he was born!

9. I am an automaton who employs the existing laws.

10. We lie deeply buried. A life like this digs us in thoroughly. Mountains are piled upon us!

11. You can buy nothing worth having, even with all the money from all the banks in the world . . . Money lowers the value. Money conceals what is genuine—money is the sorriest fraud of all!

12. It all becomes meaningless unless all are prepared at any moment to save one single life!

13. The gain of the most wonderful sensation: to have set out for the sake of a stranger.

14. In whom can I sink myself and lose this terror and this raging tumult? Who has a life, calm and good, to give for mine?

15. I have regained the paradise we have left behind us. I have stepped through its gate with an act of violence.

16. Tomorrow you will be human beings, in all their wholeness and fullness. You are dismissed from slavery and gain—settlers with the simplest needs and highest rewards—men!

17. Was he not close to me—can he go out like a light—must he not return again and again, now that one man has seen him? . . . Must I doubt any longer?

18. I shall give birth to him.

19. The Earth resounds! Your blood surges—for you are the Earth!

20. Out of all the multitudes who cannot be persuaded you have set out—you alone. Isn't this a great deal? Can more be gained?

21. I shall be pure, for my blood washes me pure. Flowing out, it cleanses the vessel I am—filled with love—as love is everything—and perfection is so rare that it must be guarded as something sacred.

22. Dream is more important than reality.

23.   Enough—enough. More cannot be endured.
No more—no more. Enough of burning pain
which my deep wounds strike into me.
It is no longer a blessing—it is a curse.

Let me enter the cold dark
where no glimmer of light penetrates.
Let me not stand up to such assault,
which forces giants to their knees.

My cry is answered by fiercer burning
and mercy recedes even further away.
More then. Strike me in my innermost depths.
Burn me—anneal me. I am ready.

SELECT BIBLIOGRAPHY

Most of Georg Kaiser's plays up to 1933 were published by Kiepenheuer (Potsdam) or Die Schmiede (Berlin). A collected edition, started in 1928, did not go beyond three volumes, containing eleven plays. Some of the plays written after 1933 were published by Querido (Amsterdam, 1938–39) and Oprecht (Zürich, 1940); the three *Griechische Dramen* by Artemis (Zürich, 1948). The rest are available only in typescript (Felix Bloch Erben, Berlin).

A collected edition, planned by Kiepenheuer & Witsch (Cologne), has so far not materialized.

ENGLISH TRANSLATIONS

From Morn to Midnight. Tr. by Ashley Dukes (London, 1920, and New York, 1922).
Gas. Tr. by Hermann Scheffauer (London and Boston, 1924).
Fire in the Opera House. Tr. by W. Katzin (In: *Eight European Plays*, New York, 1927).
The Phantom Lover (Oktobertag). Tr. by H. Bernstein and A. E. Mayer (New York, 1928).
The Coral Gas I and *II.* (In: *Twenty-five Modern Plays*, New York and London, 1931).
Vera or A Villa in Sicily (Villa Aurea). (London and New York, 1931).
The Raft of the Medusa. Tr. by H. F. Garten and E. Sprigge (unpubl.).
The Protagonist. Tr. by H. R. Garten (In *The Tulane Drama Review*, Vol. 5, No. 2. New Orleans, 1960).

BOOKS ON KAISER

DIEBOLD, BERNHARD. *Der Denkspieler Georg Kaiser.* Frankfurt a. M., 1924.
FREYHAN, MAX. *Georg Kaisers Werk.* Berlin, 1926.

LEWIN, LUDWIG. *Die Jagd nach dem Erlebnis. Ein Buch über Georg Kaiser.* Berlin, 1926.

KOENIGSGARTEN, HUGO F. *Georg Kaiser.* Potsdam, 1928.

LINICK, L. M. *Der Subjektivismus im Werke Georg Kaisers.* Strasbourg, 1938.

FIVIAN, E. A. *Georg Kaiser und seine Stellung im Expressionismus.* Munich, 1946.

KENWORTHY, BRYAN J. *Georg Kaiser.* Oxford, 1957.

PAULSEN, WOLFGANG. *Georg Kaiser. Die Perspektiven seines Werkes.* Tübingen, 1960.

Robert Walser

Robert Walser

by H. M. WAIDSON

Robert Walser was born on 15 April 1878 at Biel, where his father was proprietor of a stationery and toy shop. He had seven brothers and sisters, of whom one, Karl Walser (1877–1943), became a well-known painter. On leaving school in 1892, Robert Walser was employed at a local bank, but soon gave up this work and took a succession of posts, frequently as a clerical worker, interrupted by periods when he undertook long walks and gave himself to writing. He published individual poems and wrote some short verse dramas before *Fritz Kochers Aufsätze* was published by the Insel Verlag in 1904. For much of the time from 1905 to 1913 Robert Walser lived with his brother Karl in Berlin, where apart from prose sketches he wrote the novels *Geschwister Tanner* (1907), *Der Gehülfe* (1908) and *Jakob von Gunten* (1909), which were published by the Verlag Bruno Cassirer. His stay in Berlin was terminated by a personal crisis. He returned to Switzerland, but found the struggle to devote himself to writing continuingly difficult. The manuscript of a novel *Theodor* was lost when sent to a publisher. In 1929 Walser agreed to undergo treatment at a mental hospital in Berne, and in 1933 he transferred to the hospital at Herisau. His life during these later years is described by Carl Seelig in his *Wanderungen mit Robert Walser*. Walser died on 25 December 1956 during the course of an afternoon walk.

ROBERT WALSER'S first prose publication, *Fritz Kochers Aufsätze* (1904), anticipates his later work in its themes and presentation. It is true that here there is a tenuous framework, which the later collections of prose sketches do not have; Fritz Kocher, a boy who died shortly after leaving school, has left behind him a collection of school-essays which the editor wishes to publish. The essays are on subjects such as "Man", "Autumn" or "Friendship", themes set by the teacher and developed by the pupil into delicate arabesques that characterize them unmistakably as the work of Walser. A theme is presented with simplicity, then diverted by a small touch into satire, or less frequently into a direct expression of the writer's sensibility of heart. There is the vision of the writer and artist as representing man in his noblest state, the admission of a secret enthusiasm for art, praise of the possession of a sensitive temperament, a determination to live intensely only for the passing moment, an appreciation of the joys of friendship, descriptions of autumn and winter, contrasts between poverty and wealth, indecision about a future career, descriptions of Christmas or a fairground, and an invocation of the spirit of music. Then the fiction is tacitly dropped, and there follows a series of descriptions of the problems of a clerical worker; the essays concern someone who has now left school and who between the age of eighteen and twenty-four is making wry discoveries about the world of business. A new framework is now devised; the author brings to the reader's notice "leaves from the notebook of a painter". Here is an early indication of the relationship between Robert Walser and his elder brother Karl. The painter has been living in poverty, finds the patronage and affection of a wealthy lady, later tires of this protected life and sets off once more on his travels. "Why is it that artists can find no rest?" he asks himself. The volume concludes with an essay on "Der Wald", which is more rhapsodic in tone than the earlier ones. The author remains dissatisfied with his attempt:

Über etwas Schönes exakt und bestimmt schreiben, ist schwer. Gedanken fliegen um das Schöne wie trunkene Schmetterlinge, ohne zum Ziel und festen Punkt zu kommen.[1]

In this image one senses the seriousness with which Walser approached his writing, for all the self-deprecating gestures he often made, and one senses too the tension that he may well have felt between his volatile-impressionistic imagination and the desire to control his themes within a firm formal structure. Here was a problem which he rarely resolved successfully, and preoccupation with which seems to have caused him to express himself, apart from the novels, in a series of essays and short stories which elaborate, sometimes repetitively, themes many of which are foreshadowed in *Fritz Kochers Aufsätze*. The problem is indicated again in *Die Geliebte*, from *Die Rose* (1925), Walser's last publication before his writing ceased: "Dich binden, Macht des Geistes, wem gelänge das?"[2]

The precision of detail and lightness of touch with which Walser writes may be illustrated most simply by reproducing one of Fritz Kocher's essays. Here, then, is *Unsere Stadt*:

Unsere Stadt ist eigentlich mehr ein großer schöner Garten als eine Stadt. Die Straßen sind Gartenwege. Sie sehen so sauber und wie mit feinem Sand bestreut aus. Über den Dächern der Stadt erhebt sich der Berg mit seinen dunklen Tannen und mit seinem grünen Laub. Wir haben die prächtigsten Anlagen, unter anderem eine Allee, die von Napoleon herstammen soll. Ich glaube zwar nicht, daß er mit eigener Hand die Bäume gesetzt hat, dazu war er doch wohl zu stolz, zu großmächtig. Im Sommer geben die breiten alten Kastanien einen herrlichen erquickenden Schatten. An Sommerabenden sieht man die Bewohner der Stadt, welche spazieren mögen, in dieser Allee auf und ab wandeln. Die Damen nehmen sich in ihren hellfarbigen Kleidern besonders schön aus. Auf dem abenddunklen See wird dann mit Lust gegondelt. Der See gehört zu unserer Stadt wie die Kirche, oder wie das Lustschloß eines Fürsten zu einer Residenz in Monarchien. Ohne den See wäre unsere Stadt nicht unsere Stadt, ja, man würde sie nicht wiedererkennen. Unsere Kirche, die protestantische, liegt auf einer hochgelegenen Plattform, die mit zwei wunderbar schönen, großen Kastanienbäumen geziert ist. Die Fenster der Kirche sind mit den feurigsten Farben bemalt, was ihr ein märchenhaftes Aussehen gibt. Oft ertönt der lieblichste vielstimmige Gesang aus ihr. Ich stehe gern draußen, wenn drinnen gesungen wird. Die Frauen singen am schönsten. Unser Rathaus ist würdig, und sein großer Saal dient zu Bällen und sonstigen Anlässen. Wir haben sogar ein Theater. Alle Winter besuchen uns auf zwei Monate fremde Schauspieler, welche sehr feine Manieren haben, ein sehr feines Deutsch sprechen und Zylinder auf den Köpfen tragen. Ich freue mich immer, wenn sie kommen, und helfe unsern Bürgern nicht mit, wenn sie verächtlich von dem "Pack" reden. Es kann sein, dass sie ihre Schulden nicht bezahlen, dass sie frech sind, dass sie sich betrinken, dass sie aus schlechten Familien herstammen, aber wofür sind sie Künstler? Einem Künstler sieht man großmütig dergleichen durch die Finger. Sie spielen auch ganz herrlich. Ich habe die "Räuber" gesehen. Es ist ein wundervolles Theaterstück, voll Feuer und Schönheiten. Kann man sich auf eine feinere und edlere Weise amüsieren, als, indem man das Theater besucht? Große Städte gehen uns ja in dieser Hinsicht mit dem besten Beispiel voran.—Unsere Stadt hat viel Industrie, das kommt, weil sie Fabriken hat. Fabriken und ihre Umgebung sehen unschön aus. Da ist die Luft schwarz und dick, und ich begreife nicht, warum man sich mit so unsauberen Dingen abgeben kann. Ich bekümmere mich nicht, was in den Fabriken gemacht wird. Ich weiß nur, daß alle armen Leute in der Fabrik arbeiten, vielleicht zur Strafe, daß sie so arm sind. Wir haben hübsche Straßen, und überall blicken grüne Bäume zwischen den Häusern hervor. Wenn es regnet, sind die Straßen recht schmutzig. Bei uns wird wenig für die Straßen getan. Vater sagt das. Schade, daß unser Haus keinen Garten hat. Wir wohnen im ersten Stock. Unsere Wohnung ist schön, aber es sollte ein Garten dazu gehören. Mama klagt oft deshalb. Der alte Stadtteil ist mir am liebsten. Ich schlendere gern in den alten Gässchen, Gewölben und Gängen. Auch unterirdische Gänge haben wir. Im ganzen : wir haben eine sehr hübsche Stadt.[3]

The sketch flows in one paragraph, its sentences being short and often simple. It can be imagined as an exercise, where the thought pours out in a succession of impressions which are linked together by association, not by argument. The panorama moves from one section of the view to another, description of the physical surroundings being interrupted by factors such as the singing in church, the visits of the actors and the comments from father and mother. The frequent use of "schön", "hübsch" and "fein" can indicate an ironical sense of distance from the objects described; elsewhere Walser sometimes uses diminutives for similar effect. One senses the conflict of two worlds. Citizens like Fritz' parents are proud of the orderly world of tree-clad streets, and of the town's other amenities—church, chestnut-trees, lake and so on. Napoleon is the remote, patriarchal provider of an avenue of trees, associated with the burghers and their "dignified" town hall. Opposed to the securely established citizens are the actors and industrial workers. The actors, being artists, are not to be measured by ordinary, civic standards. They are the wanderers who do not share the stability of the settled burgher. The industrial poor are for the most part unseen and out of mind, and Fritz Kocher reflects and parodies the general attitude of the middle-class section of the inhabitants. There is no narrative tension in this sketch; the effect depends upon the unity of mood and style which is achieved. There are hints here of the inconsequentiality that at times becomes tiresome in some of the later sketches. No doubt *Unsere Stadt* is less memorable than some others of the short works, but it is recognizably Walser's work.

The short sketch, occasionally expanded into a short story, is the literary form which accompanied Walser throughout the course of his life as a writer. But although it is through this briefer form that Walser's work is likely to be introduced to readers, the present essay wishes to concern itself mainly with the author's longer works. *Der Spaziergang* (1917), of novelle length, has much in common with the shorter works. Walking is a frequent theme in Walser's writing, and is expressed here with a vigour and enthusiasm that have made this work one of his best known writings. The narrator's principal business in the town which he visits is to have lunch with a patroness, to try on a suit at a tailor's, and to convince an income-tax official that, as a poorly paid writer, he is entitled to the lowest possible assessment. These encounters are expressed as a series of speeches which are themselves sketches in miniature— Frau Aebi's comic encouragement to the protagonist to do justice to her food; his indignation about his suit and the tailor's equally indignant reply; his justification to the tax official of his way of life as a poor but independent writer. In anticipation of these central points of the outward action the protagonist describes with playful zest the figures whom he meets on the first part of the walk, the professor, the bookseller, the bank-official, the woman who, he imagines, was once an actress, a girl whose singing is heard from an open window, and a number of others. They are not important as participants in any plot, but we are asked to cherish them as impressions in their own right which have become memorable because of the vivid eagerness with which the author has seized them :

Die morgendliche Welt, die sich vor meinen Augen ausbreitete, erschien mir so schön, als sähe ich sie zum erstenmal.[4]

The quality of freshness which Walser conveys in *Der Spaziergang* endows everyday scenes with the uniqueness of a personal vision. In his statement to the tax official the narrator equates the man who writes with the man who walks, and describes his concern as being extended over the small as well as the great :

Die höchsten und niedrigsten, die ernstesten und lustigsten Dinge sind ihm gleicherweise lieb und schön und wert . . . Er muß jederzeit des Mitleides, des Mitempfindens und der Begeisterung fähig sein, und er ist es hoffentlich. Er muß in den hohen Enthusiasmus hinaufdringen und sich in die tiefste und kleinste Alltäglichkeit herunterzusenken und zu neigen vermögen, und er kann es vermutlich. Treues, hingebungsvolles Aufgehen und Sichverlieren in die Gegenstände und eifrige Liebe zu allen Erscheinungen und Dingen machen ihn aber dafür glücklich . . .[5]

The narrator combines idyllic description with fantasy. A pine forest which is "quiet as in the heart of a happy human being" reminds him of the interior of a temple or an enchanted castle. The vision of the tired giant Tomzack looms unexpectedly into the protagonist's solitude, to disappear as inexplicably as he came. The poet-walker must make considerable effort to prevent the ordered world of consciousness from disintegrating :

. . . er muß sich fragen : "Wo bin ich?" Erde und Himmel fließen und stürzen mit einmal in ein blitzendes, schimmerndes, übereinanderwogendes, undeutliches Nebelgebilde zusammen; das Chaos beginnt, und die Ordnungen verschwinden. Mühsam versucht der Erschütterte seine gesunde Besinnung aufrecht zu erhalten . . .[6]

What is seen is described with sharpness and precision, and an additional dimension is provided by the imaginative reactions of the protagonist to the scene before him. The common-sense world is continually liable to lose its shape, perhaps by being overlain with a fantasy, or by being transmuted by ecstasy or by being overcome by chaos. An important climax lies in the narrator's vision at the level-crossing shortly after the conclusion of his friendly interview with the tax authorities. After the opening of the barrier at the crossing he senses that he has come to the highlight of his walk :

> Hier beim Bahnübergang schien mir der Höhepunkt oder etwas wie das Zentrum zu sein, von wo aus es leise wieder sinken würde.[7]

The commonplace scene on the road is transfigured and is interpreted in these terms :

> Gott der Allmächtige, unser gnädiger Herr, trat auf die Straße, um sie zu verherrlichen und himmlisch schön zu machen. Einbildungen aller Art und Illusionen machten mich glauben, daß Jesus Christus heraufgestiegen sei und jetzt mitten unter den Leuten und mitten durch die liebenswürdige Gegend wandere und umher wandle. Häuser, Gärten und Menschen verwandelten sich in Klänge, alles Gegenständliche schien sich in eine Zärtlichkeit verwandelt zu haben. Süßer Silberschleier und Seelennebel schwamm in alles und legte sich um alles. Die Weltseele hatte sich geöffnet, und alles Leid, alle menschlichen Enttäuschungen, alles Böse, alles Schmerzhafte schienen zu entschwinden, und von nun an nie mehr wieder zu erscheinen. Frühere Spaziergänge traten mir vor die Augen; aber das wundervolle Bild der bescheidenen Gegenwart wurde zur überragenden Empfindung. Die Zukunft verblaßte, und die Vergangenheit zerrann. Ich glühte und blühte selber im glühenden, blühenden Augenblick . . . Im süßen Liebeslichte erkannte ich oder glaubte ich erkennen zu sollen, daß vielleicht der innerliche Mensch der einzige sei, der wahrhaft existiert.[8]

The impression of the moment has acquired visionary significance, emphasizing man's inward spirit and its closeness to the earth's beauty. After this experience, the walk takes its return journey as evening approaches with an elegiac tone and with a less emphatic manner than earlier. The author does not offer novelties to the reader, and asserts rather his conception of nature and human life as a "flight of repetitions", a phenomenon that he regards both "as beauty and as blessing". Evening brings with it thoughts of loneliness, tiredness and the transience of all life and its impressions. *Der Spaziergang* is rich in its varied associations of ideas and the luminous intensity of its prose. It blends the playful, the satirical and the sensitively imaginative aspects of Walser's writing in a form which is simple, but without the tenuousness of a number of the short sketches. This is one of the few occasions when Walser used the middle-length prose form, though he gave much of his creative energies to wrestling with the novel form, with varying success. The years in Berlin in particular saw his preoccupation with novel writing. In his *Wanderungen mit Robert Walser,* Carl Seelig reports Walser as having said that he might well have burnt three novels in Berlin; a later novel *Theodor* was written in Switzerland between 1917 and 1922, but this too has been lost. There remain the three published novels : *Die Geschwister Tanner, Der Gehülfe* and *Jakob von Gunten.* In later life Walser looked back to the period in Berlin as his time of greatest opportunity. He said to Seelig in January 1937 :

"Könnte ich mich nochmals ins 30. Lebensjahr zurückschrauben, so würde ich nicht mehr wie ein romantischer Luftibus ins Blaue hineinschreiben, sonderlingshaft und unbekümmert. Man darf die Gesellschaft nicht negieren. Man muß in ihr leben und für oder gegen sie kämpfen. Das ist der Fehler meiner Romane. Sie sind zu schrullig und reflexiv, in der Komposition oft zu salopp. Um die künstlerische Gesetzmäßigkeit mich foutierend, habe ich einfach drauflosmusiziert."[9]

Six years later he expressed regrets combined with ironic defiance that he did not meet the reading public half-way during his productive period :

"Ich hätte ein wenig Liebe und Trauer, ein wenig Ernst und Beifall in meine Bücher mischen sollen—auch ein wenig Edelromantik..."[10]

In the conversations with Seelig Walser criticizes the subjective element in *Die Geschwister Tanner* as having irritated its first readers; he feels that he has spoken too intimately of his own brothers and sisters, and that he would prefer to cut the work by seventy or eighty pages in preparing it for a new edition. The sketch *Geschwister Tanner,* from the *Kleine Dichtungen* of 1914, throws a more positive and poetic light upon the genesis of this work in the Berlin flat which he shared with his brother Karl. The act of creating something that he knows to be beautiful is a blissful experience, and is described in rapturous terms :

Der Dichter muß schweifen, muß sich mutig verlieren, muß immer alles, alles wieder wagen, muß hoffen, darf, darf nur hoffen . . . Ich hoffte nie, daß ich je etwas Ernstes, Schönes und Gutes fertigstellen könnte.—Der bessere Gedanke und damit der Schaffensmut tauchte nur langsam, dafür aber eben nur um so geheimnisreicher aus den Abgründen der Selbstnicht-achtung und des leichtsinnigen Unglaubens hervor.—Es glich der aufsteigenden Morgensonne. Abend und Morgen, Vergangen-heit und Zukunft und die reizende Gegenwart lagen wie zu meinen Füssen, das Land wurde dicht vor mir lebendig, und mich dünkte, ich könne das menschliche Treiben, das ganze Menschenleben mit Händen greifen, so lebhaft sah ich es.— Ein Bild löste das andere ab, und die Einfälle spielten mitein-ander wie glückliche, anmutige, artige Kinder. Voller Entzücken hing ich am fröhlichen Grundgedanken, und indem ich nur fleissig immer weiter schrieb, fand sich der Zusammenhang.[11]

Die Geschwister Tanner is an episodic work, liable to dissolve into series of descriptions, letters and monologues. Its unity lies in the first place in the personalities of the Tanner family, reflected through their encounters with Simon. His elder brother Klaus reproaches Simon in a letter for not having a settled career and for his restlessness in moving from one post to another. Simon is a wanderer who wants to live in the present moment; he says on first meeting Frau Klara:

Ich habe nie etwas besessen, bin nie etwas gewesen, und werde trotz den Hoffnungen meiner Eltern nie etwas sein.[12]

Rather more than a year later Simon wanders into a state convalescent home, glad of the temporary shelter of warmth in midwinter. A friendly woman-supervisor persuades him to talk about himself and his family, and the novel closes with this con-versation, which consists largely of Simon's summing up of himself and of his near relatives, reminding us of the ties of affection that exist between this group of individualists. It is here, in Simon's last speech, that he gives some hints as to the reason for the particular character of the bonds between these brothers and sisters which gives the novel its distinctive quality. The memory of their mother's dignity, the accounts of her sufferings as a child, and later the wit-nessing of the collapse of her personality in her last years form a common emotional experience of depth which her children carry with them, hardly consciously, in their adult lives. Simon says of his mother:

Ihre Eltern waren nicht gut zu ihr, so lernte sie früh die Schwermut kennen und stand, als sie Mädchen war, eines Tages an ein Brückengeländer angelehnt und dachte darüber nach, ob es nicht besser wäre, in den Fluß hinab zu springen. Man muß sie vernachlässigt, hin und her geschoben und auf diese Art mißhandelt haben. Als ich als Knabe einmal von ihrer Jugend hörte, schoß mir der Zorn ins Gesicht, ich bebte vor Empörung und haßte von nun an die unbekannten Gestalten meiner Großeltern. Für uns Kinder hatte die Mutter, als sie noch gesund war, etwas beinahe Majestätisches, vor dem wir uns fürchteten und zurückscheuten; als sie krank im Geist wurde, bemitleideten wir sie. Es war ein toller Sprung, so von der ängstlichen, geheimnisvollen Ehrfurcht ins Mitleid überspringen zu müssen.[13]

Both parents grew up in isolated mountain districts, and came into the town to share the newly developing prosperity introduced there by industrialization. Simon has not yet found the solutions to the problems involved in his parents' lives :

Ich stehe noch immer vor der Türe des Lebens, klopfe und klopfe, allerdings mit wenig Ungestüm, und horche nur gespannt, ob jemand komme, der mir den Riegel zurückschieben möchte.[14]

In the course of the novel Simon's closest ties are with his brother Kaspar and his sister Hedwig. With his firm vocation as painter Kaspar has an immediate purpose in life which Simon lacks; at the same time his carefree self-confidence enables him to take life more easily than Simon :

"Was geht alles in der Welt vorüber. Man muß schaffen, schaffen und nochmals schaffen, dazu ist man da, nicht zum Bemitleiden."[15]

Simon finds the furnished room and thus begins the connection with Frau Klara, but it is Kaspar with whom she falls in love. For Kaspar is more defined as a personality by his artistic mission and by the easiness of his approaches to the other sex. Simon rejects the possibility of a more intimate relationship with her, and asserts his independence by going for a lonely walk. As an artist and a Bohemian, Kaspar is following an expected pattern of development, and his move to Paris is in keeping with his sense of purpose. As Frau Klara says, Simon is different and "can scarcely be grasped". Simon likes to confide in his friend Rosa, but she is secretly in love with Kaspar. Simon's affection for his brother allows of no feelings of jealousy; he is glad for Kaspar when Frau Klara becomes closely bound to the latter.

When winter finds him out of work and homeless, Simon goes to his sister Hedwig, a village schoolmistress, and stays with her for three months. Hedwig's attitude to him is protective, but she is much less settled than at first appears; she is anxious to escape, perhaps as a governess in Italy, or more probably by marrying a local farmer. "Ich werde das Leben verspielt haben,"[16] she says, as she thinks of the type of marriage she is likely to make. But she feels, as Simon puts it later, a mixture of affection and contempt for him :

> "Nein, nein, Simon, wegen dir wird niemand weinen. Wenn du fort bist, bist du fort. Das ist alles. Glaubst du, um dich könnte man weinen? Keine Rede."[17]

Simon is more closely bound to Kaspar and Hedwig, who are nearer to him in temperament, than to his other brothers. For Klaus is separated from them by his more positive acceptance of the standards of normal society, while Emil, in a mental hospital, lives in total estrangement from the world around him.

Der Spaziergang focuses our attention on the events of the walk and on the immediate impressions they make on the narrator; the personality of the narrator is kept deliberately in the background. To discover a further dimension to such a personality we can turn to *Die Geschwister Tanner,* where Simon, a self-effacing wanderer, is the main personage. Of the various walks that Simon undertakes in the course of the novel, the most memorable is perhaps the three days' trek to Hedwig in the winter, in the course of which he comes across the frozen corpse of the poet Sebastian and resolves to see that his poems are collected and published. *Die Geschwister Tanner* has an emotional directness that is less clearly observed in Walser's other writings; it is a work which invites above all affectionate reading.

Der Gehülfe is in the first place a comic novel depicting the relationship of Joseph Marti with the Tobler family during the months when he is in their house as clerical assistant and secretary to the engineer Tobler. Joseph Marti seems to be less vulnerable than Simon Tanner, but at heart he too is a wanderer; the events of the novel take place during an interval between one phase of restlessness and another. He would like to keep the whole of his experience of people on a light, ironical, non-committal, distant level. His reflections as he first awaits admission to the house indicate a characteristic mood :

> Eines Morgens um acht Uhr stand ein junger Mann vor der Türe eines alleinstehenden, anscheinend schmucken Hauses. Es regnete. "Es wundert mich beinahe," dachte der Dastehende, "daß ich einen Schirm bei mir habe." Er besaß nämlich in seinen früheren Jahren nie einen Regenschirm.[18]

An attention to details of everyday life suffuses this realistic novel, and a variety of precisely observed impressions can be united in Joseph's mind to an experience of beauty. After a few weeks with the Tobler family, Joseph is permitted to take a trip to the nearby city (the novel is based on a similar period in Walser's life spent near Zürich), and he feels the impact of the sunny Sunday with a gaiety and heightened awareness :

> Es war alles so mild, so bedeckt, so leicht und hübsch, es war ebenso groß wie klein geworden, ebenso nah wie fern, ebenso weit wie fein und ebenso zart wie bedeutend. Es schien bald alles, was Joseph sah, ein natürlicher, stiller, gütiger Traum geworden zu sein, nicht ein gar so schöner, nein, ein bescheidener, und doch ein so schöner.[19]

Here it is as if Joseph is capable of double vision, of harmonizing a close examination of detail with a broad conspectus of the whole scene; the series of contrasting adjectives indicates the combination of the miniature and the panoramic which is successfully achieved in this vision of the city. He speculates about the personalities of the strangers sitting on the public seats, imagining the complexity of living that could be developed from the material of his passing glances :

> Das Leben ließ sich nicht so leicht in Kasten und Ordnungen abteilen ... Ah, das Leben machte bitter, aber es konnte auch froh und innig demütig machen, und dankbar fürs Wenige, für das bißchen süße, freie Luft zum Einatmen.[20]

From the point of view of its stylized description this impression of Zürich is one of the outstanding sequences in the work. It is perhaps inevitable, and part of the comedy, that it should later be reduced by Tobler to a commonplace level :

> "Ja so? In der Stadt sind Sie gewesen? Und wie hat es Ihnen denn dort nach der längern Abwesenheit wieder gefallen? Nicht schlecht, was? Jawohl, die Städte vermögen manches zu bieten, aber man kommt schließlich doch auch gern wieder zurück. Habe ich recht oder nicht?"[21]

The tension between Joseph and his employer is the main motor force of the novel. Tobler's first words to Joseph are an irritated enquiry as to why he has arrived two days earlier than expected, a misunderstanding for which Joseph is not responsible. The final quarrel on New Year's Day which causes Joseph abruptly to leave is not primarily about Joseph, but about his predecessor Wirsich to whom Joseph has been giving protection and shelter, though without Tobler's personal permission. It appears as if Joseph is diametrically opposed to Tobler, his own quietness, for instance, contrasting with the latter's loud and decided manner. Tobler is essentially a comic figure. Having inherited some money, he has taken over an elegant house and devoted himself to inventions such

as the "Reklameuhr", advertising novelties by means of which he
hopes to make his fortune. He makes much of the August 1st holi-
day, organizing illuminations and fireworks for the household :

> Wie glücklich sah Tobler aus! Das war etwas für ihn. Für
> Feste und deren schöne Inszenierung schien er wie kaum ein
> zweiter geschaffen zu sein.[22]

This thought comes again to Joseph Marti as he silently participates
in Tobler's celebration of the completion of his fairy-grotto,

> ... ein höhlenartiges, mit Zement ausgeschlagenes und tapeziertes
> Ding, länglich wie ein größeres Ofenloch, etwas zu niedrig, so
> daß die Besucher mehr als einmal die Köpfe anstießen.[23]

Characteristic too are Tobler's frequent, busy-seeming train journeys, which are mainly motivated by his wish not to "waste" a
season-ticket he has taken out.

Already at an early phase of the novel, we acquire little confidence in the nature of Tobler's enterprises, and as with the passing
of the months his affairs approach inevitably nearer to bankruptcy,
Tobler and his assistant seem to be bound more closely together.
Tobler is rebuffed by his mother, while Joseph is at odds with his
father; neither of them is at home in the middle-class world of
Swiss enterprise which surrounds them; they irritate and stimulate
each other, and both are romantic at heart. Joseph is a freer man
than Tobler, and Frau Tobler, tied to her husband and her four
children, tells him to count his blessings :

> "Sie, Marti, haben es eigentlich recht gut, viel besser als mein
> Mann und als ich, aber von mir will ich gar nicht reden. Sie
> können von hier weggehen. Sie packen einfach Ihre paar
> Sachen, setzen sich in die Eisenbahn und fahren nach wohin Sie
> wollen... An nichts Dauerndes sind Sie gebunden, an nichts
> Hemmendes gefangen und an nichts Allzuliebevolles gefesselt
> und angekettet."[24]

Joseph Marti's encounters with Wirsich offer a sequence of
action that forms a counterpart to his relations with Tobler. If
Joseph seems elusive and irresponsible to the Toblers or to Klara,
the friend he visits in the city, he can with justification assume a
protective rôle to the unfortunate Wirsich. When the latter and
his mother have left after their first meeting with Joseph at Toblers',
Joseph reflects upon the fatality with which suffering may fall
upon an old woman or a poor child. Although he expects to put
the man and the old woman aside as memories that will soon turn
pale, as most memories do in his vagrant life, chance is to bring
him on two other occasions into contact with the forlorn Wirsich.

Joseph's conviction of the rightness of his caritative assistance to Wirsich seems to be confirmed by the landscape around him :

> Und dazwischen war es ihm beinahe heilig zumut. Die ganze Landschaft schien ihm zu beten, so freundlich, mit all den leisen, gedämpften Erdfarben.[(25)]

Both Silvi, Frau Tobler's neglected child, and Wirsich appeal to Joseph because they are in distress and unloved; similarly Frau Weiss, Frau Tobler and Klara feel a need to offer help, sympathy or advice to Joseph; and Tobler himself, though apparently secure enough, is ultimately a figure to be loved and pitied. *Der Gehülfe* is a friendly novel, and the support which Joseph gives to Wirsich comes to take a prior place to his assistance of Tobler. The mood of the lake forms a colourful background as the narrative moves from summer to winter, while the decline of the Tobler fortunes is mirrored in the changing weather outside the house.

Although considerably shorter than the two earlier novels and written in diary form, *Jakob von Gunten* is equally distinctive. It has an elusive quality of self-conscious distance from everyday reality that marks it out as contemporary in spirit as well as in time with Rilke's *Malte Laurids Brigge* and the work of Kafka. Seelig has reported Kafka's admiration for this particular work, and Jakob's attitude to the Institut Benjamenta, together with other features of the novel, seems to foreshadow the relationship of Kafka's protagonists to their environment, particularly in *Der Prozeß* and *Das Schloß*. The Institute gives little to its pupils, whose instruction is largely limited to learning by heart regulations and studying a book on the aims of the school. There is only this one lesson, which is repeated indefinitely; it is taken by Fräulein Benjamenta, sister of the principal. Outward decorum is emphasized, and laughter is out of place. One of Jakob's first reactions is indignation at the sleeping quarters offered to him. But he soon comes to accept the lack of furniture in the classroom, to take part willingly in the scrubbing and sweeping operations, to conform with the requirement that all food should be eaten up, to be resigned to unjust punishments and to the elaborate ceremonies during interviews with Benjamenta. The pupils, Jakob comments, are cheerful but without hope. There is a derelict garden to which the pupils are forbidden access, and the "inner rooms" of the principal and his sister are also normally out of bounds. The school is placed in an apartment in a shabby city block. Inside the school complicated regulations are supposed to be followed, but from three o'clock in the afternoon onwards the pupils are left to themselves and are free to explore any part of city life that attracts them. The institution is in fact a training-school for personal servants. Walser spent a short time at such a school in Berlin and for a time tried this form of work; Simon, in *Die Geschwister Tanner*, has an episode as a domestic servant.

Kraus is the pupil whose personality stimulates Jakob most. For much of the time he is patronizing to this youth with the "monkey-like" appearance. Kraus has the temperament that will make for an ideal servant, and sees it as part of his duty to persuade Jakob to accept his point of view on such subjects as willingness to work, the need for contentment and humbleness. Kraus is never bored, and is indignant that Jakob should have such feelings. When Kraus leaves, Jakob feels that a sun has set: "Adieu, Jakob, bessere dich, ändere dich," Kraus advises him, and: "Arbeite mehr, wünsche weniger." Unlike Jakob, Kraus is indifferent to the glitter and bustle of the city. School routine and life outside the school, including the interludes when he is the guest of his artist-brother, offer Jakob neither comfort nor hope, but Kraus' personality gives Jakob a faith that he finds nowhere else:

. . . dieser ungraziöse Kraus ist schöner als die graziösesten und schönsten Menschen. Er glänzt nicht mit Gaben, aber mit dem Schimmer eines guten und unverdorbenen Herzens, und seine schlechten, schlichten Manieren sind vielleicht trotz alles Hölzernen, das ihnen anhaftet, das Schönste, was es an Bewegung und Manier in der menschlichen Gesellschaft geben kann . . . Ja, man wird Kraus nie achten, und gerade das, daß er, ohne Achtung zu genießen, dahinleben wird, das ist ja das Wundervolle und Planvolle, das An-den-Schöpfer-Mahnende . . . Ich glaube, ich, ich bin einer der ganz wenigen, vielleicht der einzige, oder vielleicht sind es zwei oder drei Menschen, die wissen werden, was sie an Kraus besitzen oder besessen haben.[26]

Jakob's presence at the school is more unexpected than that of Kraus. It is to a considerable extent an act of rebellion against his childhood environment; he has run away from his father and a wealthy home, and does not write to his mother, though he knows that she will be distressed on his account. The presence of his successful elder brother in the city gives him an opportunity of experiencing different circumstances from those of the school, but the link with Johann is less important to him than the relationships within the school. Jakob is here because he has decided to cut himself off from all dependence on his family, to build up his own life without their help; and if he fails, this will be in his eyes more creditable than remaining within the confines and protection of the Guntens. He and his fellow-pupils have as prospects only servitude. If Kraus accepts this contentedly, Jakob is pessimistic about these implications:

Vielleicht aber besitze ich aristokratische Adern. Ich weiß es nicht. Aber das Eine weiß ich bestimmt: Ich werde eine reizende kugelrunde Null im späteren Leben sein. Ich werde als alter Mann junge, selbstbewußte, schlecht erzogene Grobiane bedienen müssen, oder ich werde betteln, oder ich werde zugrunde gehen.[27]

These are among Jakob's first thoughts in his diary, and he comes back to them as he approaches its end, when he envisages the possibility of his life collapsing and decides that such a collapse is of little importance, as his individual personality is a cipher.

Yet the school dominates Jakob. At first he is indignant and rebellious (hence his first friendship with Schacht), but his hatred of the Institute gradually changes to fondness and sympathy as he realizes its precariousness and the need which Benjamenta and his sister have for his affection and support. Jakob soon comes to identify himself, in hate and then in love, with the environment he has chosen. His admiration for Fräulein Benjamenta begins as if towards a distant being, and when she approaches him alone in the darkening schoolroom, he realizes that she is in need of his sympathy. Her death is foreshadowed, though when it takes place, Jakob is surprised at the coldness of his own emotions at this point. Jakob's relations with Benjamenta undergo a comparable transformation from dislike to friendship. Fairly soon Jakob feels something akin to commiseration for Benjamenta's solitary life. An important moment in their relationship is the interview in which Benjamenta, to Jakob's astonishment, confesses his special feelings for his pupil. Love and hatred alternate for a time; the invitations become more pressing, until after the death of Fräulein Benjamenta and the departure of Kraus, Jakob agrees to throw in his lot with Benjamenta, who has hated the world until he found Jakob. The school has disintegrated into non-existence, and Benjamenta and Jakob prepare for a new life—that of the wanderer. For a time, a peculiar setting has satisfied the restless protagonist, as in *Der Gehülfe*, but here the union between the two antagonists has in the end been realized, and a strange harmony prevails at the close. The individual at first seems powerless against the rules which press upon him, but the forms of society fall away, leaving the personal relationship with Benjamenta, paradoxical as it is, as the centre and essence of Jakob's life.

The element of fantasy repeatedly breaks into the narrative of *Jakob von Gunten*. Soon after his arrival at the Institute Jakob notes:

Weiß Gott, manchmal will mir mein ganzer hiesiger Auferthalt wie ein unverständlicher Traum vorkommen.[28]

He dreams once about his mother, and another time creates in his imagination a whole series of teachers who might have held office in the school. He develops fantasies connected with wealth and power, and sees himself as a medieval leader or as a soldier of Napoleon. One of his most elaborate visions is of Fräulein Benjamenta escorting him over unknown regions of the house explaining to him allegories of happiness, poverty, deprivation, care, freedom, quiet and doubt. When he and Kraus are admitted to the "inner rooms", he is disappointed to find no element of wonder or secrecy there. Satirical humour asserts itself again :

> Es sind allerdings Goldfische da, und Kraus und ich müssen das Bassin, in welchem diese Tiere schwimmen und leben, regelmäßig entleeren, säubern und mit frischem Wasser auffüllen. Ist das aber etwas nur entfernt Zauberhaftes? Goldfische können in jeder preußischen mittleren Beamtenfamilie vorkommen, und an Beamtenfamilien klebt nichts Unverständliches und Absonderliches.[29]

His imagination can extend the apartment into a huge building with winding-staircases and a maze of corridors. And Jakob's final decision to go with Benjamenta is foreshadowed by his dream, in the course of which Jakob follows Benjamenta into the desert :

> Es war lächerlich und herrlich zugleich. "Der Kultur entrücken, Jakob. Weißt du, das ist famos," sagte von Zeit zu Zeit der Vorsteher, der wie ein Araber aussah.[30]

The closeness of reality to fantasy, of ridiculousness to magnificence, and the contrast of civilization and solitude, of stability and restlessness, are recurring themes in Walser's work. *Der Gehülfe* is the most normally realistic novel, and *Jakob von Gunten* the most elusive and problematic. The short essays and stories are often prose-poems, and are the literary form to which Walser turned most regularly and spontaneously in the main course of his career as a writer. His work as a poet, finally, may be briefly noted, for here too the proximity in themes and approach to the prose sketches is evident. The collection of *Gedichte*, published in 1909 with illustrations by Karl Walser, contains short lyrics, mostly of consciously unassuming and simple shape and content. Nature, wandering, poverty, fear, solitude and inner quiet are among the themes. "Zu philosophisch" is the title of this poem :

> Wie geisterhaft im Sinken
> und Steigen ist mein Leben.
> Stets seh ich mich mir winken,
> dem Winkenden entschweben.

Ich seh' mich als Gelächter,
als tiefe Trauer wieder,
als wilden Redeflechter;
doch alles dies sinkt nieder.

Und ist zu allen Zeiten
wohl niemals recht gewesen.
Ich bin vergeßne Weiten
zu wandern auserlesen.[31]

Walser's later verse is more rugged and reflective, often with a colloquial directness and a dry quality of language and thought. Carl Seelig records in his postscript to the *Unbekannte Gedichte* how Walser took up lyrical poetry anew in his later years, at the time when he was becoming increasingly aware that his gift of prose-writing was becoming exhausted. "Beten ist ja wie dichten. Jedes Gedicht ist eine Art von Gebet",[32] he wrote in an essay of 1919 which Seelig quotes. Poems he continued to write after he had withdrawn from the world, long after he had ceased to write prose. Perhaps the undated poem "Beschaulichkeit" belongs to this last phase of his writing; evidently it looks back rather than forward :

Die Bücher waren alle schon geschrieben,
Die Taten alle scheinbar schon getan.
Alles, was seine schönen Augen sah'n,
Stammte aus früherer Bemühung her.
Die Häuser, Brücken und die Eisenbahn
Hatten etwas durchaus Bemerkenswertes.
Er dachte an den stürmischen Laertes,
An Lohengrin und seinen sanften Schwan,
Und üb'rall war das Hohe schon getan,
Stammte aus längstvergang'nen Zeiten.
Man sah ihn einsam über Felder reiten.
Das Leben lag am Ufer wie ein Kahn,
Das nicht mehr fähig ist zum Schaukeln, Gleiten.[33]

[I should like to express my indebtedness to Herr P. Müller and Dr. M. Schäppi for their help during the writing of this essay.]

TRANSLATIONS

1. To write exactly and definitely about something beautiful is difficult. Thoughts fly around what is beautiful like drunken butterflies, without coming to a destination and a firm point.
2. "O power of the spirit, who could bind you?"
3. Our town is actually more a large, beautiful garden than a town.

The streets are garden-paths. They look so clean, and as if strewn with fine sand. Above the roofs of the town rises the mountain with its dark fir-trees and its green foliage. We have the most magnificent parks, including an avenue which is said to date from Napoleon. It is true, I do not believe that he planted the trees with his own hands, for after all he was surely too proud, too powerful for that. In summer the wide, old chestnut-trees provide splendid, refreshing shade. On summer evenings one sees those inhabitants of the town who like to take a walk strolling up and down this avenue. The ladies look particularly beautiful in their bright-coloured dresses. It is a pleasure to go boating on the evening-dark lake. The lake belongs to our town like the church, or as in a monarchy the summer palace of a duke belongs to his town-residence. Without the lake our town would not be our town, indeed, one would not recognize it. Our church, the Protestant one, is situated on an elevated platform that is adorned by two wonderfully beautiful, large chestnut-trees. The windows of the church are painted with the most fiery colours, and this gives it a fairy-like appearance. Often the most delightful part-singing is heard from it. I like to stand outside, when there is singing inside. The women sing most beautifully. Our town hall is dignified, and its large hall serves for balls and other occasions. We even have a theatre. Every winter we are visited for two months by strange actors who have very elegant manners, speak very elegant German and wear top-hats. I am always glad when they come, and do not collaborate with our citizens when they speak contemptuously of the "mob". It may be that they do not pay their debts, that they are insolent, that they get drunk, that they come from bad families, but what are they artists for? One makes generous allowances to an artist for that sort of thing. They act quite splendidly too. I have seen "The Robbers". It is a wonderful play, full of fire and beautiful passages. Is it possible to amuse oneself in a more elegant and a nobler manner than by going to the theatre? Big cities set us the best example in this respect.—Our town has much industry, the reason being that it has factories. Factories and their surroundings look ugly. The air there is black and thick, and I do not understand why people can occupy themselves with such unclean things. I don't care about what is made in the factories. I only know that all the poor people work in the factory, perhaps as a punishment for being so poor. We have pretty roads, and everywhere green trees look out between the houses. When it rains the streets are really dirty. In our town little is done for the streets. Father says so. A pity that our house hasn't a garden. We live on the first floor. Our flat is nice, but there ought to be a garden to it. Mama often complains about this. I like the old part of the town best. I like strolling in the old streets, arcades and passages. We have underground passages too. All in all: we have a very pretty town.

3. The morning world spread out before my eyes appeared as beautiful to me as if I saw it for the first time.

5. The highest and the lowest, the most serious and the most hilarious things are to him equally beloved, beautiful and valuable . . . He must at all times be capable of compassion, of sympathy, and of enthusiasm, and it is hoped that he is. He must be able to bow down and sink into

the deepest and smallest everyday thing, and it is probable that he can.
Faithful, devoted self-effacement and self-surrender among objects, and
zealous love for all phenomena and things make him happy in this
however . . .

6. . . . he must ask himself: "Where am I?" Earth and heaven suddenly stream together and collide, rocking interlocked one upon the
other into a flashing, shimmering, obscure nebular imagery; chaos begins,
and the orders vanish. Convulsed, he laboriously tries to retain his normal
state of mind . . .

7. Here at the railway-crossing seemed to be the peak, or something
like the centre, from which again the gentle declivity would begin.

8. God the Almighty, our merciful Lord, walked down the road, to
glorify it and make it divinely beautiful. Imaginings of all sorts, and
illusions, made me believe that Jesus Christ was risen again and wandering now in the midst of the people and in the midst of this friendly
place. Houses, gardens, and people were transfigured into musical
sounds, all that was solid seemed to be transfigured into soul and into
gentleness. Sweet veils of silver and soul-haze swam through all things
and lay over all things. The soul of the world had opened, and all grief,
all human disappointment, all evil, all pain seemed to vanish, from now
on never to appear again. Earlier walks came before my eyes; but the
wonderful image of the humble present became a feeling which overpowered all others. The future paled, and the past dissolved. I glowed
and flowered myself in the glowing, flowering present . . . In the sweet
light of love I realized, or believed I realized, that perhaps the inward
self is the only self which really exists. (The English passages from *Der
Spaziergang* are taken from Christopher Middleton's translation, *The
Walk and Other Stories*, by kind permission of John Calder (Publishers)
Ltd.)

9. "If I could screw myself back to the age of thirty, I would not
again write into the blue like a romantic will-o'-the-wisp, eccentric and
not caring. It is wrong to deny society. We must live in it, and fight
either for or against it. That is the fault of my novels. They are too
odd and reflective, often too slack in structure. Not caring about artistic
propriety, I simply fired away."

10. "I should have mixed into my books a little love and grief, a little
earnestness and applause—a little of the nobly romantic too."

11. The poet must roam, must boldly lose himself, must always venture
everything again and again, must hope, may, may only hope . . . I never
hoped that I should ever be able to complete anything serious, beautiful
and good. The better thought and at the same time the courage to create
appeared only slowly, but precisely because of this with all the more
secret splendour from the abysses of lack of self-respect and of frivolous
unbelief.—It was like the rising sun. Evening and morning, past and
future and the attractive present lay as if at my feet, the land close
before me came to life, and I felt as if I could grasp hold of human
activities, the whole of human life, with my hands, it looked so alive to
me.—One image came after the other, and the ideas played with each
other like happy, charming, good children. Full of rapture I clung to the

cheerful central thought, and as I just went on writing busily, the connections were established.

12. I have never possessed anything, have never been anything, and in spite of the hopes of my parents shall never be anything.

13. Her parents were not good to her, and so she knew melancholy at an early age, and one day when she was a girl she stood leaning against the railing of a bridge and considered whether it would not be better to jump down into the river. She must have been neglected, pushed about and in this way maltreated. When as a boy I once heard about her youth, my face flushed with anger, I trembled with indignation and from now onwards hated the unknown figures of my grandparents. When she was still in good health mother had for us children something that was almost majestic about her which we feared and of which we fought shy; when she became mentally ill, we pitied her. It was a crazy leap, to have to jump in this way from fearful, secret reverence to pity.

14. I still stand in front of life's door, I knock and knock, it is true with little impetuosity, and I only listen tensely in case someone should come and push back the bolt for me.

15. "What is there in the world that does not pass by. We must create, create, and again create, that is what we are there for, not to pity."

16. "I shall have gambled away my life."

17. "No, no, Simon, nobody will cry on your account. When you are away, you are away. That is all. Do you believe that anyone could cry about you? There is no question of this."

18. At eight o'clock one morning a young man stood at the door of a detached, apparently elegant house. It was raining. "I am almost surprised," the man standing there thought, "that I have an umbrella with me." For in his earlier years he never possessed an umbrella.

19. It was all so gentle, so protected, so light and pretty, it had become so large as small, so near as distant, so far as fine and so delicate as significant. Soon everything that Joseph saw seemed to have become a natural, quiet, friendly dream, not a particularly beautiful one, no, a modest one, and yet one that was so beautiful.

20. Life did not let itself be divided so easily into boxes and orders... Ah, life made one bitter, but it could also make one gay and inwardly humble, and thankful for the little that was given, for the little sweet, fresh air to breathe.

21. "Oh yes? You've been in the town? And how did you like it there again after a fairly long absence? Not bad, eh? Indeed, the towns can offer a great deal, but in the end it is always a pleasure too to come back. Am I right, or not?"

22. How happy Tobler looked! That was just right for him. He seemed to be suited almost uniquely to celebrations and to producing them in fine style.

23. ...a cave-like thing, lined and decorated with cement, longish in shape like a fairly large oven-hole, rather too low, so that the visitors bumped their heads more than once.

24. "You, Marti, are really in quite a good position, much better than my husband and myself, but I don't want to talk about myself. You can

go away from here. You simply pack your few things, sit in the train and travel wherever you like . . . You are not tied to anything permanent, not caught by anything that restrains and not bound and chained to anything that is all too endearing."

25. And in between his mood was almost holy. The whole landscape seemed to him to be praying, in such a friendly fashion, with all the gentle, muted colours of the earth.

26. . . . this ungraceful Kraus is more attractive than the most graceful and attractive of human beings. He does not shine with talents, but with the light of a good, unspoilt heart, and his bad, simple manners are perhaps, in spite of everything that is wooden about them, the most beautiful thing in the way of movement and manner that there can be in human society . . . It is true, Kraus will never be respected, and precisely the fact that he will live out his life without enjoying respect is indeed what is beautiful and purposeful, what reminds us of the Creator . . . I believe that I, I am one of the few, perhaps the only one, or perhaps there are two or three people, who will know what they have, or have had, in Kraus.

27. But perhaps I possess aristocratic blood in my veins. I don't know. But one thing I know definitely: in later life I shall be a charming, spherical cipher. As an old man I shall have to serve young, self-confident, badly brought up louts, or else I shall be a beggar or come to ruin.

28. God knows, sometimes my whole stay here seems to me like an incomprehensible dream.

29. Certainly there are goldfish there, and Kraus and I regularly have to empty the bowl in which these creatures swim and live, and fill it with fresh water. But is that something even distantly magical? One can find goldfish in every Prussian family of the middle official class, and there is nothing incomprehensible and strange about officials' families.

30. It was ridiculous and magnificent at the same time. "To get away from civilization, Jacob. You know, that's grand," said the principal, who looked like an Arab, from time to time.

31. How ghostly is my life as it falls and rises. Always I see myself beckoning to myself and disappearing from the one who beckons.

I see myself as laughter, or again as deep mourning, or as a wild orator; but all this sinks down.

And it has probably never really existed at any time. I have been chosen to wander through forgotten distances.

32. "After all praying is like writing poetry. Every poem is a kind of prayer."

33. The books had all been written, the deeds apparently had all been accomplished. Everything that his fine eyes saw derived from earlier effort. The houses, bridges and railways had something wholly remarkable about them. He thought about stormy Laertes, about Lohengrin and his gentle swan, and everywhere what was great had already been accomplished, and derived from long since forgotten times. He could be seen riding lonely across fields. Life lay on the bank like a boat that is no longer capable of swaying and floating.

SELECT BIBLIOGRAPHY

Fritz Kochers Aufsätze. Leipzig, 1904.

Geschwister Tanner. Berlin, 1907. (Second ed. Zürich, 1933.)

Der Gehülfe. Berlin, 1908.

Jakob von Gunten. Berlin, 1909. (Second ed. Zürich, 1950.)

Gedichte. Berlin, 1909. (Third ed. with preface by Carl Seelig. Basle, 1944.)

Der Spaziergang. Frauenfeld, 1917. (Second ed. Herrliberg-Zürich, 1944.)

Poetenleben. Frauenfeld, 1918.

Die Rose. Berlin, 1925.

Unbekannte Gedichte. Ed. with a postscript by Carl Seelig. St. Gallen, 1958.

Dichtungen in Prosa. Ed. by Carl Seelig. Geneva. Vol. 1, 1953: *Aufsätze, Kleine Dichtungen.* Vol. 2, 1954: *Unveröffentlichte Prosadichtungen.* Vol. 3, 1955: *Der Gehülfe.* Vol. 4, 1959: *Fritz Kochers Aufsätze, Die Rose, Kleine Dichtungen.* Vol. 5, 1961: *Komödie, Geschichten, Der Spaziergang.*

Robert Walser: Kleine Auslese. Ed. by Paul Müller, on behalf of the Stiftung Pro Helvetia for the opening of the Walser Memorial, Herisau. Herisau, 1962.

Prosa. Ed. by Walter Höllerer. Frankfurt-am-Main, 1960.

The Walk and Other Stories. Translated by Christopher Middleton. London, 1957.

HANS BÄNZIGER. *Heimat und Fremde.* Ein Kapitel "Tragische Literaturgeschichte" in der Schweiz: Jakob Schaffner, Robert Walser, Albin Zollinger. Berne, 1958.

KARL JOACHIM WILHELM GREVEN. *Existenz, Welt und reines Sein im Werk Robert Walsers.* Diss. Cologne, 1960.

CHRISTOPHER MIDDLETON. "The Picture of Nobody. Some Remarks on Robert Walser with a Note on Walser and Kafka." *Revue des langues vivantes.* Vol. 24. Brussels, 1958. pp. 404–28.

CARL SEELIG. *Wanderungen mit Robert Walser.* St. Gallen, 1957.

OTTO ZINNIKER. *Robert Walser der Poet.* Zürich, 1947.

ALBERT SOERGEL and CURT HOHOFF. *Dichtung und Dichter der Zeit.* Vol. 1, Düsseldorf, 1961. pp. 815–28.

PAUL MÜLLER. "Aufbruch, Einfahrt, Zerfall. Bemerkungen zu Robert Walsers Prosa." *Neue Zürcher Zeitung,* 17 June 1962.

"A Miniaturist in Prose." *Times Literary Supplement,* 21 July 1961.

Heinrich Mann

Heinrich Mann

by W. E. YUILL

Literatur ist soziale Erscheinung.
(Literature is a social phenomenon.)
H. Mann

Luiz Heinrich Mann was born in Lübeck on 27 March 1871, the first of five children. His father, Thomas Johann Heinrich Mann, belonged to one of the prominent mercantile families of the port and held the titles of Consul and Senator; his mother, Julia da Silva-Bruhns, was of Portuguese descent on the maternal side. Heinrich thus shared with his more celebrated brother, Thomas, that situation "between the races" which plays a significant part in the work of both writers. After a brief apprenticeship to the book-trade in Dresden Heinrich worked for a time with the publisher S. Fischer in Berlin. Desultory studies at the university there were never completed, and, after deciding that painting was not his true bent, Mann embarked on his career as a writer. He spent the years before the First World War mainly south of the Alps, with periods of residence in Munich. Not long before the outbreak of war Heinrich married Maria Kanova, a young actress from Prague. This marriage was later dissolved and in 1932 Mann married Nelly Kröger, also a native of Lübeck. The years 1914–18 were passed mainly in Berlin and Munich. In the Weimar Republic Mann achieved eminence as a political writer and was elected president of the literary section in the Prussian Academy of Arts and Sciences. Under Nazi rule the only place for so determined and influential a liberal would obviously be in a concentration camp, and Mann left Germany as soon as Hitler came to power. He settled first in Holland, then in Czechoslovakia, where, in 1935, he was granted Czech nationality in place of the German citizenship of which the Nazis had shamefully deprived him and his brother. During the years immediately before the second war Mann lived in France, and was ultimately forced to emigrate to the United States. He died on 12 March 1950 in Los Angeles, shortly before his intended departure for the German Democratic Republic.

I

"AT the age of twenty-five I said to myself : It is necessary to write novels about contemporary society." With this resolve Heinrich Mann turned away from the sterilized classicism and the ultra-sophisticated psychology of his first novel, *In einer Familie,* in which he had "devised only such tangible action as was suggested by his investigation of the human heart". Henceforth it was his aim to register the intellectual and emotional climate of an era, a social class or a nation. The climate rather than the geology, so to speak, for Mann is not a sociological novelist in the sense of one who painstakingly maps out the structure of society. His imagination is visual and poetic rather than primarily analytical : it is stimulated by patterns rather than diagrams and revels in gestures rather than graphs :

"Man gestaltet drauflos", he writes, "und bewegt Gestalten. Der Gedanke ist noch sehr unsicher. Wenn man bestimmte Meinungen hat, sind sie indessen auch nur aus der Arbeit des Gestaltens hervorgegangen."[1]

Mann's mind not only absorbs and reproduces striking gestures— it magnifies them, too, for there is in it an element of the grotesque and the histrionic. But although his visions often have the quality of nightmare, they are rarely pure fantasy : they are simply the truth writ large.

German writers of Mann's generation have had to contend with a particularly treacherous climate, and few of them have had such a sharp weather-eye as he had. When he was a young man he found himself surrounded by the autumnal richness of the turn of the century, a time of growing prosperity—if one were to judge by statistics. In the midst of the ripe beauties of the '90's, how-ever, Mann detects the signs of coming storms. He smells the odour of decay; for him the glittering surface of this European society has the iridescence of corruption. In the vulgar sybaritism of Berlin, the Bohemianism of Munich, the Ruritanian intrigues of the Balkans and Italy, the same symptoms are observed : a craving for experience and an inability to master it, a mixture of sentiment-ality and debauchery, a febrile activity that springs from anxiety— what the painter Jakobus Halm in *Die Göttinnen* scornfully calls "hysterical Renaissance". Among the wealthy vamps of "Cloud-cuckoo Land"—the Berlin of financiers and fortune-hunters— Andreas Zumsee (hero of *Im Schlaraffenland*) does not find healthy sensuality but only "effete silliness, poor nerves and unhealthy fish-blood". The decadent bourgeois, feverishly pursuing lascivious pleasures among the velvet hangings and the marble Venuses, has lost that sense of peril that gives life its zest :

Das ist's, was uns fehlt : die Gefahr! reflects Claude Marehn in *Die Jagd nach Liebe*. Ich bin das Endergebnis generation-enlanger bürgerlicher Anstrengungen, gerichtet auf Wohlhaben-heit, Gefahrlosigkeit, Freiheit von Illusionen : auf ein ganz gemütsruhiges, glattes Dasein. Mit mir sollte das Ideal bürgerlicher Kultur erreicht sein. Tatsächlich ist bei mir jede Bewegung zu Ende : ich glaube an nichts, hoffe nichts, erstrebe nichts, erkenne nichts an : kein Vaterland, keine Familie, keine Freundschaft. Und nur der älteste Affekt, und der letzte der stirbt, macht mir noch zu schaffen. Ich habe ihn kaum, aber ich gedenke noch seiner. Die Liebe : alle die Grausamkeit, alle die Lust an Gefahren, all der Wille zu zerstören und selbst aufzugehen in einem andern Wesen—woher nähme ich letzter, schwacher Bürger so viele Gewaltsamkeiten.[2]

It is a characteristic perversity of this decadent generation that its women are more virile than the men; they are the incarnation of the life-force, the rude vitality for which the male longs in "nihilistic solitude". Claude Marehn's failure to possess the actress Ute Ende epitomizes his failure to cope with life. He has neither the ruthlessness nor the stamina of the older generation, personified in the senile rake, Herr Panier, who staggers on gouty limbs from board-room to bedroom and, between thromboses, gamely seduces one after another of Claude's mistresses.

The *femme fatale* as Mann sees her is embodied in the Duchess Violante d'Assy, heroine of the trilogy, *Die Göttinnen* (*Diana, Minerva, Venus*). Violante is at once the scourge and the idol of bourgeois society; she is a reincarnation of the Renaissance, Nietzsche's "vornehmer Mensch", set apart by her mixture of Nordic and Mediterranean blood. Violante is emancipated not only by a rationalistic upbringing but also by her immense wealth; she can afford to indulge her emotions to the full and to scorn the bourgeoisie as "all those who have ugly feelings, which, in any case, they express untruthfully". Throughout this extravaganza of overpowering voluptuousness Violante pursues the sublime and the beautiful in politics, in art and in love :

> Mein ganzes Leben war eine einzige große Liebe; jeder Größe und der ganzen Schönheit habe ich meine heiße Brust entgegengeworfen. Ich habe nichts geschmäht, niemand verdammt, keinen Groll gehegt. Mich und mein Schicksal habe ich gut geheißen bis ans Ende.[3]

She is beyond good and evil, because for her "vice does not exist. She lacks the very concept . . . anything is right that gives a keener thrill to life." Violante d'Assy might be seen as a female Faust and Don Juan in one person. Her more particular features are those of the early film diva—the heavy raven hair and the sultry gaze of Pola Negri or Theda Bara. She is very much a figure of her age, a figment of its collective imagination, perhaps, reflected in the mind of Heinrich Mann.

In spite of her hedonism and her ruthless aestheticism Violante is frustrated : she suffers from the feeling that her apparently untrammelled existence is preordained and artificial. At the climax of her career she recognizes that she has done nothing but act a part :

Ich habe ja das Programm heruntergespielt, Stück für Stück, das für mich festgestellt war, schon bevor ich da war. Die drei Göttinnen haben, eine nach der anderen, mein Gewand in Falten gelegt und meine Gesten geregelt, jede nach ihrem Sinne. Mein Leben war ein Kunstwerk.[4]

This is even more the case with Ute Ende, whose immense willpower is directed to the creation of a work of art in her own flesh and blood. "Life is a work of art"—a cry of gratification for the Romantics, a cry of despair for the disciples of Nietzsche : the modern artist, as Mann sees him at this time, suffers from what Nietzsche called the "vampirism of his talent". He is debarred from emotional involvement by an exaggerated awareness of self and he plunders experience for the sake of his art. The artist is no longer a complete man—full-blooded like his counterpart in the Renaissance, for art and life have become mutually exclusive—and this is one of the marks of decadence. The poet Mario Malvolto in Mann's short story, *Pippo Spano*, confesses, "Art so saps its victim that he remains for ever incapable of a genuine feeling, an honest surrender." For a time the passionate love of a woman paralyses Malvolto's talent, making him a man instead of an actor. In the tragic climax to their love, however, he cannot bring himself to complete the suicide pact and die with Gemma : "Only now, when it is supposed to be in earnest," he says, "do I realize that it was just an act, like everything else." He survives beneath the sardonic gaze of the condottiere whose portrait hangs on the wall— "an actor who has forgotten his lines".

This particular ambiguity, the fluctuating frontier between illusion and reality, recurs in many contexts. In one of Mann's earliest stories (*Der Löwe*) he speaks of "the moment when we stand, as it were, on a dizzy ridge whose sharp edge cuts into our feet before we lose our balance and it is determined on which side we are to fall— into fiction or reality". Although he never achieved lasting success as a dramatist, Mann was fascinated throughout his life by the theatre, and there is hardly one of his novels, from *Im Schlaraffenland* to *Henri IV* in which a theatrical performance does not play a significant part. It is above all the glamorous figure of the actress that captivates his imagination : his work is full of characters like Ute Ende, Branzilla (in the *Novelle* of that name) and Flora Garlinda in *Die kleine Stadt*, bewitching monsters of artifice and pathological ambition. "Only the actress is the perfect

woman!" cries a character in one of Mann's plays. But the actress
is not only a siren, she is also an outcast; her art is a weakness as
well as a weapon, requiring her to live on that razor-edge between
truth and fiction, tragedy and comedy. Mann's understanding of
this situation is shown in the short story *Schauspielerin* and the
drama with the same title, which have plots differing only in the
ending. The heroine in each case is loved by a wealthy man who,
for family reasons, refuses to marry her. In the story (as in another
Novelle entitled *Szene*) the actress survives the crisis precisely
because of the release of tension offered by her art and the
emotional resilience it has taught her. In the drama the balance
declines on the side of tragedy. Leonie Hallmann is weary of the
emotional extravagance which the stage has inculcated in her :

> In solch ein Glück, wie ich's kenne, bricht man ein, wie
> in einen Kassenschrank. Dann wird verschwendet, vierzehn Tage
> lang—und man ist wieder fertig.[5]

She craves domestic security, and when her lover refuses to give
her it she poisons herself. The tragedy of Leonie Hallmann had
bitter significance for Mann, because his sister Carla took her own
life in precisely these circumstances. But even her death did not
cancel the ambiguity : Mann later contrived a happy ending for
the drama, while to the same period belongs *Variété*, a farcical
treatment of the theme.

For the respectable citizen the stage can be a perilous lure : it
represents a kind of pandemonium which threatens to overturn
his well-ordered society. The moral balance of a community may
in fact be judged by its reaction to the seductive world of the stage.
This is essentially the theme of *Professor Unrat* and *Die kleine
Stadt*, which depict the response of two very different communities
to the irruption into their midst of a Bohemian element. *Professor
Unrat* is more than a study of a personality grotesquely deformed
by the exercise of authority and the burden of public scorn : Mann
is concerned with the inner nature of a community as well as with
the fate of an eccentric. When the grammar-school teacher is
ostracized because he has succumbed to the grimy attractions of
the "Blue Angel", he avenges himself on the community by turning
on it the spell which caused his own downfall. Himself entangled
in a web of hatred and jealousy, he uses the "artiste", Rosa Fröh-
lich, to ensnare and deprave his fellow-citizens. Unrat's revenge
could not succeed, however, if he did not appeal to an element of
anarchy and latent hysteria beneath the apparent respectability of
this small town. This is Lübeck as Thomas Mann once described it :

> Es hockt in ihren gotischen Winkeln und schleicht durch

ihre Giebelgassen etwas Spukhaftes, allzu Altes, Erblasthaftes—
hysterisches Mittelalter, verjährte Nervenexzentrizität, etwas
wie religiöse Seelenkrankheit.[6]

It is almost by chance that the hypnotic power of Unrat—or,
rather, the power of the citizens' own vices—is broken : he is
arrested for a minor offence and at once becomes a scapegoat
instead of an ogre.

The setting of the other novel is the small town of Palestrina in
the Alban hills. The arrival of an operatic troupe touches off an
explosion of hitherto repressed lusts and jealousies. As one of the
singers remarks, "Our arrival has had a stimulating effect on the
inhabitants of this place. All at once they've found the courage to
set free their vices." The turmoil is political as well as erotic, since
the performance of the opera becomes an issue between the clerical
party and the radicals, still burning with the zeal of Garibaldi.
The town square is a counterpart to the stage and the events
enacted on it are just as melodramatic; the fervent interest of the
audience in the fate of *Die arme Tonietta* is just as whole-hearted
as their subsequent participation in a brawl between the two
parties. This is a happier race, however, than the citizens of
Lübeck—well-balanced, in spite of its ebullience, capable of
walking unscathed the razor-edge between illusion and reality.
These are Italians as Heinrich Mann knew and loved them, a breed
of whom Claude Marehn said, with more envy than irony, that
they were

... stärkere, wärmere Menschen, die nicht zersetzt waren durch
Verstehen, die nur dachten solange sie sprachen, die nicht mit
schmerzlicher Kleinlichkeit das Werden ihres inneren Schicksals
verfolgten, sondern bei denen alles von draußen kam . . .
Sie waren nicht mit ihren durchgesiebten Seelen allein.[7]

The public feud in *Die kleine Stadt* hovers on the verge of
tragedy but ends in a reconciliation between the leaders of the fac-
tions, the lawyer Belotti and Don Taddeo the priest. Violent
passions have been purged and the antagonists are united in a sense
of their common humanity. To a critic of his novel, Mann wrote :

Ich spreche von einem kleinen Volk, das, voll aller Laster und
Niedrigkeit, dennoch in einem Augenblick der Liebe, verbrüdert
auf seinem staubigen Stadtplatz, einen unwiderruflichen Schritt
aufwärts tut, zur Größe.[8]

For the community, a happy reconcilation; for the lovers, Nello
Gennaro and Alba Nardini, the balance falls on the side of tragedy.
Like the lovers in the opera, they are doomed by jealousy and mis-

understanding. But even here there is a kind of fateful propriety : unlike Mario Malvolto, Alba does not hesitate to join in death the lover whom she has killed, and the scene where they lie dead together on the sunlit square gives to the story a coda of operatic grandeur and melancholy beauty.

II

Im Schlaraffenland, Die Göttinnen and *Die Jagd nach Liebe* have an element of satire, but their social criticism is peripheral. *Professor Unrat, Die kleine Stadt* and the novel *Zwischen den Rassen*, which is concerned specifically with the schizophrenia of those who—like Mann—are situated between the Nordic and the Latin race : these are works which indicate growing concentration and a sharpening of focus. Mann begins to see his task as social critic more clearly; the pose of the outsider which may be detected in much of his early work, is dropped and the moralist and political thinker emerge more and more; Zola succeeds Nietzsche as Mann's model. Henceforth Heinrich Mann adheres to what he regards as a typically French tradition of liberal thought and writing. In the essay *Geist und Tat*, published in 1910, he compares the literary traditions of France and Germany : on the one hand, a symbiosis of writer and people, an impassioned scepticism and devotion to reason, a co-ordination of thought and action epitomized in the Revolution of 1789. In Germany, on the other hand, Mann observes a gulf between the writer and his nation, an unhappy aptitude for philosophical speculation, a total lack of coordination between ideas and things. German society is a society in which there are "icebergs of estrangement between the classes", a society in which the masses have no literary flair, and hence no vision. In Heinrich Mann's view the modern German writer has betrayed his nation :

Gerade er aber wirkt in Deutschland seit Jahrzehnten für die Beschönigung des Ungeistigen, für die sophistische Rechtfertigung des Ungerechten, für seinen Todfeind, die Macht.[9]

German poets have dwelt in an ivory tower, cut off from the concerns of the people :

Sie haben das Leben des Volkes nur als Symbol genommen für die eigenen hohen Erlebnisse. Sie haben der Welt eine Statistenrolle zugeteilt, ihre schöne Leidenschaft nie in die Kämpfe dort unten eingemischt, haben die Demokratie nicht gekannt und haben sie verachtet.[10]

There is, by and large, some truth in this view, although it does less than justice to the naturalistic writers and to an unruly genius like Frank Wedekind, for whom Mann elsewhere expresses great admiration. There is some truth, too, in Mann's contention that German society does not know its own nature because the poets have thus failed it. As he was to write later, "It is split into strata which are ignorant of each other, and the ruling class looms vaguely behind the clouds." It was to remedy this situation that Heinrich Mann embarked on his second trilogy, *Das Kaiserreich*, in which he attempts to analyse the society of Imperial Germany as Zola had analysed that of the Second Empire.

Of the three novels, *Der Untertan*, *Die Armen* and *Der Kopf*, which deal respectively with the middle class, the workers and the political leadership, the first is undoubtedly the most accomplished. The very name of its hero, Diederich Heßling, with the mixture of hatred and weakness it suggests, is an imaginative triumph. Heßling is a complex figure, embodying the contradictions of his class and yet by no means forfeiting his plausibility. He is a bully and a hysteric, a soulful sneak, a cad with a taste for Schubert. Heßling is essentially weak and neurotic : his character is splendidly summed up in the opening sentence of the novel—"Diederich Heßling war ein weiches Kind, das am liebsten träumte, sich vor allem fürchtete und viel an den Ohren litt."[11] His weakness is the inner uncertainty of a society that is outwardly sound and confident. As a child Diederich feels a compulsion to ingratiate himself with the local policeman, and on his form-master's birthday it is the cane that he chooses to decorate with a garland. He bullies a Jewish boy in his class and experiences a ravishing sense of power as the agent of public opinion : "Wie wohl man sich fühlte bei geteilter Verantwortlichkeit und einem Schuldbewußtsein, das kollektiv war !"[12]

The school community is succeeded by the student corporation that "thinks and wills for him", and by the "nation" as Heßling conceives it—embodied in the glittering figure of the Emperor. The lawyer, Wolfgang Buck, points out how falsely histrionic is Heßling's view of society :

> . . . da es in Wirklichkeit und im Gesetz weder den Herrn noch den Untertan gibt, erhält das öffentliche Leben einen Anstrich schlechten Komödiantentums. Die Gesinnung trägt Kostüm, Reden fallen wie von Kreuzrittern, indes man Blech erzeugt oder Papier, und das Pappschwert wird gezogen für einen Begriff wie den der Majestät, den doch kein Mensch mehr, außer in Märchenbüchern, ernsthaft erlebt . . . [13]

Although this miming of a bogus Romantic age serves Heßling's ethic of success, it also satisfies a deeper psychological need, a masochistic urge that is glimpsed in his sexual relationships, a longing for submission and for absorption in the might of the nation, "die Macht, die über uns hingeht und deren Hufe wir küssen! . . . Gegen die wir nichts können, weil wir sie alle lieben".[14]

The scorn of the intellectual cannot impede the rise of this paper manufacturer. His allies are too numerous and too influential : the brutish Junker, Regierungspräsident von Wulckow; the temporizing mayor; the venal newspaper editor; the paranoiac Francophobe, Professor Kühnchen; the renegade Jewish prosecutor, Jadassohn; the treacherous Social Democrat, Napoleon Fischer; the time-serving parson. Against this alliance of interests stand only the senile representative of the revolutionary tradition of 1848, the elder Buck; a progressive industrialist; a sceptical physician—and Wolfgang Buck, a German Hamlet, vacillating between the law and the theatre and failing in each because of his devotion to the other. Buck sees his contemporaries delivered into bondage more subtle than the tyrannies of the past, corrupted by social legislation designed to satisfy the people to the point where they will not fight for bread, let alone liberty : "Absolutism alleviated only by the mania for advertisement."

And so Heßling, assisted and exploited by the aristocracy, arrives at the climax of his career—the unveiling ceremony of a statue to Wilhelm I which has been erected at his instigation. With superb irony Mann puts into his mouth a fiery indictment of the French Second Empire that exactly describes the German Reich :

> Der Nerv der Öffentlichkeit war Reklamesucht, und jeden Augenblick schlug sie um in Verfolgungssucht. Im Äußern nur auf das Prestige gestellt, im Innern nur auf die Polizei, ohne anderen Glauben als die Gewalt, trachtete man nach nichts als nach Theaterwirkung, trieb ruhmrediger Pomp mit der vergangenen Heldenepoche, und der einzige Gipfel, den man erreichte, war der des Chauvinismus.[15]

As Diederich arrives at his peroration a tremendous thunderstorm breaks, the illustrious company scatters in all directions, and instead of being ceremonially invested Heßling has a decoration thrust into his hand by a soaking policeman with the words, "Da ham'se 'n Willemsorden."[16]

Seldom can a more effective symbolic climax have been contrived, and seldom can a work of fiction have been confirmed in real life with such promptitude : the final instalments of *Der Untertan* had not appeared in print when war was declared. As Zola's work was confirmed and realized by the collapse of 1870, so was Mann's by the catastrophe of 1914, and he might well have said of himself what he later said of Zola :

Einer, der äußerlich nichts vor Augen hatte, als was alle vor
Augen hatten, Macht, Glanz und Erfolg, hatte diesem Reich
und dieser Zeit dennoch stärker und tiefer in die Augen gesehen
als alle.[17]

The brother of the two poets, Viktor Mann, confirms that,
whereas Thomas was dumbfounded by the outbreak of war,
Heinrich had long expected it. The war was to become an occasion
of temporary but bitter dissension between Heinrich and Thomas—
a "Bruderzwist im Hause Mann".[18] Thomas saw the war
initially at least, as "fundamentally decent", as a solemn trial by
ordeal of the German nation, which might well "kindle the hearts
of her poets"; for Heinrich it was an unmitigated disaster. To an
essay by his brother which praised Frederick the Great and justified
his attack on Saxony Heinrich replied with astonishing boldness in
Zola (1915), once more denouncing German imperialism under the
name of the Second Empire. No intelligent reader could mistake
the import of these words :

Niemand im Grunde glaubt an das Kaiserreich, für das man
doch siegen soll. Man glaubt zuerst an seine Macht, man hält
es für fast unüberwindlich. Aber was ist Macht, wenn sie nicht
Recht ist, das tiefste Recht, wurzelnd in dem Bewußtsein
erfüllter Pflicht, erkämpfter Ideale, erhöhten Menschentums. Ein
Reich, das einzig auf Gewalt bestanden hat und nicht auf
Freiheit, Gerechtigkeit und Wahrheit, ein Reich, in dem nur
befohlen und gehorcht, verdient und ausgebeutet, des Menschen
aber nie geachtet ward, kann nie siegen, und zöge es aus mit
übermenschlicher Macht.[19]

The war, prophesies Mann, will not be an elevating but a degrading experience, dragging down in shame even those who deplore it :

Jetzt, da die Feinde dastehn, die eure Herren euch gemacht
haben, müssen noch die Letzten sich unterwerfen. Denn jetzt
sind die Unterdrücker wirklich, was zu sein sie so lange frech be-
haupteten : das Vaterland! Nicht nur mit kämpfen müßt ihr für
sie, die das Vaterland sind, ihr müßt mit fälschen, mit Unrecht
tun, müßt euch mit beschmutzen. Ihr werdet verächtlich wie sie.
Was unterscheidet euch noch von ihnen? Ihr seid besiegt schon
vor der Niederlage.[20]

In the ponderous *Betrachtungen eines Unpolitischen* Thomas
Mann replied to his brother, whom he variously termed "boulevard
moralist", "citoyen vertueux" and "European intellectual". The
main result of this work, which the author himself later called "a
rambling quixotic defence of bourgeois Romanticism, nationalism

and the German war", was to convince Thomas that his brother had been right : "hardly was it finished", he said, "than I disowned it".

Der Untertan is a splendid satire, executed with the deftness and the controlled distortions of a *Simplicissimus* caricature; it is mordant but not pitiless, full of understanding as well as anger. It has humorous scenes of unforced symbolism : Heßling squatting in a puddle before his monarch, or pursuing him with frantic hurrahs across a Roman square; dedicating his wedding night to the Emperor, or crouching under the lectern to escape the thunderbolts which his oration has apparently called down. Mann's touch is less adroit in the sequel, *Die Armen,* perhaps because the tragedy of the German situation had become more obvious. This is a sombre work with lurid highlights. Heßling has developed fully the satanic features that the elder Buck had glimpsed in his dying moments; he rules, a neurotic tyrant and the father of degenerate sons, over a colony of workers who are degraded, like the workers in Brecht's *Heilige Johanna*, by their dependence and penury : "All the people here were good people and behaved, in consequence of their poverty, as if they were evil." This is how the denizens of Heßling's industrial barracks are seen by their champion, Karl Balrich, who is determined to wrest from Heßling the wealth that is literally the wages of sin. His method is pathetically naïve : he sets about learning Latin so as to contest the legality of Heßling's estate, built up, it appears, on a loan that was never repaid, on money gained from adultery. Balrich is supported by a rancorous schoolmaster, Professor Klinkorum, and the sceptical Dr. Heuteufel; he is secretly encouraged by Wolfgang Buck, now a pensioner of Heßling. Every sort of intrigue and chicanery is practised against Balrich, but it is as much his disillusionment with his own class and their corrupt representative, Napoleon Fischer, that makes him give up the struggle. When war comes his class-hatred is diverted to the foreign enemy and he is shipped off unprotesting to the front. The pessimism of the novel is summed up by Wolfgang Buck's words :

> Die Macht—das ist mehr als Menschenwerk; das ist uralter Widerstand gegen unser Atmen, Fühlen, Ersehnen. Das ist der Zwang abwärts, das Tier, das wir einst waren. Das ist die Erde selbst, in der wir haften. Frühere Menschen, zu Zeiten, kamen los aus ihr, und künftige werden loskommen. Wir heutigen nicht. Ergeben wir uns.[21]

The capitulation of the intellectual is the theme of *Der Kopf.* This final novel of the trilogy is not a sequel to the other two, and it differs from them in that it is a semi-fictional work, in which real events feature and leading German politicians appear under pseudonyms. The documentation of the story occupied Mann for years, and it was not published until 1925. The plot revolves round two men of Mann's own generation who embark on political careers. Wolf Mangolf chooses the path of the conformist; Claudius Terra is a much more problematic character, half-idealist, half-charlatan, a disreputable Marquis Posa, a mountebank who pursues humanitarian ideals. His chief aim is to avert the coming war: "Only by means of cunning and deceit," he says, "can I swindle them out of the butchery they have set their hearts on." Terra joins the Establishment with the idea of subverting it; Mangolf, pre-occupied with personal ambitions, tries to preserve it, to maintain the system of balances between monarchy, government and industry devised by his master, Graf Lannas. Neither succeeds, because the real seat of power is occupied by the military caste and a clique of international financiers. The two men, who have lived out a love-hate relationship, commit suicide together; their bodies form a symbolic cross as they fall—and Mangolf's daughter leans from the window to cheer on the marching troops.

Der Kopf has not the clear contours of Der Untertan nor its uniformly satirical mood; it is a mixture of savage caricature and mystical symbolism. The language oscillates between brooding lyricism and the staccato style of "Neue Sachlichkeit". On the one hand there is the delicately equivocal relationship between Terra and his sister Lea—a recurrent theme in Mann's work, well illus-trated in the story, Der Bruder, written about this time. On the other hand there is the nightmarish description of the hate-feast of militarists and industrialists. The novel is altogether a sad and tortured work. Der Untertan was a prophecy; Der Kopf is an epitaph on a lost generation of intellectuals who were forced by the social pressures of their age into disingenuousness and anarchy on the one hand, irresponsible ambition and compromise on the other. It is an epitaph, too, on a nation that rushed to its doom, hypnotized by the abyss:

> Denn es wollte vollauf, was ihm bevorstand, Zusammenbruch, Chaos—unbarmherzig sich selbst, Wachs für fremde Sieger und die eigenen gierigen Verdiener. Es haßte Vernunft; wer es rettete, verriet es—und konnte es darum nur verraten, nicht retten.[22]

III

In Heinrich Mann's view the disappearance of the monarchy did not materially alter the nature of German society: "The true powers that be," he wrote, "of whom there are now so few, have abandoned their cover, we can see them. Previously they were brilliantly masked by monarchy and militarism." A superstitious faith in "the economy" replaces faith in the monarchy. The class-structure is changed only in so far as the distribution of wealth and influence becomes even more top-heavy—"anonymous powers lording it over armies of proletarians with widely varying incomes". The capitalist exploiter is no longer the grotesque Herr Panier but a financial Big Brother like the hero of Mann's short story *Kobes*, a faceless figure with appetite for nothing but power who exhorts his minions by loudspeaker :

> Kobes schlemmt nicht, Kobes säuft nicht, Kobes tanzt nicht, Kobes hurt nicht, Kobes arbeitet zwanzig Stunden am Tag.[23]

In this situation Heinrich Mann stood out as the champion and the critic of the Republic. As president of the literary section of the Prussian Academy his energies were devoted to speeches and articles in which he warned his countrymen against irresponsible industrialists, against their own innate conservatism and their vulnerability to political charlatans :

> Jeder schäbige Gauner kann dieses Volk, mit vorgemachten großen Worten, auf seine Seite bringen, der ehrliche Mann im Guten nie . . . Denn in diesem Lande ist persönliche Verantwortung bis heute unbekannt. Dieses Volk ist, wie kein anderes, im Sichausreden auf Kollektivitäten befangen. . . . Man kann es ungestraft verderben, spielt man ihm nur Betäubungsmittel in die Hände.[24]

Aware of the internal weakness of the Republic, Mann appealed to the Chancellor, Stresemann, to proclaim "a dictatorship of reason" in order to forestall the dictatorship of unreason that was already on its way. His was the thankless task of Cassandra, and yet even he could be unduly optimistic, for in 1925 he could still write :

> Voraussichtlich wird Deutschland niemals einen Diktator erleben. . . . Die ganze Vergangenheit des deutschen Volkes sollte dafür bürgen, daß eine solche fragwürdige Erscheinung seine politische Bühne nie betreten wird.[25]

Mann feared the power of the industrialist more than that of the demagogue; he was not alone in his underestimation of Hitler's appeal to the masses—the industrialists made the same mistake.

Mann continues, in his imaginative works, to record the changing social climate. In the satirical comedy, *Das gastliche Haus*, he illustrates what one of the characters calls the Bürgerdämmerung— the eclipse of the middle class. The middle-class manufacturer,

Schummer, who has ousted the aristocratic Quasses from their home, is in turn bought up by the spiv, Milbe. "In this house," concludes Schummer, "Quasses, Schummers and Milbes will in future live as one family." From the earthquake that has levelled the social edifice emerges post-war youth, disillusioned, unsentimental, cruelly honest. The type is already adumbrated by Mann in the figure of Wendlicher in *Brabach* (1916) and it is well illustrated in Wolf Schatz in the story, *Der Gläubiger*. Wolf turns with scorn on the respected judge who has for years been his mother's clandestine lover :

> Wir heucheln weniger als ihr. Wir nennen, was wir tun, beim richtigen Namen, und manches tun wir nicht. Nach Geld heiraten. Einander betrügen. Verbotenen Lebenswandel Führen : wir haben das alles nicht nötig.[26]

This younger generation is very different from that of Claude Marehn; it does not pursue sentiment, its ideal is "objectivity". The hero of Mann's musical comedy, *Bibi*, sings :

> Wir lachen nicht, wo Grund für eine Lache ist,
> Wir haben auch zum Weinen nicht viel Zeit,
> Wir haben nichts, was 'ne Sache ist—
> Aber wir haben Sachlichkeit.[27]

It was no doubt Mann's hope that these hard-boiled, self-reliant young people might prove more accessible to reason than their fathers. Rational humanism and internationalism are the ideals of Mann's political writing. The road to salvation he sees in a union of European peoples that will replace the unholy alliance of financiers. With prophetic insight Mann was appealing as early as 1924 for a political union, first of France and Germany, ultimately of all European states—for a Europe which, as he put it, "would not be complete without the birthplace of Shakespeare". Without union, Mann believes, Europe is doomed to become an economic colony of the United States, or—given another war—a military colony of the U.S.S.R. In a sense it might be said that both these things have happened since 1945. Practically the last words that Mann wrote on German soil were a plea for international understanding : *Bekenntnis zum Übernationalen*, published in December 1932. Nationalism, argues Mann, was originally the creation of the democratic movement, the cause of a nation against its despot; it has now become a function of unreason, a central idea of the irrational era that began in the second half of the nineteenth century. Internationalism represents reason restored and the only hope of Europe's survival. A prediction by Mann that the age of unreason would die out about 1940 has unfortunately not been

entirely fulfilled; he may have been naïve in thinking nationalism
the most dangerous form of political dementia. More sophisticated
ideologies, bristling with rational arguments, have since proved
themselves even more perilous and absurd. It might also be argued
that Mann's political thinking is outmoded in that it is too exclusively concerned with Europe. However, in the field where he
chose to make predictions he showed great perspicuity, and certainly his ideal of international co-operation seems to have gained
ground since 1932.

Like his short stories and plays, Mann's novels of this period
mostly exude the typically hectic atmosphere of the 1920's. In
common with Brecht, Feuchtwanger, Döblin and the artist George
Groß, Mann was fascinated by the jungle of the cities with their
jazz, professional boxers, fast cars and "big deals". This was just
the atmosphere to stimulate the romantic nerve in Mann's imagination, and often he seems less concerned with social criticism than
with the fate of individuals in a milieu that is very much that of
the detective story. In Mann, as in Brecht, mother-love is very
nearly the only emotion that remains uncorrupted in this context,
and in *Mutter Marie* and *Ein ernstes Leben* the theme is a mother's
battle for her child against the criminal designs of the Berlin underworld. In both these stories Mann also explores the near-incestuous
relationships that seemed to haunt him : the quasi-erotic feeling of
Marie for Valentin, her son, is reminiscent of the relationship
between Lili and her son in *Der Kopf*, while the intimacy of Terra
and Lea is raised to daemonic pitch in Kurt and Vicki Meier in
Ein ernstes Leben.

The action of these stories is hardly more sensational than that
of *Die große Sache*, in which, however, a concern with social and
political problems is more apparent. This is, in fact, a parable of
life during the years of the great depression. The "big deal" of the
title is a revolutionary explosive which a civil engineer, Birk, claims
to have invented. He hands the bomb over to his children, and
an insane struggle ensues, involving industrialists, speculators, spies,
spivs, a prize-fighter and his English trainer. After thirty-six hours
of breakneck journeys by car and aeroplane it turns out that everyone has been pursuing a phantom in the manner typical of their
day : the miracle explosive is indeed an "invention"—pure invention; the whole affair was a scheme devised by Birk to teach his
children a proper sense of values. The penumbra of the irrational
which not infrequently hovers round Mann's work is more marked
here than in any other of his stories. Birk is a modern mystic who
has the power to project his mind and even, apparently, his
physical presence into distant localities. To Birk's mind there are
in essence only three ways of life—honest work, wire-pulling and

crime; he tries to make his children see the unique value of the
first, and the wisdom he instils into their fevered minds is summed
up in the words: "Learn to be responsible! Learn to endure!
Learn to be happy!"

Mann's style, generally incisive, becomes even more elliptical and
terse in most of the works of this period. In an age of rapid communication, he remarks, the yardstick of style is the spoken word;
the poet's task is to model his sentences so that they retain, even in
the breathless articulation of the day, a certain aura of the sublime.
Again and again Mann's narrative condenses into dialogue, and even
descriptive passages often have the curtness of stage directions.

Amidst these hectic chronicles of the '20's and early '30's
is one work that looks back to an earlier age. *Eugénie* is set at the
very beginning of the Imperial era. Its heroine, Gabriele West, like
Lola in *Zwischen den Rassen*, Dora Breetpott in *Professor Unrat*
and Estela Vermühlen in *Der Unbekannte*—like Mann's own
mother, in fact—is an exotic creature, transported from France to
the solid respectability of Lübeck. This North German society, full
of the confidence inspired by victory, nevertheless feels a piquant
sympathy for the defeated Napoleon III and his Empress, Eugénie;
triumph is tempered with awe. The grandiose poet, Professor von
Heines (clearly a portrait of Emanuel Geibel in his old age), is
moved to compose a play in which Gabriele West acts the part of
the Empress. Once again the delicate balance between illusion and
reality is manipulated; through the play—itself a symptom of an
irrational romantic impulse in this staid society—Mann hints at the
affinities between the Second Empire and the Reich. The dubious
Herr Pidohn, a financial speculator of the type that is to supplant
the solid Lübeck merchants, acts the part of the political speculator,
Napoleon. *Eugénie* is a study of the affinity between two ill-starred
empires that is as restrained as *Der Untertan* is robust. There is
an air of nostalgia about it, and Mann seems reluctant to shatter
the idyll completely: a tragic conclusion is avoided, and Konsul
West and Gabriele, at least, achieve integrity and harmony.

IV

Cut off after 1933 from the nation whose social and political
malaise he had so faithfully recorded, Mann at last departed from
his resolve to write novels of contemporary society. The last phase
of his work is dominated by the third great pillar that supports a
span of nearly sixty years' creative writing—the two historical
novels, *Die Jugend des Henri Quatre* and *Die Vollendung des
Henri Quatre*. During a visit to Pau in 1925 Mann had been impressed by the living memory of Henry of Navarre preserved

among ordinary people—"le seul roi", he wrote later, "de qui le pauvre ait gardé la mémoire". In his exile he turned to the life of Henry, seeing in it not just an historical episode, but an exemplar of the true man and ruler, as well as an allegory of the never-ending struggle between love and hatred, reason and fanaticism, tyranny and liberty. Mann does not hesitate to idealize the character and aspirations of Henry, for the novel is designed to put into narrative patterns and symbolic scenes the liberal idealism of his political writing.

For Mann, Henry's excellence as a ruler stems from his qualities as a man : he has the emotional well-temperedness and the sound sensuality of the Mediterranean race, the critical reason of the Frenchman; he is both an intellectual and a man of action, a militant humanist. Applied to him, the traditional term "prince of the blood" has more than its traditional sense :

Il possède le mot propre par quoi il signale et ses qualités et ses droits. En appuyant sur son titre de *prince du sang* c'est en réalité sur les prérogatives de sa personnalité morale qu'il insiste. . . . C'est sa belle santé morale qui lui donne l'avantage sur tous les immodérés de son époque.

In the same way, his kingdom is "more than land and territory, it is the same thing as liberty and one with the law".

Unlike Frederick the Great as he is portrayed by Mann in his unfinished *Traurige Geschichte von Friedrich dem Großen*, Henry has survived the treacheries and brutalities of his youth without being morally maimed; he retains his balance "above the chasm of his own being". Henry is the first modern man, and his great "innovation" is humanity : "Faith in man's destiny on earth, his destiny to be rational and brave, free, prosperous and happy." He turns his back on the massacre of St. Bartholomew, which he has himself barely escaped, and looks to the future. The secret of Henry's greatness is a simple heart full of a love that runs the whole gamut from the erotic to the humanitarian. His many love-affairs are the blossoming of a nature indestructibly healthy. They are the inspiration of his deeds; the same psychic force impels the ruler and the lover :

Die Liebe (ist) die wahre Kraft seines Wesens. . . . Für alles, was er tut, ist sein ursprünglicher Antrieb das Geschlecht und die gesteigerte Kraft, die es hervorbringt durch seine Entzückung.[28]

Henry epitomizes Mann's unchanging belief that the state of a nation is ultimately a state of mind.

Henry's heart is simple, his mind is not. During his virtual imprisonment in the Louvre he learns that "totus mundus exercet histrionem"—all the world's a stage, and that he, too, must dissemble. To his enemies the young prince is a harmless buffoon, but his buffoonery is in truth a mask. Henry has the courage to discard impractical notions of honour and dignity and to grasp that the first object in diplomacy and war is—to survive. Like Brecht's anti-heroes, he practises the prudent defiance of the oppressed. But even as king he is prepared to act a part, to afford to his people—for the sake of higher aims—the spectacle of a great monarch, which is the only form of greatness they can comprehend. Here again, as in *Das Kaiserreich* or in the drama, *Der Weg zur Macht*, with its confrontation of Napoleon Bonaparte and Talma, there is the ambiguity of Kaiser and Komödiant. In Henry's case, however, the rôle is dictated by reason and played out for humanitarian ends.

Ranged against Henry are the dark and obscene forces of the past, symbolized in the grotesque creatures that haunt the labyrinthine galleries of the Louvre. At their head is Catharine de Medici, who personifies the lust for power. The panoply of tyranny, symbolized by Elizabeth of Austria in her cloth of gold, may pass away; tyranny will remain, because it is a cast of mind :

> Es sind keine Protestanten, Katholiken, Spanier oder Franzosen. Es ist eine Gattung Mensch : die will die düstere Gewalt, die Erdenschwere, und Ausschweifungen liebt sie im Grauen und in der unreinen Verzückung.[29]

The Catholic League of the sixteenth century is a paradigm of party hatred; behind Mann's descriptions of its demonstrations may be heard the delirious ovations of Nürnberg.

The story of Henry has universal significance because it describes human attitudes that are universal. At times, indeed, Mann's view of the human mind and human behaviour transcends psychology and politics and becomes almost theological. The vision of man's fight against tyranny assumes apocalyptic features. Thus Henry speaks of his enemies :

> Sie oder ich, von meinem Untergang lassen sie nicht. Sie betreiben aber mit meinem Untergang einen größeren, den der Freiheit, Vernunft und Menschlichkeit. Überwältigt hat ihre universale Monarchie und Weltherrschaft viele Glieder der Christenheit, die wird daran zum Ungeheuer, ein unförmlicher Leib und giftige Köpfe. Meine Sache ist, daß die Völker leben sollen, und sollen nicht statt der lebendigen Vernunft an bösen Träumen leiden in dem aufgedunsenen Bauch der universalen Macht, die sie alle verschluckt hat. Ich bin gemacht, um zu retten, so viele von ihnen noch die Wahl haben und wollen mit mir den engen Pfad gehen.[30]

The narrow path of salvation is none other than Mann's ideal of a league of nations, first conceived in modern times by Henry and his minister, Sully. Characteristic of Mann's thought and experience, too, is the concern for Germany that he attributes to Henry. The plague that spreads from beyond the Rhine is symbolic of moral infections, and when Henry and his vision of a united Europe are destroyed by Ravaillac's dagger, it is in Germany that the explosion of prejudice and hatred takes place some few years later : the Thirty Years War, from which many of the tribulations of modern Europe might be said to stem directly. The murder of Henry is seen by Heinrich Mann not only as a symbolic defeat for the cause of reason, humanity and freedom, but as an objective turning-point in European history.

The two novels of Henry's life were not the last of Mann's works; they were followed by volumes of essays and reminiscences, as well as by a satirical novel of the Czech resistance, *Lidice*, and by a strange and involved account of the outbreak of the 1939 war in France (*Der Atem*), which falls far short of the standard of his other work. After his death the fragmentary dramatized novel on Frederick the Great was published. None of these later works, however, embodies the essence of Mann's thought or illustrates the maturity of his art as well as *Henry IV*. It is a work of epic stamina that moves at a steady, unhurried pace. Often the narrative gives way to pure dialogue, for which Mann showed an increasing fondness, and the author does not hesitate to employ elliptical epic phrases of his own devising. The style is terse and compact, not so much German in its syntax and rhythm as French—and, indeed, the periodic commentaries and the final vision of the transfigured hero are written in French.

Over the years Mann had formed his vision of the world through the medium of his poetic creations; in *Henri IV* he finally shows "what could be done with the world". It does not matter that the world of Henry is imperfect, that it is past, that the battle has not been won. What matters to Mann is the confidence that such personalities as Henry have existed and can exist. As always, it is the individual who is of paramount importance, the human rather than the political constitution. This was in the mind of Thomas Mann when he wrote of *Henry IV* :

> . . . ein Werk erster Ordnung, in dem Güte und Kühnheit sich auf eine Weise mischen, die, aus dem Intellektuellen ins Wirkliche übertragen, einen Erdteil erretten könnte, ein Geschichts- und Menschheitsgedicht, dessen trauernde Ironie und grimmige Kenntnis des Höllisch-Bösen seinem Glauben an die Vernunft

und das Gute keinen Abbruch tut; eine Synthese aller Gaben dieses großen Künstlers, worin sich der schon politisch gespannte Ästhetizismus seiner Jugend mit der durchaus eigenartigen kämpferischen Milde seines Alters bewundernswert zusammenschließt.[31]

Die Göttinnen, Das Kaiserreich, Henry IV : pillars of a life's work that has the unity of Europe's destiny, for even the novels of Mann's youth are relevant to the evolution of European politics. They show the decaying humus from which dictatorship grew, "literary aestheticism as the forerunner of political vices", said Mann. What we see in *Die Göttinnen* is a society of the utterly irresponsible, the apotheosis of the irrational, the modish admiration of force as an aesthetic phenomenon. From this intellectual climate came a generation of men without true seriousness and already half in love with death. So, at least, Mann sees it. His vision has undoubtedly something of the enormity and the grotesque quality that marks his imagination throughout : Mann has the grand gestures of Victor Hugo as well as the intellect of Zola. Exaggeration was for him almost an artistic principle :

Die großen Romane, he writes, sind immer und ausnahmslos übersteigert gewesen. Das Denken und Fühlen der Menschen war in ihnen heftiger und entschlossener, das Schicksal gewaltiger, und die Dinge und Vorgänge erstanden stärker in einer Luft, die zugleich leichter war und erregender glänzte.[32]

The man who sees an avalanche approaching may be excused a degree of exaggeration when he warns his companions, and the occasional stridency of Mann's warnings may perhaps be pardoned in view of the accuracy of his prophecies. His gift is almost uncanny, so that one is tempted to link it with the evidences of telepathy and second sight in his stories and in his own experience. It may be that the full tale of his prophecies is not yet told; Charles de Gaulle may not be Mann's ideal reincarnation of Henri IV, but at least a union of France and Germany, and ultimately of all Western Europe no longer seems an impractical ideal.

Heinrich Mann is in some ways both an anachronism and uncharacteristic of his nation. His conception of the writer as a vital organ in the body politic, the conscience of a nation and the guardian of its liberties, smacks of the eighteenth century and may seem out of place in an era of massive political and commercial propaganda. If this conception is out of date, so much the worse for us, for this would mean that the area of individual responsibility had somehow been curtailed. In his determination to speak to the nation as a whole and to help shape its policies, Mann differs probably from the majority of German writers, who have tended to address themselves rather to the individual cultured mind. To some readers, Mann may seem naïve in his pursuit of political ideals, undiscriminating, for instance, in his unqualified enthusiasm for the Russian revolution as the worthy continuation of the revolution of 1789. It would be difficult, however, to doubt his integrity, his sincere devotion to principles which he is capable of formulating clearly and simply. Mann is essentially a rebel—not the witty, ironic, ambiguous rebel of the Brecht or Tucholsky type, but essentially a dignified rebel—a German Victor Hugo. He is also a responsible rebel and—rare phenomenon—a rebel with endurance. For Mann was not so naïve as to believe that the battle could be won for good :

> Der Kampf ist nie aus, der Sieg hat kein Gesicht, und erst die Söhne mögen feststellen, wieviel die Väter gewonnen haben. Die Wirklichkeit ist bitter und dunkel, wir können nichts tun, als unser Blut und unsere Tränen geben. Wir können nichts tun, als kämpfen für die Ziele, die nie erreicht werden, aber von denen abzusehen schimpflich wäre—kämpfen und dann dahingehen.[33]

Mann is a prophet by no means without honour in his own country—indeed, there are some who think that too much honour is paid him in the Eastern parts of it. There are reservations, however. It is understandable that there should be, for it is not easy—and, as we may see from the case of Diederich Heßling, not entirely healthy—to love the rod that beats us. It seems, perhaps, to some Germans that Mann too whole-heartedly transferred his allegiance to France—although this is an offence that may become more venial when Mann's dream is realized. Perhaps the fundamental reason, however, why Mann failed to influence his people more during his life, or to gain a place nearer their hearts after his death, is simply to be found in his character as a political moralist. Just a year after his brother's death, Thomas Mann wrote of him :

> Die Verbindung des Dichters mit dem politischen Moralisten war den Deutschen zu fremd, als daß sein kritisches Genie über ihr Schicksal etwas vermocht hätte, und noch heute, fürchte ich, wissen wenige von ihnen, daß dieser Tote einer ihrer größten Schriftsteller war.[34]

When the bitterness of two wars has faded, perhaps the justice of that final comment will be more widely recognized among Mann's own countrymen.

TRANSLATIONS

1. One just goes on creating characters and making them move. The idea is still very vague. If one has definite opinions, then they have only emerged from the activity of creating characters.

2. That is what we lack: danger! I am the end-product of generations of middle-class endeavours directed towards prosperity, security, freedom from illusion, towards an existence entirely serene and smooth. In me the ideal of middle-class culture ought to be attained. In fact, all movement has come to a standstill in me: I believe nothing, hope for nothing, strive for nothing, acknowledge nothing: no fatherland, no family, no friendship. And only the oldest of the emotions and the last to expire still troubles me. I barely possess it, but I can still recall it. Love: all its cruelty, its delight in danger, its will to destroy and to be absorbed in another being—where would I, last feeble representative of the middle class, find so many violent urges.

3. My whole life was one great love; with ardent breast I cast myself upon all that was great and beautiful. I scorned nothing, condemned no one, nourished no rancour. To the very end I acquiesced in my own nature and in my fate.

4. I have in fact played out, item by item, the programme that was specified for me before I ever came on the scene. One after another, the three goddesses have draped the folds of my garments, ordered my gestures, each to her own way of thinking. My life was a work of art.

5. One breaks into the sort of happiness I am familiar with as one burgles a safe. A couple of weeks' squandering—and it's all over once more.

6. In its Gothic nooks there crouches, and through its gabled alleyways there creeps something uncanny, something senile, some hereditary taint —medieval hysteria, superannuated neurosis, something in the nature of a religious malady.

7. ... stronger, warmer men, who were not eroded by understanding, who only took thought as long as they were speaking, who did not pursue with agonizing meticulousness the evolution of their inner destiny, but for whom everything proceeded from outside themselves ... they were not all alone with their shredded souls.

8. I speak about a small community that—full of vices and depravity —nevertheless in a moment of love, joined in brotherhood on its dusty town square, takes an irrevocable step upwards towards greatness.

9. It is he who has worked for decades in Germany to put a good face on the things that are not of the mind, to justify by sophistry what is unjust, in the interests of his mortal enemy—authority.

10. They have taken the life of the people only as a symbol for their own lofty sensations. They have accorded to life only the part of a walker-on, have never involved their fine feelings in the struggles down below, have never known what democracy is and yet have scorned it.

11. Diederich Hessling was a sensitive child who liked best to dream, was frightened of everything and suffered a lot with his ears.

12. How grand it felt when responsibility was divided and the sense of guilt collective.

13. . . . since in fact and in law there is neither ruler nor subject public life takes on the superficial colouring of poor play-acting. Political sentiment wears costume, speeches are made in the tone of Crusaders by manufacturers of tinplate or paper and the cardboard sword is drawn for a notion like that of "His Majesty", which no one seriously believes in outside fairy-tales.

14. The authority that rides over us as we kiss its hooves! Against which we can do nothing because we are all in love with it.

15. The vital nerve of public life was a mania for advertisement, and again and again it turned into a mania for persecution. Outwardly bolstered up by prestige, inwardly by the police, without any faith other than force, they sought only theatrical effect, made great play with the heroic past, and the only height they scaled was the height of Jingoism.

16. 'Ere's yer Order o' William.

17. A man, who outwardly had no more in front of his eyes than everyone else—power, brilliance and success—had nevertheless gazed with more intensity and insight than any other into the eyes of this régime and this era.

18. Fraternal squabble in the house of Mann. (The reference is to Grillparzer's historical drama, *Ein Bruderzwist im Hause Habsburg*.)

19. No one really believes in the Empire for which they are supposed to conquer. To begin with they believe in its might, believe it to be well-nigh invincible. But what is might when it is not right, the most profound right, rooted in the consciousness of duty done, of ideals fought for and won, of a higher humanity. An Empire that has rested on might alone, and not on liberty, justice and truth, an Empire in which orders were given and obeyed, in which money was made and people exploited, but in which no account was taken of the individual—such an Empire cannot prevail, even though it should go forth with superhuman might.

20. Now, when the enemies that your masters have made for you are arrayed against you, every last one of you will have to submit. For now the oppressors are in fact what they have so long and so arrogantly claimed to be: the Fatherland! You will not only have to fight along with those who are the fatherland, you will have to swindle along with them, do wrong along with them, soil yourselves along with them. What distinguishes you from them? You have lost the battle long before you are defeated.

21. Power—it is more than the work of men; it is the primordial resistance to our breathing, feeling, longing. It is the force that drags us down, the brute that once we were. It is the soil in which we were planted. Men before us have torn themselves free from it at times, and men will do so in the future. Our generation will not. Let us give up.

22. For it sought with all its heart that which was in store for it—ruin, chaos—ruthless towards itself, wax in the hands of alien victors and its own greedy money-grubbers. It detested reason; whoever tried to save it, betrayed it—and for this same reason could only betray it, not save it.

23. Kobes is no glutton, Kobes does not drink, Kobes does not dance, Kobes knows no whores, Kobes works for twenty hours a day.

24. Any shabby tramp can get this nation on his side with grand and

empty words, an honest man with good intentions, never. For in this country personal responsibility is unknown to this very day. This nation is bogged down like no other in the excuses of collective responsibility. Anyone can ruin it with impunity, provided only he sees to it that it has access to suitable narcotics.

25. As far as can be seen, Germany will never have a dictator.... The whole past tradition of the German people should be a guarantee that such a dubious phenomenon will never tread its political stage.

26. We are not such hypocrites as you. We call what we do by its proper name, and there are quite a few things we don't do. Marry for money. Give each other away. Live a dishonest life: we are above that sort of thing.

27.   We do not laugh when there's something to laugh at,
         Nor have we got much time to cry,
         We've nothing that you'd call an object,
         But we do have objectivity.

28. Love is the real driving force of his being.... In everything he does his ultimate impulse is sex and the heightened power that comes from its stimulation.

29. It is not the Protestants, the Catholics, the Spaniards or the French. It is a breed of men: they seek a murky power, the lethargy of the earth, they love to wallow in horror and in unclean rapture.

30. It is them or me: they are intent on destroying me. But with my destruction they seek the destruction of something greater, the destruction of liberty, reason and humanity. Their universal monarchy and hegemony have overwhelmed many of the limbs of the Christian body; it has become a monster, a misshapen trunk and venomous heads. It is my concern that the nations should live and should not, for want of the living power of reason, suffer evil dreams in the swollen belly of the universal power that has devoured them all. I was created to rescue as many of them as have the choice and as will walk the narrow path with me.

31. ...a work of the first rank, in which good nature and vigour are mingled in a manner which, if it were transferred from the world of the mind to the real world, could be the salvation of a continent, a poem of history and of humanity, in which melancholy irony and savage insight into infernal wickedness do not impair faith in reason and goodness; a synthesis of all the talents of this great artist in which his youthful aestheticism with its political overtones is admirably linked with the characteristic valiant urbanity of his maturity.

32. Without exception great novels have been products of exaggeration. The thoughts and emotions of men in them were always more vehement and more resolute, destiny was more potent, and things and events arose with sharper contours in an atmosphere that was more rarefied and that shed a more exciting glow.

33. The fight is never done, victory has no face, and only the sons may tell how much their fathers have won. Reality is bitter and dark, we can do nothing but give our blood and tears. We can do nothing but fight for objectives that will never be attained but from which it would be shameful to avert our eyes—fight and then pass on.

34. The combination of the poet and the political moralist was too alien to the Germans for his critical genius to have much influence on their fate, and even today, I fear, few of them realize that the dead man was one of their greatest writers.

SELECT BIBLIOGRAPHY

WORKS

Heinrich Mann entrusted his works to a number of different publishers, and there is as yet no definitive edition. The following is a complete list with the year of first publication in each case. Those marked * are available in an edition now being produced by Claassen Verlag, who have also published a volume of selected essays. Aufbau Verlag have published the complete plays in one volume; *Professor Unrat* is published by Rowohlt.

1893: *In einer Familie* (Novel)
1897: *Das Wunderbare* (Short stories)
1900: *Im Schlaraffenland* (Novel)
1902/03: *Die Göttinnen* (*Diana, Minerva, Venus*: novels)
1903/04: *Die Jagd nach Liebe* (Novel)
1904/05: *Flöten und Dolche* (Short stories)
1905/06: *Eine Freundschaft* (Essay)
         Schauspielerin (Short story)
1905: *Professor Unrat* (Novel)
1906: *Stürmische Morgen* (Short stories)
1907: *Zwischen den Rassen* (Novel)
1908: *Die Bösen* (Short stories)
*1910: *Die kleine Stadt* (Novel)
         Das Herz (Short stories)
         Variété, Der Tyrann, Die Unschuldige (One-act plays)
1911: *Rückkehr vom Hades* (Short stories)
         Schauspielerin (Drama)
1912: *Die große Liebe* (Drama)
1913: *Madame Legros* (Drama)
*1914: *Der Untertan* (Novel: published in book form, 1918)
1915: *Zola* (Essay)
1916: *Brabach* (Drama)
1917: *Die Armen* (Novel)
1918: *Der Weg zur Macht* (Drama)
1919: *Macht und Mensch* (Speeches)
1920: *Die Ehrgeizige* (Short story)
1923: *Kobes* (Short story)
         Diktatur der Vernunft (Speeches)
         Das gastliche Haus (Drama)
         Der Jüngling (Short story)
1924: *Abrechnungen* (Short stories)
1925: *Der Kopf* (Novel)
1926: *Liliane und Paul* (Short story)
1927: *Mutter Marie* (Novel)

*1928: *Eugénie* (Novel)
   Sieben Jahre (Speeches)
1929: *Sie sind jung* (Short stories)
1931: *Die große Sache* (Novel)
*1932: *Ein ernstes Leben* (Novel)
   Das öffentliche Leben (Essays)
   Das Bekenntnis zum Übernationalen (Essay)
1933: *Der Haß* (Essays)
*1935: *Die Jugend des Königs Henri Quatre* (Novel)
1936: *Es kommt der Tag* (Anthology)
*1937: *Die Vollendung des Königs Henri Quatre* (Novel)
1939: *Mut* (Essays)
1943: *Lidice* (Novel)
1945: *Ein Zeitalter wird besichtigt* (Memoirs and essays)
1949: *Der Atem* (Novel)
*1950: *Empfang bei der Welt* (Novel)
*1962: *Die traurige Geschichte von Friedrich dem Großen* (Dramatized
   novel. The edition includes an essay on Frederick the Great, first
   published in 1949.)
   A detailed bibliography will be found in the periodical, *Aufbau*,
   vol. 6 (1950).

BIOGRAPHY AND COMMENTARY

IHERING, H. *Heinrich Mann*. Berlin, 1951.
KANTOROWICZ, A. *Heinrich und Thomas Mann*. Berlin, 1956.
LEMKE, K. *Heinrich Mann. Zu seinem 75. Geburtstag*. Berlin, 1946.
MANN, V. *Wir waren fünf. Bildnis der Familie Mann*. Constance, 1949.
SCHRÖDER, W. *Heinrich Mann. Bildnis eines Meisters*. Vienna, 1931.
SINSHEIMER, H. *Heinrich Manns Werk*. Munich, 1921.
WEISSTEIN, U. *Heinrich Mann*. Tübingen, 1962.

Stefan Zweig

Stefan Zweig

by W. I. LUCAS

Stefan Zweig was born on 28 November 1881 in Vienna. After a Gymnasium education, he studied Literature and Philosophy at the Universities of Vienna and Berlin, and obtained the doctor's degree of the University of Vienna. At the age of eighteen, while still at school, he was already writing for some of the best periodicals in Vienna. In 1902 he visited Verhaeren in Brussels and later spent some time in Paris where he met many of the cultural leaders of the day. In the years before the First World War he spent the greater part of his time in travel—Paris, London, Florence, Berlin, Rome, India, China, Africa and the North American continent. He was in Vienna during the First World War; but in the autumn of 1917 he received permission to travel to Switzerland to become a newspaper correspondent and later to attend the first production of his play *Jeremias*; whilst there, he was in close touch with his friend Romain Rolland. After the war he settled in a house on the Kapuzinerberg in Salzburg. It was here that he was able to welcome many famous people to his home. In 1938 he was driven into exile by the Nazis and migrated to England. Later he went to North America, and finally to Brazil. He and his wife committed suicide on 22 February 1942.

"WIDER meinen Willen bin ich Zeuge geworden der furchtbarsten Niederlage der Vernunft und des wildesten Triumphes der Brutalität innerhalb der Chronik der Zeiten; nie—ich verzeichne dies keineswegs mit Stolz, sondern mit Beschämung—hat eine Generation einen solchen moralischen Rückfall aus solcher geistigen Höhe gelitten wie die unsere. In dem einen kleinen Intervall, seit mir der Bart zu sprossen begann und seit er mir zu ergrauen beginnt, in diesem einen Jahrhundert hat sich mehr ereignet an radikalen Verwandlungen und Veränderungen als sonst in zehn Menschengeschlechtern ... So verschieden ist mein Heute von jedem meiner Gestern, meine Aufstiege und meine Abstürze, daß mich manchmal dünkt ich hätte nicht bloß eine, sondern mehrere, völlig voneinander verschiedene Existenzen gelebt. . . . Jedesmal wenn ich im Gespräch jüngeren Freunden Episoden aus der Zeit vor dem ersten Kriege erzähle, merke ich an ihren erstaunten Fragen, wieviel für sie schon historisch oder unvorstellbar von dem geworden ist, was für mich noch selbstverständliche Realität bedeutet. Und ein geheimer Instinkt in mir gibt ihnen recht: zwischen unserem Heute, unserem Gestern und Vorgestern sind alle Brücken abgebrochen."[1]

These words are from the preface to Stefan Zweig's autobiography. He—an Austrian, a Jew, a writer, a humanist, and a pacifist—belonged to a generation that was convulsed by two world wars with all the turmoil and changes that went with them. Three times, he relates, he was deprived of his home and his means of existence; he was forced into exile, and finally ended his life by suicide having seen every one of his ideals shattered. Outwardly he lived a life of detachment from all these convulsions; inwardly he clung firmly to his own convictions and never once did he compromise with the political powers that dominated his homeland.

Vienna, at the time when Stefan Zweig was born—28 November 1881—was still the metropolis and cultural centre of a large empire. It had a long tradition of readily assimilating ideas and movements in the arts from all over Europe. Zweig acknowledged generously the debt that he owed his native city for his development both as a thinker and as an artist: "Aufnahmewillig und mit einem besonderen Sinn für Empfänglichkeit begabt, zog diese Stadt die disparatsten Kräfte an sich, entspannte, lockerte, begütigte sie; es war lind, hier zu leben, in dieser Atmosphäre geistiger Konzilianz, und bewußt wurde jeder Bürger dieser Stadt zum Übernationalen, zum Kosmopolitischen, zum Weltbürger, erzogen."[2] And in another passage he wrote: "das Genie Wiens—ein spezifisch musikalisches —war von je gewesen, daß es alle volkhaften, alle sprachlichen Gegensätze in sich harmonisierte, seine Kultur eine Synthese aller abendländischen Kulturen; wer dort lebte und wirkte, fühlte sich frei von Enge und Vorurteil. Nirgends war es leichter, Europäer zu sein, und ich weiß, daß ich es zum guten Teil dieser Stadt zu danken habe, . . . daß ich frühzeitig gelernt, die Idee der Gemeinschaft als die höchste meines Herzens zu lieben. Man lebte gut, man lebte leicht und unbesorgt in jenem alten Wien."[3] Many Jewish families played a brilliant rôle in Viennese society, among them Stefan Zweig's own family. He was born into a prosperous upper middle-class home: his father, who came from a Moravian family of merchants and industrialists, amassed a considerable fortune; his mother came from a family of international bankers, professors, lawyers, and doctors and had connections with related families all over Europe, and even America. Stefan felt more at home with his mother's relatives than with his father's, and he valued their sense of tradition more than the wealth of his father.

The affluence of his parents made life too easy for Zweig during his childhood years, and he admitted in his autobiography that he had been spoilt as a child. Nor did he experience any need to struggle or face difficulties in the world outside. Yet his first wife, Friederike, writing about her husband's childhood,[4] indicates that he never overcame a feeling of resentment at the prohibitions and restraints he had to endure amidst the parental luxury. "His sensitive emotional apparatus had been—sometimes without apparent cause—manifestly irritated and injured. Consequently, he was exposed to strange reflexes and fluctuations of mood."[5] It appears that the financial security of his home was balanced by an inner sense of insecurity as if he were always expecting some sort of a shock. This paradox may well be the reason for the reticence and the reserve before strangers that was so characteristic of him in later life. His modesty was such that he tended to avoid public service, to remain detached from politics, and to decline any honours or titles or to participate in any kind of organization however much he approved of its aims. Yet he could be generous in helping others, especially younger writers who sought his advice, and he had many friends who were deeply attached to him.

Zweig began his literary career by writing for the best periodicals of Vienna whilst he was still at school. The enjoyment of art and literature and the writing of poems were natural to him and to some of his school-fellows. "Schon im Gymnasium war nicht nur mir allein, sondern einer ganzen Gruppe künstlerische Betätigung das uneingestandene Ziel und Kunstgenuß die gemeinsame Leidenschaft. Wir bildeten gleichsam die letzte Generation jenes heute fast nicht mehr rekonstruierbaren Kunstfanatismus, der diese alte Theater- und Komödiantenstadt von je auszeichnete."[6] At the age of nineteen he had already published his first slim volume of poems, under the title *Silberne Seiten,* poems, like those of his second volume, *Die frühen Kränze,* published in 1906, that are little more than the romantic dreams and fantasies of adolescence.

Zweig was not misled by his early success in securing publication for these early efforts. He knew he lacked the maturity to devote himself exclusively to these literary pursuits as yet. In his autobiography he wrote of his student days in Berlin : "Innerlich war mir mein Weg für die nächsten Jahre jetzt klar geworden; viel sehen, viel lernen und dann erst eigentlich beginnen! Nicht mit voreiligen Publikationen vor die Welt treten—erst von der Welt ihr Wesentliches wissen!"[7] He needed several years to gain a wider experience of life so as to enrich his imagination, and to learn more of the art of writing. To do this he had first of all to escape from the atmosphere of Vienna : he had come to hate the sheltered and secure life of his youth, he was oppressed by the superficiality and hypocrisy of middle-class society there and longed to be free and independent : "Es war doch der eigentliche Sinn meiner Eskapade, jener gesicherten und bürgerlichen Atmosphäre zu entkommen und statt dessen losgelöst und ganz auf mich gestellt zu leben. Ich wolte ausschließlich Menschen kennenlernen . . . und möglichst interessante Menschen."[8] Next, he completed his university studies in order to comply with what was expected of him by his family. Then he spent several years in travel : Paris, London, Florence, Rome, farther afield to India, China and Africa and finally to North America and Cuba. For the future writer these travels provided a wealth of material and impressions which later found their way into his fiction. The fourth step he took was directed towards developing his powers of expression and gaining fluency and ease in the handling of language, by translating literary works from other languages, mainly French and English, into his native German : "dem Rate Dehmels ... entsprechend, nützte ich meine Zeit, um aus fremden Sprachen zu übersetzen, was ich noch heute für die beste Möglichkeit für einen jungen Dichter halte, den Geist der eigenen Sprache tiefer und schöpferischer zu begreifen."[9] Baudelaire, Verlaine, Keats, William Morris are among the authors he translated.

The search for suitable material to translate led Zweig to discover the Belgian poet Emile Verhaeren who at that time was still almost unknown in Germany. Zweig was attracted to the poetry, but he was even more fascinated by the man. What impressed him about the Belgian poet was the contemporary and modern approach he had adopted in his art and his European, rather than national, outlook; he felt too that here was an older man who could be useful to him as a model and a guide, for he recognized that Verhaeren's achievements had been the result of hard work rather than of any innate genius. Zweig went to Brussels in 1902, some four years after he had started to translate the Belgian's poetry into German, with the deliberate intention of meeting Verhaeren and out of this visit there grew a friendship between the two men that lasted until the war of 1914 intervened. Stefan Zweig was proud of the fact that he was the one to introduce Verhaeren to Germany, firstly by the translations he published and secondly by his critical biography which appeared in 1910. Moreover, his admiration for the Belgian had also helped Zweig to acquire a sense of purpose and of direction for his own future as a creative writer.

This study on Verhaeren was only one of a whole series of biographical works, mainly on contemporary French writers whom Zweig admired and helped to introduce to German readers. Biography was a genre that was popular in Germany and was being successfully cultivated by other writers (e.g. Emil Ludwig) as well as Stefan Zweig. His first study, on *Verlaine,* was published as early as 1902. The work on *Verhaeren* (1910) was followed by a portrait of *Romain Rolland* (1921), a Frenchman whose friendship and ideals he shared during the First World War. In 1927 he published a study of *Marceline Desbordes-Valmore* whom he regarded as

the greatest poetess of France; it was through this work and translations of it into other languages that she acquired an international
reputation. Later biographies—*Joseph Fouché* (1929, his last work
to be published in Germany during his lifetime), *Marie Antoinette*
(1932), *Triumph und Tragik des Erasmus von Rotterdam* (1934),
Marie Stuart (1935), *Castellio gegen Calvin* (1936), *Magellan*
(1938)—dealt with historical personages from other countries as
well as France who illustrated in various ways that enlightened
humanism upon which Zweig based his own faith. His last critical
biography was devoted to Balzac, but death intervened before he
could complete what he had hoped would have been the major
work of his life. This work "was to be a summing up of his own
experience as an author and of what life had taught him. Balzac
seemed to him to be a unique theme, appropriate to his own
special gifts and, as it were, destined to be treated by him. Since
his early days in Vienna he had been deeply interested in Balzac's
writings and the Balzac legend."[10] Other Austrian writers had been
deeply impressed by Balzac in their youth besides Zweig—Hugo
von Hofmannsthal, for example—but Zweig was the only one who
retained this interest throughout his life. He had published a number of essays on Balzac and had been accumulating material for
many years. The task of writing this substantial work was begun
in 1939; the first volume was more or less completed, but the
second and third volumes remained a torso.

The lives of famous authors fascinated Zweig. His interest in
the study of psychology and, to a lesser degree, sociology, enabled
him to approach his subjects from an angle that was comparatively
novel at the time. Besides the full-scale biographies just referred to,
he published three volumes under the general title, *Baumeister der
Welt*, each containing three essays on authors of particular interest
to him, such as Balzac, Dickens, Dostoevsky, Tolstoy, Hölderlin and
Kleist. The essay is a literary form that has not found favour in
Germany as it has in England, and Zweig was almost unique in
the way he cultivated this medium between the years 1919 and
1933. The symmetry—three volumes containing three essays each
—may have been the result of chance as much as design, but
whichever it was in this case, it was evidence of Zweig's fondness
for a symmetrical pattern if he could achieve it. One other volume,
Die Heilung durch den Geist (1931), stands rather apart, for
although the method of presentation is the same, the three essays
are psychological studies of three personalities, Mesmer, Mary
Baker Eddy, and Freud, who represented three types or methods
of psycho-therapeutic treatment of mental distress. Except for the
essay on Freud it is the least successful volume of all these essays.

Zweig's reputation as an author during his lifetime was largely started when he ventured into this field of literature.

What was it that attracted Stefan Zweig to write these many volumes of biographical studies? And why were they so successful? He set out on these investigations as a learner who wanted to know how other, older, writers lived and how they worked. Some of these writers, the Belgian Verhaeren in particular, served as models for his own life and work as has already been mentioned —companions on the way as he called them. What he learnt from France he then wanted to transmit to the German world, or perhaps better said, he wanted to impart to Germany something of his admiration and enthusiasm for modern French writers. To him they were modern in the sense that they dealt with contemporary themes in a contemporary idiom as German writers at that time did not. Moreover, it was characteristic of his heritage as a Jew that he was always so anxious, and unsparing in his efforts, to act as a mediator between nations and to interpret a different culture using another medium of expression in terms of his own. The success of these biographical works depended to a large extent on his method of presenting history. Before he wrote a word he always undertook the most thorough and intensive researches into his subject: "bei einer Biographie wie 'Marie Antoinette'," he wrote,[11] "habe ich tatsächlich jede einzelne Rechnung nachgeprüft, um ihren persönlichen Verbrauch festzustellen, alle zeitgenössische Zeitungen und Pamphlete studiert, alle Prozeßakten bis auf die letzte Zeile durchgeackert." Such thoroughness was typical of Zweig. But he was primarily an artist, not an historian, and he could only portray history with the eyes of a poet. "Ideen in Gestalten darzustellen" was his aim as he explained in the preface to *Die Heilung durch den Geist*—ideas made incarnate through personalities from history. It was the artist in him who saw history through the lives of certain human beings who had significantly altered the course of events. Zweig laid bare their essentially human qualities; he saw them against the background of their age and culture; he freed them from any narrowly national interpretation; and he drew out the significance of their achievements as a means of interpreting what was happening in his own day. Erasmus, for example, was presented to his generation as a great humanist and as the first European and cosmopolitan. This work was a testimony to Zweig's personal convictions at a time when the very spirit represented by Erasmus was being crushed in Germany by the hysterical fanaticism of Hitlerism: "es ist ein stiller Lobgesang an den antifanatischen Menschen, dem die künstlerische Leistung und der innere Friede das Wichtigste auf Erden ist—ich habe mir damit die eigene Lebenshaltung in einem Symbol besiegelt", he wrote to Richard Strauß in 1934.[12] Zweig summed up what he considered to be his task in writing all these biographies in the epilogue to his *Marie Antoinette* : "not to deify, but to humanize, is the supreme task of creative psychological study."[13]

These biographies are so vividly and dramatically portrayed that the characters seem to come to life before our very eyes. It was this dramatic element in them that made them so popular with the public. The care that he devoted to the form of these—and indeed of all his works can be seen by reading his own remarks on his methods : "denn kaum daß die erste ungefähre Fassung eines Buches ins Reine geschrieben ist, beginnt für mich die eigentliche Arbeit, an der ich mir von Version zu Version nicht genug tun kann. Es ist ein unablässiges Ballast-über-Bordwerfen, ein ständiges Verdichten und Klären der inneren Architektur; während die meisten andern sich nicht entschließen können, etwas zu verschweigen, was sie wissen, und mit einer gewissen Verliebtheit in jede gelungene Zeile sich weiter und tiefer zeigen wollen, als sie eigentlich sind, ist es mein Ehrgeiz, immer mehr zu wissen, als nach außen hin sichtbar wird. Dieser Prozeß der Kondensierung und damit Dramatisierung wiederholt sich dann noch einmal, zweimal und dreimal bei den gedruckten Fahnen; es wird schließlich eine Art lustvoller Jagd, noch einen Satz oder auch nur ein Wort zu finden, dessen Fehlen die Präzision nicht vermindern und gleichzeitig das Tempo steigern könnte. Innerhalb meiner Arbeit ist mir die des Weglassens eigentlich die vergnüglichste."[14] It is no disparagement of academic research—which has a different function —to say that Zweig consciously adopted methods that appealed to the imagination of the public. One needs to add, too, that he only wrote about persons that meant something to him and in that respect they represent a confession of his personal preferences. His art in the field of biography was one of popularization without descending into vulgarity. During his life he was the most important exponent of this art and in Germany at any rate it seems to have died with him.

It was this technique of elimination of every unessential detail and of dramatization, carried to the point of exaggeration that enabled Zweig to excel in one other form of biographical writing— what has been called the miniature biography. The five historical miniatures contained in the volume *Sternstunden der Menschheit* which Zweig published in 1927 in the famous *Inselbücherei*—a venture, incidentally, he helped to launch—were something entirely new. Its success with the public was immediate—some 250,000 copies were sold within a very short period and it has remained a favourite with the public ever since. (Later it was enlarged to include five more essays and the 1947 edition has added two more.)

History, psychology, and poetry are here fused into a unity : the historian's love for the great characters of the past and their historical significance are here combined with the author's profound understanding of the human soul and the poet's eye for a good story. Zweig succeeded in creating gems of a beauty that is peculiarly his own and has never been equalled since.

Zweig selected for each of these miniature essays what to him was a pregnant moment in the history of Europe from the sixteenth to the twentieth centuries, that is to say, moments of destiny in the lives of human beings who have influenced the course of history. The scene is not always Europe—it is, for example, America in the essay *Die Entdeckung Eldoradoes*, the South Pole in *Der Kampf um den Südpol*, but the events described are part of the history of Europe. In the preface to the original edition Zweig calls these pregnant moments of decision "explosive moments" which give history its dramatic forms. He confidently asserts he has made no attempt to colour the essential facts by any invention of his own. He made his attitude clear when he described history as the greatest poet of all times, but like the artist, incapable of incessant creation. However, Zweig's attempts to justify his method of selection will hardly satisfy any professional historian! He was really fascinated by the lives of men whose intentions were radically affected or changed by the unpredictable element of chance in life. In most cases he picks on a decision that leads to frustration. Thus, Vasco Nunez de Balboa, after triumphantly mastering the obstacles of nature and man and after being the first European to discover the Pacific Ocean and the rich territories along its shores, ends his life ignominiously as a rebel through the envy of a frustrated rival (*Die Flucht in die Unsterblichkeit*); Napoleon is finally defeated at the battle of Waterloo through the incompetence of one of his generals (*Die Weltminute von Waterloo*); Captain Scott's energetic pursuit of the South Pole ends in tragic frustration (*Der Kampf um den Südpol*). Fate, however, does not always lead to tragic frustration : through will power Georg Friedrich Handel was able to rise, phoenix-like, from what should have been his death-bed and so was able to give the world his *Messiah*; Goethe, enjoying a rare favour of fate, was able to give Germany one of its finest poems (*Die Marienbader Elegie*). Each little essay provides a thumb-nail sketch of the character and a vivid description of human endeavour face to face with human frailty, frustration, and death, but in every instance some lasting achievement remains. Whether we think of these miniature essays as history, as Zweig would have us do, or prefer to look upon them as fiction, they lead naturally to a consideration of his narratives.

The Novelle or short story was the genre that best suited Zweig's genius as a writer. He was a prolific writer of stories that reveal astonishing powers of invention. It was the publication of the collection of four stories entitled *Erstes Erlebnis* (1911) that marked the beginning of his reputation in this field. This was followed by two further volumes, *Amok* (1922) and *Verwirrung der Gefühle* (1927). The three volumes formed a series to which Zweig later gave the title of *Die Kette,* a cycle which corresponded to the three volumes of biography entitled *Baumeister der Welt.* The three volumes deal with three stages in the life of man: the first is centred on children and young people just becoming aware of adult problems, the second introduces men and women in their middle years who have become the slaves of passion, whilst the third presents episodes and adventures from the lives of older people. Other volumes which he published during his lifetime were also built around some central theme. His last story, *Schachnovelle,* published in 1943 after his death, showed no diminution of his powers. Collectively they reveal that Zweig combined a fertile and lively imagination with a strong sense for form and structure.

At first sight it might appear somewhat surprising that Zweig did not turn to historical sources for the material of his stories. There is, however, a close connection between them and his life. This is not to suggest that they are in any way autobiographical, but they are essentially the outcome of his personal experience of contemporary life and of his own age. Stefan Zweig was, to quote Hermann Hesse, "der kluge und feinsinnige Einfühler"; others who knew him draw attention to his ability to enter into and absorb emotions he could not have experienced himself—to his capacity of being a "sponge" (Antonina Vallentin). It was as if feminine insight into, and understanding of, the sufferings of others had entered into a marriage with masculine curiosity. For curiosity is his other major characteristic: again and again in memoirs on Zweig we can read that the dominant expression in his eyes was that of curiosity, the curiosity of a man who was always on the look-out to meet new people and to acquire knowledge of experiences that were outside his own range. Zweig was, we are told, easily affected by the experiences, especially the sufferings, of others. He was an acute listener to and and keen observer of the human drama, sensitive and responsive to people from all walks of life. In this way he obtained the raw material which he then transformed imaginatively into the episodes and the poetry of his stories. Friederike Zweig relates how, for example, a boyish attachment to a governess is mirrored in two early stories, *Die Liebe der Erika Ewald* (1904) and *Die Gouvernante* (in *Erstes Erlebnis*), but, she adds significantly, this can only be guessed through allusions in the stories. Again, it is Friederike Zweig who indicates that

Buchmendl may well be based on Zweig's familiarity with "the whimsical, shrivelled antiquaries, with their fanatical love of books, whom he had observed behind the dusty window-panes of the shops in the Palais Royal".[15] His art seemed to depend on fertilization by experience. During the First World War Zweig visited friends who lived by Lake Geneva. Here he met people who had found their way into free Switzerland in devious and adventurous ways— he met, for example, one young couple who had escaped by swimming the broad lake. Such, and similar incidents that came his way, inspired the pathetic story *Episode am Genfer See* in which the agony suffered by individuals from hostilities between nations, in which they are involved without their knowing why, is starkly illustrated. This story tells how a soldier, completely nude, is picked up exhausted by a Swiss fisherman; the soldier, who belonged to one of the Russian divisions sent to France, was so overwhelmed by his longing to return to his home, his wife and children and to the simple life he understood that he deserted; in his ignorance he thought that Lake Geneva was the lake he knew so well in his native land.

By drawing upon the rich resources that came to him in this way Zweig could epitomize the experience of an age. He had the ability to translate the major issues of his day into terms of human suffering and of ordinary human lives. There is little or no attempt to educate or instruct his readers or to pass moral judgments : he just tells a story in which human destiny and human lives are affected, usually disastrously, by events outside their control as individuals. He "humanizes" events, to use a rather ugly word. Two examples are worth mentioning to illustrate this. The first, *Die unsichtbare Sammlung,* is the story of an art-dealer who, in his search for art treasures to satisfy the demands of the *nouveaux riches* in the inflationary period after the First World War, visits a former customer of the firm only to discover that the wonderful art collection had been sold by the wife and daughter piece by piece to rapacious and unscrupulous dealers for worthless money. The collector himself was unaware of what was happening because the women replaced the drawings with cheap copies and—he was blind. Again, the last story he wrote, *Schachnovelle* (known in English as *The Royal Game*) is pure fiction, yet it conveys in a terrifying manner the brutal inhumanity of National Socialism. It is, in fact, one of the most penetrating and powerful portrayals ever written of the suffering inflicted on countless millions by this twentieth-century tyranny over mind and soul. What Stefan Zweig suffered personally was negligible in comparison with the tale he tells, but it is a revelation of his creative powers. The artist is here speaking for his age in a way that documentary evidence never can.

Zweig's range is thus conditioned by the circumstances of the contemporary world with which he was familiar. He is creative when he is inspired by the places and people he knew either in his youth or from his many travels about the world. The setting is often his native city Vienna, "die weiche und wollüstige Stadt Wien, die wie keine andere das Spazierengehen, das nichtstuerische Betrachten, das Elegantsein zu einer geradezu künstlerischen Vollendung, zu einem Lebenszweck heranbildet" as it is described in *Phantastische Nacht*.[16] More often than not he chooses a hotel, or a ship as the starting-point for his stories—the sort of place where casual acquaintances are made and adventures experienced or exchanged in conversation. It is a cosmopolitan world in which people of all nationalities meet and talk together.

"In meinen Novellen ist es immer der dem Schicksal Unterliegende, der mich anzieht"[17]—thus Zweig wrote in his autobiography. Who are these victims of fate that people his stories? Most of them belong to a social world that has long disappeared. We meet the idle rich of an upper middle-class society and lower aristocracy, pleasure-seeking libertines bent on amorous adventures, members of the professions such as artists, lawyers, diplomats, doctors, officers, and senior civil servants. On the fringe of this social set there is a host of secondary figures ranging from minor government officials to singers, actresses, governesses and servants of all kinds. Then there are the adventurers who escape from their bourgeois world to live a more natural or primitive life in less civilized surroundings. A typical example of the type of irresponsible character that inhabits Zweig's Novellen describes his life in the following words : "Der Mensch, der ich damals war, unterschied sich in wenigem äußerlich und innerlich von den meisten seiner Gesellschaftsklasse, die man besonders bei uns in Wien die 'gute Gesellschaft' ohne besonderen Stolz, sondern ganz als selbstverständlich zu bezeichnen pflegt. Ich ging in das sechsunddreißigste Jahr, meine Eltern waren früh gestorben und hatten mir knapp vor meiner Mündigkeit ein Vermögen hinterlassen, das sich als reichlich genug erwies, um von nun ab den Gedanken an Erwerb und Karriere gänzlich mir zu erübrigen. Ich hatte nämlich gerade meine Universitätsstudien vollendet,... als dies elterliche Vermögen an mich als einzigen Erben fiel und mir eine plötzliche arbeitslose Unabhängigkeit zusicherte, selbst im Rahmen weitgespannter und sogar luxuriöser Wünsche. Ehrgeiz hatte mich nie bedrängt, so beschloß ich einmal dem Leben erst ein paar Jahre zuzusehen und zu warten bis es mich schließlich verlocken würde, mir selbst einen Wirkungskreis zu finden. Es blieb aber bei diesem Zuschauen und Warten, denn da ich nichts Sonderliches begehrte, erreichte ich alles im engen Kreis meiner Wünsche."[18] This character leads an aimless life; his irresponsible attitude leads him to commit a theft, by accident as it were, which, if discovered, would have made him a social outcast; the realization of his situation provides the necessary shock and in this character the life of drift is transformed into a useful life of helping people who are in need, so that he overcomes the limitations of class and convention to embrace all mankind in a spirit of brotherhood. But not many of Zweig's stories end so happily! This is the sort of society that is met with in the works of a number of Austrian writers and artists who, like Zweig, grew up in Vienna in the years before the outbreak of the 1914 war—Arthur Schnitzler, Richard Beer-Hofmann, Arthur Schnabel, Hugo von Hofmannsthal among others. Zweig felt at home in the old Imperial Austria and never quite succeeded in coming to terms with the radical changes that followed : the title of his autobiography is, significantly, *Die Welt von gestern*. As a student in Berlin he had reacted against the security of his home life by seeking contact with people whose lives were threatened with the insecurity that comes from degrading poverty or from demoralizing behaviour. It is best to let Zweig describe what this meant to him in his own words : "Ich lebte plötzlich in einem Kreise (in Berlin), wo es auch wirkliche Armut mit zerrissenen Kleidern und abgetretenen Schuhen gab, einer Sphäre also, die ich in Wien nie berührt. Ich saß am selben Tisch mit schweren Trinkern und Homosexuellen und Morphinisten, ich schüttelte—sehr stolz—die Hand einem ziemlich bekannten und abgestraften Hochstapler (der später seine Memoiren veröffentlichte und auf diese Weise zu uns Schriftstellern kam). Alles was ich den realistischen Romanen kaum geglaubt hatte, schob und drängte sich in den kleinen Wirtsstuben und Cafés, in die ich eingeführt wurde, zusammen, und je schlimmer eines Menschen Ruf war, um so begehrlicher mein Interesse, seinen Träger persönlich kennenzulernen. Diese besondere Liebe oder Neugier für gefährdete Menschen hat mich übrigens mein ganzes Leben lang begleitet; selbst in den Jahren, wo es sich geziemt hätte, schon wählerischer zu werden, haben meine Freunde mich oft gescholten, mit was für amoralischen, unverläßlichen und wahrhaft kompromittierenden Leuten ich umging. Vielleicht ließ mir gerade die Sphäre der Solidität, aus der ich kam, und die Tatsache, daß ich selbst bis zu einem gewissen Grade mich mit dem Komplex der 'Sicherheit' belastet fühlte, all jene faszinierend erscheinen, die mit ihrem Leben, ihrer Zeit, ihrem Geld, ihrer Gesundheit, ihrem guten Ruf verschwenderisch und beinahe verächtlich umgingen, diese Passionierten, diese Monomanen des bloßen Existierens ohne Ziel, und vielleicht merkt man in meinen Romanen und Novellen diese Vorliebe für alle intensiven und unbändigen Naturen."[19]

Women, too, play a notable rôle in these Novellen. Like the men they are very much members of their particular social class and display all the characteristics of their class. Yet, in comparison with the men, they are on the whole rather less hide-bound by class, more naturally themselves, and more feminine than the men are masculine. Like the men they experience adventures that shake them to the very roots of their being and are overpowered by the demonic and uncontrollable force of their deepest instincts and urges that leads them to throw aside all the restraints of social conventions. Antonina Vallentin, in drawing attention to Zweig's remarkable gift of perception of the human emotions, asserts that he was particularly well suited to be the ideal interpreter of those who were unable to express themselves—women and children. She adds that he had a remarkable gift for reading the soul of women and that millions of women readers felt they were understood for the first time : "il mettait la couleur de l'aventure dans la grisaille de leur existence".[20] When a German lady in *Vierundzwanzig Stunden aus dem Leben einer Frau* makes the comment "es gäbe einerseits wirkliche Frauen und anderseits Dirnennaturen" about a married woman who has eloped with a Frenchman after no more than a few hours' acquaintanceship in a hotel, the narrator in the story retorts "daß eine Frau in manchen Stunden ihres Lebens jenseits ihres Willens und Wissens geheimnisvollen Mächten ausgeliefert sei".[21] This is the kind of woman Zweig likes to portray in his Novellen.

This story of the amazing adventure of an Englishwoman called Mrs. C. attempting unsuccessfully to save a hardened gambler from committing suicide, impressed Sigmund Freud. "This little masterpiece," he wrote, "ostensibly sets out only to show what an irresponsible creature woman is, and to what excesses, surprising even to herself, an unexpected experience may drive her."[22] He then proceeds to subject the story to a psycho-analytical interpretation which, as Freud admits, was strange to Zweig's knowledge and intention. It is an interpretation that would certainly not occur to anyone but an expert in Freudian psycho-analytical methods; its value, however, lies in the evidence it provides of Zweig's capacity for understanding the innermost secrets of the soul of both men and women. And Freud was surely right when he finished his appreciation with the words : "the brilliantly told, faultlessly motivated story is of course complete in itself and is certain to make a deep effect upon his reader."[23] Mrs. C.'s maternal instinct led her to submit to the embraces of the gambler she hoped to save Like Mrs. C. most of the women in Zweig's Novellen—if we except the prostitutes and those women of easy-going virtue who play a subsidiary rôle—enter into conventional marriages, possess a strongly developed maternal instinct, and at some stage in their lives succumb to the magical attraction of adventure.

One of the strangest female figures ever created by Zweig was the woman nicknamed Leporella (after Leporello, the servant of Don Giovanni in Mozart's opera) in the story named after her. She forms a striking contrast to the society ladies in most of the stories : she was an orphan who had been degraded and humiliated by being treated as a burden on the community; she is described as boorish, inarticulate, lacking in all human friendships or any interest in the world around her. She was obsessed with a mania for work which she pursued robot-like without interruption from morning to night with the sole object of saving money. Not even the change from a remote village to service in a fashionable Viennese home could change her ways until a few friendly remarks and a slap on the buttocks by her employer aroused an instinct that had remained dormant. This chance incident was the turning-point for both their lives. What was meant light-heartedly by the man and quickly forgotten was instinctively significant for her. She transferred her mania to the man and became his devoted slave to the extent that she unashamedly aided him in his amorous adventures during his wife's absence. Her limited intelligence took the baron's casual remark after one of his quarrels with his wife, "da muß einmal ein Ende gemacht werden",[24] quite literally and murdered his wife by a ruse that deceived everybody except the baron. She committed suicide when he discarded her, horrified by her inhuman obsession.

Zweig's Novellen are filled with people whose lives are controlled by an obsession. The words "besessen" and "Besessenheit" are used again and again to describe the dominating feature of his characters. They are all monomaniacs in varying degrees. Jakob Mendel in *Buchmendl* was the victim of his mania for books : "dieser Jakob Mendel sah und hörte nichts von allem um sich her. Neben ihm lärmten und krakeelten die Billardspieler, liefen die Marköre, rasselte das Telephon. . . . In diesem kleinen galizischen Büchertrödler Jakob Mendel hatte ich zum erstenmal als junger Mensch das große Geheimnis der restlosen Konzentration gesehen, das den Künstler macht wie den Gelehrten, den wahrhaft Weisen wie den vollkommen Irrwitzigen, dieses tragische Glück und Unglück vollkommener Besessenheit."[25] The Russian soldier in *Episode am Genfer See* is obsessed with the longing for home. Mrs. C. in *Vierundzwanzig Stunden aus dem Leben einer Frau* is bent on saving a man who had developed a mania for gambling. The highly intelligent and cultured lawyer in *Schachnovelle* was threatened with insanity after his release from confinement unless he could keep under control a mania for chess which had been forced upon him to counter the subtle methods of his prison torturers. It has often been said that sex is a major obsession of this century and it is certainly a problem that appears in many different guises in Zweig's Novellen. The sexual attraction of man for woman, woman for man, and even man for man is a basic theme, and it drives its victims to their destruction. The relation between the sexes tends to be an unequal or unbalanced one : the men turn light-heartedly from one woman to another in the search for satisfaction where the woman tends to display a greater constancy and sense of devotion. It is a demonic passion that plays havoc with lives. Zweig's Novellen are full of sad, overwrought, demented people.

The angle of vision that is given to us is a limited and narrow one. The men and women in all these stories are treated as individuals who live as individuals. Their problems are largely personal and private. They live their real lives in opposition to society rather than as members. The bourgeois society to which they belong is exposed as full of hypocrisy. *Die Gouvernante,* for example, is only a slight story of scandal in a typical bourgeois home with its conventional morality that brings tragedy to a young governess who is pregnant by a student related to her employers. Today the story seems outdated, but it contains a protest against the lies, the evasion of reality that characterized the kind of society Zweig knew in Vienna. The narrator in *Vierundzwanzig Stunden aus dem Leben einer Frau* registers the protest of the individual who is in revolt against society when he says to Mrs. C. : "Die staatliche Justiz entscheidet über diese Dinge (der Moral) sicherlich strenger als ich; ihr obliegt die Pflicht, mitleidslos die allgemeine Sitte und Konvention zu schützen : das nötigt sie, sie zu verurteilen statt zu entschuldigen. Ich als Privatperson aber sehe nicht ein, warum ich freiwillig die Rolle des Staatsanwaltes übernehmen sollte : ich ziehe es vor, Verteidiger von Beruf zu sein. Mir persönlich macht es mehr Freude, Menschen zu verstehen, als sie zu richten."[26] The way of escape from this hypocritical bourgeois world is flight into the world of adventure. "Flucht" and "Abenteuer" are again favourite words of Zweig, and Zweig's characters are usually involved in one way or another in an attempt to escape from convention to a more "real" kind of life in which they can give full play to their deeper instincts : this is, in fact, the fundamental problem in all Zweig's Novellen. It is the conflict that was Zweig's own : the conflict between the material and moral security of his home and his own inner sense of insecurity that was prepared for any reversal of fortune.

Thus the urban and cosmopolitan world of these Novellen is only a backcloth to the drama that is played out between individuals. Nature, too, has only a minor rôle to play. The weather sometimes serves as a foil to the human situation : in *Vierundzwan-zig Stunden aus dem Leben einer Frau* the storm that rages on the sea-front corresponds to the storm that rages within the characters. As a rule natural phenomena are described in terms of the human sphere : "Jene weißen, unruhigen Wolken flatterten am Himmel ... jene weißen, selbst noch jungen und flattrigen Gesellen,... die sich bald wie Taschentücher zerknüllen ...";[27] "Wie ein Seiden-bonbon schmeckte sie (die Luft)."[28] There is even less awareness of God; religion has no place except as a trapping in one or two stories : in *Untergang eines Herzens* the father, overwhelmed with shame on discovering that his nineteen-year-old daughter was hav-ing an illicit love-affair with a hotel acquaintance, turns religious, but this piety is treated as little more than a psychological reaction of a broken-hearted man.

Zweig produced a few plays which met with considerable success during his life but are hardly known today. One drama, *Jeremias,* owed its success to its topicality : it is a biblical drama written during the First World War and banned by censorship because of its anti-war tendencies. The drama is a confession of his belief in the brotherhood of man. To the English reader it is of interest to mention that he wrote a comedy, *Volpone,* an adaptation of Ben Jonson's play; it was composed in a matter of a few days and was performed at hundreds of theatres all over the world. He used another of Jonson's comedies, *Epicoene or the Silent Woman,* for his libretto to Richard Strauß's opera *Die schweigsame Frau.* The co-operation between Zweig and Strauß might have been more fruitful for opera if the political situation had been different.

"Rätselhafte psychologische Dinge haben über mich eine geradezu beunruhigende Macht, es reizt mich bis ins Blut, Zusammenhänge aufzuspüren, ..."[29] These words by the narrator in *Der Amokläufer* could have been written by Zweig to refer to himself, for he was passionately addicted to the possibilities of interpreting human action and motives with the help of modern psychology. He was a great admirer of his Viennese compatriot Sigmund Freud and, as has already been mentioned, he wrote an essay on him in his *Heilung durch den Geist.* He considered Freud's discoveries impor-tant as a means of enrichment to creative literature, although he objected to what appeared to him to be the one-sidedness of Freudian doctrine. He applied what he learnt from the teachings of Freud and the Viennese school of psycho-analysis to his own works as no Austrian before him had done. Indeed, Zweig could dissect human emotions in a way that was new to German litera-ture. The Novelle *Angst,* for example, could almost be described as a case-book history of the emotional disturbances experienced by a wife who is afraid of her romance with another man being discovered by her husband : the whole range of fears from a knock at the front door to the terrors of her dreams are laid bare with the masterly precision of a surgeon operating on the physical body.

Zweig used the term "Novelle" to describe his stories. They are not Novellen in any strict sense of the term. He had a powerful sense for the artistic construction of his stories, but his main concern was not with the artistic or poetic angle. His emphasis is always on the human interest he can extract from some dramatic episode or anecdote. It is not action that he presents; he aims at portraying the reaction of people who are emotional, passionate and extreme in temperament. This emphasis on the psychological aspect led to the use of the confession to a narrator as his main literary device. One of the most striking examples of this is in *Vierundzwanzig Stunden aus dem Leben einer Frau* : the anguished confession of Mrs. C., "die weißhaarige, vornehme, alte englische Dame," is brought about by the chance remark of the narrator, "vierundzwanzig Stunden könnten das Schicksal einer Frau vollkommen bestimmen";[30] within her confession there is the confession to her of the gambler, and finally there is the gambler's confession in Polish to God in church which she hears but does not understand. A variation of this device is the story consisting of a letter as a means of confession with just a few introductory remarks by an imaginary recipient, e.g. *Brief einer Unbekannten*; or the story can take the form of a chronicle as in *Phantastische Nacht*.

Zweig's mastery in the handling of language is such that at its best he can achieve a quality of crystalline clarity. He knows how to hold the attention of his reader with his vivid, racy and colloquial style, by the rapid rhythm of his prose, and by the tension and dramatic intensity he imparts to his language. At its worst his language suffers from repetition, overemphasis, and exaggeration, almost to the point of obsession. "He insists a little too much, perhaps," as Jules Romains wrote kindly in an essay on Zweig. He often introduces an excessive amount of sheer sensationalism, sometimes of the very worst kind. He employs skilfully, but not always successfully, the techniques of modern journalism or perhaps better, of the modern film with its close-ups, its flash-backs, its emotionalism and, at its worst, its superficiality. The effects he aims at are at times marred by the too obvious attempts to impress the reader.

Zweig belonged to a generation of Austrian writers from Rilke and Hofmannsthal to Kafka and Musil who between them produced some of the finest literature of this century in the German language. During his life he enjoyed almost unparalleled success and popularity in Germany and abroad. He had little connection with current literary trends, belonged to no literary "school" or

movement; he preferred to go his own way as a writer. He believed
that he expressed in his works something of the spirit of his age—
the brilliant but decadent world of Viennese society in the early
years of this century. It is this that gives him his place in the
history of German literature.

TRANSLATIONS AND NOTES

1. Against my will I have been the witness of the most terrible defeat
of reason and of the wildest triumphs of brutality in the chronicle of the
ages; never—I record this in no way with pride but with shame—has one
generation suffered such a moral relapse from such a spiritual height as
ours. In the one small interval between the time my beard began to sprout
and the time it begins to turn grey, in this one century more radical
changes have occurred than in ten generations at any other time . . . So
different is my today from each of my yesterdays, my ups and downs,
that I sometimes think I must have experienced not just one but several
totally different existences. . . . Every time I relate episodes from the time
before the first war to my younger friends, I notice by their astonished
questions how much has become historical and inconceivable to them
that is still obviously real to me. And a secret instinct in me tells me they
are right: between our today, our yesterday and beyond all bridges have
been destroyed.

—*Die Welt von Gestern,* p. 8f.

2. Responsive and gifted with a special sense for receptiveness, this
city attracted the most diverse forces, slackened, loosened and quietened
them, life was gentle here, in this conciliatory atmosphere, and every
citizen of this city was consciously educated to be international, cosmopolitan and a world-citizen.

—ibid., p. 23.

3. The genius of Vienna—a specifically musical one—has always been
able to harmonize all national and linguistic contrasts, and its culture has
always been a synthesis of all Western cultures; whoever lived and worked
there, felt himself to be free of any narrowness and prejudice. Nowhere
was it easier to be a European, and I know I have largely to thank this
city that I early learnt to love the idea of fellowship as the highest of
my heart. Life was good, easy and carefree in that ancient Vienna.

—ibid., p. 33.

4. See Chapter 1 of her biography.

5. Friederike Zweig, p. 9.

6. Even at the grammar school not only to me but to a whole group
artistic activity was the secret aim and appreciation of art our common
passion. We were, it seems, the last generation with that fanaticism for
art, which has been as good as lost today but always distinguished this
ancient city of the theatre.

—ibid.

7. Inwardly my way for the next few years was clear to me: to see
much, to learn much and only then to begin. Not to come forward with

immature publications, but to get to know the essential things about the world.

—Die Welt von Gestern, p. 116.

8. The real meaning of my escapade was to get away from the sheltered and bourgeois atmosphere and to live free and independent instead. I was concerned only with getting to know people—and as far as possible interesting people.

—ibid., p. 111.

9. Following the advice of Dehmel I used my time translating from foreign languages, and still today I look upon this as the best possibility for a young poet to understand more deeply and creatively the spirit of his own language.

—ibid., p. 116.

10. Richard Friedenthal, who prepared a version for the press after Zweig's death, in the Introduction (p. IX) to the English edition, translated by William and Dorothy Rose, London, 1948.

11. With a biography like "Marie Antoinette" I actually examined every account in order to establish her personal expenditure, studied all contemporary papers and pamphlets, worked through all legal papers to the very last line.

—ibid., p. 293.

12. It is a calm song in praise of the anti-fanatic man to whom artistic achievement and inner peace are the most important things on earth—with it I have sealed in a symbol my own attitude to life.

—Richard Strauss—Stefan Zweig Briefwechsel, p. 63.

13. Friederike Zweig, p. 155.

14. About as soon as I have copied out the first version of a book there begins for me the real work which is incessant from one version to another. It is a constant throwing ballast overboard, a constant compression and clarification of the inner architecture; whilst most (authors) cannot be reticent about anything they know, and with a certain infatuation with every successful line want to show off as being more profound and more advanced than they really are, it is my ambition to know more than is outwardly visible. This process of condensation and dramatization is repeated once, twice, three times with the printed proofs; in the end it becomes a kind of enjoyable chase to find one more sentence or word, the omission of which could not diminish the precision and at the same time increase the tempo. The most pleasurable task in my work is that of erasion.

—Die Welt von Gestern, p. 293.

15. Friederike Zweig, p. 12.

16. The tender and sensuous city of Vienna, that as no other raises the stroll, the idle looking-on, and elegance to artistic perfection and the aim in life.

—Ausgew. Nov. p. 278.

17. In my Novellen it is always the victim of fate that attracts me.

—Die Welt von Gestern, p. 159.

18. The man I was at that time differed little either outwardly or inwardly from the majority of his social class which we in Vienna were

accustomed to calling "good society" without any particular pride but rather as a matter of course. I was just turning thirty-six, my parents had died young and, just before I became of age, had left me a fortune which proved ample enough to make it completely unnecessary for me to think of earning or a career. I had just completed my university studies ... when I as the sole heir acquired this parental fortune and was suddenly assured of independence without the necessity of work, even within the framework of far-reaching and even luxurious wishes. Ambition had never bothered me, so I decided to spend a few years as a spectator of life and to wait until I would finally be tempted into finding some sphere of activity. I remained in this state of being a spectator and of waiting, for as I longed for nothing in particular, I gained everything within the narrow circle of my wishes.

—Ausgew. Nov. p. 278.

19. Suddenly I was living in a circle (in Berlin) where there was real poverty with ragged clothes—a sphere I had not met in Vienna. I sat at the same table with heavy drinkers and homosexuals and morphine addicts, very proudly I shook hands with a fairly well known and well-punished crook (who later published his memoirs and so came into contact with us writers). The small pubs and cafés I had been introduced to were full of the people I had hardly believed existed in realistic novels, and the worse a man's reputation the more I was interested in meeting him. This special fondness or curiosity for compromised people has accompanied me my whole life; even in those years when I ought to have been more fastidious, my friends reproached me for mixing with such amoral, irresponsible and thoroughly compromised people. Perhaps the very sphere of solidity from which I had emerged and the fact that I felt myself to some extent saddled with the complex of "security" led me to find all those people fascinating who were prodigal with and even contemptuous of their lives, their time, money, health and their good reputation—people who were passionate, monomaniacs without an aim in life—and one can observe in my novels and short stories this preference for all intensive and wayward natures.

—Die Welt von Gestern, p. 114.

20. Antonina Vallentin, p. 51.

21. That a woman is at times in her life at the mercy of mysterious powers that are beyond her will and knowledge.

—Ausgew. Nov. p. 144.

22. S. Freud, *Collected Papers,* vol. V. London 1950, p. 239.

23. ibid., p. 240.

24. There must be an end to all this.

—Ausgew. Nov. p. 512.

25. Jakob Mendel saw and heard nothing of what went on around him. Nearby the billiard players squabbled and bawled, the waiters ran around the telephone rattled away. . . . In this short second-hand book-dealer from Galicia I had seen for the first time as a young man the great secret of complete concentration that is the making of the artist as well as the scholar, the really wise man as well as the madman, this tragic fortune and misfortune of complete obsession.

—ibid., Nov. p. 225.

26. The laws of the state certainly decide these matters of morality more severely than I do; they are obliged to protect without mercy the accepted morals and conventions; that leads them to condemn rather than to excuse. I as a private individual do not see why I should voluntarily take the rôle of public prosecutor: I prefer to be by profession the counsel for the defendant. It gives me more pleasure to understand men than to judge them.

—*Ausgew. Nov.* p. 147.

27. Those white, restless clouds floated in the sky . . . those white, still very young and fickle companions . . . that were soon crumpled like handkerchiefs.

—*Brennendes Geh.* p. 7.

28. The air tasted like a sweet. —ibid., p. 169.

29. Enigmatical psychological matters exercise a disturbing power over me. I am stirred to my very marrow to trace connections.

—*Ausgew. Nov.* p. 17.

30. Twenty-four hours can completely determine the fate of a woman.

—ibid., *Nov.* p. 217.

SELECT BIBLIOGRAPHY

I. THE WORKS OF ZWEIG

References in the text have been taken from the following post-war editions:

Ausgewählte Novellen. Bermann-Fischer Verlag. Stockholm, 1947. Contains ten of the best Novellen.

Brennendes Geheimnis und andere Erzählungen. S. Fischer Verlag. Contains eight Novellen, two of which (*Die Mondscheingasse* and *Leporella*) are included in *Ausgewählte Novellen.*

Schachnovelle. Fischer Verlag. 1961.

Sternstunden der Menschheit. Zwölf historische Miniaturen. Bermann-Fischer Verlag. Stockholm, 1947.

Zweig's autobiography, *Die Welt von gestern. Erinnerungen eines Europäers,* S. Fischer Verlag. 1951. Is important.

Richard Strauß—Stefan Zweig. Briefwechsel. Fischer Verlag. 1957.

II. The following is a selection of Zweig's original works in order of their publication and with their original titles:

Silberne Saiten. (Poems) 1901.
Die Liebe der Erika Ewald. (Novellen) 1904.
Verlaine. (Critical biography) 1905.
Die Frühen Kränze. (Poems) 1906.
Tersites. (Play) 1907.
Emile Verhaeren. (Critical biography) 1910.
Erstes Erlebnis. Vier Geschichten aus Kinderland. 1911.
Jeremias. (Play) 1917.
Drei Meister: Balzac, Dickens, Dostojewskij (Biography) 1920.

Marceline Desbordes-Valmore. (Biography) 1920.
Angst. (Novelle) 1920.
Romain Rolland: der Mann und das Werk. (Critical biography) 1921.
Amok. (Novelle) 1922.
Der Kampf mit dem Dämon: Hölderlin, Kleist, Nietzsche. (Biography) 1925.
Ben Jonson's *"Volpone".* (Play) 1926.
Die Unsichtbare Sammlung. (Nouvelle) 1927.
Der Flüchtling. (Episode) 1927.
Verwirrung der Gefühle. (Three Novellen) 1927.
Abschied von Rilke. (An address) 1927.
Sternstunden der Menschheit. Fünf historische Miniaturen. 1927.
Drei Dichter ihres Lebens: Casanova, Stendhal, Tolstoi. (Biography) 1928.
Kleine Chronik. Vier Erzählungen. 1929.
Joseph Fouche: Bildnis eines politischen Menschen. (Biography) 1929.
Die Heilung durch den Geist: Mesmer, Mary Baker Eddy, Freud. (Biography) 1931.
Marie Antoinette: Bildnis eines mittleren Charakters. (Biography) 1932.
Triumph und Tragik des Erasmus von Rotterdam. (Biography) 1934.
Maria Stuart. (Biography) 1935.
Baumeister der Welt. 1935. (Zusammenfassung in einem Band von: *Der Kampf mit dem Dämon*; *Drei Meister*; *Drei Dichter ihres Lebens.*)
Castellio Gegen Calvin. (Biography) 1936.
Gesammelte Erzählungen. 1. Band; *Die Kette,* 1936. 2. Band: *Kaleidoskop,* 1936.
Magellan. (Biography) 1938.
Balzac. (Biography) English edition, London, 1948.

III. WORKS ON ZWEIG

Friederike Maria Zweig. *Stefan Zweig.* London, 1946. The German edition was published in 1946 with the title, *Stefan Zweig, wie ich ihn erlebte.* A valuable appreciation by Zweig's first wife.
E. Rieger. *Stefan Zweig. Der Mann und das Werk.* Berlin, 1928.
Jules Romains. *Stefan Zweig. Great European.* New York, 1941. (Translated from the French.)
H. Arens. *Stefan Zweig. Sein Leben und sein Werk.* Esslingen, 1948.
Antonina Vallentin. "Stefan Zweig", article in *Europe*, Revue Mensuelle, 25 année no. 22, October 1947, pp. 48–67.
Alfred Matthis. *Stefan Zweig as Librettist and Richard Strauß.* Music and Letters, vol XXV, London, 1944.

Hermann Hesse

Hermann Hesse

by EVA J. ENGEL

Gruss eines Wanderers... der... im Dunkel
geht, aber vom Licht weiss und es sucht.
May 1943[1]

Hermann Hesse (2. vii. 1877–9. viii. 1962) was born of a devoutly
Pietist family in Calw (Württemberg). Hesse, technically a Swiss citizen
by birth and later by act of will, spent all his life in Switzerland after
1912, except for one long journey to East India in 1911. Both Hesse's
parents had experience in missionary work out East; from them and
from his maternal grandfather derived his considerable interest in Indian
and Chinese teaching. From his parents, too, he inherited the gift for
poetry and narrative. Despite a family tradition to take up theology,
Hesse ran away from school at Maulbronn. After a period of great
turbulence and indecision (during which he was briefly apprenticed to
a clockmaker) he spent several years in Tübingen, ostensibly to learn to
sell books, but mainly following up extensive boyhood reading at home.
In 1899 he went to Basle, and came upon Burkhardt's ideas on history.
In Basle he married the highly musical daughter of the mathematician
Bernoulli in the same year in which he won acclaim as the author of
Peter Camenzind (1904). By Lake Constance, a period of apparent well-
being and success followed, to be shattered by his first wife's mental
breakdown and the declaration of war in 1914. Hesse regarded this as the
second period of decisive conflict in his life. He was helped by advice
and friendship of the psychiatrist Lang, by taking up water-colour
drawing, and, from 1919 onwards, by intensive study of Chinese and
Indian thought. From 1919 he lived almost a hermit's life in Montagnola
near Lugano. Gardening and painting were his relaxations but the harvest
of those years from 1919 to 1943 rests in his great novels, in recognition
of which the poet was given the Nobel prize in 1946.

I

"ICH bin ein Dichter, ein Sucher und Bekenner, ich habe der
Wahrheit und Aufrichtigkeit zu dienen (und zur Wahrheit
gehört auch das Schöne, es ist eine ihrer Erscheinungsformen),
ich habe einen Auftrag... : ich muss anderen Suchenden die Welt
verstehen und bestehen helfen."[2] Again and again in the course
of a long lifetime Hesse affirms the conviction of his poetic purpose
and of man's essential function. This we are to regard as the key,
the poet's key in which his oeuvre is set. At the outset the search

251

leads him to a sensitive, unflinching examination of his own self in the past; growth and development in their turn bring the over-powering experience of a continuous sequence of transformations, instil a sense of awe, and convey a measure of relativity of man and universe. This innate awareness confers life-giving momentum both to the very young "romantic" poet and to the wise, ageing inventor of Josef Knecht, the magister ludi, director of the game, and teacher of the young.

As a young man of twenty-one Hesse wrote : "Incipit Vita nova. I have become a new man—as yet a miracle to myself. I am at rest and active at the same time. I receive and I give. I own treasures but perhaps I am too ignorant as yet to know which is the most precious."[3] And the man of sixty-five years was to feel : "Transzendieren... war mir seither, gleich dem 'Erwachen' ein rechtes Zauberwort, fordernd und treibend, tröstend und versprechend. Mein Leben, so etwa nahm ich mir vor, sollte ein Transzendieren sein, ein Fortschreiten von Stufe zu Stufe, es sollte ein Raum um den andern durchschritten und zurückgelassen werden, so wie eine Musik Thema um Thema, Tempo um Tempo erledigt, abspielt, vollendet und hinter sich lässt, nie müde und schlafend, stets wach, stets vollkommen gegenwärtig."[4] Between these two works, between the years 1899 and 1943 in which *Eine Stunde hinter Mitternacht* and *Das Glasperlenspiel* were published lies a wealth of intense documentation. It would be difficult to exclude even one of Hesse's prose writings (*Der Lauscher*, 1901; *Unterm Rad*, 1901; *Peter Camenzind*, 1904; *Gertrud*, 1910; *Rosshalde*, 1914; *Knulp*, 1915; *Demian*, 1917; *Märchen*, 1919; *Wanderung*, 1920; *Klingsors letzter Sommer*, 1920; *Siddharta*, 1922; *Kurgast*, 1924; *Steppenwolf*, 1927; *Narziss und Goldmund*, 1930; *Morgenlandfahrt*, 1932) or the poems and essays, or the host of less accessible water-colour drawings which came into being after Hesse's fortieth year.

In contrast to Hesse's earlier public, the present-day reader is thus a privileged participant. Up to 1932 and the esoteric *Morgenlandfahrt*, it would have been prophetic guesswork to say that Hesse would consciously achieve a journey's end, and to see his search leading with set purpose to its summit of integral harmony.

Nowadays, when Hesse's work can be seen as a whole, the earlier delusions of piecemeal analysis may be avoided. We are for instance not so likely to discuss two of his narratives out of context with the whole by seeing them solely in relation to each other, or perhaps even by presuming on an "absolute" valuation. In 1921 Hesse himself seems to have been despondently aware of the incomplete nature of his work; he considered, and then refused his publisher's request for an anthology.[5] But by now the collected works are clearly an edifice of "Dichtung und Wahrheit", a poetic crystallization of experience; they represent the strata of his life, the successive stages of his inner development. Individual tales can be appreciated as complete in themselves, and yet each story is one facet in a many-sided crystal. In 1930, Hesse himself speaks of Knulp : the vagabond, the hypnotic Demian, Siddharta : the sinner-saint, Klingsor: the man possessed, the Steppenwolf and the wood-carver Goldmund as "brothers, each a variant of my theme".[6] They are, in a significant way, at successive stages of experience, precursors but also successors one of the other.

If, however, this inner continuity of concepts and problems is ignored, the narratives emerge solely as a chronicle account, as "Seelenbiographien" of the same individual at different stages in his life. (The child : Unterm Rad; the adolescent : Demian; the young poet : Peter Camenzind; the musician : Gertrud; the painter : Rosshalde; the artist and the conflict of matrimony : Gertrud, Rosshalde; the Dionysian : Klingsor; the ascetic : Siddharta; the "man of fifty" : Steppenwolf; and mature wisdom in Glasperlenspiel.) Such a "serial" approach entirely ignores the multiplicity of characters in each tale, the specific mood of each narrative, and above all the progression and interplay of experience and themes from narrative to narrative. With every new beginning, Hesse believed himself to be dealing with new problems and new figures. But on looking back in 1953 he realized that he had been concentrating all the time, from differing levels of experience, on "the few problems and types that are appropriate" to him.[7] The demarcation of the poetic potential of his themes—though this seemed meagre to him then—is irrelevant, for at a later stage it enabled Hesse to look back on groups of individuals and to discern in them resemblances of character. He sees in them a multiform entity (Personenknäuel), and thus he is confirmed in the belief not only that each individual needs to "awake" and be "reborn" but that this is the way in which the evolution of man will come about.

II

The recurrence and variation of problems and types to which Hesse himself refers[8] does not result from any poverty of imagination. The metamorphoses of the basic theme are breathtaking. In each of its numerous settings in space and time the theme is equally convincing and meaningfully different. The journey through life which man must undertake becomes the object of the poet's "knowledge, presentiment, thought and feeling", it is captured in the colours and the landscapes of the painter's "Bilderhandschrift",[9] and speaks to him from music. While the poet in

Hesse can be intoxicated by the "magic of the visionary", the story-teller Hesse calls his narratives "monologues in which a single human being and his relations to the world and to his own self are being scanned".[10] In music, classical music, Hesse recognizes "awareness of the tragedy of being human, an affirmation of mankind, its bravery and serenity",[11] and the painter in him is gripped by the "indomitable passion of seeing, observing, and the proud, secret feeling of sharing the creative impulse".[12] This compound of feeling, thinking, hearing and seeing in unison disperses into "tröstende Seifenblasen"[13] of lyric and painted landscape, where colours can rise to the crescendo of a concert[14] and the poet takes notes "in sketches, as an artist would".[15]

The most gripping of what might be called "autobiographical monologues", *Flötentraum* and *Der schwere Weg* are written after a period of international upheaval and domestic disaster, as part of the *Fairy Tales* (1919). These two tales record the focal moment of new experience, and relate it by means of a journey that covers about twelve hours. In *Flötentraum* the journey is by river and at night; in *Der schwere Weg* there is a steep, wearisome ascent through mist, and up a dark, dank, frightening gorge to the summit. In both, a bright and beautiful world that he is reluctant to leave lies behind the wanderer : in both he is restored and set free by light, whether it is the lantern on the river or the intoxicating inrush of light as he emerges on the mountain top. In this instance light is not a symbol for insight itself but for the necessity of striving after it. In both tales the ego is given an imperturbable and serenely adamant guide. By precept and example the guide instils firmness of purpose and an awareness of the necessity to go forward. In the grand simplicity of idiom and setting, in sage, firm and ethical undertone, *Flötentraum* and *Der schwere Weg* recall the parables of old with their symbolic quality and their essential, universal truth.[16]

From these tales too speaks Hesse's ability to see time three-dimensionally. At any given moment of the present he can look on life, capable of weighing up the present but also ready to anticipate the presumable course of life in the future. The notion of such "conjectural biographies" is derived from Jean Paul (1763–1825) and no one since him has experimented so brilliantly as Hesse with this idea. It seems possible to speak of three such separate experiments in this form undertaken by him. The first concerns individual long narratives in which for instance Emil Sinclair and Demian (*Demian*), Siddharta, Harry Haller (*Steppenwolf*), Narziss as well as Goldmund give varying accounts of "what might have been" in the case of Hesse himself. There is no restriction in form : both the first person singular and the device of the narrator are used. By 1930 Hesse had come to abstract from all these different incarnations of himself the figure of the man "who is called"; and in the *Glasperlenspiel,* written between 1931 and 1942, we have the "Versuch einer Lebensgeschichte"[17] of one such man, told by one of his disciples. To emphasize the inherent truth of his kind of life (and final sacrifice) there is the appendix containing three *curricula vitae,* professedly written in adolescence by Knecht, the central figure, himself. These three "lives" are represented as intellectual and literary training, as specimen essays of the yearly account demanded of the intellectual élite. The fact that two of these three "Lebensläufe" were published in the early stages of work upon the main biography[18] helps us to see that Hesse was working on an anatomy of man in which a knowledge of individual variants was in fact a *sine qua non* for the final study. As the watershed between the autobiographical conjectures of the maturing Hesse and their "superindividual" abstraction in Josef Knecht we encounter *Kurzgefasster Lebenslauf.*[19] Here Hesse gives an account of himself, primarily to himself, yet ending with a superbly witty repartee to a world that troubles him with its impertinent, incontinent questioning.

Hesse records how he realized at the age of twelve that he wanted to be "a poet or nothing". "But to become a poet was impossible, to want to become one was shameful and ludicrous, as I was soon made to understand."[20] At the end of adolescence and in the utmost despair at seeing intellectual life so stifled by the present he came upon the historian Burkhardt. Through him he gained an insight into the meaning of history and of the past, and came to see that it is just such reference to what is "past, old and ancient" that alone makes intellectual existence possible. In the summer of 1914 however, he was shaken out of the feeling that all is well with himself and with the world, and that all the suffering must have some cause. In considerable conflict with his own self and with the world around him he tried to see *his* part in the total confusion and guilt. Once more he was misunderstood and found himself isolated. To some extent, this led to retrogression, for in his search for causes, he is once more delving mainly into his own self—and trying to uproot what he finds there. But the transformation which this process started, though it impaired belief in his poetic nature, also brings to him new vision. His feelings, his perception, his mind now go beyond self-analysis to the meaning and fate of man. So-called "reality" therefore ceases to have any meaning; past and present form part of him and so does life in the future. He imagines himself, twenty years later, in a prison cell and to have painted a landscape of his own. The painting is complete with all that makes the world of nature beautiful to him : rivers, mountains, sea, clouds and harvesting peasants. Moreover, this make-believe ideal world offers also a means of escape. Into the painted mountain leads a tunnel, and into this chugs a Lilliputian railway. And one fine day when the interrogation becomes too harassing, Hesse disappears into the painting and clambers on to the train which vanishes into the tunnel. Left behind are the warders; unlike him they have no access to the Chinese art of withdrawing from the world of phenomena and into the magic of what Wilhelm Busch called the poet's dimension.

And a poet's dimension it remains, despite Hesse's later disbelief in his calling, and despite his ironic escape from public acclaim and from the request to give a factual account of himself. If we could have hoped for any theoretical comments from him, it would not be on his life but on his works that we should welcome them. As in Hofmannsthal's *Ad me ipsum* we might then hope to comprehend how the poet himself might have interpreted his writings as a whole. For Hesse the evidence has to be pieced together from widely scattered references. For instance he helped us to understand how at the age of twelve, in a very sudden flash of insight, Hölderlin's poem "Die Nacht" convinced him that he must become a poet. The "sacramental" nature of this happening is analysed in *Glasperlenspiel*.[21] "There are many forms of dedication to a mission (berufen sein) but the nucleus and the meaning of this happening remain identical : the soul is awakened, transformed, heightened,[22] and in place of dreams and presentiments that affect you from within there is a sudden call from without : a fragment of reality confronts and takes hold of you." Quite clearly such an experience is something like a miracle which can be encountered only once in a lifetime. The individual thus summoned, alone and wondering, doubting his own fitness is suddenly aware that he is completely set apart from all those around him by a heightened capacity, the capacity of "individuation". As part of this painful and yet wonderful process of "coming into being" he will experience shocks which reveal things that were hidden to him and stood in the way of his inner progress.[23] The experience of being "awakened" will enable him to shed the past,[24] to be transformed and to go forward.[25]

If we look back to the very young poet Hesse, these recurrent shocks which are to project him on to other levels of awareness are still to come. So far he observes and feels. He sees clouds and flowers, butterflies, water and trees. He remembers feelings, the loneliness of the cripple, of the child, of death. Landscape as yet means more to the young man than human and intellectual experience. He treasures the wooded, still landscape and moves in the countryside of the little South German towns of his childhood. He goes fishing, climbs mountains, looks up to the clouds and sees stretched out below and in the distance the gleaming blue of mountain lake or river. Earlier generations in somewhat sentiment-alizing, adulatory fashion loved in Hesse the sensitive poet who extolled clouds, and saw in them the symbol of longing and wanderlust :

Oh die Wolken, die schönen, schwebenden, rastlosen! Ich war ein unwissendes Kind und liebte sie, schaute sie an und wusste nicht, dass auch ich als eine Wolke durchs Leben gehen würde—wandernd, überall fremd, schwebend zwischen Zeit und Ewigkeit.[26]

Not for long do clouds remain for him airy shapes that float away in rhythmical beauty. By the time the boy is old enough to climb his first mountain he views with new and awestruck understanding the size and proportion of the heavens, and the vast distances that the clouds travel. They accompany him all his life, minutely observed, loved and part of him : "I should find it impos-sible to decide whether this sky with its clouds, its filaments, and serenely set on its own course is mirrored in my heart or whether on the contrary after all I read into that sky the sort of life I wish mine to be."[27]

Even stronger is the appeal of water. The lake in its beautiful clarity, scintillating in a rich range of colour appeals primarily to the eye. Running water wells with all the mystery of "Dauer und Wechsel";[28] fountain and river speak to anyone who submits to listen willingly to the "ancient, lovely symbol" of surrender to the merging element of eventual perfection. To understand the secrets of the element that is "always and ever the same, and new at each moment" would mean to understand many conundrums of exist-ence.[29] Solitary trees will reveal the essence of this secret :

In ihren Wipfeln rauscht die Welt, ihre Wurzeln ruhen im Unendlichen; allein sie verlieren sich nicht darin, sondern erstreben mit aller Kraft ihres Lebens nur das Eine : ihr eignes, in ihnen wohnendes Gesetz zu erfüllen.

Bäume sind Heiligtümer. Wer mit ihnen zu sprechen, wer ihnen zuzuhören weiss, der erfährt die Wahrheit. Sie predigen nicht Lehren und Rezepte, sie predigen, um das Einzelne unbekümmert, das Urgesetz des Lebens ... Mein Amt ist, im ausgeprägten Einmaligen das Ewige zu gestalten und zu zeigen.[30]

Thus to Hesse, contact with nature brought joy and fulfilment of the longing for manifestation of the divine; it gave him insight into the beauty, the mystery of nature and disclosed to him the kinship of all forms of organic life. Such a panorama of beauty of symbolic meaning sums up the very personal interpretation which he puts upon the word felicity (Glück) : "completeness, existence not confined by time, the perpetual tunefulness of the world".[31] With all the impulsive fervour of the young, Hesse the poet longed to communicate his Song of the Earth, and the visionary in him wanted to teach his fellow-men the art of perceiving. To him, this project is so revolutionary that it calls for entirely new means of structure and language : "All this I hoped to convey not by means of hymns and Song of Songs. I hoped to present it simply, truth-fully, objectively."[32]

It has been said that Hesse's style does not alter. Not only is this a surprisingly falsifying statement : if true it would amount to an accusation of something like plagiarism. We should be left to imagine for instance that extreme skill in stylistic pastiche thwarted the growth of the poet's own style and condemned him for ever to be expressing himself in the language and the style of great predecessors : Nietzsche, Keller, Eichendorff, Goethe. Such exer-cises in style which Hesse engaged in, sometimes involuntarily, sometimes deliberately[33] may be attributed to a variety of causes. There is however the persistent dread of the limitations of lang-uage, of words. Hesse envies the musician, for he has a language all his own in which to express his ideas. The poet has to use words for his notation, and words are used also at school, in business, in the law courts.[34] Even in writing Hesse wants to paint, to express himself in music. This accounts for a predilection for specific, generally onomatopoeic words, and, above all, for the rhythmic pattern of his prose. The prose is as flexible as the theme, and yet has a recognizable musicality of its own (only the *Glasperlenspiel* must be excepted). The sentence structure is beautifully clear, characterized by a throng of adjectives and a complex differentia-tion of content and emphasis by paraphrase. Antithetical structure has as much symbolic significance as the tripartite, gradated state-ment. Though Hesse's prose flows so beautifully, there was a time when he deliberately trained himself "slowly in that mysterious skill to say only what was simple and unassuming yet in so doing to churn up the soul of the listener as the wind does the mirroring surface of the water".[35]

That it is in his power to do so depends as much on the poetic use of language as on the craftsman's discipline of form. Among his lyrics numerous poems stand out, as different from each other perhaps and as memorable for their diction as the onomatopoeic *Scheingewitter*,[36] the philosophic *Leben einer Blume*[37] or the majestic tone poem *Zu einer Toccata von Bach*.[38] In each lyric the immediacy of expression is clearly felt. In narrative prose however, Hesse works and refines. He is beset by doubt, he regards "story-telling" as an art for which he suspects he lacks the necessary talent and training (Voraussetzungen). On the one hand he considers that early twentieth-century writers used fossilized forms and merely imitated structural patterns of the past. On the other hand writers are separated from one another by individual discrepancies in outlook, belief, "language"; and each writer stands apart from his public.[39] Yet this in no way absolves them from doing their utmost to bridge the gulf. We know from letters[40] and of course from internal evidence that Hesse clearly went to great pains in the matter of structure. This is true particularly for his writings after 1925; above all the conscious care of structure and thematic development takes effect in the *Steppenwolf*.

As in Goethe's *Die Leiden des jungen Werthers*, an "editor's" preface introduces an ironic fiction (that the hero despairs of ever finding himself and commits suicide). There is further a pathetic discrepancy between the "message" of the preface, the common interpretation of the main text itself and the interpretation which the poet intended to have put upon it. In bringing to our attention Haller's autobiographical account and the mysterious "Treatise of the wolf from the steppes" the editor does not fail to give facts as he sees them a factual interpretation. To him Haller's account is merely a case-history, not of the patient but of the time-bound disease itself (Zeitkrankheit): the suffering which is brought about by the overlap of two civilizations, two periods in history.[41] Dissatisfaction with his own self is the starting point of Haller's reflections, and thus his entire philosophy is called into question. Instead of seeing himself as a unity he finds that he is confronted by a dual self. If there is no such constant thing as a unified ego we must, on looking into our own selves, be dismayed by a "Fiktion vom Ich". It is here that the treatise sets in. Despite its apparent mystification, and beyond, it presents thesis, antithesis and synthesis of Haller's perplexity.[42] It also gives a detailed examination of the central thesis of the theme: the division of man into two diametrically opposed creatures, in this case man and Siberian wolf. In view of the Karamasoff essay (*Die Brüder Karamasoff oder Der Untergang Europas,* 1919), it appears to me that Hesse used ciphers for the antimony "European man/Russian", "amoral man/moral man".[43] (The fallibility of "good" and "bad" in this context being easily demonstrated later in the narrative by the wolfish man and the servile wolf of the Magic Theatre.) The antithesis of Hesse's theme in the Steppenwolf's Magic Theatre reduces ad absurdum any belief that man is *only* a duality. If man can look into the mirror of his own self and laugh at the image, i.e. not take himself seriously, then he can enter this magic theatre, this "picture

gallery of his soul". There, set free from time, reality, and space
he will find a multiplicity of selves. And, as foretold in the treatise,
he will gain insight into the infinite possibilities of transformation
that lie ahead of man, and the numerous courses that his life may
run : "Der Mensch ist ja keine feste und dauernde Gestaltung . . .
er ist vielmehr ein Versuch und Übergang."[44] But this same sentence continues : "man is nothing more than the narrow, dangerous
bridge between 'Natur' and 'Geist' "—in itself a revealing paraphrase of Nietzsche's "man is a rope fastened between animal and
superman—a rope above an abyss".[45] While this statement sheds
light on the meaning which "Geist" and "Natur" held for Hesse
it also underlines his concern for structure. If structure is to be
maintained "so streng und straff wie eine Sonate",[46] Hesse's
narrative would follow on the architectural lines of traditional
philosophic disputations : a thesis is stated and then rigorously
examined from all angles in the form of question and answer until
a conclusion can be worked out. For the Steppenwolf freedom of
will exists only in so far as one may accept one's fate or rebel
against it. He is taught to accept himself as a multiplicity. He must
look on life not as something that he can master : it is a complicated game with endless variants. In our day-to-day life, values
can easily become distorted, they cannot be destroyed (Hesse illustrates his meaning by the distortion of sound in the early radios).

The complex embroidery of the basic structural form, its triadic
argument, antithetical treatment, prefiguring of motifs and concepts is of course not restricted to Steppenwolf. Amongst examples
that might be drawn upon we have already referred to the overall
structure in *Glasperlenspiel*. Here the essential concepts of intellectual service to a cause, demanding even sacrifice of self, is restated
in the three "lives" of the pagan rainmaker, the Christian hermit,
the Indian sage that are appended to the main work. Another
example of such interrelated study of a character and his estrangement from his own world was given by H. Ball[47] in his analysis
of the three tales that have more in common than their common
title : *Kinderseele, Klein und Wagner,* and *Klingsors letzter
Sommer*. We should do Hesse an injustice if we regarded such
"relatedness" as subconscious :

> In einer Blume Rot und Blau,
> In eines Dichters Worte wendet,
> Nach innen sich der Schöpfung Bau,
> Der stets beginnt und niemals endet.
> Und wo sich Wort und Ton gesellt,
> Wo Lied erklingt, Kunst sich entfaltet,
> Wird jedesmal der Sinn der Welt,

Des ganzen Daseins neu gestaltet,
Und jedes Lied und jedes Buch
Und jedes Bild ist ein Enthüllen,
Ein neuer, tausendster Versuch,
Des Lebens Einheit zu erfüllen.
In diese Einheit einzugehn
Lockt euch die Dichtung, die Musik,
Der Schöpfung Viefalt zu verstehn
Genügt ein einziger Spiegelblick.[48]

Once the young poet's spontaneous nature-poetry had been submitted to the conscious discipline of thought and form, the content of Hesse's work began to show more and more clearly that it was a groping towards "Erkenntnis".[49] This search begins with innumerable attempts to seek and describe the individual self, the real self, the essential self. As from time immemorial the search carries with it the need for utmost sincerity and severity towards one's self. "Do not deceive yourself as to the nature of your calling, heed it and fulfil yourself by serving it.[50] If you have really done that there is no room for regrets whether you were a Knulp or a Klingsor, a tramp or a genius." The tramp will fill all sober-minded citizens with faint longing for freedom,[51] the painter will thirstily take hold of the world by means of the senses and give way to the urge to create.[52] In moments of real inspiration the artist in his self-portrait can reveal himself for what he is : Faust as well as Karamazov.[53] In other instances friend helps friend, master helps disciple to find himself. Thus Max Demian rouses the adolescent Emil Sinclair to think and to doubt; the Brahmin Siddharta imagines that he no longer wants teachers, since he has rejected the highest of them all : Gotoma; but as time goes on he realizes that life is a never-ending quest for "cognition", especially for one so ignorant about himself and the world. In Narziss and in Goldmund we have the friend who may be faced with a seem-ingly destructive task : the ascetic Narziss helps Goldmund the Dionysian to realize that they are completely different and must therefore fulfil themselves in different ways.

Not always of course does the search for the real self end happily : truth may be far too strong. In a gripping, uncannily cynical story, the worthy, humdrum young "man by name of Ziegler" finds out, by that very alchemy for which he as a modern man has such a healthy scorn, why animals despise us so much. His attempt, however, to join the animal world (by stripping off his clothes) is merely regarded as an outbreak of insanity. Thus he is trapped in both worlds. But where the searcher believes in magic, the mirror (as in the Magic Theatre) can help to unlock doors kept firmly bolted. On a higher level of "cognition" than the Steppenwolf's, the searcher realizes that all the images have in fact been reflections of his own self, so that the mirror itself was as it were non-existent; it was no more than the "top layer of a surface made of glass".[54] We are led to see that not only is the search for self a journey on which each sets out by himself; it is also a pilgrimage in search of self in which all mankind is engaged. As Hesse moves from *Demian* to *Siddharta,* to *Morgenlandfahrt,* we encounter descriptions of more and more highly differentiated aspects of the quest. The goal of the search is not the self but "Menschwerdung" ("to develop into a human being"). The *Glasperlenspiel,* finally, calls on aesthetic and ethical qualities of different teachers : Thomas an der Trave (modelled on Thomas Mann), paragon of Castalian irony and form, the nameless Master of music, the "Elder Brother" as initiator into Chinese studies, and the defender of historical truth, the friar Jacobus (written with the historian Jakob Burkhardt in mind). The *Glasperlenspiel* seeks to work out a harmonious synthesis between the intellect and the individual who after all must come to terms with the world in which he finds himself. We are shown symbols and abstractions of the qualities that are instrumental towards achieving "cognition". Of these, the three that claim our attention are music, the Immortals (i.e. genius) and the Magic Theatre. In music we have the symbol of harmony between heaven and earth;[55] music has beauty of form, mathematical structure, a wealth of ideas and feeling, and lends itself to those improvising variants of thought which for Hesse belong to the art of meditation. Among the Immortals he numbers Bach, Goethe, Mozart. To them we owe inspiration and joy. In them we admire the greatness of their surrender, their readiness for suffering and the enduring of suffering itself.[56] The third symbol, that of the Magic Theatre, represents critical self-analysis. This mirror is a glass that cannot be deceived. Whatever we see in it, hinges on "inner reality," what it teaches is the "art of living".[57]

III

And yet the creator of this mirror of self-analysis in the twentieth century is frequently spoken of as a Romantic. The original words which by now have become an accusation, go back to H. Ball's biography of Hesse. But his discussion must be replaced in its context. By calling Hesse "the last of the knights in the resplendent cavalcade of Romanticism",[58] Ball is in the first instance pursuing an association of thought that suggests kinship with Jean Paul : "a heart brimming over with love for the stars in heaven, for butterflies and parrots, for colourful Gardens of Eden, quixotic anchorites; sensitively able to pour out his feelings, and ever ready to welcome whatever exploits friendship might hold in store". At all times it will be a foolhardy undertaking to assume that the term "romantic" can be given a generally accepted definition. Moreover, it becomes clear that the emphasis for Ball lies in the qualifying "last"; and in any case the entire statement becomes prophetic (since Ball was writing before 1927) solely because of the conclusion that Ball drew from his character study. He describes Hesse as indebted to such widely different Romantic poets as C. Brentano and Hölderlin (and many would hesitate to think of Hölderlin as a Romantic); to Ball Hesse seems to share the Romantics' piety, grace and sense of "malheur d'être". Assuredly, therefore, as is evident, Hesse has inherited from the Romantics the sum-total of their experience, their longing, their anguish, their aloofness. And Ball reminds his readers once more, that Hesse to him is the *last* knight of Romanticism : "will he suddenly wheel round, this knight, and face an altogether new front?"

And yet in Hesse's earlier work there is undoubtedly a Romantic tendency to escape from the world of his day,[59] to be "ein Sucher nach rückwarts".[60] In his ultimate work, the *Glasperlenspiel*, however, only one noble ideal of Romanticism is left, the catalysis of "universality". It is indeed this close union of the sciences and the arts which is to be understood by his symbol of the "crystalline game". By the Utopian nature of this ideal alliance Hesse refers us to accomplishment, to endeavour in a foreseeable future. He would not have turned to the future if he had considered the present congenial to such ideas. He could not reject the present without looking at it closely. Hence, his search is no longer concerned with the "self in the past" but with the self in the present-day world. We are first of all concerned with the ego and the intellectual stimulus it received. Intellectually, young Hesse owes much to three men. Of these, Kierkegaard plays a part that would repay looking into; his influence pales by the side of that of Nietzsche and Burkhardt.

Nietzsche's scathing analysis, one is tempted to call it diagnosis, of his time found many attentive minds in young Hesse's generation. In Hesse himself it would seem to be primarily responsible for three very disturbing thoughts that affect his ethical, his aesthetic and his historical sensibilities. Though he would never join Nietzsche in his clamouring for a "revaluing of all values", Hesse does accept, with distress, that "God is dead";[61] he accepts the consequences that the individual must rethink metaphysical concepts by himself, that is without the support of recognized religions.

Between 1919 and 1922 this search was to lead him, the son and grandson of Protestant missionaries, to a study of Chinese and Indian thought. Sanskrit literature, and Nietzsche, too, introduced the goddess Maya, the divinity of illusion. It is she who created "outer reality", the world of illusion, and it is this veil which shrouds the true world. Hence the poet, the thinker must fear that poetry and ideas are obscured by worldly values as well as divorced from outer reality, i.e. the everyday world. From Goethe's *Tasso* to the figures in Thomas Mann's novels, modern literature shows itself aware of this problem and distressed by its apparent antinomous character. Hesse attempts to work out an aesthetic solution in all his major narratives from *Siddharta* (1922) onwards (*Steppenwolf, Narziss und Goldmund, Morgenlandfahrt*) but it is doubtful whether even the *Glasperlenspiel* succeeds in effecting a truly harmonious synthesis. In the course of this tale Hesse argues that history may be the one field in which the man of intellect can find the outer world merging with inner reality, with inner truth. Ideas and mimesis of reality both undergo a process of growth, they are equally variable and dependent on subjective interpretation. This does not affect the inner truth. Where accounts of one and the same event can be, and are, distorted by the mirror of the individual,[62] truth will be concealed but it will nevertheless be present. Like the poet, the historian lives in the world, takes from it and gives to it. Both have an equally serious, perhaps tragic task. In order to find out what history is, the historian must live it, prophesy it, help to fashion it, he must learn to see historical reality in his own life.[63] He can achieve it only by transforming his own personal life into history.[64] If we assume that poet and historian represent outer and inner reality respectively, correspondences between these two worlds can be established. In both worlds there is "striving, growth and ever new beginning".

Through Burkhardt the historian, Hesse had come into contact with history and historiography, its laws and contradictions. As a poet-prophet he joins both worlds in the *Glasperlenspiel*. Our present world is depicted in the "outer world" of that universe. Occasionally chosen visitors from it can enter Castalia, the world within. This is not a Utopia but the world of the future; by its name it suggests a source dedicated to the Muses and to Apollo, god of the sun, of poetry, inspiration and music. The inhabitants of this land are ascetic devotees of knowledge and all that is understood by "Geist" (for Hesse "mind", "soul" and "feeling"). Like the residents of that other "pedagogic province" (in Goethe's *Wilhelm Meister*) they mainly depend on each other in their search for knowledge but are, on occasion, also sent into the outer world to seek it.

IV

It is into this outer world that Hesse went to search for a historical grasp of his own world. And where the historical and sociological aspect enters his narratives—as he feels they should in the modern novel[65]—Hesse emerges as "Kulturkritiker". In the *Kurzgefasster Lebenslauf* Hesse explains that the bestiality and madness of war result in the second of two basic experiences in his own life. A sense of guilt and degradation completely overpowers him; the degradation heralds the destruction of all but material values and ushers in an age where everything else may easily go under;[66] the guilt causes men and women to accuse the other side and not themselves. We find a reflection of this in the pestilence raging in Goldmund's lifetime: "The worst off were the living. Under the burden of terror and fear of death they seemed to have lost eyes and soul. Weird and terrible things were reported to him on all sides: parents deserted their children, husbands their wives when these fell a prey to the disease. . . . and worst of all, each one in all this misery was eagerly looking for a scapegoat."[67] In Hesse's own life there sprang from the experience of utter dejection and collapse an individual reborn with a new heightened sense of awareness. It brought home to him the necessity of a new way of seeing the world. In his old way, he had seen and judged it adversely as an unending sequence of antinomies, bedevilled further by the anti-intellectual attitude of militarist and industrialist alike,[68] by man's servitude to machines,[69] in short, by the entire non-sense and distortion of the modern world.

The new mode of vision is first indicated in *Demian*. Where Nietzsche speaks of the downfall of the European world, Hesse predicts the "rebirth and downfall of all that is now",[70] and sees in the soul of Europe the fettered animal that will repay liberation by initial bloodshed. This exploration of the future finds disquieting confirmation and extension in the reading of Dostojewski. Hesse's reaction may be judged from his thought-provoking essay *Die Brüder Karamasoff oder Der Untergang Europas*; in it Hesse foresees the moral and intellectual (geistig) downfall of European man by the stealthy, cumulative control that an age-old Asiatic ideal is allowed to gain over the European mind. In the first instance the European mind will be devoured and utterly destroyed; on a positive level the "devouring" can be regarded as a "return": to Asia, the motherland of mankind. Symbolically, (in the tradition of alchemy, as also in Goethe's *Faust II*) this return to the "mothers" is the preliminary essential to rebirth. For Hesse, the Karamazovs signify the "amorality of thought and feeling, and the ability to seek and feel all that is divine, necessary, predestined

—even in the "utmost evil and ugliness".[71] He feels that in this, Russian man is seeking to dissolve the concept of dualism and to "return behind the veil shrouding the *principium individuationis*". To achieve it, Dostojewski depicts men in whom there is no vain regret at having "zwei Seelen, ach" like Faust, but who accept the coexistence of good and evil, of the divine and the diabolical.[72]

By the time that Hesse begins to work on *Steppenwolf,* he is earnestly trying to persuade himself that he must learn to accept, "smilingly" (i.e. without illusions) the twentieth-century world under this new guise, just as he must learn to see in himself both man and wolf, artist and bourgeois, and even, paradoxically, Faust and Karamazov. Indeed, by 1932 (*Dank an Goethe*) Hesse grows to realize that for him the essential Goethe is characterized by the existence of both "apollinische Klassizität" and "den, die Mütter suchenden, dunklen Faustgeist"[73] in all the mystery of Bipolarität.

V

Convinced belief in dualism, faith in the complementary nature of opposites are usually held to represent two entirely different outlooks on life. Each philosophy claims men of such different temperament that it is Hesse's extraordinary achievement, and good fortune, to have been able to jettison belief in dualism and to attempt to see life in terms of integration of phenomenon and idea. From a belief in opposites (Gegensätze),[74] he advanced to the acceptance of polarity (Gegenpole). Such bipolarity he had experienced in himself, he is both painter and poet, "stillborn" and "a child of the gods", attracted to Buddhist as well as to Protestant dogma.[75] As two symbols for bipolarity he used hermaphrodite and "Doppelfigur" in a complex structure where the central figure is complemented by one other dual character. The hermaphrodite Hermine, the Steppenwolf's mentor and guide bears the female counterpart to Hesse's own Christian name. Similarly, in *Morgenlandfahrt,* the complementary figure is also an allegorical interpretation of antinomy. Andreas Leo (i.e. man-lion) is wise servant as well as Grand Master of the League. As in dreams, the individual pilgrims are free to participate in fusion of experience;[76] they can "shift time and space like the flats on a stage" and interchange opposites. For the pilgrimage to the source of light is an individual one, transcending time, nationality and individuality. Should a pilgrim desert the company, the admission of guilt absolves if he can pay the penalty of self-cognition. In the archives of the League the narrator discovers that his essential self is represented there as a "Doppelfigur", as a Siamese-twin sculpture of the poet himself and of the figure of his creation, Leo. Like a mirror, the statue's glass-like substance reveals progressive, dynamic fusion between the two figures, thus illustrating Hesse's belief that the poet, like a mother, gives of his own strength and substance to whatever he creates. The reciprocal fusion of the two statues, though both life-giving and life-consuming, is clearly to be understood as ultimate integration.

As the *Morgenlandfahrt* suggests, this quest for self cannot be undertaken at will or just when the individual chooses. The condition is that he overcome the temptation to accuse himself of inclination towards suicide, sensuality, or sensuousness. The process of self-cognition is advocated as remedy because it sets the penitent free. To this end psycho-analysis and also the art of meditation will play their part, two processes which juxtapose the demands of "Natur" and of "Geist". Meditation in itself is a source of strength;[77] it becomes this by the preparations needed for it : the "neutralizing of the self".[78] Psycho-analysis can be regarded as a new, excellent instrument, and useful as a key. As such, however, it has no magic qualities and the artist in particular must guard against overrating its effectiveness. Despite this, which was in 1918 a most timely note of caution, the poet Hesse finds psycho-analysis valuable : it emphasizes the importance of imagination, it brings about a closer relation to one's own subconscious, and above all it makes obvious the fundamental demand of truthfulness towards oneself.[79] Hesse's verdict would thus seem to be : life does not resolve the conflicts it engenders, but it does confirm that we must accept the fact that in us life "is bipolar and is not called on to make a choice between Natur and Geist".[80]

Once more then it is not a question of choice between opposites. Sage, poet, scientist, artist all of one accord construct "the cathedral of the intellect with its one hundred portals",[81] and Hesse desires the harmony of "Natur" and "Geist".[82] Therefore, to bring this about the intellect and man's soul can only be comprehended as that force which complements nature : "In der Natur kann der Geist nicht leben, nur gegen sie, nur als ihr Gegenspiel."[83] Hence, the search on which the poet set out continues. In its early stages it had been a search after man's nature, but then begins a journey towards the East, in search of illumination and "Geist".

VI

We remember that Hesse spoke of man as the "transition between Natur and Geist",[84] and that he described this link as dangerously fragile. As Hesse emphatically suggests, the need to maintain the link with either side, and if possible to bring them close together, is imperative and calls for a frank, courageous inspection of all component parts of the structure. This introspective survey reveals deficiencies that are bound to impair the individual human structure sensually as well as intellectually. Thus, at the outset of his life, Hesse in his quality of poet and human being, is overcome by an intensity of suffering. If he shrinks from facing antitheses, it is because at that time he believes himself called upon but incapable of making a choice between artist and bourgeois, "libertine" and saint, between Sansara and Nirvana. Fear of loneliness is his worst enemy. He has watched the imposed isolation of the cripple, experienced the essential loneliness of the artist, and for a time he regards loneliness as the "disease of our time".[85] In contrast with this mood of self-pity we ought to recall the brave resolution of the poem *Allein*[86] : we must eventually face death by ourselves, therefore let us realize that all difficult things have to be faced in solitude. Death itself, however, has a seductive aspect which rests on its powers to release from life by an act of will, through suicide, or in its sublimity as it brings the "solution of a great conundrum".[87] A reverence for the experience of seeing a human being die, accompanies him all his life. To the individual, death brings fulfilment (as through Knecht's final sacrifice in *Glasperlenspiel*), to the onlooker, death brings "glad tidings of metamorphosis, change of form and transition to new life".[88] But the transition he watches in his own era Hesse instinctively regards as the "downfall of Europe", as destruction. Intellectually he tries to understand and welcome it : "this decay like any death will of course lead to rebirth".[89]

This rebirth will come about under two conditions. It presupposes the experience which Hesse describes as "Erwachen" and the willingness of the awakened to take action. "Awakening" is too gentle a word to describe the shock experienced when a place of no return has been reached. The sleeper becomes conscious, and summons all his determination to leave, and to go forward.[90] He is startled as if he had suddenly been shown a mirror that stripped him of all pretence. His reaction is that of the young bird "fighting its way out of the egg".[91] He destroys the egg because he must survive, and because he must worship and serve God. Only those who possess the innate knowledge of powers worth worshipping (i.e. the "Immortals"), can be thus awakened : only those in whom the ability to serve, the virtue of reverence is found. Of these qualities, it is not reverence that appears to be most in demand (as it is in Goethe's *Wilhelm Meister*) but the willingness to serve and the humility which makes service possible. Again it may be said, nearly all of Hesse's writings illustrate the development of this concept to its ultimate perfection in *Glasperlenspiel*. Service can be an act of friendship (*Demian*), service never impairs essential freedoms : the ascetic Siddharta serves a worldly merchant, and is yet independent of all material wants that might compel him to sell his services. On a higher stage, intellectual service links disciple to master in loyalty and reverence, irrespective of the status of the master. He may be a ferryman (*Siddharta*) or a steward like Leo (*Morgenlandfahrt*) and he reaches a final symbolic concentration in the servant who becomes Grand Master of the League (*Morgenlandfahrt*) and in that other "servant" Josef Knecht. He, like the J. K. of Kafka's *Trial* is seeking unattainable truths. Knecht both serves and is in command. But his service is neither to individuals nor to a community. His service is both symbol and reality, and as such becomes the ideal of service in a higher cause : "Dienst am Überpersönlichen".[92] Intellectually, physically, and emotionally it sets the individual free of himself.

The wisdom that can be gathered from the abstraction "to serve" is attainable on the level of "Natur" to all who try to understand the meaning of "Spiel". All men must learn to play the game of life but for each of them this will amount to a different kind of playing. Once more we are dealing with an idea that can be traced right back to Hesse's earliest work. Children must be found time to play their childhood games even in the midst of preparing for scholarship examinations (*Unterm Rad*). The unworldly, the ascetic must learn to play at living, at loving (Siddharta, Goldmund). The Steppenwolf, who cannot master life in the present-day world at all, is taught to regard life as a game of chess, a game in which infinite variants are possible. He is confronted with some of these in the Magic Theatre. The "pilgrim to the East" is deeply perturbed by finding that "all life's a stage" ("Maskenspiel des Lebens"). And from all these preliminaries Hesse develops a higher kind of magic theatre in his "thought game". This crystalline game he describes as a highly developed secret language, a language which "toys" with "all the contents and values of our civilization". "Its structure is musical, it rests on meditation."[93]

So, ultimately, the symbol "Spiel" connotes transformation, progressive development. Its foundation is based on the three principles of knowledge, worship of the beautiful and meditation.[94] Freedom attained by "serving" and by "playing" releases the individual from himself and helps to prepare his way to super-individuality. As in *Der schwere Weg,* as soon as the climber overcomes his desire to look back and his unwillingness to ascend, the path becomes more manageable, the sky widens and at the summit the radiance bursts upon him. This symbolic search leads towards "Geist" : "Göttlich ist und ewig der Geist. Ihm entgegen

... Führt unser Weg."[95] Moreover, the reaching of the summit represents in symbolic form the attainment of a new stage of perceptiveness. In a similar quest Siddharta had gradually come closer to the goal of his search, and had only then realized what he was seeking :[96] to conceive the idea of unity until it became part of himself. This idea evolves antithetically from the multitude of sights that lie before the traveller. Hesse had experienced it in his journey in 1911 to Singapore, Penang, Sumatra and Ceylon. That this variegation is basically no more than a unity is for him yet another instance of "Gegensatz" and "Gegenpol", though it defies illustration in terms of words. The musician, Hesse suggests, could recreate it by a harmony of tunes in which two voices are seen to diverge, to come together and to contend with each other but at all times to move in intricate interrelation to each other.[97] Presumably, the outer and the inner world of the *Glasperlenspiel* are an attempt to illustrate this idea of "Einheit der Welten".

The idea of the unity of the worlds has an obvious ethical corollary : if the world is seen as one, the doctrine of "love thy neighbour" becomes irrelevant, for it is only illusion, Maya, that makes us believe in the separateness of "you" and "I".[98] Furthermore, the idea of the unity of the worlds rephrases the idea of synthesis, a synthesis in the realm of noumena and phenomena. It is thus another way to set man free.

Yet a further way may be sought in the idea of transcendence. Each human individual makes his way through life up a series of steps. Outwardly it is a progression in age and maturity. Inwardly it corresponds to three stages which Hesse regards as fundamental. The first stage is one of innocence. The stage where innocence is lost, sharply divides child and awakened man, for the individual now despairs under the feeling of guilt. From here two roads are open to him : he can go either to his downfall or on to life itself.[99]

Ideally, once set on the road to life, man's journey should proceed rhythmically, fluidly like a harmony in music. In human life the path does not run quite so smoothly. When Hesse's figures have followed their "road into life" they have had to overcome self-centredness, to battle a way out of the world that confined them and yet make their peace with it. Though not even Siddharta or Knecht reach the longed for harmonious synthesis of both worlds, they yet approach it : "Every earthly phenomenon is a symbol and every symbol an open gate. Through it—if only it hold itself in readiness—the soul may make its way into the interior of the world. There, both you and I, day as well as night are all one."[100]

As with the work of any poet of eminence, Hesse's prose, the fabric of his ideas becomes more and more profound and universal. An intricate web of thought and symbol, nobility of language, a rhythm of its own accompany it to the end.

NOTES AND TRANSLATIONS

(Unless otherwise indicated, all quotations are taken from *Hermann Hesse, Gesammelte Schriften,* 7 vols., Suhrkamp, 1957.)

1. vii, 636, letter. "Greetings of a wanderer who journeys in the dark though he knows of the light and is in search of it."

2. vii, 773, letter. "I am a poet, I seek and profess. It is my task to serve sincerity and truth (and the beautiful is part of truth—it is one of the guises under which truth appears). I have a mission: those who also search I must help to understand and to endure life."

3. i, 35 (*Eine Stunde hinter Mitternacht*).

4. vi, 511, *Glasperlenspiel.* "From that day onward, to transcend, rather like to awake, too, was a truly magic term for me. It was demanding, encouraging; it consoled and promised. My life, so I decided, was to consist of transcendence. It was to move with measured tread from step to step. I was to pass through and leave behind one zone after the other in the way in which a piece of music deals with theme after theme and different tempi by playing them, completing them, dismissing them, never wearying or falling asleep, on the contrary, fully awake and alert."

5. vii, 249f., *Vorrede eines Dichters zu seinen ausgewählten Werken.*

6. vii, 493, letter.

7. vii, 865, *Rundbriefe,* Engadiner Erlebnisse (1953).

8. op. cit. loc. cit.

9. "Pictorial writing".

10. vii, 303, *Eine Arbeitsnacht.*

11. vi, 116, *Glasperlenspiel.*

12. ii, 633, *Rosshalde.*

13. iv, 632, *Beim Einzug in ein neues Haus.* "Bubbles in the air, but comforting."

14. iii, 609, *Klingsors letzter Sommer.*

15. i, 330, *Peter Camenzind.*

16. *The Flautist's Dream,* in fact, might be taken to illustrate the *Bhagavad Gita* ii, 69: "In the dark night of all beings awakes to Light the tranquil man. But what is day to other beings is night for the sage who sees." And *Journey Laborious* similarly would have as its starting point the *Bhagavad Gita* vi, 3-4: (3) "When the sage climbs the heights of Yoga, he follows the path of work; but when he reaches the heights of Yoga, he is in the land of peace". (4) "And he reaches the heights of Yoga when he surrenders his earthly will: when he is not bound by the work of his senses, and he is not bound by his earthly works." (tr. Juan Mascaró, Penguin, 1962.)

17. "Prolegomena to a biography."

18. In the literary journal *Neue Rundschau,* May and December, 1934.

19. "A deliberately abridged autobiography."

20. iv, 472, *Kurzgefasster Lebenslauf.*

21. vi, 126 and 129, *Glasperlenspiel.*

22. A technical, literary term: "raised and intensified".

23. iii, 144 and 220, *Demian.*

24. iii, 646, *Siddharta.* The concept of "being awakened" Hesse would have encountered in the *Upanishads.* The *Mandukya Upanishad* describes the fourth (and last) "condition" of the self as taking place in the awakened life of supreme consciousness.

25. iii, 301, *Flötentraum.*

26. i, 230, *Peter Camenzind*: "Clouds, beautiful, floating, restless clouds. I was an ignorant child and loved them, looked at them and did not know that I too would pass through life like a cloud, always journeying, a stranger wherever I went, and aloft between time and eternity."

27. iii, 422, *Wanderung.*

28. Goethe's poem by this title is one of several in which he explores the concept of cyclical transience.

29. iii, 633f., *Siddharta.*

30. iii, 405, *Wanderung.* "The tops of the trees commune with the world, their roots rest in the infinite. Yet the trees do not lose themselves in the infinite, for with all their vital strength they strive after one thing: to bear out their own inheritance. Trees are sacred. He who knows their language and he who heeds it will learn truth. Trees do not preach or prescribe doctrines, succinctly they teach the primeval law of life . . . : it is my task (says the tree) to fashion and signify the sempiternal in meaningful uniqueness."

31. iv, 891, *Glück.*

32. i, 329, *Peter Camenzind.*

33. See for instance *Zarathustra returns,* vii, 200f.

34. vii, 56, *Sprache.*

35. iii, 292, *Der Dichter.*

36. v, 739, poems.

37. v, 744, poems.

38. v, 748, poems.

39. iv, 844, *Der Bettler.*

40. e.g. see vii, 495.

41. iv, 205, *Steppenwolf.*

42. iv, 204f., ibid.

43. vii, 163f., *Die Brüder Karamasoff.*

44. iv, 247, *Steppenwolf.*

45. *Thus spoke Zarathustra,* preface, §4.

46. vii, 495, letter. "As austere and concise as a sonata."

47. H. Ball: *Herman Hesse,* Zürich, 1947. p. 197.

48. v, 724, from the poem *Sprache*: "In the red or the blue of any flower, in the words of a poet, the edifice of creation turns towards its centre. It has innumerable beginnings and ceases never. Wherever word and tune are joined, a song is heard and art comes into its own, then each once, the meaning of the universe, of existence itself is fashioned anew. Every song, every book, every painting reveals a new attempt, one of thousands, to accomplish the unity of life. Music and poetry entice

you to comprehend this unity, and yet one glance into the mirror suffices to grasp all creation in its diversity."

49. For Hesse this word would seem to stand for "gaining insight into existence and its meaning".

50. v, 287, *Narziss und Goldmund.*

51. iii, 96, *Knulp.*

52. ii, 528 and 570, *Rosshalde.*

53. iii, 608 and 610, *Klingsors letzter Sommer.*

54. vi, 35, *Morgenlandfahrt.*

55. vi, 100, *Glasperlenspiel.*

56. iv, 248, *Steppenwolf.*

57. iv, 388, *Steppenwolf.*

58. Ball, op. cit. p. 24.

59. iii, 890–91, *Das schreibende Glas.*

60. iii, 218, *Demian:* "he who looks backwards in pursuance of his quest".

61. v, 523, the poem *Im Leide.*

62. vi, 71, *Morgenlandfahrt.*

63. vi, 250, *Glasperlenspiel.*

64. vi, 278, *Glasperlenspiel.*

65. vii, 20, *Wilhelm Meisters Lehrjahre.*

66. vi, 472, *Glasperlenspiel.*

67. v, 226, *Narziss und Goldmund.*

68. iv, 327, *Steppenwolf.*

69. vi, 90, *Morgenlandfahrt.*

70. iii, 238, *Demian.*

71. vii, 163, *Die Brüder Karamasoff.*

72. vii, 165, ibid.

73. vii, 381, *Dank an Goethe:* "Faust in the fierce, sombre mood that impels him to seek out the 'mothers'."

74. v, 255, *Narziss und Goldmund.*

75. vii, 370f., *Mein Glaube* (1931).

76. vi, 24, *Morgenlandfahrt.*

77. vi, 151, *Glasperlenspiel.*

78. vi, 673, ibid.

79. vii, 139, *Künstler und Psychoanalyse* (1918).

80. vii, 633, letter.

81. v, 349, poem: *Stunden im Garten.*

82. vii, 570, letter.

83. v, 68, *Naziss und Goldmund:* "mind, soul and feeling cannot exist in the everyday world, unless they are pitched against it and complement it".

84. iv, 247, *Steppenwolf.*

85. ii, 128, *Gertrud.*

86. v, 554.

87. i, 249, *Peter Camenzind.*

88. iv, 593, *Bei Christian Wagners Tod.*

89. vii, 162, *Die Brüder Karamasoff.*

90. iii, 185, *Demian.*

91. iii, 185f., ibid.
92. vi, 81, *Glasperlenspiel*: "service in the cause of the superindividual".
93. v, 348f., in the poem *Stunden im Garten*.
94. vi, 420, *Glasperlenspiel*.
95. v, 740, poem, *Besinnung*: "Everlasting and of God is the mind. Our path takes us towards it (and Him)."
96. iii, 716, *Siddharta*.
97. iv, 113f., *Kurgast*.
98. vii, 674, letter.
99. vii, 391, *Ein Stückchen Theologie* (1932).
100. iii, 367, *Iris*.

A complete reference to the literature on Hesse's writings can be found in:

H. WAIBLER. *Hermann Hesse Eine Bibliographie*, Bern, 1962.

Amongst the large number of books listed, the following will be found particularly helpful for their insight into the poet's mind:

H. BALL. *Hermann Hesse sein Leben und sein Werk*. Berlin, 1927. (In later editions A. Carlsson contributes: *Vom Steppenwolf bis zur Morgenlandfahrt* and O. Basler, in a rather different style, a chapter on Der Weg zum *Glasperlenspiel*.)
P. BÖCKMANN. *Hermann Hesse* (in *Deutsche Literatur im Zwanzigsten Jahrhundert*, ed. H. Friedmann and O. Mann. Heidelberg, 1954. pp. 288–305.

SELECT BIBLIOGRAPHY

ENGLISH TRANSLATIONS (SELECTION)

The Prodigy (Unterm Rad), tr. W. J. Strachan, London, 1957.
Demian, tr. Henry Holt, New York, 1948.
——, tr. Peter Owen, London, 1958.
In Sight of Chaos (The Brothers Karamazoff), tr. S. Hudson, Zürich, 1923.
Siddharta, tr. H. Rosner, London, 1954.
Steppenwolf, tr. G. Creighton, London, 1929.
Death and the Lover (from *Narziss und Goldmund*), tr. G. Dunlop, London, 1932.
The Journey to the East (Morgenlandfahrt), tr. H. Rosner, London, 1956.
Magister ludi, tr. Mervyn Savill, London, 1950.

Gertrud von le Fort

Gertrud von le Fort

by IAN HILTON

Gertrud von le Fort's autobiographical sketch, *Mein Elternhaus* (1941), provides us with a knowledge of her early life and upbringing. Of Huguenot descent, she was born on 11th October 1876 in Minden. Her background is that of the upper middle class. Her early years were spent in different garrisons to which her father, a Prussian army officer, had been posted. She was brought up in the Protestant traditions of the family and her father supervised her education for a long time. From him Gertrud inherited her love of history. From her mother, who was a deeply religious Protestant believer, stemmed her interest in religion. It seemed natural that she should carry on to study History and Theology at the universities of Heidelberg (where she came under the famed philosopher of the day, Ernst Troeltsch), Marburg and Berlin. Following the death of the father, Gertrud had travelled widely with her mother, including a visit to Rome, which undoubtedly had no small effect upon the mind of Gertrud in connection with her subsequent conversion to the Roman Catholic faith in 1925. By this time Gertrud was living in South Germany, having moved from Mecklenburg to Baierbrunn near Munich. Gertrud von le Fort was opposed to the Hitler régime and was forbidden, like so many, to publish after her criticism had become noticeable. The old family estate of Boeck am Mueritzsee was confiscated by the National Socialists and eventually she fled to Switzerland. She returned to Germany soon after the war to live in Oberstdorf in the Allgäu, where she still resides today. Her literary activities embracing fiction and non-fiction, prose and verse, span some fifty years. In 1948 she was awarded the Droste-Hülshoff prize, four years later she received the Schweizer Gottfried Keller prize and in 1955 the Grosser Literatur Preis von Nordrhein Westfalen. Most of her works are translated into a variety of foreign languages (in this connection it is noticeable that her work has made an impact in the Orient as well as in the West judging from the recent spate of Japanese translations).

NIETZSCHE'S "God is dead" cry, the spiritual chaos resulting after the First World War—Spengler's *Untergang des Abendlandes* illustrated the mood of the day quite decisively—the literature of the "Lost Generation" of Hemingway and others, all this was indicative of man's increasing concern since the turn of the century with the immanence of life rather than with transcendental values. At the same time, however, running counter to this attitude of mind, was a general renewal of a

Catholic spiritual life in Europe, which also expressed itself in literature. In France the "Renouveau catholique" was to be seen in the literature of Claudel, Bernanos, Péguy, etc. Across the Rhine Karl Muth in particular sought to incorporate the Catholics into the spiritual life of Germany in an active form, with his founding in 1903 in Munich of the "Kulturzeitschrift", *Hochland*. With this encouragement a new generation of Catholic writers came to proclaim in their work a belief in a world order created by God. And in the '30's this resurgence of Catholic religious literature was given a further impetus by such writers as Bergengruen, R. Schneider and Elisabeth Langgässer. To these names can be added that of Gertrud von le Fort. She is, in fact, a convert to Catholicism, but that she has not become narrow-minded about Protestantism is made clear enough in her fiction in the portrayal, for example, of Frau Bake (*Die Magdeburgische Hochzeit*) and Marie Durand (*Der Turm der Beständigkeit*) as Protestants endowed with the true Christian spirit, who act as examples for others. It is interesting to read the authoress's own words on the subject of the convert :

> Der Konvertit ist nicht, wie missverstehende Deutung zuweilen meint, ein Mensch, welcher die schmerzliche konfessionelle Trennung betont, sondern im Gegenteil, einer, der sie überwunden hat.[1]

In her heart Gertrud von le Fort feels the unity of the two Christian Churches, and in her fiction she stresses the need for unity, since she sees religion as the sole means whereby man and culture may be saved. This is the message of *Die Magdeburgische Hochzeit* (1938), a story built around the resistance of Protestant Magdeburg during the Thirty Years War and its storming by Tilly's troops in 1631. The Protestant Dr. Bake is passing the cathedral on his way out of the destroyed city when he hears the Credo being sung by the Catholics. Only the thickness of a wall separated them. In spirit they were united :

> Bake lauschte auf : das war doch das grosse christliche Glaubensbekenntnis, das er da vernahm, das gleiche, das er selbst so manches Mal in der hohen Domkirche in tiefster Ehrfurcht gesprochen hatte . . . er vergass völlig einen Augenblick lang, dass es die Papisten waren die es angestimmt hatten— er meinte nichts anders als dass ein vielstimmiges Echo dort drinnen seine eigene Stimme widerhallend aufgenommen habe . . . es war Bake, als werde mit jedem dieser kurzen majestätischen Sätze ein zeitlosgewaltiges Fundament freigelegt, auf dem die im hohen Dom Versammelten und er selbst, der Ausgeschlossene, . . . gleicherweise standen.[2]

Gertrud von le Fort's views on the poet and the function of poetry are quite definite. She sees poetry as a religious concern (one recalls the words of Eichendorff : "Die wahre Poesie ist durchaus religiös und die Religion poetisch.")[3] and (in common with Bergengruen) the poet's function as "Erbarmer und Offenbarer". Like her character Friederike in *Die Opferflamme*, Gertrud von le Fort could say :

Ich begriff, dass die ungeheueren Gaben an die Vernichtung, welche eine verfinsterte Welt heute dem Hass und der Verzweiflung darbringt, von uns, die wir diesen Hass und diese Verzweiflung nicht teilen, umgewandelt werden müssen in die Opfer der Liebe und der Hoffnung.[4]

And it is the theme of love which runs through all her writings; love which is constantly propounded in religious terms ("Die Liebe stammt von Gott und führt zu Gott", declares one of her characters). Thus her first major work, *Hymnen an die Kirche* (1924), is based on the First Commandment—"Love the Lord thy God".

In actual fact Gertrud von le Fort's literary activities commence as early as 1902—"Juvenilia", comprising some poetry and short stories. The themes of some of this early work indicate an interest in matters religious right from the start (e.g. *Spökenkieken* (1907), *In hoc signo vinces* (1908)), though the "problems" that are developed in her later works do not really appear here. The short stories are perhaps more interesting in themselves because of certain formal and stylistic ties with later writings of hers—the use of the framework technique, the symbolic meaning given to certain natural phenomena, first examples of the imagery that is to adorn all her work. It is not until 1924, some months prior to her conversion, however, at a time when she was already forty-eight, that the name of Gertrud von le Fort reached a wider audience for the first time with the publication of her hymns to the Catholic Church. These hymns, which Paul Claudel praised highly in the preface to the French translation, are a songful expression of spiritual exaltation and worship. The poetess treats the word "hymn" in accordance with the original meaning of the Greek verb. The theme running through the volume, which consists of a prologue and forty-four hymns, is that of the meeting of the Voice of the Soul and the Voice of the Church, and is a poetic account of the overcoming of the Soul's fears and its final union with the Spirit of the Church. The form and style are reminiscent of the Psalms of David. As in the Psalms, so too in the *Hymnen*, the verse consists of two "members". Sometimes the sense runs on in them, more often there is a definite and deliberate parallelism in the couplet, a parallelism that can be antithetic in nature. Common

to both Psalm and *Hymnen* is the direct and familiar style of
address, for each is an expression of a secret communion of the
individual with God. This accounts for a freshess of language with
images so often drawn from natural phenomena. In all there is a
careful balance between imagination and control over form and
theme, between rhapsodic language and a conscious following of
the pattern of the Church's liturgy. By means of the "dialogue"
of the Voice of the Soul and the Voice of the Church a positive
Catholic Christian interpretation of life is adopted as a point of
reference and expressed by the poetess in this, her first major work,
as in all her later writings.

Her companion hymn-cycle, *Hymnen an Deutschland* (1932),
with the theme of "love thy neighbour", is important for the light
it sheds on Gertrud von le Fort's concept of "das Reich". Words
from *Mein Elternhaus* provide an insight into and understanding
of her conscious association of Christianity and Germany:

> So ward in der Tradition unserer Familie das Ringen um die
> beiden grossen letztverpflichtenden Güter des Menschen,
> Religion und Vaterland in sehr eindrucksvoller Weise sichtbar.[5]

Despite her own personal sufferings at Germany's hands—she
experienced the horrors of the '30's and after, when she lost
all that represented the old traditions with the seizure of the family
estate by the National Socialists and was forced to flee abroad—
her native land means very much to her. Her love for Germany
Gertrud von le Fort reveals in such a poem as *Wie oft, mein
Vaterland*:

> Doch immer bleibst du die Heimat:
> Immer bleibst du
> Das eine geliebte Land, vor dem es kein Grauen und Zittern
> Gibt, und kein Vergessen in allen Weiten der Erde![6]

But this love stems ever from a Christian attitude and not from
political motives. Gertrud von le Fort's concern is with the reunion
of the soul with God, and in an attempt to point the way back to
Him she unfolds the history of the German people before their
eyes. What the poetess is advocating in these hymns is a return to
the original concept of the "Reich" of the Middle Ages, where
Church and Empire were unified. Whereas in the first hymn-
cycle Gertrud von le Fort was concerned with the soul of the
individual and the language was accordingly rhapsodic in nature,
here in the *Hymnen an Deutschland* the soul in question is that of
a whole people and the poetess employs a more direct approach.
The language is simple to match the urgency of her appeal to a
nation, and the use of free rhythm especially helps in this cycle to

effect the note of immediacy with her readers. This feeling of being bound up with the fate of Germany, her pride in its Past, her concern over its Present and its Future (though a social awareness and realism, as found in Böll, is not present in her work, even in *Dar Kranz der Engel*) is very real and makes itself felt in her prose as well as in her verse. Her immediately following works, *Das Reich des Kindes* (1935), *Die Vöglein von Theres* (1937) and *Die Magdeburgische Hochzeit* (1938), all dealing with the theme of "das Reich", clearly continue to express this same concern over the fate of Germany at that time.

With regard to Gertrud von le Fort's presentation of nature, descriptions of nature merely as landscape settings are used sparingly in her imaginative writings. Really the treatment of nature (as in *Die Opferflamme*, for example) is to stress the authoress's profound belief in the close relationship of nature and God. Thus in *Der Kranz der Engel* descriptions of natural scenery are not so much to establish topographical features in and around Heidelberg, as to create (as far as the heroine, Veronika, is concerned) a feeling of harmony and an acknowledgment of the presence of a divine power. As Eichendorff saw in the greatness and beauty of nature the wisdom and goodness of God, so in Gertrud von le Fort are similar religious feelings awakened by nature. She sees in nature an eternal law and rhythm. For many years she has lived in the mountains, first in Arosa and currently in Oberstdorf, and the mention that she makes of these places, either in prose fiction (*Die Opferflamme*), verse (the cycle *Gesang aus den Bergen*) or essay form (*Wahlheimat Oberstdorf*), provides evidence of her conviction that there in the mountains and valleys is peace and tranquillity to be found, the very innocence of nature in contrast to the artificiality and superficiality of everyday life. It is perhaps significant that the words of the 121st Psalm are repeated in *Die Opferflamme*: "Ich hebe meine Augen auf zu den Bergen, von welchen mir Hülfe kommt."[7] The authoress loves to compare the permanence of nature with the impermanence of human life. But in her presentation of death Gertrud von le Fort does not present the horrifying aspect of it; rather does she present death symbolically as a homecoming, as does Eichendorff. Her characters may at first fear death, but eventually this fear is overcome when actually faced with its presence. They learn, like Kort in *Spökenkieken*

... jenes bisher in Gedanken gemiedene Reich des Todes als ein fernes schönes Land zu betrachten und zu begreifen dass unser Schicksal in alle Ewigkeit beschlossen liegt in einer Macht, deren Wesen nichts anderes sein kann als eine tiefe grosse Freundlichkeit.[8]

The sense of innocence that she finds in nature is often symbolized in her fiction in the portrayal of children in contrast to the picture of the adult who can be and so often is a tool of evil. Thus one recalls the simplicity of the child in *Die Unschuldigen*, one remembers that the birth of the fifth child of Frau Bake in *Die Magdeburgische Hochzeit* symbolized the idea of innocence and purity that was to be found in the visionary hopes for the future. Again, the picture comes to mind of the two small boys walking hand in hand with Bice in *Die Tochter Farinatas*; these youngsters stand in direct contrast to the base wickedness of their elder brothers. In *Das fremde Kind* it is the Jewish child Esther who is instrumental in alleviating Jeskow's sense of guilt.

Fundamental to any understanding of Gertrud von le Fort is her essay, *Die Ewige Frau* (1934).

> Dieses Buch (the authoress writes) behauptet für die Frau von ihrem Symbol her eine besondere Hinordnung zum Religiösen . . . es geht um die Bildhaftigkeit des Religiösen.[9]

Clearly she does not treat woman in the manner expounded by the "Jung Deutschland" group of writers. One does not see in her a representative of the modern woman's movement. Her views are founded upon the Veneration for Mary, which was required of her by Catholicism. She calls for an end of self-willed subjectivism (das Religiöse beginnt dort, wo das eigenwillig Subjektive endet)[10] and does not see self-sacrifice as a purely negative action :

> Das Passiv-Empfangende des Weiblichen erscheint in der christlichen Gnadenordnung als das Positiv-Entscheidende : das marianische Dogma bedeutet . . . die Lehre von der Mitwirkung der Kreatur bei der Erlösung.[11]

A sign or symbol of this readiness on the part of woman to serve is the veil. It is a veil that the nun wears, a veil that the bride wears. Turning to the question of woman's rôle in present-day life, Gertrud von le Fort sees woman in three ways—as *virgo, sponsa* and *mater*. The authoress calls for a return to the former concept of the virgin who was held originally in high respect :

> Die Jungfrau bedeutet gestalthaft die religiöse Heraushebung und Bejahung des Personwertes in seiner letzten Unmittelbarkeit zu Gott allein.[12]

However it is the positive side of virginity she calls for, not the negative side :

> Für die Frau, welche ihre Jungfräulichkeit nicht als Wert auf Gott bezogen erkennt, bedeutet Ehe—und Kinderlosigkeit in der Tat eine tiefe Tragik.[13]

The virgin may be thought of as the *sponsa Christi*, but woman also has to be considered in the rôle of *sponsa des Mannes*. Man and wife, Gertrud von le Fort asserts, should be of one spirit as well as of one flesh. Woman must act as a mirror to man so that a true fulfilment of cultural activities may result (in this connection one thinks, for example, of the assistance afforded by the Schlegel women in the creative work of their husbands). Nor is this assistance confined to husband and wife, but can be afforded to man by a loved one, a friend or companion (again, one thinks of the relationship of Goethe and Frau von Stein; "Ach du warst in abgelebten Zeiten meine Schwester oder meine Frau,"[14] the poet wrote on one occasion). Woman becomes at one and the same time "das Mitwirkende" and "das Mitschaffende". But since "die sponsa des Mannes bleibt zur sponsa Christi berufen", woman should not seek to imitate man and his actions (das Religiöse bedeutet in erster Linie Demut).[15] At a time of man's senselessness and brutality there is special need, Gertrud von le Fort feels, for woman as *sponsa*. The "mysterium caritatis", the union of the spirit as well as of the flesh, must not be denied. As for the *mater*, she is "das Bild der irdischen Unendlichkeit".[16] The love of a mother, which is unending and natural, signifies "das Sichaufgeben und Opfern bis zur Gefahr der eigenen Unpersönlichkeit und Gestaltlosigkeit".[17] This self-sacrifice is to be found not only in the case of "leibliche Mütterlichkeit" but also "geistige Mütterlichkeit". Gertrud von le Fort sees a relationship between motherhood and the Church. She feels that woman's mission in the Church is closely bound up with the very essence of the Church : "Die Kirche selbst ist, als Mutter betrachtet, ein mitwirkendes Prinzip— der in ihr Wirkende ist Christus".

> Das Apostolat der Frau in der Kirche ist in erster Linie das Apostolat des Schweigens...sie ist vor allem berufen, das verborgene Christusleben in der Kirche darzustellen; sie ist also als Trägerin ihrer religiösen Sendung in der Kirche die Tochter Mariens. Damit ist das mütterliche Apostolat der Frau in seiner letzten Tiefe angedeutet.[18]

Though the work is based on dogma and thus in that sense contains eternal values, at the same time it had a special significance for its day and was very much a "Zeitbuch" in its attempt to combat the prevailing attitude of the time :

> Im Blick auf das mysterium caritatis stellt das Dritte Reich die schmerzliche Epoche dar, welche das Geheimnis der Liebe als das eigentlich schöpferische Prinzip nicht mehr kannte.[19]

This fact Gertrud von le Fort decried. Nor was she alone, for it was noticeable that in the '30's several articles on the same theme, mostly written by women (amongst them Sigrid Undset and Maria Schlüter-Hermkes) appeared in *Hochland*. It is also not without point that *Die Ewige Frau* was revised in 1960, for the '50's as reflected in European literature were a period of doubt, despair and feelings of insecurity on the part of the individual in society. No one illustrated this lack of purpose and direction in women better than Françoise Sagan in her novels. Gertrud von le Fort's treatise with its message once again stands as a challenge to our present way of thinking.

Why *Die Ewige Frau* is fundamental to an understanding of Gertrud von le Fort and appreciation of her work is because what she expresses in the essay about woman as philosophy, as theology, is then propounded in practice in her literary creations. The female characters in these books symbolize one or other aspect of woman as revealed in the treatise. Thus Blanche in *Die Letzte am Schafott*, and Barby in *Die Abberufung der Jungfrau von Barby* symbolize the aspect of "Jungfräulichkeit", and their characters must be viewed in this light. (Noticeably several of Gertrud von le Fort's works have for their setting a convent, where, of course, the veil is a sign of woman's readiness to serve. Besides the two above-mentioned stories, *In hoc signo vinces, Die letzte Begegnung* and in part *Plus Ultra* come into this category.) Both Blanche and Barby choose God and become through their bodily and spiritual sacrifices living victims. They are like the "agnus dei" and can be compared with the figure of the "victim" in Mauriac's novels, such as Alain Forcas in *Les Anges noirs* or Marie in *Le Noeud de vipères*. (It is, incidentally, important to note that Gertrud von le Fort's characters in even the earliest works are depicted in accordance with the Veneration for Mary, even before her thoughts on the subject find a compact formulation in her treatise.) Likewise in *Die Opferflamme* Friederike has to be understood as an example of the *sponsa*. On two occasions in the story she acts as the means for the "Wiedereinsetzung des mysterium caritatis als der einen göttlichen Ordnung, in der sich Mann und Frau, gleichviel wo, schöpferisch begegnen können".[20] The figure of *mater* is to be found in Anne de Vitré in *Das Gericht des Meeres* and in Anna Elisabeth in *Die Verfemte*. In the first story Anne de Vitré has to choose between patriotism and motherly pity for a child entrusted to her care. The climax comes when she becomes conscious of the fact that "eine Frau kann sich doch nicht zum Werkzeug des Todes hergeben—eine Frau ist doch dazu da, um das Leben zu schenken!"[21] In the second Anna Elisabeth also has to decide between patriotism and motherly feelings for a Swedish officer seeking to escape after the battle of Fehrbellin. She helps him to escape to freedom across the moor after his appeal to her; "Mutter, Ihr seid eine Mutter, rettet mich!"[22] It is in fact possible to see in such characters as Anna Elisabeth or Veronika (*Das Schweisstuch der Veronika*) examples of that familiar literary figure, the "outsider". But unlike Amis' or Wain's "outsider", who is usually a social misfit, Gertrud von le Fort's "outsider" is a spiritual outsider; a person who, while feeling happily integrated in society, becomes an outcast because society tends to divorce itself from him following a decision on a spiritual conflict that person makes, which though it be a correct decision from a Christian standpoint, nevertheless puts the individual in a decided minority against the general consensus of opinion which is either agnostically, atheistically or even apathetically religiously inclined. So often in Gertrud von le Fort's stories one finds a contrast of two women characters. On the one hand will be presented the figure of a woman who stands completely "unter dem Schleier" and corresponds to one of the three types, *virgo, sponsa* or *mater*; directly contrasted to her can be found the female who, far from subordinating her own will to that of God and revealing a readiness for self-sacrifice, expressly seeks to impose her own will. Thus in *Die Magdeburgische Hochzeit* the characters of Frau Bake and Erdmuth Plögen stand in contrast to each other, and likewise do those of the Carmelite nun, Luise von la Vallière, and Frau von Montespan in *Die letzte Begegnung*.

Finally it is necessary in Gertrud von le Fort's writings to view certain of her male characters in the light of *Die Ewige Frau,* and treat them from the aspect of "Jungfräulichkeit" :

> Hier trifft die Linie der Jungfrau mit der des Mannes zusammen. Auch er wertet die Virginität als Förderung und Steigerung zur Höchstleistung; zur religiösen Heraushebung und Bejahung des Personwertes in seiner letzten Unmittelbarkeit zu Gott allein.[23]

Though in her stories man may be more readily associated with acts of evil, it would be wrong to imagine that the authoress does not envisage the possibility of man being endowed with certain "feminine" characteristics of kindness and devotion, humility and sacrifice. For it is in this mould that the characters of Tilly (*Die Magdeburgische Hochzeit*), Heinrich (*Die Vöglein von Theres*) and the Prince of Beauvau (*Der Turm der Beständigkeit*) are formed. The number of instances where man stands "under the cross" as opposed to "against the cross" are limited indeed, but because of this very fact they stand out in stark contrast to the more common picture of man as an instrument of senseless evil and destruction, to an Enzio (*Das Schweisstuch der Veronika*) or a Pappenheim

(*Die Magdeburgische Hochzeit*) or a Burdoc (*Das Gericht des Meeres*).

At the same time, however, because the authoress tends to approach the problem of Grace in her works in a spiritually intellectual manner, her characters often cease to be individuals of flesh and blood and become instead stylized and recurrent types. Consequently, and in contrast to the realistic attitude to sex of other Christian writers such as Greene, Mauriac or the Norwegian authoress, Sigrid Undset, the relationship between man and woman sometimes becomes artificial in Gertrud von le Fort's stories, as one finds, for example, in *Das Schweisstuch der Veronika*, a two-part work portraying the clash of classical, materialistic and Christian attitudes at the end of the nineteenth and the start of the twentieth centuries.

If *Hymnen an die Kirche* brought Gertrud von le Fort into prominence for the first time, then *Der römische Brunnen* (1928) established her as an authoress of note. This work and its sequel, *Der Kranz der Engel* (1946), go to make up the most ambitious of her works, *Das Schweisstuch der Veronika*. *Der römische Brunnen* is thematically akin to *Hymnen an die Kirche*, for both works contain the idea of the "Berufung zur Kirche"—the Catholic Church. The story is, in fact, that of the spiritual development of the heroine, Veronika. The setting is Rome, the time is the period just prior to the First World War, and the activities of the members of a household constitute the action. The Grandmother represents the old Winckelmann traditions. For her Rome is the centre of culture and classical beauty. Theological knowledge is of no interest to her. Yet, even when her world of ideals is eventually shattered, she cannot and will not deny her existence. Befriended by the Grandmother is Enzio, a blond young German, who writes verse in remembrance of the glories of Imperial Rome. Obsessed with the pessimistic and nihilistic philosophy of Nietzsche, he allows no place for the godly element in his life. Tante Edelgart, however, likes to call herself a Christian, but the thought of the grace of God terrifies her and as long as she hesitates to take the sacraments she is denying God. In turning to the psychiatrist with her spiritual problems, she (other literary examples include Frau von Montespan in *Die letzte Begegnung* and Max in Julien Green's *Chaque Homme dans sa Nuit*) illustrates the predicament of so many people today who, through lack of faith, prefer to turn to everyone with their spiritual problems rather than to the priest, with whom they formerly used to discuss them. In the heroine, Veronika, one sees the breakthrough of godly grace. Feeling the worlds of the Grandmother and Enzio to be insufficient, she turns to the Church and freely makes her decision. Significantly

for her Rome is "Die Ewige Stadt". The second volume is concerned with the sacrament of marriage and deals with the problem
of a Catholic in relation to an apparently impossible physical love.
The action of *Der Kranz der Engel* takes place some time after
the First World War and the scene is shifted to Heidelberg.
Veronika meets Enzio again; they fall in love and become engaged.
Enzio, very much a non-Christian refuses to marry in the Church
and a crisis arises. Veronika is resigned to a civil marriage since
she is unwilling to forsake Enzio, for, paradoxically it might seem,
her earthly love is basically a religious love. It soon becomes
obvious to the reader that Gertrud von le Fort is creating in
Veronika an example of the "Jungfrau", as formulated in *Die
Ewige Frau*. Veronika is being regarded as a tool of God chosen
to carry out a mission on His behalf. Clearly Veronika feels herself
to be carrying out the will of God by sticking by the godless Enzio,
even though her confessor, the Dean, accuses her of committing a
sin against God and threatens to refuse her the sacraments.

It is interesting to compare Gertrud von le Fort's treatment of
this problem with that given by Graham Greene to a similar
problem in *Brighton Rock*. There Rose marries Pinkie out of
Church in a Registry Office. She is willing to run the risk of
damnation for him, out of love and a blind trust in the mercy
of God. But, one feels, it is from a physical love. In *Der Kranz
der Engel* Veronika is willing to run the risk of possible damnation
out of love for Enzio, but here it rather stems from a spiritual love.
Moreover hers is not a blind trust in the mercy of God so much
as an overwhelmingly clear decision on her part to put her faith
in God. Or again, compare the attitude of Greene's heroine in *The
Living Room,* who, when faced with the enormity of her sin
through her affair with a married man, replies that she can live
a lifetime without the sacraments, with that of Veronika, who,
when faced with the loss of the sacraments, feels as if her world
has come apart, and one realizes that with Gertrud von le Fort
the spiritual aspect of love comes before the physical in her works.
The key to all this is found in *Plus Ultra* : "Es gibt in alle Ewigkeit nur eine Liebe, die stammt von Himmel, auch wenn diese
Welt sie irdisch nennt...".[24] But one may be forgiven for thinking
the character of Veronika to be a little anaemic. Preoccupied with
inner problems, she seems sometimes to be unaware of the actuali-
ties of life. All the world may love a lover, but can one wholly
believe in Veronika, especially when one considers, for example,
character portrayals in the work of Greene or Mauriac. They
are writers who, whilst offending many by their treatment of
sex and sin in their work, still seek to strike the balance between
"passion" and "belief". In their stories the sinner who is capable

of passion is also capable of love in the end, and for Greene
and Mauriac love is religion just as it is for Gertrud von le
Fort. But passion as such is missing in her work. (Thus in *Plus
Ultra* Arabella's love for the Emperor, Charles V, turns into a
religious love, a love of God; in *Die Tochter Farinatas* Guido
Novello's hoped-for night of love with Bice does not materialize.
It is a seduction scene which does not take place.) And because
of her tendency to present types, the sinner is sometimes abstractly
drawn. Thus Guido Novello, sufficiently a sinner to think in terms
of adultery, is subsequently dissuaded from such thoughts in a
moment. Enzio's evil thoughts are not matched by his actions, and
his sudden conversion and agreement to marriage in the Church
after such aversion remains unconvincing. Since there is no real
evidence of a breakthrough of godly grace in his case, his conversion seems to be one to tolerance. One is reminded of Rex's
answer in Waugh's *Brideshead Revisited* in connection with the
difficulties in the proposed "mixed" marriage of Julia and himself : "Oh that, well if that's all, it's soon unmixed. I'll become a
Catholic. What does one have to do?"

The reader of Gertrud von le Fort's works will immediately
perceive that they have practically without exception, an historical
basis. Historically her writings cover all the significant epochs of
the Christian world, from the very beginnings of Christianity (*Die
Frau des Pilatus*) to pre- and Carolingian times (*Das Reich des
Kindes*), through the Middle Ages (*Die Tochter Farinatas*) to the
wars of religion (*Die Magdeburgische Hochzeit*), the French Revolution (*Die Letzte am Schafott*) up to the time of the two World
Wars (*Das Schweisstuch der Veronika*). Paul Claudel was accused
of being cut off from the realities of the world and modernity. His
use of history, it was argued, weakened into nostalgia. The same
cannot be said of Gertrud von le Fort. Her use of history is, in
fact, no more an evasion of present-day realities than Bergengruen's employment of history in *Der Grosstyrann und das Gericht*,
for example. What part, then, does history play in her work? Her
interpretation of history is not personal but religious. She interprets
history for its significance in the eyes of God, as did the Hebrew
writers of the Old Testament. Basically the authoress is interested
in mankind and she employs history as a background for the portrayal of human life. Her choice of a particular epoch is not an
unconscious one. She deliberately chooses those which, in her view,
present an interesting case of "Dämonie" in a cultured age, and
which she can use to illustrate that, basically, the fears, evils, tempta-
tions besetting man are always the same : "Es ist Welt, wo immer
wir gehen; es ist Welt, wo immer wir stehen; Empörung und
Gewalt, Stolz und Gewalt, Geld und Gewalt, Hass und Gewalt",[25]

runs the verdict in *Der Papst aus dem Ghetto*. Furthermore, she is not interested in the great historical characters as such but rather as human beings, and so her characters, be they of royal blood or of the aristocracy, be they nuns or soldiers, all are treated as ordinary human beings. The writer with a message to put across runs, of course, the risk of sacrificing art at the expense of beliefs. With Gertrud von le Fort this risk is limited with her employment of an historical background to her work, where she can confine her energies to building up her story around one historical event, so that the whole is controlled by this one particular event at a specific point in history. One realizes this when placing, for example, *Das Schweisstuch der Veronika* and *Die Magdeburgische Hochzeit* side by side. One might argue that the first story is in effect historical in that it deals with a piece of contemporary history, but the authoress deals not with one event, but covers a vast era of the transitional age at the end of the last century and the start of the present one, which she presents through her characters. Compare that with the crisp treatment in the second work, where the action is centred around the storming of the city of Magdeburg, and one finds here a better balance of action and thought. Undoubtedly an historical narrative of this kind gives her work more drive.

Though Gertrud von le Fort deals with a oneness of theme, the authoress does present and develop her theme in a variety of literary forms. Since *Hymnen an die Kirche* she has been a fairly prolific writer. As for Friederike in *Die Opferflamme,* so too for Gertrud von le Fort herself is "Dichtung eben keine Arbeit neben dem Leben, sondern eine Form des Lebens". In the period since 1924 she has produced, besides a second hymn-cycle and other verse and miscellaneous essays, some twenty works of prose fiction all dealing with the problem of Grace. The interesting thing is to trace the authoress's experimentation over the years to find a literary medium most suited to her ideas and beliefs. Unlike Raabe, who found his feet with short stories and then branched out on the lengthier novel form, Gertrud von le Fort has turned to the novel but three times, and these early on in her literary career. The works concerned are the two parts of *Das Schweisstuch der Veronika* (the second part was started as early as 1939) and *Der Papst aus dem Ghetto* (1930). In this last work the authoress penetrates into an interesting and generally little-known period in the history of the Church, for the story has the background of Pope Anaklet II and his election, which brought about the schism in the Catholic Church in 1130. Her use here of the style of the chronicle of the Middle Ages, which is artistically complementary to the story and the setting of the novel, hints at the authoress's readiness to experiment. Her next work, chronologically, is *Die Letzte am Schafott* (1931) and this is a "Novelle". And on examination of her writings the fact gradually emerges that it is to this literary form and to that of the "Erzählung" that Gertrud von le Fort returns time and time again in preference to all other genres. This must be construed as a deliberate usage of the shorter prose form as the best medium of expression for her ideas. The German Romantics had found the short prose form a congenial form of expression. Often this was dictated by policy, as they had not got the staying power for long mental creativity (there are exceptions, of course). Gertrud von le Fort's preference for the short prose form is also dictated by policy but for different reasons. She has the mental strength for long works (*Das Schweisstuch der Veronika* shows this) but she sees the shorter prose form as the most effective means at her disposal of presenting with thoroughness and insight the clash of two diametrically opposed worlds of good and evil.

She does not see evil as something new but as something which has always revealed itself in cruelty, hate, sadism, war, destruction of the inner man, etc., as she made clear in her essay, *Unser Weg durch die Nacht*. That she is concerned with the concept of evil is especially indicated in her "Erzählung", *Die Consolata* (1947). The scene of this story is thirteenth-century Padua, where Ansedio, a nephew of Ezzelino da Romano, rules supreme. Seeing so much destruction on his arrival in the city, the Papal Legate is forced to query the existence of God (a similar *cri de cœur* is heard in *Die Abberufung der Jungfrau von Barby* and *Am Tor des Himmels*) and he sets out to discover the nature of evil. The answer he finally arrives at is namely that "das Böse hat wirklich keine andere Macht als die Ohnmacht des Guten",[26] and that this faint-heartedness is the result of a lack of the spirit of Christian love (significantly the message in *Die Tochter Farinatas* runs: "Jeden Ort, welchen die Liebe verlässt, den gewinnt der Hass").[27] Meeting evil with evil is negative, Gertrud von le Fort feels, and she asserts that the overcoming of evil is only to be achieved by the spirit of Christian love—"christliche Liebe, das heisst: die ganze Fragwürdigkeit und Abgründigkeit des Menschen kennen und dennoch lieben" (*Unser Weg durch die Nacht*).[28] So in all her fiction Gertrud von le Fort consciously presents either through character, or situation, or both, the face of evil as "Kontrastmittel zur Aufhellung der Liebe". At the same time, since the problem of godlessness is seemingly a growing one, she tries to impart a sense of urgency in her work. The novel with its "loose" form tends to develop in its own time, so she turns more to the closely bound form of the "Novelle" with its few characters, concentration upon one main incident, application of the "Wendepunkt" (which plays an important rôle in Gertrud von le Fort's "Novellen" since it represents the "Entscheidungsmoment", the moment of decision for or against God, which every individual is called upon to make) and perhaps even the "Falken", all of which help to provide a dramatic note in keeping with the urgency of her message. Gertrud von le Fort has never turned her attention to the drama form as a medium for her Christian beliefs, (as Claudel did), which may in part be explained by the fact that for a long time she had little if any opportunity for direct contact with the world of literature or the theatre. But it is noticeable that the authoress has indicated her liking for the "Novelle" because of its "high dramatic form". One recalls the words of Theodor Storm :

> Die Novelle ist die Schwester des Dramas und die strengste Form der Prosadichtung. Gleich dem Drama behandelt sie die tiefsten Probleme des Menschenlebens; gleich diesem verlangt sie zu ihrer Vollendung einem im Mittelpunkt stehenden Konflikt, von welchem aus das Ganze sich organisiert, und demzufolge die geschlossenste Form und die Ausscheidung alles Unwesentlichen. (*Sämtliche Werke.* Koster. Band VIII.)[29]

Just as Kleist called his "Novellen" in actual fact "Erzählungen," so is it clear that in Gertrud von le Fort's eyes the "Erzählung" often comes to assume the guise of a "Novelle". The authoress is indeed familiar with Kleist's "Novellen" and one may detect in her works certain Kleistian touches in the formal approach to the genre even if not thematically speaking; for example in the way in which her story will plunge the reader "medias in res", cutting out lengthy exposition. The opening of *Die Consolata* illustrates this point :

> Wenige Tage, nachdem das Kreuzheer der verbündeten Venezianer und Mantuaner sich der Stadt Padua bemächtigt hatte, um dort die Herrschaft des Ansedio, eines Neffen des schrecklichen Ezzelino da Romano, aus dem benachbarten Verona, zu zerschlagen, hielt der päpstliche Legat Filippo Fontana seinen feierlichen Einzug in den eroberten Mauern.[30]

The conciseness and directness of this opening is reminiscent of Kleist's *Erdbeben in Chili*. Another Kleistian touch found in Gertrud von le Fort's work is the method of building up of tension over a period. *Die Consolata, Die Unschuldigen* and *Die Magdeburgische Hochzeit* especially provide good examples of this.

Die Letzte am Schafott, Gertrud von le Fort's first attempt at a "Novelle" since she came into the public eye, is also probably her best known. In 1960 a film was made from Bernanos'

Dialogues des Carmelites, which was, in fact, drawn from Gertrud von le Fort's story. Two years earlier an opera by Poulenc had been performed at Covent Garden, based on Bernanos' version of that same text. *Die Letzte am Schafott* has an authentic historical background, namely the French Revolution and the death on the guillotine of sixteen Carmelite nuns in Paris on 17th July 1794. Around this historical fact Gertrud von le Fort has composed a fictional story with the theme of martyrdom and fear. The heroine, Blanche de la Force, has from childhood suffered from fear. Since she fears the outside world, it is recommended that she enter a convent. With the outbreak of the French Revolution she becomes so frightened that she is almost barred from the convent. Eventually she flees the convent and goes to her father in Paris. However the grace of God is still with her and by the time the actual execution of the nuns takes place, Blanche has been drawn into the midst of chaos, and having allowed the divine will of God to act within her, she is prepared to meet her own death alongside the nuns. There is here the same basic thesis and antithesis of evil and good as in all her works. The force of evil reaches its highest point in the scenes round the guillotine, where chaos rules supreme and against this backcloth the spirit of Christian love is exemplified in Blanche. She is an example of the true martyr who willingly lets the will of God work within her. Acting as a foil to Blanche is Marie de l'Incarnation, who is strong and self-willed. She wishes to carry out her own will which is not true martyrdom as she is made to realize. The work adheres closely to the usually recognized form of the "Novelle". It treats of one single, unique event. It is the story of a weak person who at the decisive moment becomes strong spiritually. The "Wendepunkt" occurs when Blanche flees the convent. The "Novelle" is written in epistolary form, an account reputedly given to a friend by the Herr von Villeroi. This "correspondence" provides, therefore, a framework for the story as such, a technique which is so reminiscent of Storm.

Exactly the same kind of framework is employed in *Die Frau des Pilatus* (1955). In this work the authoress sets out to show that it has always been man who has rejected God and not vice versa, and illustrates her point here by turning to the drama of Christ Himself as a background to her story of the conflict of worldly and spiritual forces. Using the Gospels as a source of information, the "Novelle" is basically the fictional account of the crucifixion of Christ and the resulting relationship between Pontius Pilate and his wife, Claudia. These two are seen as the prototypes, so to speak, of man and woman through the ages, Pilate representing man's rejection of God, Claudia serving as the first woman in time after the Virgin Mary to act in the symbolic religious manner ascribed to woman by Gertrud von le Fort in *Die Ewige Frau*. Again in keeping with the traditional form of the "Novelle", the story deals with one central event, the "Wendepunkt" is the moment of realization on Claudia's part of how unchristian she had been, when she hears of the death of the Christians constant in their faith. There is also a "Falke" in this work, the leitmotif being the words of the Creed : "Crucifixus etiam pro nobis sub Pontio Pilato." The use of the framework technique here as in *Die Letzte am Schafott* is interesting in that the story in both cases is related in the form of a report, not by one of the chief protagonists as in *Plus Ultra* for example, but by one who witnessed the events. In common with *Die Letzte am Schafott* the story-teller in *Die Frau des Pilatus*, the Greek girl Praxedis, is herself converted to new spiritual values and beliefs as a result of witnessing Claudia's self-sacrifice on behalf of her husband, just as the Herr von Villeroi was changed after witnessing Blanche's death on the scaffold. Such a technique has the hope and purpose of making the reader also more aware of the spiritual values involved, and of course the use of the direct form of the report especially assists in making the tale more vivid and real.

There is yet another way in which Gertrud von le Fort employs the framework technique, which is connected with her use of history. As already mentioned, her works have an historical setting, but at the same time a connection with the present day. A "link in time" is thus established (just as a "link in space" is created by the authoress's treatment of the relationship of man and God through the admittance of Grace). This can be either an indirect link, through implication as it were, as in *Die Consolata*, where Padua and the fate of Ansedio find a resemblance in the last days of Hitler in Berlin, or a more direct connection by means of the framework technique as in, for example, *Die Verfemte*, where a thread runs through the story from the times of the Thirty Years War to 1945; or in *Am Tor des Himmels* (1954), where the seventeenth and twentieth centuries are connected by a manuscript. This latter work especially provides an answer to those critics who might complain that Gertrud von le Fort always lives in an ivory tower. In this book the state of affairs, the fears and doubts in God, which resulted from Galileo's discoveries in the seventeenth century are mirrored in the parallel situation confronting man today following the splitting of the atom. In no other work has the authoress shown such concern over the problem and mood of contemporary disillusionment of man. Even in a scientifically streamlined age the crisis facing man is still a religious one, as was indicated in *Der Kranz der Engel*: "Und im übrigen...gibt es nur eine einzige wirklich ernsthafte Krise, die jung und alt gleicherweise angeht, es gibt einfach die religiöse Krise."[31] Significantly the story ends with a question which is left unanswered : "Wie würde sie (die Entscheidung) ausfallen?"[32] The work is an open challenge to man to find his way back to God.

Reviewing the authoress's fiction one realizes that her prose with its simplicity of style and lucid neo-classical language (which with its sense of calm contrasts with the staccato outbursts of many present-day "angry-young writers") lends tremendously to the effectiveness of her stories. The reader is not bogged down by a mass of descriptive irrelevancies, possibly detrimental to the central theme. Over the years, while her themes and characterization have remained basically the same, her style has if anything become even more simple and direct and in a way more dramatic (to a point in *Die letzte Begegnung,* for example, that the Unities are fairly strictly adhered to in order to increase the element of tension) so as to match the sense of urgency of her message.

To heighten this message and to colour the story, Gertrud von le Fort makes considerable use of symbols. What is important about the twentieth-century writer is that he is making a conscious use of symbols and also possibly to a greater extent than did his predecessors. Certainly this is true of the Christian writer of today. Gertrud von le Fort has indicated the character of the symbol and her use of it in *Die Ewige Frau* :

> Symbole sind Zeichen oder Bilder, in denen letzte metaphysische Wirklichkeiten und Bestimmungen nicht abstrakt erkannt, sondern gleichnishaft anschaubar werden; Symbole sind also die im Sichtbaren gesprochene Sprache eines Unsichtbaren. Zu Grunde liegt die Überzeugung einer sinnvollen Ordnung aller Wesen und Dinge, die sich durch die Wesen und Dinge selbst als göttliche Ordnung auszuweisen vermag : eben durch die Sprache ihrer Symbole.[33]

Thus the symbol constitutes a most important means of indicating to man the meaning and purpose of life in accordance with Christian principles. For this reason Gertrud von le Fort employs not private and obscure symbols, but, following the pattern of writers during the Catholic literary resurgence after the First World War, symbols as found in the liturgy of the Catholic Mass and the Bible because they are readily understandable. Hence the significance of the cross in her work as a symbol of love and salvation, not just of death but of life also, hence her treatment of the sacraments to symbolize the communion of man with God, and her employment of the fountain as a symbol of Divine Grace. Hence one comes to understand the significance of titles of works such as

Das Schweisstuch der Veronika, the names of characters such as Blanche *de la Force.*

Gertrud von le Fort has remained constant in her belief in Christianity as the panacea for the world's ills from first to last. Her latest book, *Das fremde Kind* (1961), confirms this view. The edifying tone of her work is clear, for, after all, she is writing for a generally agnostic community, but she is not concerned only with edification. She never ceases to be a story-teller. The risk for the "committed" writer, a convinced Christian believer such as Gertrud von le Fort, that aesthetic considerations and religious convictions may not always be in harmony, is inescapable. One might point to seemingly weak motivation in *Das Schweisstuch der Veronika,* the reliance on ruse and intrigue in *Der Turm der Beständigkeit,* but generally speaking the result with Gertrud von le Fort has been a careful balance. Truly can it be said that, as a member of the older generation of writers, Gertrud von le Fort has helped in bridging the gap in twentieth-century German literature, those "arid wastes" of which so much mention has been made. The references that she has made to Claudel, Bernanos, Pasternak, Camus and Graham Greene, bear witness to Gertrud von le Fort's awareness of a European literary heritage. She becomes an interpreter in the crisis facing Christianity today.

TRANSLATIONS

1. The convert is not, as is sometimes mistakenly imagined, a person who accentuates the painful confessional differences, but on the contrary one who has overcome them.

2. Bake listened: that was indeed the great Christian creed which he heard there, the same which he himself had intoned in deep reverence so many a time in the lofty cathedral church ... he completely forgot for the moment that it was the papists who had uttered it—he thought only of the fact that a multi-voiced echo inside there had taken up the sound of his own voice ... it seemed to Bake as if with every one of the short majestic sentences a timelessly powerful foundation was laid bare, on which those assembled in the lofty cathedral and he himself, the one shut out, stood in like manner.

3. True poetry is thoroughly religious and religion poetical.

4. I understood that the monstrous talents for destruction, which a darkened world today offers to hatred and despair, must be changed into the sacrifices of love and of hope by those of us who do not share this hatred and despair.

5. And so in accordance with the tradition of our family the struggle for the two great binding possessions of man, religion and one's homeland, was evident in a very impressive manner.

6. Yet you always remain my home:
    Ever you remain the one beloved land; you do not induce
    horror nor trembling, nor are you forgotten
    in all corners of the earth.

7. I lift mine eyes up to the hills whence cometh my help.

8. ... to regard that hitherto mentally avoided kingdom of death as a distant beautiful land and to understand that our fate lies for all eternity in a force which really can be nothing other than a deep and great friendliness.

9. This book affirms from the aspect of the symbolic significance of woman a particular affinity to the religious idea ... it is concerned with the figurative application of the religious idea.

10. The religious idea begins at the point where the wilfully subjective element ceases.

11. The passive, accepting character of woman is seen in the Christian divine ordinance as a character of positive action and decision. The dogma of the Virgin Mary signifies ... the teaching of co-operation of God's creatures in the Redemption.

12. The figure of the Virgin signifies the religious elevation and affirmation of personal values in the final immediacy with God alone.

13. Not being married and not having any children is indeed a tragedy for the woman who does not recognize her virginity as of value to God.

14. Ah, you were in times long ago my sister or my wife.

15. The religious idea signifies in the first instance humility.

16. The image of earthly infinity.

17. The self-surrender and sacrifice even at the risk of losing one's personality and form.

18. The Church itself when considered in the rôle of mother is a principle of co-operation—the one operating in her is Christ ... The apostleship of woman within the Church is in the first instance the apostleship of silence ... above all she is called to represent the hidden life of Christ within the Church; she is therefore in her rôle of bearer of her religious mission in the Church the daughter of Mary. And thus is indicated the motherly apostleship of woman in the final run of things.

19. In its view of the "mysterium caritatis" the Third Reich represents that painful epoch which does not recognize any longer the secret of love as the real creative principle.

20. Re-establishment of the "mysterium caritatis" as the one godly order in which man and woman can meet creatively.

21. A woman cannot commit herself to becoming a tool of death—a woman's function is rather the giving of life.

22. "Mother, you are a mother, save me!"

23. Here the paths of the virgin and man converge. He too values virginity as a means of furtherance and intensification towards one's best performance; towards the religious elevation and acknowledgment of one's personal value in his final immediacy with God alone.

24. There is for all time but one love, which comes from Heaven, even if this world calls it earthly.

25. "It is the world wherever we go; it is the world wherever we stand; rebellion and power; pride and power; money and power; hatred and power."

26. "Evil has really no other might than the faint-heartedness of the good."

27. "Every place that love leaves is won over by hate."

28. "Christian love—that means to know and still love the whole questionableness and fall of man."

29. The "Novelle" is the sister of the drama and the strictest form of prose writing. Like the drama it treats the deepest problems of human life; like it, it demands for its completion a central conflict from which the whole may evolve, and accordingly the most closed form and the exclusion of all unessentials.

30. A few days after the army of the allied Venetians and Mantuans had seized the town of Padua in order to crush the mastery of Ansedio, a nephew of the terrible Ezzelino da Romano from the neighbouring Verona, the papal legate Filippo Fontana made his triumphal procession by the conquered walls.

31. "And for the rest ... there is but one single, really serious crisis, which affects both young and old equally, and that is simply the religious crisis."

32. "How would the matter be decided?"

33. Symbols are signs or images, in which final metaphysical realities and definitions are recognized not abstractly, but become as it were visible according to their image; symbols, therefore, are the language of the invisible spoken in terms of the visible. There is the basic conviction of a sensible order of all beings and things, which can be revealed as a godly order through the beings and things themselves; through the very language of their symbols.

SELECT BIBLIOGRAPHY

WORKS

EHRENWIRTH VERLAG, MUNICH. *Gertrud von le Fort: Erzählende Schriften,* 1956 (3 volumes). A collected edition of the authoress's prose fiction from 1928–55.
Hymnen an die Kirche.

INSEL VERLAG. *Der Turm der Beständigkeit; Die letzte Begegnung; Das fremde Kind; Gedichte.*

KÖSEL UND PUSTET, MUNICH. *Die Ewige Frau; Hymnen an Deutschland.*

WORKS OF REFERENCE

A. FOCKE. *Gertrud von le Fort.* Graz, Verlag Styria. 1960.

N. HEINEN. *Gertrud von le Fort, eine Einführung in Werk und Persönlichkeit.* Luxemburg, Editions du Centre. 1955. (A perceptive study.)

H. JAPPE. *Gertrud von le Fort, das erzählende Werk.* Meran, Verlag H. Unterberger. 1950.

T. Kampmann. *Gertrud von le Fort. Die Welt einer Dichterin.* Warendorf, Verlag J. Schnellsche Buchhandlung. 1948. (A sound introduction.)

M. Kohnen. *Gertrud von le Fort e o retorno a ordem crista.* Rio de Janeiro, Irmaos Pongetti. 1952.

Helene Kuhlmann. *Vom Horchen und Gehorchen. Eine Studie zu Gertrud von le Fort.* Recklinghausen, Paulus Verlag. 1950.

Also worthy of note are R. Faesi's essay on Gertrud von le Fort in *Christliche Dichter der Gegenwart,* Heidelberg, W. Rothe Verlag, 1955; and the section on the authoress in Grenzmann, *Dichtung und Glaube,* Bonn, Athenäum Verlag, 1953.